Quentin Bates

AN ICELANDIC MURDER MYSTERY

COLD BREATH

CONSTABLE

CONSTABLE

First published in Great Britain in 2018 by Constable

A CIP catalogue record for this book is available from the British Library.

ISBN: 978-1-47212-776-1

Typeset in Bembo MT by TW Type, Cornwall
Printed and bound in Great Britain by CPI Group (UK) Ltd, Croydon CR0 4YY

Papers used by Constable are from well-managed forests and
other responsible sources.

MIX
Paper from
responsible sources
FSC® C104740

Constable
An imprint of
Little, Brown Book Group
Carmelite House
50 Victoria Embankment
London EC4Y 0DZ

An Hachette UK Company
www.hachette.co.uk

www.littlebrown.co.uk

For Astrid

Chapter One

No jokes, she decided, at least not at the boss's expense.

'Coffee, Gunnhildur?'

The circle of a brand-new, carefully trimmed goatee gave Ívar Laxdal's face a malevolent look. Gunna thought the grey-shot black beard suited him and longed to ask the reason for it, but decided that regardless of how close their working relationship had become, it still wasn't the kind of question she could ask.

She lifted her feet from the desk and nodded towards the coffee room in the corner.

'Help yourself.'

The beard turned his smile into something sinister.

'No, I thought I'd invite you out. Just for once. You're not busy, are you?'

'We're always busy. You know that better than anyone. I'm forever bitching to you about how short of everything we are.'

Ívar Laxdal nodded. 'I know, and I assure you that your observations don't pass unnoticed. But you're not overrun with work right now, this minute, are you?'

Gunna shrugged her coat over her shoulders.

'Hold the fort, would you, Helgi?' she said to her colleague at the desk opposite hers. 'Duty calls.'

'Go for a walk,' the pale man suggested. 'Don't go far. Don't go out of sight.'

1

The plump man opened his mouth to speak and then quickly shut it. It had been an instruction, not a suggestion.

'How long?' he asked, his voice quivering. Next to him his wife could not hide the helpless hatred in her eyes.

'Twenty minutes,' the dark man said, pointing to the wavelets being whipped up on the surface of the lake by a bitter wind. 'Leave your phones on the table. Go that way and walk around the lake. Be where we can see you.'

'You . . . ?' the woman began.

'Come on, Hanne. We don't have a choice,' the man muttered to his wife, taking her arm. He stared steadfastly ahead as they walked away, while she shot a single furious glance over her shoulder towards the two men.

It was supposed to be the holiday they had been looking forward to. For the first time there was no need to hurry. There were no longer projects to manage, classes to teach, meetings to attend, deadlines to meet, or jobs waiting for them to return to. Retirement meant they could spend as long as they wanted touring this rocky island they had long wanted to visit, arriving before the tourist season got underway and taking things slowly, dawdling around the northern coastline as they made their way to Reykjavík, stopping whenever and wherever they saw fit.

That had been the plan, she reflected bitterly, until the unwelcome visitors had arrived one night before they had got as far as the ferry, with an offer they dared not refuse.

'How long should this take?' the pale man asked, watching as the tubby man and his stick-thin wife walked stiffly, arm-in-arm, around the shore of the lake.

'Not long. Under the driver's side bunk. Tools?'

They disappeared into the camper van, and the dark man opened a compact tool box on the table as he looked around.

'Nice truck,' he said. 'House-proud people. Very tidy.'

'Maybe they wanted the place to look its best for their visitors.'

The elderly couple, still arm-in-arm, returned windblown after a slow walk around the grey waters of the lake where the wind filled the air with spray.

'We're finished. Thanks for your co-operation,' one of the men said, standing up from his seat in the camper van's back door as the couple approached.

'It's not as if we had a choice in the matter,' the woman snapped at him, her voice loaded with helpless anger.

He shrugged. 'It's not our choice either, I'm afraid. Now we'd like you to go away and enjoy the rest of your holiday. Forget you ever saw us. It goes without saying that you won't say a word to anyone, ever. In which case you'll never hear from us again.'

The pale man dipped a hand into his pocket and took out a sheet of paper folded into four. He held it up and handed it to the woman.

'What's this?'

'Take a look.'

She unfolded it carefully and stiffened as she saw it. Her husband's face sagged as she showed it to him.

'Your house. Your daughter's house,' the pale man said, his finger sliding over each of the four pictures. 'Your son-in-law's business.' His finger moved across the paper. 'And this is where your mother lives. Just so you know. Not one single word.'

Gunna wondered what was going on as they crossed the road and skirted the Hlemmur bus station, leaving the Hverfisgata police headquarters behind. In the years they had worked together Ívar Laxdal had kept his officers at arm's length, not the length of an unfriendly arm, but at a definite distance. All the same, Gunna knew that she was different, as far as he was concerned. Ívar Laxdal had been to sea with both of the men in her life, and she quickly directed her thoughts away from Ragnar Sæmundsson, knowing it would bring a familiar stab of pain deep in her chest and that her eyes would prick with tears demanding to be shed.

He pushed open the door of Café Roma, a coffee house around the corner from the police station. Early in the mornings police officers snatching a quick coffee was a frequent sight, but by mid-morning the place was quiet.

'Coffee? Ordinary or something fancy?'

'Ordinary will do for me, thanks,' Gunna replied as he went to the counter, leaving her to take a seat by the window overlooking the windblown street outside, where bags and wrappers were swept along by the stiff breeze off the sea.

'To what do I owe the honour?' she asked as Ívar Laxdal sat down, removed his coat and poured a precise amount of milk into his coffee.

'Biscuit?' He snapped a saucer-sized pastry in two and passed the larger segment to her. 'How's the family?'

'The usual. Steini tinkers with anything mechanical. Gísli's longlining and doesn't like it much, but it gives him time at home with Drífa and Kjartan. Laufey is . . .' She paused.

'Laufey is . . . ?' Ívar Laxdal asked with immediate concern.

'Let's say she's going through a turbulent patch. When she started university in Reykjavík she lost touch with her old group of friends and has fallen in with a very different crowd.'

'A bad crowd?'

'No. Just different, new friends and a new environment. I think she's struggling a little to fit in.'

'She will. She wouldn't be Ragnar Sæmundsson's daughter if she weren't resourceful.'

'That's true. But it's taking her a while to find her feet.'

'And how's Serious Crime?'

'Busy, as always,' Gunna said, wondering when Ívar Laxdal was going to get to the point. 'Helgi's chasing witnesses for the assault case we've been working on, the guy who lost an eye.'

'And you?'

'The Sugarberries rape case. Eiríkur's working on that with me. It's delicate, and I'm not convinced we'll get a conviction.'

'Why?'

'It's too woolly. There's no forensic evidence and she didn't do herself any favours by coming forward more than a month after the event. Plus both parties were extremely drunk, by all accounts.'

Ívar Laxdal broke off a chunk of his biscuit and chewed it, nodding sagely.

'Can they get by without you for a week or two?'

'Eiríkur and Helgi? Why, what do you have in mind?'

He scowled and glanced around. It was done so theatrically that Gunna wanted to laugh, but resisted the temptation.

'I have a particular assignment to take care of, and I've been asked to recommend a suitable officer.'

'Not cloak-and-dagger stuff, surely?' Gunna grinned, but her smile disappeared as Ívar Laxdal's face remained stony.

'Yes, pretty much.'

She cupped her chin in one hand as she wondered what to say, while Ívar Laxdal's expression remained impassive.

'I'm intrigued,' she said at last. 'But you know spies are normally younger and slimmer than I am, and male.'

'This comes from high up. I didn't want to accept it. But for good reason I decided we were better off doing as we're asked on this. It's sensitive. I need someone competent and reliable who can be discreet, while keeping their eyes and ears wide open,' he said as he sipped his coffee. 'So I thought of you.'

'Tell me more.'

He shrugged. 'There's not a great deal I can tell. Essentially, you'd be a bodyguard with a few additional duties thrown in.'

'A bodyguard who reports back to you, you mean?'

A trace of a smile appeared from within Ívar Laxdal's sinister goatee.

'Something like that. You understood exactly why I thought of you rather than . . .'

'Sævaldur?'

'Forget Sævaldur. This requires tact and a delicate touch, and while Sævaldur has talents, he doesn't possess either of those qualities.'

'Starting when?'

'As soon as you've completed the firearms refresher.'

'Firearms?' Gunna's jaw dropped. 'I did one a while ago, yes. But come on . . .'

'So that would mean you could start on Friday.'

'Friday? This Friday? There isn't a firearms course for weeks.'

Ívar Laxdal's sinister smile returned.

'There's a refresher especially for you tomorrow. Half-day intensive,' he said and hesitated. 'Assuming you're up for it.'

'It looks like you've already decided I am,' Gunna said, trying not to sound hurt. 'Do I get to know who I'm looking after, where, how and all that stuff?'

'Excellent.' Ívar Laxdal finished his coffee and ignored the question. 'Hand your casework over to the boys and I'll make sure they manage without you. The firearms refresher starts at eight tomorrow. Once you're finished I'll fill you in on the details.'

Gunna shivered, trying to work her neck a little deeper into her scarf to keep out the biting wind and the rain it was hurling at her. She wondered why she had been pulled off normal duties and instructed to be at Reykjavík's little domestic airport on a cold, wet weekday evening when the city was as quiet as it was ever likely to be.

Ívar Laxdal appeared silently at her side. Muffled in a thick coat, which she decided had to be warmer than hers, he grunted a wordless greeting.

They stood in the scant shelter the control tower offered and she wondered what they were waiting for. She opened her mouth to ask, but he beat her to it.

'There,' Ívar Laxdal said.

Points of light approached and the sound of the aircraft could be heard over the wind only when it was making its approach to touch down. It landed smartly, and once its wheels were on the ground its wings trembled in the wind. Three cars appeared from the gloom.

'Pay attention, Gunnhildur,' Ívar Laxdal told her needlessly.

There was no need to check luggage or passport. The aircraft came to rest at the edge of the apron and the sole passenger eyed the dark Patrol that pulled up next to it, watching as a young man with raindrops on his glasses and wearing an old-fashioned belted raincoat that flapped in the wind got out and stood waiting.

The co-pilot looked back into the cabin and gestured to indicate that it was safe to disembark. The passenger nodded and put on his long overcoat, first winding a pale grey scarf around his neck.

At the bottom of the steps, the young man in the raincoat extended an arm, contriving at the same time to take the visitor's bag.

'Welcome to Iceland, sir,' he said. 'My name is Valgeir Bragason. Mrs Strand asked me to meet you.'

The passenger muttered a gracious reply in a deep voice, noticing that the young man could hardly see for the raindrops on his glasses.

The Patrol sped away through the gate, with a wave to the guard, and into the night. The passenger felt a nagging uncertainty, but reassured himself. This country was supposed to be safe, wasn't it?

'What do you have planned, Mr Bragason?' he asked as the lights of the city flashed past.

'We have secure accommodation ready for you tomorrow. Tonight you are Mrs Strand's guest.'

Ívar Laxdal looked to one side and allowed himself a smile as the cars disappeared back the way they had come, into the evening gloom.

'That was exciting, wasn't it?' he asked. They had worked together for five years and she still couldn't figure out when he was joking, so she took the default position that her senior officer was always deadly serious unless there was a good reason to assume otherwise.

'Good,' he said. 'Excellent. Let's warm ourselves up, shall we?'

Once the smartest the city could offer, the hotel that overlooked the airport now looked tired, she felt. All the same, in response to a nod from Ívar Laxdal, a uniformed receptionist scuttled away and returned with mugs and a flask of coffee.

'Unless you'd prefer something stronger?' Ívar Laxdal asked.

'A double cognac would go down well. But we're here on business, aren't we?'

He grunted and poured coffee, handing her a cup.

'So, are you going to tell me why we're at the city airport watching a private jet land and one passenger be whisked away, no customs?'

Ívar Laxdal sank into one of the lobby chairs and Gunna perched on the edge of another as he looked around.

'The man's name is Osman. He's here at Steinunn Strand's invitation.'

'Which is why it wasn't easy to say no?'

'On the contrary. It wouldn't have been difficult to tell her this kind of thing isn't part of our remit. He's not an official visitor to Iceland, more a personal guest of Steinunn's. If he'd come here on an official visit, then we'd know where we stand.'

'Security, and all the usual stuff?'

'Exactly. He'd be in a hotel in the city, with a security detail to keep an eye on him.'

'So, can I ask why . . . ?'

'His presence is to be kept as low-key as possible. From what I've been able to find out from Steinunn's department, he heads some kind of charity outfit that supports refugees. I had never heard of this person before, but it seems he's a controversial figure and hasn't been shy of pointing the finger when he feels not enough is being done about refugees arriving in Europe, which is pretty much all the time. He has some influential friends and it seems he's made a few enemies as well.'

'And the security aspect and the Glock?'

'Just in case, Gunnhildur. Just in case,' he assured her. 'Let's say you're the close range security, as well as the eyes and ears. There's a heavy squad just out of sight who'll be keeping an eye on the rest of us.'

'Where?'

'Einholt. It's on the coast near Gufunes. Not exactly isolated, but still pleasantly secluded.'

'I don't get the feeling you're entirely happy with this,' Gunna said, watching Ívar Laxdal frown.

'There's too much I don't know, and that's what concerns me. I don't know if this man is what he says he is, and Steinunn's people haven't been able to come up with much, which is hardly a surprise as this is all very short-notice. I was only handed this yesterday morning, and I was pretty much told that the guy was arriving tonight and it's our job to look after him and keep him sweet. From the few crumbs of information I have from Steinunn, he's here partly to negotiate with a couple of Icelandic charity organizations, as well as to have a little rest and recuperation at her invitation.'

'Well, I'm not entirely happy either,' Gunna said. 'It takes me away from my family, which isn't ideal. Steini never complains about anything I do, but we were going to take Gísli's boat over the bay at the weekend if the weather's reasonable. And I don't want to be away from Laufey for long at the moment either as she's having a tricky time.'

'How's the lad?'

'He's fine. They've managed to find a place to buy and he's on one of the Grindavík longliners. It's decent money and he gets regular trips off.'

'That's good. You shouldn't be away too long when you have youngsters,' he said absently. 'You haven't complained about the lack of promotion for a while, have you?' he added in a throwaway tone.

'Well, no, I haven't. But I can if you've been missing it.'

Ívar Laxdal stroked his unfamiliar beard.

'Let's say that if you carry out this assignment successfully then I can assure you there'll be no obstacles to promotion.' He jerked his chin upwards. 'As I said, this comes from upstairs. They want to be sure this person remains safe and sound, and I'll make damned sure a good job done doesn't escape their notice.'

The Glock was an uncomfortable lump under her armpit. Gunna shifted awkwardly, telling herself to get used to it, then a moment later reminding herself that this operation would only take a few days, so there would be no need, or even opportunity, to become accustomed to carrying a firearm.

The weapon made her nervous, even though the pistol was

empty and the clip was in her pocket. She wondered how to tell Helgi and Eiríkur that she was going to be away for a few days as she elbowed the door open and looked inside. Eiríkur waved from his desk where he sat with the phone to his ear and held up one finger.

Gunna went to the coffee room and poured herself a mug of dark brown liquid, which she sipped absently, looking at the cartoons pinned to the walls, most of them clipped from newspapers, and most of them poking fun at the upper echelons of the police force or the various ministers of justice who had been the force's overlord at one time or another.

'Leaving us for pastures new?' Eiríkur asked with a grin.

'Why? What did the Laxdal tell you?'

Eiríkur poured himself a mug of hot water from a Thermos, sat down and dunked a teabag in it.

'He didn't say a lot. Just that you're off normal duties for a while. You haven't upset someone, have you?'

'Not yet, Eiríkur. Well, no more than usual.'

He squeezed the teabag and sipped. Gunna could sense the host of unasked questions he wanted to put to her, and realized that he and Helgi had probably been told to not ask too much.

'Never mind,' he said. 'I'm sure you will soon enough.'

'You cheeky . . .' Gunna began and returned the grin to let him know the rebuke wasn't to be taken seriously.

She and the middle-aged Helgi had clicked from the first day they'd worked together. Much the same age and both of them from coastal regions, they had a great deal in common, while the younger Eiríkur, a city child born and brought up in Reykjavík, had taken longer to become part of the team. It was only in the last year or so that he had started to give rein to an irreverent sense of humour. Gunna had taken a while to get to know him properly, and had wondered if he would remain with the force, or if the church would one day reclaim him.

'I'll be off for a day or two. To be honest, I can't tell you what it's all about because I don't know myself yet.'

'But you'll have something to tell us when you're back, I hope?'

Gunna drained her mug and put it in the sink.

'I would hope so. Unless I completely screw things up and get demoted to running the canteen.'

'Somehow I don't think so,' he said slowly, looking at her with one eye half closed, and Gunna felt a surge of discomfort when she realized that in spite of the loose-fitting fleece she'd kept zipped up, Eiríkur had still detected, with obvious alarm, the bulge under her left arm.

'All on one level. No basement. Garages there; keep your car in the one on the right,' Ívar Laxdal instructed, striding from his black Volvo towards the house while Gunna levered herself out of the car-pool Daihatsu.

The house was a long, low building, its walls the pale blue of duck eggs and the high roof set with a shallow pitch and tiled in matt-red shingles.

She surveyed the low-slung house, its barren garden and the view of the shoreline and the deserted promontory of Geldinganes lurking on the far side of a few hundred metres of white-capped waves.

'Is the causeway passable?' she asked, jerking a thumb at the long hump of Geldinganes.

'At low tide and with a four-wheel drive it might be. At this time of year, don't even think about it.'

'Is there anything over there?'

'Nothing. There's an old shelter that goes back years, but otherwise it's deserted, and it's likely to stay that way until the developers finally move in,' he said. 'That's if they ever get permission to build there. There are plans for houses eventually, but it's a few years away yet.'

'And this place,' Gunna said, nodding towards the house. 'Lonely, isn't it?'

'I know,' Ívar Laxdal replied. 'Perfect, isn't it? It's called Einholt. Or the farm that used to be here was called Einholt, until the farmhouse was pulled down and this place was built. Shall we continue?'

He opened the door and handed Gunna the key as the alarm system chirped.

'Seven–two–seven–six,' he said, punching in the code so the sound died away. 'The alarm goes on at night, please. All the windows and doors are linked to it, so if you get a visitor, you'll know about it. So will the emergency line, and they'll treat it as an absolute priority, so no false alarms, please.'

'The garage doors are on the same circuit?'

'I'm not sure. Check,' he said, striding through the living room on two levels that seemed to disappear into the distance.

'Four bedrooms, all of them en suite. You use the one at the end, closest to the front door. Our friend gets the master bedroom. Kitchen's there,' he indicated with a wave of his hand. 'Stores will be delivered as required. Let us know what you need.'

Gunna stopped in her tracks.

'Hold on a moment. How many people are going to be in this place, and for how long?'

'Two of you. Our friend and you.'

'So I'm a cook and housekeeper, as well as a bodyguard?'

Ívar Laxdal scratched his beard and a sly smile appeared behind it.

'That's for you and our guest to work out between you, isn't it? If you want takeaways for every meal, then that's fine by me.'

'Who's doing the deliveries?'

'Over here, Gunnhildur.' He walked to the end of the long living room and took the two steps to the higher end of the split-level living room in one bound. The long wall of the living room was taken up with a picture window that almost filled it, providing a view across the sound. The lights of Akranes on the far side of Faxaflói Bay could be seen between the Geldinganes promontory and the island of Viðey. There was a single window in the end wall and Ívar Laxdal tapped the glass with his finger. 'Up there, you see the first house on the end? We have that place as well, for a few weeks. The owners were very happy to get an all-expenses paid holiday in Sicily. In the meantime, two officers from the Special Unit are there around the clock. If there's a panic, that's what they're there for.'

'So to get back to my original question, did you want an offi-cer with ovaries for this role because a suitably domestic type was required, or what?' Gunna demanded, wondering if she could still turn down the assignment.

'Far from it, Gunnhildur,' Ívar Laxdal said. 'I'm aware that you're not entirely the domestic type,' he added, his sly smile returning. 'I wanted you for this particular job because I can trust you not to fuck things up, because you're competent without being intimidating, in the way that a six-foot guy with designer stubble might be, and finally, because I felt you deserved the opportunity. I'm not saying it won't be a challenge, because it will be.'

'A feminine touch, you mean?' Gunna growled, mollified but not convinced. 'So when does he get here?'

'Ah, I expect the minister will want to bring him here herself.' He looked at his watch. 'Very soon.'

Gunna made coffee, while Ívar Laxdal rolled up his sleeves. She watched with amusement and then mounting admiration as he cracked six eggs into a bowl, one-handed and two at a time, chopped onions, added a crushed clove of garlic and sliced a pepper and two tomatoes.

She sat back and watched his concentration on the task in hand until he split the omelette neatly onto two plates.

'Some fresh bread would have been good, and so would a salad, but we have to make do with what we have,' he said.

'It's good,' she told him after the first few mouthfuls. 'You'd better give Steini the recipe.'

'I assure you Steini knows how to cook an omelette. It's all in the wrist and the timing.'

'I hope our friend has an idea of what he's letting himself in for if I'm supposed to be feeding him as well.'

'You'll be fine. Just make a list of what you want.'

Gunna nodded as she wolfed the omelette, surprised at how hungry she had been.

'It'll be bog-standard Icelandic food, I reckon.'

'Meat and potatoes?'

'That's about the shape of it.'

'His diet is the least of my worries.'

'So what *are* you worried about?' Gunna asked. 'And when are you going to tell me who this character is and why I need to have a Glock stuck in my armpit.'

'You have your phone with you?'

'Of course I do.'

'Keep it on silent, and you can log into the wifi network. In any case there's a jammer in your room that blocks mobile traffic within about ten metres of the house. There's a landline with an extension in every room. If you need to call, use that. If anything personal crops up, then it'll have to wait.'

'Ívar, just how long is this expected to last?'

'A week, I would imagine. We'll rotate after a couple of days.'

Gunna sat back, trying to take it all in. 'And who's my relief?'

'I am, probably. We have to keep this discreet, and we achieve discretion by involving as few people as possible,' Ívar Laxdal said, finishing his omelette. 'The Special Unit guys up the road only know there's an VIP here and that they're to keep watch for intruders; they don't know who's going to be here and they aren't to know unless something crops up.'

The new office was a relief, Skúli Snædal told himself, adding that having an office at all, at long last, was the real relief. He shivered as he waited for the bus that would take him to work, and reminded himself that in spite of the biting spring wind, the sun was appearing earlier with every passing day, winter was almost behind them and he was again working in his chosen profession.

The last couple of years had been difficult ones. He had left a comfortable and secure but low-paid position as a staff journalist on one of Reykjavík's freesheets to take a precarious but interesting job on an established newspaper that had only a few months later been taken over by new owners. The new proprietors had installed a new manager whose task was to weed out those without a history of toeing the company line, and as one of the last in, and with a known habit of taking little at face value, Skúli had found himself among the first out.

He had even resorted to teaching to make ends meet – he shuddered at the thought. Then the new venture had been nerve-wracking, and he had put everything he had into throwing in his lot with a group of other young journalists in much the same position as himself in setting up a news website. It had been an anxious few months as *Reykjavík Pulse* had launched with fanfare, immediately becoming popular, only for the readership to gradually fall away in the ensuing months before surging again in the wake of a couple of government scandals that *Pulse*'s small team had been able to report in a way the established media had failed to do, achieving a vivacious style that bordered on satire.

Pulse was now steadily gaining ground. Its readers seemed to like its lack of political affiliation and its habit of asking embarrassing questions, and the growing readership was bringing in advertisers. In spite of some of them having reservations about *Pulse*'s frequently irreverent tone, advertisers were aware that the age demographic they were anxious to reach was reading it, without understanding that the abrasive tone was precisely what brought those readers in.

Skúli heard his phone buzz in his pocket as he got on the bus, but waited until he was seated before digging it from his pocket and scrolling through his messages, peering at the screen.

A headshot of a man with curly dark hair, gazing at a point somewhere to one side and far behind the camera, filled his screen. At first glance there was something attractive about the shape of the man's sculpted chin and elegant, narrow nose, a reassurance about the straightness of the man's shoulders. But a closer look showed an unsettling hardness behind the deep brown eyes.

He scrolled down to read the message that went with the photo and saw that it had come from a contact in Europe, someone he had worked with in his brief stint on a local newspaper in Jutland who had moved on to work with an NGO in Brussels.

You know who this guy is?

Skúli was perplexed. There was something familiar about the face, although he couldn't place it. He thought of doing a web search, so as not to have to admit that he didn't recognize the man, but decided it was too much bother.

He keyed a reply into his phone.

No. But I guess you're going to tell me?

The two black Patrols, one with its windows tinted to match the bodywork, turned up exactly as Ívar Laxdal had predicted. Gunna was half expecting a group of black-uniformed Special Unit officers to tumble out, but instead the two Patrols were manned by young men who looked out of place with the spring wind tugging at their office suits.

She saw the minister's blonde head emerge from the back of the second Patrol with the black windows, smiling and glancing about her. A moment later a lanky figure stepped out, a man with olive skin, a trimmed black beard and obsidian hair that curled over his ears. He hugged a laptop bag, looking around as if he hadn't seen daylight for a long time. He was reassured by the minister, who stopped herself, about to place a hand on his arm as he slung the bag over his shoulder.

The group swept past. Once inside, the suited young men shivered with relief to be out of the wind and the minister's eyes darted around the living room.

'Ívar, everything's ready, I assume?'

'Of course, Steinunn. Just as instructed.'

'And the team?'

'Two officers at the last house you passed on the way here, one officer here.'

The minister looked around again. Gunna had seen her often enough in print and on the screen, but was unprepared for the fact that the politician often depicted as the government's most senior female rottweiler looked decidedly homely close up, tired and with cheeks delicately pitted by ancient acne. Her trademark blonde mane looked attractively windblown and her piercing eyes had an unmistakably determined ruthlessness about them.

'Who?' she asked, looking at Ívar Laxdal with one eyebrow lifted.

'This is Gunnhildur Gísladóttir from the Serious Crime Unit. She will be looking after our friend. I'll be relieving her myself.'

The minister looked Gunna up and down before her unsettling gaze stopped to rest on her face, staring into Gunna's eyes. Gunna longed to snap back, but resisted and held the minister's eyes. She had the distinct feeling of being searched.

'If you say so, Ívar,' she said and extended a hand to Gunna. 'Look after our friend, please,' she said quietly. 'He's a remarkable man.'

Gunna took her time grasping the minister's hand. 'I'll do my best.'

'Gentlemen,' the minister said, and the young men in suits were suddenly silent. She turned and took the tall man's hand in both of hers, looking into his eyes with an intensity that did not escape Gunna, before turning to leave, the young men in suits making haste to follow her.

The man looked from Ívar Laxdal to Gunna and back.

'My name is Osman,' he said in English, his voice warm and with a clear, soft accent.

'Ívar Laxdal. I'm a senior officer with the city police force,' Ívar Laxdal said, with no less of an accent in his English. Gunna wondered if she would sound as harsh with those rough consonants dropping off her tongue. 'This is my colleague Gunnhildur Gísladóttir.'

Gunna felt herself being inspected as the stranger's heavy-lidded eyes travelled from her boots to her eyes, and the slow smile that finally gave some light to his face was clearly one of appreciation, as well as surprise.

'Gunna,' she said and watched him nod as she met his eyes and inspected him in return; seeing a tall man with a spare frame, soft brown eyes, black curly hair and a thin beard with a touch of grey.

'Arrangements are for Gunnhildur to be here with you at the house. We have a squad deployed close by to keep an eye on the approaches and they are a minute away from here,' Ívar Laxdal said.

'I will relieve Gunnhildur periodically. Only Gunnhildur and I know of your presence here, as do, of course, the minister and her staff. We have taken every possible precaution to ensure that your presence here remains between ourselves.'

'Good. Tell me, this place has been swept, has it not?'

'It has. And it's clean,' Ívar Laxdal said.

'Good. You have internet here?'

Ívar Laxdal's lips pursed. 'In the interests of security, we would ask you to be careful with any device that could indicate your location.'

Osman's eyes half closed. 'I have to communicate, but don't worry. I can be discreet and I know how to be careful. I've been keeping out of sight for some time now.' He waved at the laptop bag he had placed on the table. 'I bought the computer at the airport, so I can be sure that it's safe. Anything I need to put into it is here,' he said, placing a finger to his temple.

'Gunnhildur can show you where to connect your computer. Just so you know, our communications division monitors internet traffic here.'

'Fine. A few emails to trusted people and a little searching for information. That is all.'

'Fair enough,' Ívar Laxdal said grudgingly. 'If there's anything you need, then Gunnhildur will list it for delivery. Any problems, and one of us will be here.'

'Thank you,' Osman said in a gracious voice that narrowly escaped being condescending. 'It is very kind of Mrs Strand to go to all this trouble, and it is appreciated. Now, will you show me my room? I would like to rest.'

It was late in the day by the time Skúli had a chance to look again at the message from Lars.

He and Lars had been interns for a few months on a regional newspaper in Jutland that both of them had seen as a valuable experience, but not one that either of them had been inclined to continue. Skúli had returned to Iceland, not without a few regrets, while Lars had found his way to Copenhagen, and from there to

Brussels and a job with Plain Truth, a poorly funded, obscure but energetic NGO.

With his feet on the heavy desk that had been bought from the Red Cross along with every other piece of furniture in *Pulse*'s office, he thumbed a message into his phone.

So tell me who this guy is?

He dropped the phone back on his desk as an email popped up on his computer screen, demanding immediate attention before he could check his phone again.

He calls himself Ali Osman, he read a few minutes later. *We think his name's Osman Ali Deniz.*

OK, Skúli texted back, wondering what Lars was driving at, but sure that an answer would appear. While he waited, he typed Ali Osman's name into a search engine and found himself looking at a bewildering screenful of entries before trying the other name.

Where's this going? he punched into his phone as a second screen of information appeared, including the picture he had already seen.

We think he's in Iceland. Call me later and I'll tell you more, Lars's message read.

OK. Speak later.

Cool. Google the guy if you haven't already.

Way ahead of you . . . Skúli texted back and dropped his phone back onto the desk.

He sat back in thought, closed the document he'd been working on and began to read.

The smell of cooking brought him from his room, yawning and sleepy. Gunna had decided to keep it simple with grilled chicken, rice and vegetables. The man took his plate wordlessly and sat at the table. He paused for a moment with his eyes closed and then set to, dismembering the chicken and sprinkling it with pepper.

He stopped and his eyes widened as Gunna put her plate opposite him and sat down to eat. She poured water into two glasses from a jug, pushing one towards him.

'Enjoy your meal,' she said.

'Thank you, officer. I didn't expect you to be joining me.'

Gunna shrugged. 'Is there a reason I shouldn't?'

'No, of course not. I'm used to being alone, that's all.'

He ate fast, with the speed of a man who can't be sure that the food won't be snatched away before he has finished it. Bones collected in a pile at the edge of his plate, gnawed clean. He left nothing.

'Good?' Gunna asked and immediately regretted it. It wasn't good, but it was acceptable.

'Not bad.'

He sat back in his chair with his water glass in his hand, sipping nonchalantly, watching Gunna finish her meal.

'You are a cook?' he asked finally.

'No. I'm a police officer.'

'For many years?'

'Around twenty.'

'And now secret police?'

Gunna shook her head. 'I'm a regular police officer. We don't have secret police in this country.'

'Really?' There was a blend of amazement and disbelief in his voice.

'Really.'

'You are not in uniform like your friend.'

'This isn't an assignment that calls for uniform. And he's not my friend. He's my boss.'

'Your name. Gunnhildur.'

He pronounced it *Goon-hild-ar*.

'Gunnhildur,' she corrected him. 'Everyone calls me Gunna, except for Ívar. But he likes to keep things formal.'

'Gunna,' he said softly in a closer approximation of her name. 'My name is Osman.'

'So you said.'

'That is my family name. You don't know my first name?'

'I'm not asking questions,' she said and watched his teeth appear in a smile.

'But you would like to ask questions?'

She had to admit to herself that she was struggling to contain

20

her natural curiosity, faced with this languidly handsome man, his beguiling dark eyes and an easy familiarity as he lounged comfortably in the rigid upright kitchen chair, as she cleared her plate. Again she had the feeling she was being scanned and labelled.

'A lot of police work is asking questions. But occasionally you have to know when not to ask.'

'You are married?' he asked, his voice dropping.

'I have been.'

She asked herself if that was a look of disapproval that flashed across his face.

'You are separated from your husband?'

Gunna stacked the plates in front of her before answering.

'No. He died. Are you washing up or am I?'

Osman watched as Gunna loaded the dishwasher and she wondered if it would be worth getting one at home. Maybe when Laufey had left home, she decided. Until then her daughter could do most of the washing up in lieu of bed, board, laundry and a great many lifts.

She took her time, hoping that Osman would go back to his room and sleep or occupy himself with his new laptop, but he appeared to have no such inclination. With the pans dried and put away, and the dishwasher hissing quietly in its corner, she sat down again at the table.

'I'll probably be here with you for a few days. My colleague will be here to relieve me after that, then I'll be back the following day. All right with you? We're keeping this as low profile as possible. I gather the minister doesn't want too many people to know you're here.'

'That's what she told me as well,' Osman said. 'She said this place is very quiet and I can work without interruption. Mrs Strand is a wonderful lady, and so generous.'

Gunna fought back the comment that the minister was being generous with public resources rather than her own, and nodded in reply.

'She's quite a character,' Gunna said, wondering if that was a suitably diplomatic thing to say.

'You don't like her?' Osman asked, as if he had read her thoughts.

'Let's say that our opinions probably wouldn't coincide on very much.'

Osman's smile was broad this time and his teeth flashed.

'Gunna. Do you know why I'm here?'

'Actually, no. I haven't been told a great deal and I gather that seems to be part of the overall plan. The less we know, the better, from what I can make out.'

Osman leaned forward, placing his elbows on the table and cupping his face in his hands. His fingers were long and delicate, and Gunna noticed that the first finger of his left hand was short, ending abruptly at the first joint.

'I will explain, but without saying too much,' he said, as if speaking to an innocent. 'I am here because I know too much. There are secrets in my head that some people would prefer I did not know. They are so worried about their precious secrets that they would be glad to take my life to make sure I don't pass them on to anyone. You understand?'

Gunna felt her mouth go dry at the thought.

'In that case, I understand.'

'And they would take the life of anyone they thought I might have passed their secrets to.'

'Like me or Ívar?' Gunna asked. 'Or Steinunn?'

'I met Mrs Strand at a conference where I was speaking, and she invited me to come to your country for a few months as Iceland is so safe and I could work on the book I would like to write.'

Gunna felt her heart sink at the reference to months.

'I see. Your life is in danger in your own country?'

'I think my life is in danger in every country,' he said seriously and Gunna was conscious of the weight of the Glock at her side.

Gunna prowled the bare garden, shivering with her hands deep in her jacket pockets, the bulk of the Glock bumping under her arm as she familiarized herself with the layout of the building and its surroundings, wondering what she had let herself in for. Unlike the house itself, where little expense had been spared to make it comfortable, the garden had received little attention. In the corner behind the garage a hot tub had been installed with a wooden screen around it, its plastic cover glazed with frost.

The garden had been planted and then neglected. What had been intended to become flower beds were being invaded by grass, and Gunna guessed that by the end of the summer they would be indistinguishable from the scrubby grass surrounding them. A row of bare shrubs planted to turn into a hedge around the place looked like a row of forlorn sticks waiting for summer to bring them back to life. The outside of the house looked bare, and had an abandoned feel compared to the smartly furnished interior.

Looking around, she could see the next house half a kilometre away along an unmade track. It was a fairly new building, at the furthest edge of a spreading estate, and the tall, narrow windows in the end wall overlooked Einholt. Gunna hoped that in one of them was a Special Unit officer with his eyes to a pair of binoculars on a tripod. She waved a hand at the house, fairly confident that she would know whoever might be watching.

On the lower side of the house the ground shelved away gently downhill to the shoreline. On a day like today, with no sunshine breaking through the clouds, the dark rocks by the shore faded seamlessly into the sea that lapped against them, while the grey sea and sky merged together in the distance beyond the black hump of Geldinganes.

A sudden flurry of snow startled her and Gunna huddled deeper into her coat, blinking the sharp grains from her eyes. There was no noise beyond a practically indiscernible hum of distant traffic and the mutter of waves nagging at the rocks below.

The grey landscape would be fading into darkness soon. Her circuit complete, Gunna was sure that everything was quiet. With a final look around her, she unlocked the door and stepped inside the lobby, double locking the door behind her as Ívar Laxdal had instructed.

Skúli was tired, and little Markús laughed with delight to see him home. The last year had been a tough one, but in the past few months fate seemed to be smiling on them. First an elderly relative of Dagga's had given them a basement flat in Seltjarnarnes – a part of town they would never otherwise have been able to afford – in return for a rent they could actually manage. Then, after much soul-searching and calculating how long they could survive on their remaining savings, they had taken the plunge and joined the group setting up *Pulse*, providing news of the kind the newspapers rarely touched, as well as often controversial comment and opinions.

'Good day?' Dagga asked as Skúli shrugged the laptop bag from his shoulder and kicked off his shoes.

'Not bad. And you?'

'It's been all right. There's some dinner left if you're hungry.'

Dagga's unplanned but nonetheless welcome pregnancy had thrown all their plans into disarray. Now she spent most of her working time at a laptop at the kitchen table when Markús was with her parents while Skúli commuted to *Pulse*'s office in an old building on Hverfisgata that would undoubtedly be demolished sooner or later, but in the meantime they made the most of the place. Best of all, *Pulse* had stopped losing money after only a few weeks.

Skúli admitted to himself that this had been a surprise, and although it wasn't making huge amounts, each of them was now able to take a modest wage from the venture. Best of all, there were investors sniffing around with real interest, looking to buy a stake with an injection of cash that would be enough to lift them off the ground properly, or so they hoped.

'Great. Has Markús been fed yet?'

'Yeah. But he's still hungry. Can you take over? I deserve a long bath.'

'Right away?' Skúli asked, slightly dismayed as he still had his coat on.

'Yes. As close to right away as possible. I love our son with all my heart, but I'll go nuts if I have him on my hip for a minute longer.'

There was a note of determination in Dagga's voice which Skúli knew from experience he should ignore at his peril. So as water roared into the tub in the flat's cramped, old-fashioned bathroom, he arranged himself a plate of microwaved goulash and a tub of yoghurt for his son on the kitchen table. Then he opened his laptop out of reach of Markús's inquisitive fingers.

They ate in a desultory fashion as he spooned food alternately into himself and then Markús, checking *Pulse*'s website and social media channels in between. He checked Lars's profile and logged into Skype, looking to see Lars appear in his list of contacts and puzzled to see 'offline' against his name.

'Still in the tub?' he called out to Dagga.

'Yes.'

'Going to be long?'

'Yes. Why?'

Dagga had left the bathroom door open. Skúli carried Markús in and grinned to see her lying stretched out in the bath with a candle burning by her head and a book in her hands.

'Has Markús had a bath?'

'No, not yet.'

'Drop him in with you for a minute?'

'Uh-huh,' she agreed, eyes on the paperback in her hand.

Skúli closed the toilet lid and sat on it to undress Markús, then leaned over and lowered him into the water as Dagga moved her legs aside to make room for him. The little boy splashed happily, then gasped and shook his head as Skúli gently poured warm water over his head, smoothing his hair back from his eyes.

'Good book?'

'Uh-huh.'

Skúli peeked at the cover and saw an Arctic landscape. A thriller, nothing romantic this time, he reflected as he lifted Markús clear of the water and wrapped him in a towel, then in his arms.

'Going to be long?' he repeated gently.

Dagga lowered the book. 'Why do you ask?'

'Nothing special,' he said with a smirk, enjoying what he could see of her beneath the milky water. She arched her back slightly and stretched. For a moment her dark bush broke the surface and he felt a rush of excitement before she sank back into the depths. 'I have a call to make in a minute, then I'm all yours once Markús is asleep.'

'If you're lucky,' Dagga told him. 'Once the water's cooled off I might be all yours, young man.'

It was a private joke in their circle of friends that Dagga was a shameless cradle-snatcher, having ensnared a man a couple of years younger than herself. Occasionally it irritated him when it was alluded to in company, but between the two of them it was mentioned with a tenderness that hinted at good things to come later.

They had known each other for a long time, as colleagues and friends, long before they had found themselves on the same interminably dull press trip to the east of Iceland, during which their shared sense of the ridiculous had gelled into something deeper. On the last morning of the trip, the group of invited journalists had listened to a long and intense presentation without two of their number, much to the consternation of the press officer, who had been determined to shepherd the group around every nook and cranny of a new factory and its offices.

Markús was soon asleep in his cot and Skúli went back to the kitchen table. He found himself brooding, thinking back to the press trip where he and Dagga had finally fallen into each other's arms and a hotel bed that had creaked and squeaked alarmingly.

He shook his head, telling himself to snap out of it and concentrate. But a vague suspicion formed distressingly at the back of his mind, something he desperately wanted not to think through as the shadow of his deeply buried fear snaked around his ankles like an unwelcome mist.

Lars was still logged out of Skype, so Skúli tapped in his mobile number and listened to it ring. He was about to give up when it was finally answered.

'Yah?'

'Lars? It's Skúli. What's new?'

'Ah, Skúli. I'm really sorry. I'm in a bar, I forgot you were going to call.'

'You busy? I can call back tomorrow.'

'Yeah, that's best,' he heard Lars say, half-distractedly, and Skúli could hear the hubbub of a busy bar in the background.

'Listen, what did you find out about Ali Osman?'

'Not that much,' Skúli admitted. 'He's a dissident of some kind? From Lebanon? That's what I read anyway.'

Lars laughed. 'He's a dissident right enough, but not for the right reasons.'

'How so?'

'He's a dissident because he fell out with the wrong people over a lot of money. He says he's Lebanese originally, but I have my doubts.'

'OK. So what's your interest in him?'

'As always,' Lars said, 'human rights. He's been involved in people trafficking, or at least in the finance side of it.'

'So he's not everything he claims to be?'

'Is anyone?'

'And why bring this to me?'

Lars laughed again. 'Because Ali Osman, or Osman Ali Deniz, whichever name he happens to be using at the moment, but I guess he's Ali Osman right now, is a discreet and honoured guest of your Minister of Justice. He arrived yesterday or today, as far as we can work out. You might want to ask a few questions.'

'And report back to you?'

'Of course. I get to know where this bastard is, and you get a scandal to put on your front page. Everybody wins, eh?'

'Cool. Thanks, Lars.'

'Listen, Skúli. I have a meeting to go to in a few minutes.'

Skúli could still hear the buzz of a happy crowd in the background.

'Is she pretty?'

'What did you say?'

'I said, this meeting you have to go to, is she pretty?'

Lars guffawed. 'You think of only one thing, Skúli. But you're right, legs up to here. Listen, my friend, call me in the morning and I'll tell you more about Ali Osman, yeah?'

'Yeah, OK, Lars. Have fun . . .'

'And you,' Lars replied as a flurry of laughter enveloped him and the call came to an abrupt end.

He sat back and nodded to himself, deep in thought, not noticing Dagga's towel-swathed presence until she placed her hands on his shoulders.

'Who was that?'

'Lars. He's in Brussels at some meeting.'

'In a bar?'

'Of course. Probably surrounded by a troop of travelling pole dancers. But he gave me a story, or at least a lead.'

'Something juicy?'

'Steinunn Strand's involved.'

'Then it's bound to be crooked. It's late and I'm going to bed. Coming?'

'Uh-huh,' he said with a feigned lack of interest that led to an affectionate punch on the shoulder. She stalked past him, the towel around her waist falling away in the bedroom doorway – Skúli was out of his chair almost before it hit the floor.

Gunna listened to the house ticking. It was surprising what you could hear when the building should have been entirely silent. The bedroom nearest the front door was hers, while Osman had made himself comfortable in the spacious master bedroom that occupied one end of the long building.

Restless, irritable and unable to sleep, she pulled on a sweater and made a tour of the darkened building. Peering through the living-room window, she could see the window of the next house gazing blindly back at her. Outside, the wind seemed to have dropped away and the bare ground of the garden was lit by the fitful moon when it appeared between the clouds.

She checked every window, tried the doors and sat in the kitchen listening to the quiet house. The heating hummed faintly and the oven clock ticked, its sound as low as to be inaudible during the day but now as loud as clicking heels on a hard floor.

Satisfied that the place was as secure as it could be, she sat in one of the vast armchairs in the living room, feeling herself enveloped in it, and lifting her feet onto the stone-topped coffee table. She clicked on a lamp and picked up a magazine from the rack at her side, flipping through the articles on houses and gardens belonging to people with much greater wealth and far more time on their hands than she would ever have.

She woke to feel movement at her side, a stealthy hand creeping inside her jacket. Her eyes snapped open and she gripped the searching hand, wondering how long she had been asleep in the chair, or even if she had been asleep at all.

Osman crouched before her. The suit was gone, replaced with grey tracksuit trousers and a dark singlet. She could see the tightness of his lips as her thumb dug deep and hard into the soft underside of his wrist. Their eyes met and she held his gaze as the hand that had been reaching for the Glock under her arm went numb. She maintained her grip, watching his face as it went blank.

'Enough,' he said quietly.

Gunna slowly relaxed her grip.

He stood up languidly, a quizzical smile on his face, and nodded to himself as if he were in possession of some private piece of knowledge.

'I'm delighted to see you're alert, Goon-hil-dar,' he said quietly, rubbing his wrist. 'I might have said something about a woman and a gun not being an ideal combination, but I don't think I need to.'

He turned and padded away on bare feet and Gunna heard the door of his room click shut.

Chapter Two

Ívar Laxdal arrived early, bearing fresh fruit and still-warm rolls for breakfast.

'All shipshape, Gunnhildur?' he asked after she had checked who was at the door before unlocking it twice and locking it again behind him.

'All quiet. Coffee?'

They talked quietly in the kitchen over mugs of better coffee than anything that ever graced the Hverfisgata police station's canteen.

'Nothing to report?'

'Not a thing,' Gunna said, hesitating. 'I had a long walk around the garden yesterday and there's nothing to be seen anywhere. There's a clear line of sight all around the place, so if anyone were trying to get here, it wouldn't be a problem for the boys up the road to spot them in good time, assuming they're on the ball.'

'They are and that's why this place was chosen.'

'So who owns this house?'

Ívar Laxdal's face broke into a rare smile.

'It belongs to the minister and her husband.'

'This is Steinunn's place?'

'It is. I gather her husband inherited it quite a few years ago. They pulled down the old farmhouse that was here and built this. It's an investment, I reckon. Property doesn't lose value for long. I understand they rent it out to distinguished visitors during the summer. We had to beef up the security with extra locks and cameras, though.'

'Like an up-market Airbnb?'

'Exactly. But it's not advertised anywhere and her clientele is pretty exclusive. How's our friend?'

'Very superior, in a discreet kind of way. Doesn't say a lot. He ate everything I gave him for dinner and he didn't offer to help with the washing up.'

Ívar Laxdal smiled fleetingly. 'Do you imagine he's ever washed a dish in his life?'

'So, do I get to know who he is?'

'I don't rightly know myself. All I can tell you is that the man's a dissident of some kind, had something to do with the protests in Egypt a couple of years ago, and he daren't go home.'

'So he's claiming asylum here?'

'No idea. Not as far as I know. All I can be sure of is that he's Steinunn's guest, and he's clearly something special as far as she's concerned.'

'So if he does decide he likes it here, then I guess she'll put in a good word for him at the Immigration Directorate?'

'I don't imagine he'd have to wait as long as some of them do,' Ívar Laxdal said drily.

Skúli brooded while Markús dutifully swallowed one spoonful after another of yoghurt mixed with cereal and Dagga spread honey on toast for them both.

He felt a faint but definite lethargy, a distant voice calling to him from somewhere in the back of his mind, telling him not to be too pleased with himself, not to let himself get carried away. He knew the voice and tried to hustle it out of his mind, ordering himself to ignore it, to banish the lurking self-doubt that had chosen this moment to tug at his ankle, to remind him that it was still there in the depths, waiting to break the surface.

'You're going to the office today?' Dagga said, crunching toast.

'I ought to. But I should be back in good time.'

'Something juicy?'

'Not sure,' he said absently. 'That lead Lars gave me, I'm not sure if it's something good or not, but it looks interesting.'

'So you need to chase it up? What's it about?'

Markús shut his mouth firmly and refused to be tempted to take another mouthful.

'He's had plenty,' Dagga said.

Skúli tenderly wiped his son's mouth.

'I had no idea small children could be quite so messy,' he said with sorrow.

Dagga snorted. 'Wait until he's fifteen, then you'll see what messy really is.'

'I'm not sure I was ever like that,' Skúli protested.

'I don't suppose you were. But your family are the weirdest people in the world. You were expected to be forty the day you turned fourteen.'

Skúli shivered at the thought of his parents, which instantly brought back the nagging dark feeling he wanted to be rid of.

'True,' he admitted and forced a smile. 'They are pretty nuts.'

'Nuts? I'm amazed you escaped unscathed.'

'You mean when you snatched me from the bosom of my family?'

'Something like that. I don't recall that you needed a lot of persuasion,' she said through a mouthful of toast. 'What's this story Lars put you on to?'

'This dubious character who's come to Iceland as Steinunn Strand's guest.'

'He'd have to be something shady if he's a friend of hers.'

'Careful. My dad thinks she's wonderful.'

'Has he met her?'

'Undoubtedly. Anyway, Lars reckons there's a story in it for us, and we could do with something scandalous to get our teeth into.'

'On top of that right-wing nutjob who's supposed to be holding a public meeting on Sunday? Or is that tonight?'

'The American? McCombie? Tonight and again tomorrow. Arndís is interviewing him today.'

'Poor her.'

'Don't you miss this stuff?"

Dagga thought for a second as she plucked Markús from his high chair and bounced him on one knee.

'I used to,' she said. 'But when I think of having to interview shitbags like McCombie, I don't miss it any more.'

Ívar Laxdal ate much of the breakfast he had brought himself.

'Our friend's still asleep?'

'I assume so. I haven't seen him yet this morning.'

He peered at his watch. 'It's still early.'

'Early for some. It's almost ten. That's half the day gone.'

Ívar Laxdal stretched for the coffee and poured himself another mug, munching one of the pastries he'd brought with him.

'If Sleeping Beauty's not up in time for breakfast, then I suppose we'll have to eat it ourselves,' he said, opening a notebook. 'He's going into town today, so we have a few security headaches to deal with. He has a meeting at the Vatnsmýri Hotel, and that means us as well.'

Gunna helped herself to a fresh kringla twist and took a critical bite, reflecting that they always took her back to her childhood in the West.

'Not a patch on the ones from back home,' she said, but finished it anyway. 'So what does Osman's social whirl have in store for us?'

Ívar Laxdal looked up from his hardback notebook. Anyone else would have made a note in their phone.

'Today there's the meeting with Kyle McCombie at Hotel Vatnsmýri. There's dinner with Steinunn at her house, date to be confirmed. Then there's a day in Thingvellir lined up, depending on the weather, and after that there's a visit to Parliament. He also has a couple of other meetings pencilled in.'

'And are we joining him for all of these? Including the meeting with the weirdo?'

Ívar Laxdal coughed.

'Weirdo?'

'McCombie. The crazy white supremacist from the other side

of the Atlantic. I was reading an interview with him and he's completely mad.'

Ívar Laxdal nodded sagely.

'I would be inclined to agree with you. There have been petitions to get him denied entry to the country and there's a demonstration supposed to be taking place outside the public meeting he's holding this evening – every available officer has been drafted to jump in if it boils over.'

'Laufey was talking about him last week. I have a feeling she's going to be at the demo, so I'd appreciate it if she didn't find herself in a cell.'

'She won't.' He chuckled. 'As long as she just shouts and doesn't throw bottles, she should be fine. Anyway, we take him to meet McCombie at the hotel. Once that's over, we bring him back here. Osman's not going to the meeting.'

'I wonder what they have to talk about,' Gunna mused. 'A dissident Middle Eastern philanthropist and a hardline string-'em-up right winger; what do they have in common?'

'Extremism, I imagine, Gunnhildur,' Ívar Laxdal said. 'Who knows? Maybe they'll hate each other?'

When Ívar Laxdal had left, Gunna walked a circuit of the garden, enjoying the freshness of the morning air and the wind blowing off the sea bringing a sharp tang of seaweed with it. The upper slopes of Mount Esja were decked with a thicker covering of snow than the day before and she was sure it was only the warmish southerly wind that was keeping the snow down here at sea level at bay. The thought of her son Gísli, back at sea in this weather, was uncomfortable but nothing alarming. He was working on a smaller boat than the one he'd spent the last few years on, sacrificing a level of comfort for shorter trips that would bring him home to his young family every few days instead of once a month.

Gunna shivered. Gísli was the least of her worries at the moment. This assignment to look after the mysterious Osman meant that she was out of touch with Laufey and Steini, although she had no doubt that they would look after themselves well enough during her absence, possibly with more frequent visits to the Chinese takeaway in Keflavík than would be normal; the bin would be crammed with foil cartons by the time she next got home.

She unlocked the door, glancing around to make sure she wasn't being watched, took a last breath of salt-laden sea air and stepped into the house's warm interior. Boots off and replaced by sandals, she completed a circuit indoors, checking the windows and doors, making sure the back door leading to the hot tub was secure and satisfying herself that everything was as it should be.

In the kitchen she checked the time, saw that it was three hours before they would be collected. She sat in the living room's largest armchair, trying to concentrate on a book, but felt herself constantly conscious of the Glock under her arm and the communicator earpiece, as if she were waiting for something to happen. When Osman appeared, casual in jeans and an open-necked shirt, she was happy to put the book down.

Osman lounged on the sofa opposite.

'Have you been able to work?' she asked.

'Yes, thank you. This is a very peaceful place. A lovely little house,' he observed, looking round at the walls hung with paintings that Gunna suspected included a few genuine Kjarvals. He poured himself a glass of juice, and draped himself across another armchair as he sipped it. 'Tell me about yourself, Gunna,' he said, that brilliant smile returning. 'Tell me again: how long have you done this job?'

'Twenty years, with a break or two.'

'And is being a policeman in Iceland exciting?'

'I didn't join for the excitement.'

'So why did you join the police? You must have been young, no?'

'More for the variety, I guess. I couldn't stand the thought of doing the same thing day after day in some office or factory. The opportunity was there and I took it,' Gunna said, reluctant to go into her own life story in any detail. 'What brought you to Iceland, if you don't mind my asking? It seems a strange place for someone who's used to a warmer climate.'

The smile flashed again.

'I met Steinunn at a human rights conference in Helsinki where I had been asked to speak, and again in Paris several times at receptions and meetings. She invited me here if I wanted to get away from everything for a while. I wanted to work on a book, so it seemed the perfect opportunity.'

'What's the book about?'

Osman thought for a moment, and Gunna could see him deciding what he ought to tell her.

'A little about my life when I was younger, when things were very difficult. And there will be a lot about the situation as it is at present in the Middle East, where I am not as popular as I would prefer to be.'

'You must be in a difficult position if your life's in danger if you go home.'

'Much danger.' He laughed. 'But I'm not sure I should tell you too much. In my country we do not talk to the police willingly.'

'So where is your country?'

Osman winked and his teeth gleamed.

'I have several countries, and at the moment I'm not welcome in any of them.'

'So where do you live?'

'In Brussels mostly. It's the most convenient place for me to work as it's central. It's not as grey as London, but it's less interesting. The authorities there are sympathetic to my position – for the moment, in any case – but it's not a safe city.'

'And Iceland's safe?'

'I hope so,' he said and the dazzling smile flashed back into action. 'Gunna, I think a cup of coffee would be welcome, don't you?'

It took a moment for her to realize that he expected her to make coffee.

'Help yourself,' she said. 'It's in the cupboard at the end.'

This time his smile was tinged with regret, but not embarrassment. 'I don't make coffee.'

Or cook, or wash up, Gunna thought as she got up from the chair. I wonder what's going to happen when we get to laundry?

'It's easy enough. I'll show you.'

She filled the jug with water and poured it into the percolator while Osman stood next to her, closer than was necessary. She could smell a spicy fragrance to him, elusive but with a hint of warmth to it.

'Water in there,' she explained, filling the machine before opening the drawer to put a paper filter inside. 'Then the coffee,' she added, and froze for a moment as a hand alighted on her waist and slid gently downwards to rest on one buttock. 'Three spoonfuls,' she said through gritted teeth, counting them out as his hand gently kneaded.

She flipped the machine's drawer shut and could feel Osman's breath on her neck as his hand travelled up and snaked back around her waist.

'Switch on here and in a few minutes you'll have coffee,' she said, flipping the switch and twisting out of his grasp. She lifted the hand that was reluctant to be moved and placed it firmly on the worktop. 'I'm afraid there are some things that are definitely not included in the minister's hospitality, Mr Osman.'

The pale man was checking the pistol again, turning it over in his hands.

His broad-chested, black-bearded companion lay in the hollow and peered through binoculars set up on a tripod behind tufts of long grass.

'Nothing's happened since he turned up yesterday.'

'She'll have to come up here herself if she wants to be sure it's him.'

'She's sure.'

The dark man shivered and looked over the binoculars at the grey skies and light frosting of snow on the brooding mountain in the distance.

'Weird country,' he grunted.

'We've seen worse.'

'Would you rather be back in Chad or Niger?' the dark man asked.

'Niger? God forbid,' he shuddered and cradled the revolver in his hands.

'Happy with that antique, are you?'

'It may be an antique, but it's simple, and that means not much to go wrong.' He lifted the pistol and looked along the sight. 'The sooner we can deal with this, the better. I don't like this cloak-and-dagger shit. It feels wrong, somehow.'

Lars appeared, with his trademark grin filling the screen.

'Hey, Skúli.'

'Hi Lars.'

'How's life?'

'Not bad. *Pulse* is doing pretty well. Oh, and I'm a dad now.'

'*Mazel tov*, my friend! Girl or boy?'

'A boy. He's ten months, crawling everywhere.'

Lars beamed. 'That's wonderful, Skúli. I knew you could do it.'

'Well, the technical part of it wasn't exactly difficult, it's all the stuff since then that's been hard.'

'Well, I wish you many more.'

'Practising for the next one,' Skúli said, and hoped Arndís on the other side of the office wasn't listening to his conversation. 'Now, pleasantries and family news aside, what's all this about?'

The grin vanished from Lars's face and he was suddenly all business.

'The guy whose picture I sent you, yeah? We've been watching him carefully for a while now and we're as sure as we can be that he's not everything he makes out he is. In fact, he's a lot more, and it's not pleasant.'

'OK, and where do I come in to all this?'

Lars leaned forward, close to his own screen, and his voice dropped.

'He's in Iceland, as far as we can figure out. I'll email you all the docs so you have all the background to play with. There are gaps, but we've figured out the money's coming from a bunch of unidentifiable sources, which probably means carrier bags full of cash being paid into bank accounts in countries that don't ask too many questions. This then finds its way to Osman's organization via a few jumping-off points along the way. As far as anyone's concerned, these are donations to a charitable cause.'

'Which isn't as charitable as people would like to think it is?'

'Precisely, Skúli,' Lars said, his enthusiasm for the subject bubbling over. 'It's a scam, I suppose. A really efficient scam. Look through the details and you'll see it's all there, or most of it.'

Skúli sat back and glanced over at Arndís, seeing that she had the phone to her ear and a ballpoint in her hand as she quickly scribbled notes.

'And what are you proposing?'

'A grand slam,' Lars said with satisfaction. 'We all share information, and we each come up with a story that goes live at the same time.'

'When you say "we all", what do you mean?'

'Ah . . .' Lars said. 'I want to bring Sophie in on it if that's all right with you.'

'Sophie?'

'You remember Sophie. You met her that time you came to Antwerp?'

'French? Tall? Terrifying?'

'That's her. I see you recall all the main points.'

Lars disappeared for a moment, then the screen flickered and a new window opened.

'Can you hear me, Sophie?' Lars said, and an impassive face under an ink-black fringe appeared in the third window.

'I'm here. Good to see you again, Skúli.'

'And you, Sophie,' he said politely.

'You've discussed everything? And you know what this is about, Skúli?'

'I will when I've read through the docs Lars is sending. What's the plan? When do you want this to go live?'

'Tomorrow,' Lars said. 'Is that too soon for you?'

'I'll know when I've read through the info,' Skúli said, and paused as his laptop bleeped an alert, 'which looks like it's just dropped into my inbox. Can you tell me what makes you think this guy's in Iceland?'

'He's been very friendly with your minister for a while now. She visited one of the camps in Greece that his foundation provides with support, and they've been seen at conferences, in particular one in Helsinki recently where they spent a long time talking.'

'Have you seen him, Skúli?' Sophie broke in. 'He's a good-looking man. He charmed your minister.'

'True,' Lars agreed. 'I met him once, about a year ago, and he should be selling second-hand cars or yachts. He's a genuinely charismatic person. He charms everyone.'

'So we go live tomorrow?' Sophie said impatiently. 'I'm ready to go and I don't want to hang around until someone else gets there first.'

Skúli scratched his chin as he thought, his thumbnail rasping on the bristles along the side of his jaw.

'How time-sensitive is this?'

'For me, very,' Sophie said. 'For Lars, not quite so pressing, but I guess for you it's best to get this out there fast?'

'I'll have to approach the ministry. I can't run this without giving them a chance to comment. I'll be strung up otherwise.'

He saw Lars and Sophie look to a corner of their respective screens, as if glancing at each other from their different countries.

'If you think you have to,' Lars said. 'I suppose we ought to try and be ethical journalists.'

'We're going live at what time?' Skúli asked.

'Tomorrow morning. Ten European time.'

'That's nine here,' he said and hesitated. 'I'll call the ministry press officer at the end of the day and ask for a comment. She might decline, but hopefully she'll say no comment. That way I can put my hand on my heart and say I approached them, but they declined to confirm or deny. That would be ideal.'

'Good,' Sophie said in a curt tone. 'It was good to see you again, Skúli. We'll speak tonight if anything changes, otherwise we'll share any new information? All right?'

'Agreed,' Skúli said.

'Good. Goodbye,' she replied and her screen vanished.

'You heard the lady,' Lars chuckled. 'Give me a call if you have any questions. Now get to work, Skúli.'

It had taken every ounce of persuasion he could muster to persuade Valgeir to meet, and only then for a hasty beer after work.

Sólon wasn't the quietest place they could meet, but it had the advantage of being close for them both. Valgeir seemed preoccupied, twisting his phone in his hands and checking it every few minutes.

'Beer?'

'It's a bit early, but yeah. Make it a small one.'

Skúli returned with a tall glass for Valgeir and a fruit juice for himself. He forced Valgeir to put his phone away for a second by holding his glass out to clink them together.

'You're not drinking?'

Skúli shook his head. 'Medication. Best to keep away from it,' he mumbled.

He felt suddenly embarrassed and hoped Valgeir wouldn't push the conversation in that direction. He had no desire to explain that he had stopped taking the anti-depressants a few months ago and was feeling fairly well, just vulnerable and over-sensitive, something that alcohol would only exacerbate. He only dared have a glass of wine at home in his own secure environment where it was safe to let down his defences. It worried him that he could feel the old symptoms starting to creep up on him again, and so far he hadn't told Dagga that he'd stopped taking his meds.

'So what's this all about?' Valgeir asked, sipping his beer and looking down at his phone on the table in front of him.

'Steinunn's keeping you busy?'

It was Valgeir's turn to shake his head.

'Just a bit. Run off my feet at the moment.'

Skúli reflected that Valgeir had changed out of all recognition since they had been at university together; he wondered if he had changed as much. Valgeir had been the class joker, and he tried to

41

think back to the last time he'd heard him tell any kind of joke. He felt a moment's guilt at using an old friendship and the fact that he was one of Dagga's relatives to squeeze out a lead for a story, but decided it wasn't worth agonizing over. Two beers was all it normally took to get Valgeir to share ministry gossip, after which it was more of a challenge to stem the flow of indiscretions.

'What is it you're after?' Valgeir asked, jolting Skúli from his thoughts.

'Who says I'm after anything?'

Valgeir's eyes narrowed.

'Journalists don't buy people like me a drink unless there's something in it.'

'Normally you wouldn't be right. But this time you are,' he said. 'I hear Steinunn has a guest.'

Valgeir spluttered into his beer and coughed violently.

'How do you . . . ?' he said once Skúli had patted his back. 'I mean, what makes you think that?'

Skúli winked.

'I hear all kinds of rumours, so I was wondering if this one's true.'

Valgeir shuddered and looked around. Sólon's upstairs bar was still relatively quiet this early in the day, with only a group of man-bunned hipsters hunched over a laptop at the far end of the room.

'I hear he's a Mr Osman,' Skúli prompted.

'Hell, Skúli. Do you want to get me strung up?'

'Of course not. Complete confidence and not a word to anyone. I'm just testing the water, wondering if I'm on the right track.'

Valgeir took a deep breath, his face blank as he stared at Skúli. 'I could do with another of these,' he said, tapping his empty glass. 'But I have to go back to work, so you'd better get me a coffee.'

'If that gets me answers, no problem.'

Valgeir was pecking at his phone with a forefinger when Skúli returned with a mug and placed it in front of him.

'So?'

'So what?'

'Osman.'

Valgeir screwed up his face in a scowl and sipped his coffee, as if buying himself time and deciding what he could safely say.

'Not a word?'

'Absolutely. Not a word.'

'Can I trust you on that?'

'Come on, Valgeir. I can't afford to burn my sources.'

'I'm a source, am I?'

'Friend, relative, source, in that order.'

'Fuck you, Skúli. You're putting me in a lousy position.'

'And you're helping a gentleman of the press who will be for ever in your debt.'

'All right. His name's Osman. He's from somewhere in the Middle East, and that's about all I know. There's a dossier on him but I haven't seen it and I don't think Steinunn has either. At any rate, she has access but hasn't read it.'

'What's he doing in Iceland?'

Valgeir shrugged.

'Search me. He's Steinunn's guest, and he's here at her invitation. She's met him a couple of times before and lapped up every word he said at a conference in Helsinki last month. She thinks he's some kind of guru and saint all rolled into one; she believes the sun shines out of his arsehole.'

'Is she . . . ?'

'Hell, Skúli,' Valgeir said with a grimace. 'She's fifteen years older than he is, plus Steinunn's married. Now you've given me a mental image I could have done without. In any case, it couldn't happen. There's always someone there and he's being minded by a security detail. They wouldn't be able to get thirty seconds alone together without one of us knowing exactly what they're up to, so put that thought out of your filthy mind.'

'So what's he doing here?'

'Working on his memoirs, or so he says.'

'And what's he really up to?'

Valgeir closed his eyes.

'Don't push it, please. I'm in enough shit already.'

★ ★ ★

There was a brooding menace to the darkening weather, as if winter was playing games and refusing to give up its hold until the last possible moment. There was still a chance of snow carried by the icy north wind, and Gunna hoped that winter would relax its grip before too long.

It felt strange to be cooking a meal so early in the day, but she resigned herself to domestic duties being part of the assignment, silently regretting that she couldn't draft Steini in to handle some of the kitchen duties he performed with such flair when he had time.

Osman smiled as Gunna filled two plates and handed one of them to him.

'Thank you,' he said with a slight bow.

He poured wine the colour of blood into a glass and gestured to her. Gunna shook her head.

'Not for me. I'm on duty, remember?'

They ate in silence to begin with. Osman cleaned every shred of meat from the bones, one by one, daintily licking his fingers.

'So, Gunnhildur,' he said with a satisfied sigh and a smothered belch. 'You will have a glass of wine when you are no longer on duty?'

'Maybe. Whenever that is.'

His face opened into a warm smile, white teeth contrasting with the jet black of his thin beard.

'You have always lived in Reykjavík? You like this place?'

Gunna laid down her knife and fork.

'No. And not really.'

'Two answers?'

'No, I haven't always lived in Reykjavík. In fact, I don't live in Reykjavík now. My house is in a village by the coast. So I have an hour's drive to work every day.'

'Why do you not move to a house in the city?'

Gunna wanted to tell him to be quiet until she had finished her meal.

'I'm not all that fond of Reykjavík,' she said, to give him as brief an explanation as she could. 'I quite like to work there, but I prefer to live by the coast.'

'But you are married?' Osman asked, and she sensed that he had been curious about this since the moment he had set foot inside Einholt.

'Like my great-grandmother used to say, I have a husband but he's dead.'

'I am so sorry,' he murmured, two fingers of his right hand tapping his chest in a rapid gesture of sincerity.

'It's a long time ago now,' she said.

'But you must miss him?' Osman's voice was warm and rich, a tone perfect to deliver comfort or elicit a confidence.

'Of course. I think of him every day. I see him in my daughter's face every time I look at her. But I don't brood on it. He's no longer here and, although I miss him, I still have things to do. Children and grandchildren to look after. Work to be done.'

'You are not lonely?'

'No, Mr Osman. I have a . . .' She paused, wondering how to describe Steini. 'I have a friend or, as my daughter calls him, Mum's boyfriend.'

'And he is a good man?'

'Of course,' Gunna said, raising an eyebrow. 'You think I'd let a bad man into my house? He's a decent guy. He has children and grandchildren of his own.'

She stacked the plates and stood up to rinse them and fill the dishwasher. Gunna could feel Osman's eyes following her every move, until she finally wiped down the counter and clicked the coffee machine on.

'And you, Mr Osman? Do you have a family somewhere?'

All three of them had promised their respective partners that today would just be a couple of hours and then they would switch off for the rest of the day. Darkness had fallen and the buzz of rush hour traffic outside told them they had all broken their promises again.

'Editorial conference,' Agnar said with a sideways glance at Skúli as they sat around the low, round table in the centre of *Pulse*'s office, an arrangement chosen because it meant moving away from the desks and the screens that demanded their constant attention. 'An hour or three later than planned.'

'Yeah, sorry,' Skúli apologized. 'I had a meeting with a contact that went on a bit longer than it should have.'

Outside Sólon, Valgeir had shivered in his duffel coat, glancing along Laugavegur as if he'd been expecting someone from the ministry, accompanied by a posse of policemen, to appear from around the corner with Ingólfsstræti and handcuff him on the spot.

'What do we have?' Agnar asked.

'You go first,' Arndís suggested.

'All right. A hefty series of ads from Sunwise Travel, and they want to know if we can run a puff about them.'

'If there's a week in Tenerife in it, then I'm in,' Arndís said before Skúli could open his mouth. 'I'm prepared to sacrifice journalistic integrity for a decent holiday.'

Agnar looked sour. 'Not a chance. They'll supply the copy, but it has to at least be written by someone we know, so it won't be total crap or appear anywhere else.'

'Fair enough. I'm used to not getting lucky with freebies.'

'I met Dagga on a freebie,' Skúli said. 'So I reckon I've already had more than my share of luck.'

'Speaking of which, we ought to get Dagga into the office more often, shouldn't we?'

'Childcare,' Skúli shrugged.

'Yeah, I know, but just so we can all talk together for once.'

'OK, we can do that. But she'd probably have to bring Markús with her. What have you got for tomorrow?'

The even more sour expression on Arndís's face outdid Agnar's effort.

'Kyle McCombie, the American ultra-right nutcase who's holding a public meeting tonight. I've interviewed him and I'll go to the meeting tonight as well, so we can have that for tomorrow. It'll make a splash. And you? What have you been quietly digging into, young Skúli?'

'This guy,' Skúli said, leaning forward to place his phone on the table, to show them Osman's face on the screen. 'Ali Osman. He's a businessman, Lebanese or Turkish, or so we think, involved in all kinds of unpleasant deals in the Middle East. Lived until recently in Northern Cyprus, now resident in Brussels where he runs a charitable foundation. He's here as Steinunn Strand's guest, a very secret guest, and under police protection.'

Arndís sat back.

'Shit, where did you get that from?'

'The lead came from a friend who works for a human rights NGO. He's been following this guy and he's dug up all kinds of shit about him. The question is, Why is he here at all? Why is it such a big secret? And does the delightful Steinunn know what kind of person she's got herself mixed up with? The answer to that last question is undoubtedly no.'

'And when do you want to run this?' Arndís asked quickly.

'Tomorrow at nine. Lars is making his information available at the same time, and a website in France has its story timed for then too. So it's a triple whammy. If it's published abroad as well, then Steinunn can hardly go for an injunction.'

'She could, but I'm not sure she'd get it,' Agnar said. 'Not if the story's already out there.'

'That clashes with the McCombie interview,' Arndís broke in. 'We have to run with that as well before it's cold.'

'We can do both, can't we?' Skúli asked, reluctant to offend Arndís but determined to push his own work forward.

'But . . .' Arndís instantly protested before Agnar put his hands up.

'Children . . . Please,' he said. 'How about we run your story this evening, Arndís?'

'We always run with a strong morning story.'

'I know, and we have two that we need to run, so we have to make them both hit hard,' Agnar agreed. 'Listen, we run Arndís's interview now, an hour ahead of this rally McCombie's holding tonight. It's outside our usual schedule, so that adds weight to it. Then we run all the social media shit first thing so it hits people checking their iPads over breakfast, followed by the report on the public meeting so it goes out before eight. Then we run Skúli's story at nine; if it's important it goes live at the same time as the European versions, then the usual digest at ten. How's that?'

Skúli glanced at Arndís and caught her eye as she chewed her lip.

'I'm happy with that,' he said. 'And you?'

She thought for a few seconds, nodded and snapped her fingers.

'Yep. Let's do it. We can come back later in the day with something on the fallout from the rally, assuming it's as crazy as I expect.'

'Excellent,' Agnar said with satisfaction. 'That way we have several loads of shit hitting the fan in quick succession. That's what I like to see, plenty of cats among the pigeons.'

Chapter Three

Steingrímur gave a thumbs-up from the door and Gunna nodded to Osman, who was sitting casually in the back seat of the ministry's Patrol with its tinted windows.

'All clear. But please don't forget that we must stay in the bar area away from the window,' she told him. 'These people you're meeting will already be there, so you go straight over to them. I'll be right behind you and will stay in the bar, but the three of you will be away from anyone else so you can talk without being overheard. If anyone tries to come close, I'll head them off. If anything gets awkward, then the boys are there as well. Clear?'

'Very clear, Gunnhildur,' Osman said, a shadow of a smile crossing his face in the darkness.

'When you're finished, let me know and we'll leave the same way we came in. OK?'

'Of course. And I'm not a naughty child,' he retorted, the smile still on his face as he opened the car door.

He strolled towards the hotel's main entrance and slipped through the door that Steingrímur held open for him, nodding his acknowledgement. Gunna glanced from side to side as she followed, uncomfortably conscious of the fact that the Glock under her arm seemed five times as heavy as usual.

'Let's hope he behaves,' she muttered to Steingrímur.

The bar was far from full. Gunna picked out the two men Osman was there to meet before he did, and took his arm.

'By the wall, under the picture,' she instructed. 'Go over to them and I'll have one of the staff come over to you in a moment to get your order. All right?'

'Got you, Gunnhildur.'

'I'll be watching from the bar.'

Osman leaned in towards her. 'It's not me you need to watch, Gunnhildur,' he whispered. 'It's everyone else.'

'Don't worry,' she said with a humourless smile. 'They're being watched as well. They just don't know it.'

Osman walked over to the two men sitting under the landscape painting that adorned one wall. One had a weatherbeaten look about him, tall and with eyes that pierced, whose face lit into a bright smile as he greeted Osman and hugged him, while the other appeared to be a younger version, even down to the same style of high-buttoned dark suit. Only the cowboy boots both wore indicated they weren't a pair of missionaries. Moments later they were deep in conversation.

Gunna hoisted herself onto a barstool in the far corner, where she had a view over the whole room, then beckoned to the barman, who hurried over.

'I'll have a cup of coffee, but you see those three over there by the wall?'

'You're Gunnhildur?'

'I am, and I guess you're Kristján. I'm minding those men by the wall, and I'd like you to go and get their order first.'

As the barman approached them, Gunna scanned the room. Half a dozen of the tables had people around them. Once one of the city's classiest places to enjoy a drink, the hotel remained exclusive but was now forced to compete with a host of similarly upmarket hotels and a city centre bursting with bars and restaurants of every description. The hotel's position outside the city centre had left it off the beaten track, and the bar's clientele made Gunna feel young. Couples past middle age occupied some of the tables, while the majority of drinkers appeared to be there alone; she assumed they were guests. Three young men in the far corner by the window speaking loud English to two Asian men, and a woman with an open book and a glass of red on the table in front of her hardly seemed suspicious, as none of them seemed to be paying the slightest attention to Osman, Kyle McCombie and his sidekick.

Skúli picked up his laptop as the Skype icon began to wink at him. He hit the reply button.

'Hi, Sophie,' he said, standing up with the laptop held in front of him. 'Can you hear me?'

'Hello, Skúli. Of course I can hear you. I can see you as well. What are you doing, running a marathon?'

'Just taking this to the boardroom,' he said, meaning the tiny side office that was kept for when anyone had a confidential call to make, needed a secluded place for a discreet interview or simply needed an hour's solitude.

'Have you finished messing about?' Sophie asked, her face filling the screen as Skúli sat down in front of the laptop.

'Yes. I'm all yours now.'

'You're keeping bad company, that's all I can say.'

'Go on.'

He saw Sophie draw back from the screen and flip through notes.

'It's a can of worms,' she said. 'The White Sickle Peace Foundation was set up three years ago, a small but smart office on the rue de la Loi, right next to all the pressure groups.'

'Go on,' Skúli repeated.

'The charity itself is based in Panama, so any info on its finances looks pretty murky; there's no way of telling what's real or where the cash comes from. Its activities are lobbying for peace, goodwill, understanding, tolerance and all that shit, but as far as I can make out, it's a money pit.'

'And Ali Osman?' Skúli asked, trying not to sound too excited.

'He really is a mystery man. People either don't want to talk about him or else they just don't know.'

'No gossip?'

'Plenty of hearsay,' Sophie said with a scowl. 'But precious few facts.'

'Hit me with the gossip, then.'

Sophie took a deep breath and he watched the grainy image of her frowning as she flicked through scribbled notes.

'He's been seen in Syria, Lebanon, Turkey and Russia, according to the gossip that nobody wants to be quoted on. He was involved in shifting oil through the top end of Syria and into Turkey at some point, but had to back out of that when some bigger operators wanted that business.'

'Meaning?'

'Someone higher up the pecking order wanted the business and he wasn't given much of a choice.'

'An offer he couldn't refuse?'

'An offer it would certainly have been fatal to refuse. For a while he was based in Cyprus, supposedly shipping what's referred to as essential equipment from somewhere in Cyprus to quiet beaches on the Syrian coast, and returning with passengers – anyone who had five thousand dollars in cash. They would get dropped off within sight of somewhere they could paddle or swim ashore to. That means arms one way and people the other.'

'That's the north of Cyprus? The Turkish side?' Skúli asked.

'Of course. He did his business in the north of Cyprus and his banking in the south, or so the rumours say, until Panama became a less transparent option.'

'And he's still involved in this?'

Skúli watched Sophie dissolve as the pixels on his screen couldn't keep up with her shoulders lifting in a shrug. 'Who knows? Nobody seems to know if he's still involved, but at any rate, he made a pile of money and a lot of enemies out of it before he decamped to Brussels.'

'The enemies being the reason he's now re-invented himself as a man of peace and reconciliation living in Brussels?'

'Exactly, Skúli. What was the expression you used the other day? Hiding in plain sight, and hoping nobody reminds him of what he used to do. Now he claims his life is in danger and that he can't return to the Middle East. Fortunately for him he has a dual nationality, thanks to a former wife, and has an Italian passport, so it's not as if he's likely to be sent back anywhere. Tell me, do you think your minister has any idea what sort of character she's got herself mixed up with?'

'I've no idea,' Skúli said with a dry laugh. 'She's not the sort who takes advice willingly and I gather she invited him to Iceland on the spur of the moment and on her own initiative.'

Sophie shrugged again and Skúli could hear her giggle.

'Is this going to cause maximum embarrassment?'

'I hope so.'

'Sounds good to me, as long as we're both sure of our ground.'

'As sure as we can be, I guess,' Skúli said. 'At the moment I think I have this to myself, but it won't be long before someone else smells a rat. So far I'm the only one here who knows about Ali Osman, and that's only because Lars tipped me off.'

'It's being kept secret?'

'I guess so. It's obviously being kept discreet, but we'll find out when I start asking awkward questions.'

'And when are you going to do that?'

'About five minutes after we finish this conversation.'

She picked out the man with the broad shoulders and dark hair that fell in an untidy fringe before he spotted her.

'Ready?' she asked, taking off and folding into her pocket the faded baseball cap with the Real Madrid emblem that he'd been looking for. 'You have a car?'

They walked from the bus station out to the hired Rav in the car park without a word.

'Real name?' she asked as soon as the door had shut.

'Michel. My mate's Pino. And you?'

'Ana will do. What's the situation?'

'We're watching the place at the moment. Pino's watching right now. I'll take over later.'

'Any movements?'

'The target's there. It looks like two security taking turns. They haven't been there long enough for us to identify a routine.'

'You're certain it's him?'

'If it's the guy in the photo, then yes. Pretty sure, but I need a closer look to be certain.'

She nodded and gazed through the windscreen into the grey drizzle.

'That ties in with my info.'

'You have some inside information?'

Ana half closed one eye and tilted her head as she looked at him.

'What do you think? I'm not going into this completely blind, but it's an indirect contact, so no details. You have the gear?'

'Yep. Retrieved, checked and safely stowed away.'

'And an approach plan, if that's the way we decide to go?'

'Yeah,' he said. 'I think so. There's a second security detail in a house about half a kilometre away. They're trying to be discreet, but not succeeding very well. A bunch of big guys who are rotating shifts. They look like muscle rather than brains, but who knows?'

'Can you bypass them?'

'Sure. We'll do a recce to see how it looks close up. Will you know by then what the brief is?'

She cracked her knuckles and smiled briefly.

'I need to weigh up the options. One is a take-out, which isn't going to be easy, although we might be able to work around the extraction side of it. The other is a straightforward elimination, plus we have an additional target for surveillance.'

'No real obstacles if you just want the guy dead,' Michel said with a thin smile. 'We've done it plenty of times before.'

'Yeah, but not in this weird place, and we all want to get away in one piece to enjoy our bonus.'

'Hello, there.'

A man in a suit, his tie loosened, lifted himself onto the barstool next to her and raised a finger to summon the barman.

'Hello,' Gunna said with a frown, not wanting to be rude to the man, but hoping that he would take himself off as soon as possible.

'Drink?' he asked in English.

'I speak pretty good Icelandic,' Gunna replied coldly. 'And thanks but no thanks.'

'Ach, come on. You're not staying here, are you?'

'No.'

The barman appeared silently.

'I'll have a vodka and Coke, and give this lady whatever she wants,' he said. 'Make mine a double. Make hers a double. Charge it to nine-oh-six,' he added. 'I like a room high up. Great view over the city, y'know.'

Kristján delivered the man's double vodka and Coke and pointed to Gunna's coffee cup.

'Same again?'

'Just half a cup.'

'Coffee?' the man asked in disbelief and laughed. 'Who comes here to drink coffee?'

'I do. And some of us have to drive.'

'That's fair enough, I suppose. I guess you're not here for an afternoon off, then?'

'Not exactly,' Gunna said, peering past him for a view of Osman, which the man mistook for an expression of interest.

'My name's Sigurjón, by the way.'

'Pleased to meet you.'

'And you are . . . ?'

'Gunnhildur.'

He took a long pull on his drink, smacked his lips and dug a finger under his collar to loosen his already adrift tie a little further.

Gunna kept her eyes fixed on Osman as the man pushed his chair back, wondering if he was ready to make a move. Instead, he stretched his long legs out, turned and beckoned to the barman again for a couple more drinks.

'And what brings you here?' he asked.

Gunna glared.

'Work.'

'You work at the hotel?'

'Sort of.'

He looked at her quizzically.

'Go on, tell me. What sort of work do you do here?'

'Just making sure nobody has any trouble.'

'There's never any trouble here,' Sigurjón declared. 'I've been coming here for years. I live in Oslo, you see. I have to come home to the old country every few weeks for business. Always stay here.'

'All right.'

'This place has been good to me over the years. The company's paying, obviously. But I always like to come back to this place when I can. Had my wedding reception here,' he said, running a hand through his hair. 'But that was a couple of wives back . . . Are you married, Gunnhildur?'

'As good as.'

'Children?'

'And grandchildren, if you really want to know.'

'Well,' he laughed, 'you must have started early to be such a glamorous young grandmother.'

Gunna wondered how black trousers, boots and a fleece made her in any way glamorous, but she let it pass. She listened to Sigurjón talk about his first two wives, the one who had run off with his best friend and the present one he had taken with him to Oslo, and how different their social life in Norway was to Iceland where they had so many friends.

'Why don't you bring your wife with you, then?'

'I would, but Solla works as well – she's in insurance – and then there's the dogs,' he said, and she both regretted having started him off on a new tack and welcomed the conversation that made her less conspicuous as a lone woman in a bar.

She started when his hand crept along the bar to rest on hers.

'You're a good-looking woman,' he said, his voice dropping.

Gunna retrieved her hand.

'Is that so?'

'And you like to play hard to get.' Sigurjón laughed. 'I like that.'

Gunna sighed inwardly.

'I'm sure you're a lovely guy, Sigurjón. But I'm just not interested,' she said firmly.

She straightened and looked over his shoulder as Osman craned his neck to look around the room, his gaze finally alighting on her. He lifted two fingers and nodded once when she caught his eye.

'Come on, sweetheart,' Sigurjón said, putting his glass down on the bar harder than he had meant to, just as the loud group by the window got to their feet. Osman stood up and shook his friend's hand, while the woman on her own drained her glass and closed her book.

With everything happening at once, Gunna slipped off the barstool, and Sigurjón's words dried up as he caught sight of the Glock in its holster as her fleece flapped open.

'Hanne, we have to report this. We should.'

The force of her swift anger took him by surprise.

'No! No, We can't. Absolutely not.' She shook her head, lips a bloodless narrow line, and closed her eyes as she took a deep breath and held it. 'No, Carsten. We mustn't.'

The camper van was parked off the road, overlooking a white-capped sea a few kilometres from Akureyri. They had spent three days travelling to this place that they had both wanted to visit, this time at their leisure instead of the hurried summer holiday trips they had taken before.

They'd hardly taken in any of their surroundings in the days they'd been driving since leaving the spot where the two men had found them, retrieved whatever it was that had been hidden in their van, and then disappeared.

'They said so, Carsten. Not a word. Not a single word to anyone. That way nothing happens to anyone.'

'They must be going to do someone harm. What else could they have forced us to carry? Drugs? Weapons? Who knows? Either way, these people are criminals of the worst kind. We have a moral duty to report this.'

'No, Carsten!' Hanne yelled. 'Don't you understand? They're going to hurt someone we don't know, someone who isn't our daughter, or our son-in-law, or my mother. I don't care who they hurt as long as it's not one of our family.'

'But . . .'

'Fuck you, Carsten!' Hanne yelled, her face inches from his, eyes wide and furious. 'I can't let you endanger our family!'

'But it's wrong! It's totally, completely wrong. It's against everything you and I have ever stood for.'

'Do you think I don't know that?' she snapped back, huddling deeper into the thick coat she had bundled herself into. A second later she fumbled in a pocket, pulled out a phone, found the number she wanted and waited as it rang.

'Dorthe? Hi, it's Mum. Yeah,' she said. 'Everything all right with you? Just wanted to check.'

Carsten sat numbly in the driver's seat and listened to the conversation, imagining their daughter's bemusement and hoping she wouldn't be alarmed.

'Yes, we're in the north somewhere and it's cold but beautiful. Yes, of course,' Hanne chattered, mouthing 'all OK' to Carsten. 'Yes, fine. No problem. Just check on your grandmother, would you? Bye, darling. Love to Inge.'

'We'll have to live with this. It's going to stay with us for the rest of our lives, you realize?'

'What will stay with me is that we had no choice,' Hanne retorted.

Skúli's fingers hovered over the keypad of the phone on his desk.

He wasn't entirely happy with his article, so he'd kept it short. He had laid out what was known, dropped in a little speculation, hinted at a significant failure of judgement on Steinunn's part, and ended with the blank statement that the ministry had been approached to verify aspects of *Pulse*'s report, but had declined to comment.

Now all he needed to do was make the last line of his article a reality.

Skúli punched in the numbers, listening to his heart thumping as the phone rang on her desk at the other end, and reflected that he actually liked Elinborg and hated to do this to her.

After a dozen rings an automated system kicked in and invited him to leave a message.

Skúli cursed and dialled her mobile number, again listening to it buzz.

'Elinborg.'

'Hi Ella, it's Skúli here at *Pulse*. Do you have a couple of minutes?'

She didn't respond immediately and he could feel the reluctance to speak to him through the hissing connection.

'Sure, Skúli. I'm a little busy right now, so it'll have to be quick.'

He took a deep breath before plunging in.

'OK, Ella. I need a response to this,' he said. 'We have some copper-bottomed reports that Steinunn has a guest called Ali Osman Deniz staying in Iceland at her personal invitation. So obviously I'm looking for confirmation from the minister that this is the case, plus I have a few more questions on top of that.'

There was a wintry silence and the phone echoed.

'Ella, you still there?' Skúli asked, wondering if he could hear the wind through the phone or if it was Ella sighing in resignation.

'No comment, Skúli,' she said eventually.

'Is the minister aware that there are serious allegations about Ali Osman Deniz, that he has been involved in trafficking fuel out of Syria and into Turkey, as well as shipping weapons into Syria?'

'I . . .'

'And there are also some well-supported allegations that he's involved in people smuggling, mainly by sea from southern Turkey to Greece, and involved in trafficking people from Libya to Italy?'

'I . . .' Elinborg said and dissolved into a round of coughing. 'What sources do you have for these allegations?'

'Come on, Ella, you know I can't tell you that.'

'I'm not asking who they are, Skúli. I'm just asking how reliable these sources are before I talk to Steinunn.'

'Reliable. More than one source. So I'm looking for confirmation that Ali Osman Deniz is in Iceland right now and that he's here at Steinunn's invitation.'

'Fuck . . . Skúli. You really know how to screw up a quiet day, don't you?'

'All part of the job. Can you confirm this guy's here in Iceland right now?'

'I can't confirm or deny it.'

'You reckon Steinunn will want to respond, or just pretend it hasn't happened?'

He heard her sigh again.

'I don't know. Look, you know that I work for the ministry. What the minister does in a private capacity is beyond my remit.'

'But a prominent government figure entertaining someone who could be an international criminal has a real bearing on the ministry's credibility, surely?'

'Sure . . .' Elinborg said. 'Listen, Skúli. How long can you sit on this?'

'I've been sitting on it a while already, so the answer is, not long. You're not asking me to spike this, are you?'

'Of course not!' Elinborg replied immediately. 'But you know Steinunn is . . . Let's say she isn't the easiest of people to handle, and as you and I have known each other for a long time, I know I can trust you to keep that comment off the record.'

'Is the Prime Minister aware of this situation?'

'That's a question for his office,' Elinborg said quickly. 'So no comment.'

'How long is he staying in Iceland?'

'Again, no comment. And that's all I have to say. That's all I *can* say.'

'Fair enough. I've asked and didn't get an answer. But I guess the PM will know when this story goes live.'

'Skúli, she'll burn you. Steinunn will never speak to *Pulse* again.'

'Why should I be worried? She won't talk to us anyway.'

Elinborg ended the call without another word and Skúli sat back in his chair. Arndís glanced at him, a questioning look on her face.

'She didn't take it well?'

'Nope. But we all know what a handful Steinunn can be and I don't think she'll react well.'

★ ★ ★

'What?' Sigurjón muttered and opened his mouth, one hand in the air.

Furious with herself, Gunna put a finger to her lips.

'Listen, Sigurjón. I'm sure you're a delightful guy who loves his wife and would never try and pick up a lady on her own in a bar. Like I told you, I'm not here for the fun of it. This is police operation, and if you know what's good for you, you'll sit over there in the corner and keep out of the way until the fun and games are all over, all right?'

He nodded dumbly, took what was left of his drink, and tottered unsteadily to a table as far from Gunna and the bar as he could find.

She clicked her communicator and muttered into it.

'Steingrímur, we'll be out in a few minutes. All clear?'

'Ready when you are. All clear out here,' came the crisp reply as she went towards the group.

Kyle McCombie towered over Osman as the two shook hands, and with a moment's hesitation embraced, while the younger version of McCombie stood back, hands clasped in front of him.

Gunna zipped up her fleece, determined not to let the Glock be seen a second time.

'Gunnhildur, are we ready?' Osman asked.

'We are.'

'This is Kyle McCombie, who has flown from America to meet me,' Osman said with a touch of pride in his voice.

'Good evening,' Gunna said, and shook the spade-like hand extended towards her, which gripped hers like a clamp.

'Pleased to meet you. I hope you're taking good care of this guy,' he said with an accent that immediately put her in mind of childhood and Saturday afternoon cowboy films.

'We do our best,' Gunna replied, trying to reconcile the friendliness of the man's blue eyes with what she had seen in the newspapers about his views and the reports of his public meetings.

Kyle McCombie's face creased into a warm smile, displaying gaps between his teeth.

'Let me tell you, this is a good guy,' he said. 'A real ally.'

'Thank you, Kyle,' Osman broke in. 'It's been great to see you, and my Brussels people will be in touch shortly to make the arrangements.'

'Good. Speak soon. James, we'd best get ready. We have a big evening ahead of us.'

The younger man led the way, Osman and Kyle talking in undertones as they walked out into the lobby, while Gunna scanned the people around them and noticed that the woman who had been reading a book in the bar was close behind them.

Gunna dropped back a couple of steps and drew down the zip of her fleece, nervous that the woman was close to Osman. She felt a buzz of adrenaline run through her as she watched for sudden movements.

When Kyle and his companion said a final farewell, and he had pressed a button to summon the lift, Gunna felt the tension relax as the woman stood next to the two men, relieved that she was only trying to get to her room. She watched as the two men stood back with exaggerated courtesy to let the woman enter the lift first. Once the steel door had shut and the light above it flickered upwards, her attention returned to Osman.

She glanced from side to side as they left the building, shepherding Osman towards the Patrol parked a few yards from the door, its engine running and Steingrímur at the wheel.

'All present and correct?' she asked as Osman clicked his seat belt and Steingrímur drove away fast. 'Back to the ranch, my good man.'

Skúli was at his happiest at the kitchen table, surrounded by the chaotic paraphernalia of cooking and the needs of a young child. There was space for a laptop, and he only needed to close the lid and move it to one side at mealtimes.

He found himself revelling in working as Dagga bustled around him, sometimes with Markús balanced on one hip, at other times with the boy sitting in a high chair at the same table, gnawing a crust as his teeth were beginning to appear.

The old-fashioned radio on top of the fridge muttered in the background, and occasionally he would stretch over to turn up the volume for a news bulletin or an interview that sounded interesting.

It was so different from the house he had been brought up in, where the kitchen had been his mother's spotless domain, and he and his father and brothers had been shooed out whenever they edged past the door. Food had belonged in the dining room, not the kitchen, and his mother had stayed out of the room when his father brought acquaintances to the house for dinner.

These had never been friends. He wondered if his father had anyone he could call a friend, or if they were all just people who were somehow useful to him? Anyone who wasn't useful in some way, or who lacked the potential to one day be influential, was of no consequence and deserved no attention.

He thought ruefully that those principles even seemed to extend to family. His brothers were in the same investment business as his father; they comfortably wore tailored suits and had acquired smart wives who looked and acted the part. He, on the other hand, was the youngest of the brood – he suspected he had been a mistake, an unintended child seven years after the family had reached its optimum size, meaning he had grown up almost as an only child.

'You want some tea, Skúli?' Dagga asked, squeezing past him to click the kettle into life.

'Please.'

'What are you working on?'

'The minister's special guest, the one I told you about.'

'Making yourself unpopular again?'

Skúli smiled. 'I hope so. This goes live tomorrow and it's going to make a few people uncomfortable.'

'As long as Steinunn's one of them, then you're probably doing the right thing.'

It was the wrong time of year for tourists, but there was still a trickle of them to be seen, Illugi Gunnarsson reminded himself as he took out his earphones and shrugged on his thick quilted jacket. He pulled on a hat emblazoned with the fuel company's logo and tucked his earrings under it as he stepped outside, shivering as the wind snatched at him.

An unwieldy camper van had pulled up at the pumps and a plump, grey-haired man stepped out, stretching as he did so.

'Diesel?' Illugi asked, glancing at the plates to see the driver's nationality. 'Gas oil?' he added.

'Gas oil,' the man confirmed with a nod and Illugi yawned as he began pumping fuel into the camper van's capacious tank.

A thin woman with a lined face joined the plump man and Illugi didn't try to listen as they had a tense conversation behind him, the woman's voice loaded with concern.

'We pay inside?' the man asked as Illugi replaced the fuel tank cap.

'Yes. Inside,' he said. For a moment he thought of trying out his rudimentary Danish, but decided to stick to English after all.

Behind the till he took the man's credit card and swiped it without bothering to check the name on it. This guy wasn't the type to steal credit cards, he decided.

He replaced his earphones and leaned on the counter, idly looking out of the window. The Danish couple seemed to be having a discreet argument on the forecourt, the man nodding and the woman's hands emphasizing her every word. They got back into the huge camper van, and a moment later it lumbered off the forecourt and into the distance.

Illugi watched it make its sedate progress until it disappeared into the distance. He wondered how long it would be before another car appeared in this remote spot, and turned up the volume on his iPod as he played a magnificent flourish on an imaginary set of drums on the counter.

The wind whistled and rattled the steel shutter over the window. Gunna realized that it was later than she had thought and that they had already talked for more than an hour since returning to Einholt.

'You don't check the building outside tonight?'

'No. The boys are doing that.'

'You mean the men in the black uniforms?'

'That's them. We decided they'd keep the area covered while it's dark.'

Osman's eyes gleamed.

'Are you uncomfortable, Gunnhildur?' he asked, and she wondered if she could hear a stifled laugh behind his words.

'No,' she said. 'I wouldn't say that. But I'll admit this is something of a new experience for me. Why do you ask? Are you nervous?'

'Of course,' he said softly. 'Although I am used to this. Moving from house to house, always checking who is following, wondering who is behind me, who is around the next corner.' He emptied the wine bottle into his glass and sighed as he sipped. 'It's always a concern, not knowing if people around you are what they seem to be, or if they have been bought. Trust is not easy.'

'Are you going to tell me why your life is so dangerous?'

Osman swirled the wine in his glass, leaned back and lifted his feet onto another chair. He looked at the ceiling and then his eyes snapped back to meet Gunna's gaze.

'When you do things that threaten powerful people, when you stand up for what you believe is right but which might not be popular, then you will make enemies. Here in the north if you make an enemy, then someone might say something hurtful about you on Facebook. You told me yourself that the men who plundered your country's banks are free to walk the streets and nobody will harm them,' he said, his voice low but earnest. 'Where I come from, each one of them would be dead, somewhere on a hillside with a bullet through the back of the head, or else a bomb in his car, or a fire in his house. That is to say, if they had stayed. We have these people as well, of course. But they don't stay. They live in places that are safer for them, maybe a western city or a resort overlooking the sea, or a villa surrounded by men with Kalashnikovs, paid handsomely to keep them undisturbed and alive.'

He shrugged and held Gunna's eyes, as if daring her to challenge him.

'And what has made you these people's enemy?' she asked, her voice as low as his. 'What did you do?'

This time he laughed and twirled the stem of the wine glass in his fingers.

'There are so many things that I can hardly count them.'

'You said before that your family has enemies. But you also said they wouldn't follow you all the way to Iceland.'

'That's right. Old feuds like that stay where they were born and wait for people to reappear. However, there are others, whose reach is so much longer.'

'Who don't forgive?'

'They don't forget, and they never forgive,' Osman said, a shiver passing through him like a ripple as he dropped his feet to the floor and leaned his elbows on the table, holding his glass containing an inch of wine in front of his face. 'I made mistakes, Gunnhildur. I made some mistakes in business, which is easily done, and for the right amount of money such errors can be put right. But we are talking very large amounts of money. Maybe enough to buy this whole island,' he said, putting the glass down. 'But I also embarrassed people, I made them angry and damaged their pride. That's not something you can fix with a handful of dollars.'

'All right. Tell me what it is that was so bad it put a price on your head?'

'Plans?' Ana asked.

There was no food in the apartment, so they were in a dimly lit Indian restaurant a few doors along the street.

'That's what I was going to ask you,' Michel said, snapping a poppadom and helping himself to pickle.

'What's happening? Tighter security?'

'Surprisingly, he's still there. Comes and goes.' He drew breath sharply as the spice hit his tongue. 'There's no pattern to what he does; he just seems to spend his time holed up in the house. When he goes anywhere there are always two official cars that collect him and he's not away for more than a few hours.'

'What's the security?'

'A minder at the house,' he said. 'And some goons with heavier artillery keeping watch at a house up the hill. They're watching the road.'

'And?'

'They're watching the road. Not the way we go in.'

'And?' Ana asked, regarding him carefully.

'By water. Easy.'

Ana shifted in her seat, still sizing up the bear of a man she had been told to work with. 'They don't suspect?'

Michel shook his head. 'I don't think so. I spent an hour this morning observing them. They don't have a clue. Pino has spent longer watching them than I have, and we're sure of it.' He grinned and fell silent as a waiter appeared and made a performance of placing each dish in the right place, flicking imaginary dust away with a spotless cloth.

He drained his beer and put it down.

'Another of those, please,' he said to the waiter and looked over at Ana. 'Same for you?'

She shook her head.

'This one will last me for a while. But some water, please.'

The waiter bowed almost imperceptibly and departed.

'What do you reckon?' he asked, spooning rice onto his plate.

'I don't know yet. I need to scope the place out.'

'It's pretty straightforward, I'm telling you.'

'Like I said, I want to take a good look first.' Her voice was firm and Michel's eyes widened for a second at her tone.

'If that's what you want to do.'

'That's what I want to do,' she responded and tasted her lamb curry.

She fell silent as the waiter appeared with a full glass of beer and placed it in front of Michel. He lifted it and held it out, waiting for Ana to do the same.

'Here's to a successful and quick operation,' she said as they clinked glasses.

★　★　★

Hanne wondered how Carsten could sleep so soundly, before she realized that he was lying in the semi-darkness with his eyes wide open.

'You're awake,' she said, making a statement rather than asking a question.

'Of course.'

They had left the camper van for the night, booking into a hotel for a change, to make the most of a real bed and a shower with as much hot water as they could wallow in. Tomorrow they would be back on the road and would stop where they felt like it for the next few days. They had vague plans, but with no deadlines and no jobs to return to, there was no hurry.

'I keep thinking of . . .' Hanne said, eyes on the ceiling. A single street light cast a dim orange glow through the gap in the curtains. The shaft of light shook slightly as the lonely light at the top of its metal pole vibrated in the fierce wind coming off the sea.

'I know,' Carsten said quickly. 'You don't have to tell me.'

For the last two days hardly a word had passed between them, only the occasional few functional sentences, but each knew what the other was thinking and feeling.

The day before, Carsten had found Hanne sitting in the back of the van with tears streaming down her face and a handkerchief twisted into a tight strip between her fingers.

There had been nothing he could say. All he had been able to do was take her hand and squeeze it.

Osman stretched and she could hear his back click as he sat straight and flexed his shoulders.

'I have been to Turkey, Greece and Italy. I have seen what has happened to the people from my country, washed up on the beaches and living in doorways and tents, hoping for a little charity. Men who were dentists and lawyers begging for a few handfuls of rice or fruit, children with swollen bellies and girls being led away to be sold. I made a stand. That was my crime in their eyes. I named some of them, and that made them angry. I called them what they are, which is criminals. But worst of all, I did something.'

Gunna sat in silence, watching him and hearing a clock tick somewhere in the room.

'I used the money I had to make more. I set up an organization to help the people who are washed up on the beaches or left in leaking tubs far out to sea. The Aegean is a beautiful sea, but in winter it can turn angry.'

His voice dropped to a warm, dark murmur, mesmerizing as it acquired a rhythm.

'I have been to the beaches. I have seen the people staggering ashore with only the clothes they are wearing and what they can carry, children in each hand. I have seen the bodies, mourned those of my compatriots who lost their lives within sight of safety, some sort of safety, the chance to stay alive for a few more days. Do you hear what I am saying, Gunnhildur?'

Gunna nodded, fascinated by the depth of passion and anger in his words.

'I know exactly what they are fleeing. I've seen it with my own eyes. Ruined cities, ravaged villages, a dry, sunburned countryside that once was fertile and now is gradually becoming a desert. The trees are dying, the crops refuse to grow without water and the livestock are long gone. People became desperate and went to the cities and found there was no help for them there.'

'So what happened?' Gunna asked, looking into Osman's piercing eyes, points of light with his face in shadow.

Dagga lifted Markús from his chair and took him through to the other room, where Skúli could hear her crooning to the little boy as he fell asleep in her arms. He was fairly sure that within a few minutes they would be asleep together on the sofa.

He was happy with his article as he read it through. It was punchy and he had picked out the key points so they hit the reader right between the eyes, editing it for busy people who skim the news on a phone rather than a computer.

Osman's face, with its striking cheekbones and an enigmatic, faraway look, was prominent, and he peppered the article with a couple of links to both Sophie's and Lars's websites. Satisfied that everything was uploaded, he double-checked the dates and times for the article to go live, and sat back, hands behind his head, listening to the silence in the other room, wondering how much of a storm would erupt around his ears tomorrow.

He twisted around in his chair, clicked the kettle and tried to congratulate himself on a job well done, telling himself that this was the tip of an iceberg, that once the initial furore had died down, he would have to do whatever he could to get close to Osman himself. The man must have a tale of his own to tell, but as far as he had been able to find out, he had only given short interviews in elegant French to a couple of TV stations, answering slowball questions about the wonderful work the White Sickle Peace Foundation was doing.

He wondered what he would ask Osman if he could one day track him down, and decided that he would have to apply some more pressure to Valgeir. He wondered if he could approach Elinborg at the ministry once her anger had cooled, although he had the feeling that after tomorrow's story had appeared on the *Pulse* website, he would be *persona non grata* for some time to come, at least until the next elections had taken place and new people had been appointed.

Skúli's mood darkened as the sun dipped behind the house across the street and he tried to stop his thoughts going to places that would leave him jaded and dissatisfied. He had come to recognize that this restlessness was part of finishing a story that had some value to it, as if he knew he had done well but wanted to do better and was unable to work out exactly how.

The light faded and a street light outside flickered into life. He listened to Dagga's steady breathing in the next room, trying to force himself to ignore the fizzing buzz in his ears and keep his thoughts, as always when he was alone or trying to sleep, from turning to regrets and mistakes, things he had managed to do spectacularly wrong, people who had got the better of him, petty humiliations from his younger days.

'Stop it, stop it, stop it,' he muttered angrily, telling himself not to be such a fool, not to brood on things he could not change, none of which mattered, and hating the fact that there was no way on earth that he could banish from his mind these things that troubled him so relentlessly.

Osman's hand stretched out across the table in front of him, fingers spread wide, palm down, one finger tapping a slow beat.

'Those in charge were not capable of understanding. Their only tool is the stick and so they used it unsparingly. At first people were surprised there was no help for them, then angry, and after that they fought back. You have seen the news, I'm sure,' he said with a deep sigh. 'Civil war, family against family, extremists and opportunists taking the chance to snatch power, foreign governments desperate to extend their influence and supplying arms to both sides. It's frighteningly complex, much more so than the Western news reports are able to convey. There are so many groups of men with guns desperate for power, forging and breaking alliances, settling old scores under new pretexts, betraying people who were their allies the day before. There's oil, land and influence to be fought over. What began as a desperate need for water and food turned with terrifying speed into a bitter, vicious war, and millions of people losing their homes.'

'And needing somewhere to go?'

'Precisely,' Osman said. 'Many are in Turkey, and Turkey does not want any more of them. The number you have seen reaching Europe is a drop in the ocean, the handful who could afford a place on a boat – a chance, and only a chance, of ending up somewhere safe.'

'And you were able to escape?' Gunna asked.

'Ah. I had already left, Gunnhildur. I was already an émigré. I had offended people who do not take kindly to criticism, and their response to that kind of thing is to make sure the critic does not see many more sunrises. I was warned. I was lucky. My family was wealthy enough that I could slip away.'

'But you wanted to help?'

'I may be an outcast, an unwilling emigrant, but these are my people, and I understand better than anyone their anguish. This was the place where we had settled only a generation before, where we had arrived ourselves as refugees, and it was turning to chaos and violence. Can you imagine? You have to leave your home now, and all you can take is what will go in your pockets and a bag you can carry on your back. You have no idea if you will be able to return one day, or if there might be anything to return to. You don't know if you will be welcome anywhere else, but you expect not. So I have tried to do what I can to help.'

Osman half closed his eyes, clasped his hands together and folded them over his chest.

'You see, Gunnhildur? Trying to help people is much more dangerous than doing nothing. It shines a spotlight on other people's shortcomings. I raised money to set up an organization to provide practical things; I attracted attention to the plight of these people. For a while I was a prominent figure, in the newspapers and on TV, acting as a spokesman for these refugees, advocating that they should be helped, while some people wanted to string barbed wire along the beaches or drive them back into the sea. Have you any idea what it's like to be hated?'

'No, I can't say I do.'

Osman shook his head.

'There was hatred in the media, fury at what I was suggesting. You see, I'm the kind of émigré they like, the kind who has come to a new country with a degree and four languages. Not a hungry refugee who smells bad because he has no other clothes and nowhere to wash. Now I have people on every side who would do me harm.'

'So what can you do? What options do you have?'

Osman's face flattened into an impassive mask.

'I don't think there are many options. Steinunn was generous enough to invite me to Iceland for a rest and I hoped that everything could be kept secret so that I would have at least a little time without having to look over my shoulder. The price on my head is high enough to tempt anyone.'

'You know this?' Gunna asked.

Osman's musical laughter broke through the gloom.

'Of course I know. Some millions of dollars, or so I'm told.'

'How do you know that? How can you be sure?'

His eyes shone.

'I know, Gunnhildur,' he said, his voice dropping. 'I know because they made sure I knew. They wanted me to know that it's very much worth someone's while to take my life, and that I would spend the rest of the time I have left looking over my shoulder.'

Thór gave Fúsi a low whistle and jerked his head. Fúsi looked, grinned and gave him a thumbs up. Easy money.

They followed at a distance, watching the couple, who looked like they had just emerged from a restaurant. The pair walked side by side, in no hurry, but there were no interlinked hands, no outward displays of affection. It was a date that hadn't struck sparks, or else the pair had been together for years and felt no need to be in each other's pockets.

Not that it mattered. They'd corner them somewhere quiet between here and whatever hotel or rented apartment they were staying in and quietly relieve them of wallets and phones. Thór's sheer bulk and the raw anger that came off him in waves was enough to terrify any normal person who preferred to stay in one piece.

An apartment, Fúsi decided as he followed fifty metres behind them, fingering the flick knife in his pocket. The pair seemed deep in conversation, and they didn't seem to be heading for any of the myriad hotels that had sprung up around central Reykjavík.

He could be patient. Thór had gone around the corner and would be hurrying along a parallel street; any moment now he would appear in front of the hapless couple. Two phones, which he had to admit wouldn't be worth a lot once their erstwhile owners had locked and remotely wiped them, and a handful of cash would be enough for them to call it a good night's work.

He walked faster, sensing that the next corner, leading to a quiet street off Snorrabraut, would be the spot; it was one they had used before.

The couple up ahead came to a dead stop, just as Fúsi knew they would. Thór had bustled round the corner and walked straight into

73

the man, who had taken a step back, hands raised defensively in front of him as the woman stood to one side. Fúsi took the knife from his pocket. It wasn't much of a knife, and he knew it would barely cut through butter, but it didn't need to. The sight of it had always been enough to make tourists dig into their pockets.

'Sorry, man,' Fúsi heard the man say to Thór, who bridled, sticking out his chest and giving his natural anger full rein.

'You walked right into me,' he complained in his gruffly accented English.

'I didn't mean to. You just came round the corner; you're the one who walked into me.'

The man made to step around him and be on his way, but Thór moved to block him.

'I think you owe my friend an apology,' Fúsi said, pressing the button and hearing the snick as the blade clicked into place. 'So if you'll hand over your phones and cash, we'll leave you to it.'

The man half-turned and took in Fúsi standing there with the blade held in front of him. A smile flickered across his face.

'So this is a robbery, is it? I thought there wasn't any crime in Iceland?'

'Don't give us any shit,' Thór rumbled, grabbing the arm of the woman, who had taken a step aside. He hauled her roughly off her feet, wrapping a thick arm around her neck. 'You don't want your bitch to get hurt, do you?'

The look of amusement stayed on the man's face and Fúsi suddenly felt uneasy. Normally valuables were handed over with hardly a word, and by now they should have been on their way.

'Just do it, all right?' Fúsi snapped, the flick knife pointed at the man's chest.

He felt sick as he wondered what had gone wrong. He saw the woman twist herself out of Thór's grasp in a single fluid move-ment and spin in a circle, his hand in her grasp as his arm twisted grotesquely. As Thór howled and stumbled, trying to retain his balance, her left arm whipped upwards, the heel of her hand catch-ing his nose to send his head snapping backwards. A stabbing blow to his throat brought Thór's head forwards onto his chest and, as another connected with his temple, Thór dropped in an undignified, unconscious heap.

Fúsi heard the clatter of metal on stone and realized the knife in his hand had been sent flying across the pavement. A second later the breath was knocked out of him as he was propelled rapidly backwards and slammed against a wall.

'Bad idea, pal,' the man said.

There were already flashing lights and blue and white tape fluttering in the night breeze as Eiríkur appeared, still yawning. On the way out of the house, he had given himself time to brush his teeth but not his hair, and as he lived closer to the scene than Helgi, he had beaten him to it.

The scene was only a short walk from the central police station on Hverfisgata and the response had been rapid. Someone walking home had stumbled across the two comatose figures and a panicky call had altered the emergency services.

'What do we have?' Eiríkur asked the motorcycle officer standing guard at the scene as he looked round instinctively for Gunna before remembering that she was busy on other duties.

'One dead, one unconscious. They've both had the shit beaten out of them,' the officer replied.

'Do we know who these guys are?'

The officer's eyes twinkled. 'The stiff is Thór Hersteinsson and the one with the broken bones is Fúsi Bjössa.'

'Thór's dead?'

'They don't come much deader. May he rest in peace.'

'You almost said that as if you meant it,' Eiríkur said.

'We can probably disband half the police force now that thug's off the streets for good.'

'Indeed. Couldn't have happened to a nicer guy. All right, do we know anything?'

'Not a lot. A drunk guy walking home found them and called in. That's all. The ambulance got here a minute before we did and they've already taken Fúsi away. Thór hasn't been touched, other than to confirm that he's dead.'

'Anyone touched anything?'

'Only the medics and the guy who found them.'

Eiríkur nodded. 'That's good. I gather forensics are on the way, so if you could keep people clear, that would be ideal. Helgi should be here soon.'

'No problem,' the motorcycle officer replied. 'It would be useful if we could open up Snorrabraut again before morning, otherwise the traffic's going to be murderous. On the other hand, my shift'll be over by then, so it'll be someone else's problem.'

Chapter Four

A woman tugging on the belt of an old-fashioned raincoat that flapped around her knees swept out of the door just as Helgi was about to push it open.

'Don't mention it,' Helgi muttered under his breath, stepping back as the woman barged past him through the hospital's doors and into the darkness outside.

Helgi looked through the window in the hospital room door. The forlorn patient he could see looked vaguely like the petty criminal Helgi had arrested a dozen times over the years, generally for the same offences again and again. He had no fondness for Sigfús Björnsson, known to everyone as Fúsi Bjössa, who he was sure had never once been troubled by a pang of conscience for any of his misdeeds, but he was still shocked by the sight of him.

Fúsi lay in bed, a monitor humming at his side and a drip in his arm. His face appeared to be one vast bruise, as if whoever had attacked him had set out to leave nothing untouched; it was hard to see where one injury began and another ended.

'Is he able to talk?'

The duty doctor shrugged.

'He can mumble. There are no major injuries, just a lot of painful ones. His jaw isn't broken, but he doesn't have many teeth left. He's pumped full of painkillers.'

'Has anyone been to see him yet? You've spoken to his next of kin?'

'Yes, there was someone. Just gone.'

'Tall woman in a raincoat?'

'I don't know. You'd have to ask the nursing team.'

'I'll do that,' Helgi said. 'But first I ought to have a word with this gentleman.'

The doctor's grim smile contained no trace of humour.

'I'm not sure that this guy could be classed as a gentleman,' he said quietly. 'But good luck.'

'*Hæ*, Fúsi,' Helgi said as he sat down uninvited by the bed. 'You've been upsetting people again, have you?'

Fúsi opened the one eye that wasn't entirely swollen shut.

'I was attacked,' he mumbled through broken teeth. 'I mean, we were attacked.'

'Your mate Thór hasn't come out of this well, Fúsi. Thór is here as well, but he's flat on his back in the morgue. Sorry, but I thought you ought to know.'

A single tear welled from Fúsi's good eye.

'Bastard.'

Helgi leaned closer.

'Listen, this isn't a formal interrogation. You're full of painkillers, so no statement yet. All I'm after right now is for you to tell me who did this. Answers first, statement later. This is going to be a murder charge, no two ways about it. So it's serious. You know who did this?'

Fúsi nodded, wincing at the pain in his neck as he did so.

'Rikki,' he mumbled, looking away. 'Rich Rikki. Rikki the Sponge.'

'Alone?'

'Yeah. It was just Rikki. He came after us, smacked Thór a couple of times and he went down like a sack of spuds. I tried to stop him and then he turned on me. I don't remember much after that.'

'Why? Why was Rikki coming after you two? And single-handed?'

'There was some other guy there as well, didn't see who it was. But it was Rikki who did the business.'

'You don't know the other person?'

Fúsi tried to shrug his shoulders and whimpered as he shifted in bed.

'Didn't see him,' he muttered. 'Big guy, like all the lads who hang around with Rikki. Dark hair. Grey tracksuit. Look, I had other stuff on my mind.'

Helgi sat back, puzzled. Everyone knew Rich Rikki, but it wasn't normal for him to carry out a beating somewhere so public where there could be witnesses.

'You're telling me that you witnessed Ríkharður Rúnarsson beating Thór Hersteinsson to death last night on the corner of Snorrabraut and Njálsgata?'

Fúsi nodded.

'That's it. That's what happened,' he said with as much emphasis as his puffed lips and broken teeth would allow. 'It was Rikki.'

'G'day, Rikki,' Helgi said, pulling the duvet back to reveal a face that was both bewildered and furious.

Rikki's current girlfriend stood in the doorway, arms crossed and a hopeless look on her face, trying to convey that she'd had no choice but to let the police into the apartment.

'What the fuck do you want?' he demanded, sitting up quickly, eyes flickering from Helgi to the two uniformed officers behind him. In the dim light of the stuffy bedroom intricate tattoos chased each other around the bulging muscles of Rikki's torso.

'What? Aren't you pleased to see us?' Helgi asked, wishing he could move out of range of those fists, should Rikki decide to swing a punch, but unable to with the officers and Chief Inspector Sævaldur Bogason crowded behind him into the little room.

'What does the filth want with me?' Rikki grunted.

'Rikki, where were you last night?' Helgi replied. 'It's serious, so don't mess us about.'

'Out with the guys. Why?'

'Where were you between eleven and half-past midnight?' Sævaldur demanded, his voice harsh in the thick air.

'Out,' Rikki said slowly, casting a glance at the tight-lipped woman now peering past the crowd of police officers. 'I was out. Why?'

'Where were you and who were you with?'

'I reckon you'd better get my lawyer before I say anything,' Rikki said, rasping a hand over the millimetre of stubble on his head. 'Is this an arrest, or what? I know my rights. I'm not saying anything unless you arseholes want to make it real.'

Helgi could almost feel Sævaldur's grin of delight behind him.

'Then let's make it real, shall we?' Sævaldur said with satisfaction he made no effort to conceal. 'You're coming down to Hverfisgata with us, right now. Tell him, Helgi.'

Helgi took a deep breath.

'Ríkharður Rúnarsson, you're under arrest for the murder of Thór Hersteinsson. You have the right to legal representation at every stage of proceedings. You do not have to say anything that might incriminate you. You have an obligation to tell the truth.'

Rikki's mouth hung open.

'Thór?' he said, dazed. 'I haven't seen that fuckwit for months. What's all this about?'

'You heard, Rikki,' Helgi said. 'This just got serious.'

'But you . . . I know where you bastards live, y'know.'

'Shut your mouth before you make it worse, Rikki,' Helgi snapped. 'Don't give yourself another six months for threatening behaviour. Come on, get your trousers on and we're going.'

Sævaldur gloated from the doorway and jerked his head at Rikki.

'Bring him out, will you?' he said to the two uniformed officers. 'And cuff the bastard.'

Eiríkur liked Miss Cruz, the city police force's forensic pathologist, who'd arrived five years ago from Spain on a six-month placement and never left. As much as he liked Miss Cruz, he hated the place where she worked, and a visit to the sterile room with its corpses on trays was always a trial. Eiríkur made a habit of encountering death by closing his eyes in a moment's silent prayer before opening the door.

Miss Cruz was washing her hands when he arrived. She gave him a smile as he pushed open the heavy door with trepidation, aware of how much the place put him on edge.

'Good morning,' she greeted him in her habitual precise English, drying her hands and shaking out inky curls as the surgical cap came off.

'Hello. Finished?' he asked hopefully.

'I've done a preliminary assessment. Do you want to take a look at the victim?'

'Sure,' Eiríkur said and instantly regretted it.

Naked, pale and laid out on a steel tray, Thór Hersteinsson looked smaller and sadder than he ever had during his short, angry life. For the first time that Eiríkur could remember from the many hours Thór had spent in interview rooms and numerous nights in the cells, he looked almost at peace, the familiar buzzing aggression sucked out of him.

'What do I need to know?' Eiríkur asked, relieved that Miss Cruz's work with the scalpel had not yet begun.

'Impact trauma to the throat and left temple,' Miss Cruz said, switching to lecture mode. 'Two powerful blows, as far as I'm able to see without taking him to pieces, which we'll be doing this afternoon. And his nose has been practically ripped off.'

'His nose? Eiríkur asked, feeling stupid.

'Exactly. I would say an upward strike to the face that caught his nose; either a fist, or more likely the heel of the attacker's hand,' she said, jabbing a hand upward into the space over Thór Hersteinsson's face to demonstrate.

'A short attacker?'

'Not necessarily,' Miss Cruz mused. 'But close, very close. The attacker would have been standing right in front of him. An extremely powerful blow, so someone either very strong or skilled at what they were doing. Or they could have got lucky while this guy got very unlucky. But all that stuff's your department.'

Eiríkur surveyed the dead man in front of him and wondered if he ought to feel some kind of pity for Thór Hersteinsson, who had spent most of his adult life making the lives of those around him difficult and unhappy. He knew his father would have said something wise about being charitable to the unfortunate, but quickly brushed those thoughts aside.

'This would have been extremely painful, surely?'

'Of course,' Miss Cruz said. 'The nose is a highly sensitive part of the body, so the pain would have been massive, though not life threatening, but . . .'

'But?'

'If it's pain we're talking about, then my guess is that he would have been more preoccupied with his left arm. That would have been both extraordinarily painful and entirely debilitating.'

'Why? What happened to his arm?' Eiríkur asked, leaning over the body and noticing for the first time that the arm looked awkward, as if it hardly belonged to the body it was attached to.

'His arm has been dislocated at the shoulder, wrenched right out of the socket.'

Eiríkur stood up and looked at her in surprise.

'Pulled his arm out, smashed his nose and then a couple more blows to the head? In that order, do you think?'

Miss Cruz shrugged.

'That's what it looks like. I imagine the trauma to the head meant it was lights out.'

'Somebody really didn't like this guy and wanted to hurt him.'

'Someone very skilled in a close-quarters martial art – aikido, ju-jitsu, something like that.'

'Someone with dangerous skills,' Eiríkur said, 'and who's prepared to use them.'

'Sit down,' Helgi told the woman. It felt odd that he was telling her to take a seat in her own home, but he could see her twisting her hands as she shot sideways glances at him.

She took a seat behind the kitchen table, sitting awkwardly, perched on the edge of a stool.

'How long has Rikki been living here?' Helgi asked.

'Not long,' she said slowly. 'A couple of months, on and off.'

'He lives out of a carrier bag, right? A few nights here and a few nights there?'

The woman nodded, her face grey. Helgi guessed that she would never step outside without her face made up and her long hair, so pale it was almost white, in perfect order. He'd encountered Rikki in the past and knew that he liked his girlfriends to conform to type.

'You don't mind, do you?' she asked, clicking a lighter without waiting for a reply.

Helgi coughed and glared.

'When did Rikki show up? Don't tell me he was here with you all evening and you watched *Star Trek* for an hour before having an early night.'

'He lets himself in. I was out and he was already here when I got home.'

'What time?'

'Around one.'

'Where had you been?'

'What's that to you?' she asked, sending a plume of grey smoke high over Helgi's head.

'I might need to verify it, so who will confirm that for you?'

'I work at the 10–11 on Grjótháls. It's open round the clock. I finished at twelve, picked up a pizza and came home. So I was back before one and Rikki was already asleep in the armchair. The supervisor's name is Gróa Gunnlaugsdóttir. She'll confirm I was at work.'

'I'll check,' Helgi assured her.

She turned away to stub out her cigarette and he studied her profile, checking for the marks that Rikki had made a habit of leaving on his girlfriends over the years. He wasn't shy of administering a slap, or worse, when they didn't meet his standards.

Reassured that there were no remnants of a black eye to be seen, he stood and zipped up his jacket.

'Thanks for the information. I'll leave you to it.'

'Rikki'll be back soon, won't he?' she asked, and Helgi wondered whether the plaintive tone indicated that she was missing him already, or that she was hoping he would be in a cell for years to come.

'It's not for me to say,' he said, 'but I wouldn't bank on it.' He folded his arms as the woman hunched on the stool in the corner of the kitchen. 'Unless you've anything to add?'

'No,' she said, shaking her head. 'Rikki was here when I got home before one. That's the truth of it.'

'Fair enough. But you can give me a call any time you like if there's anything you feel we ought to know.'

Rikki looked smarter wearing a clean shirt. The stubble on his head glittered silver in the harsh light of the interview room. He scowled, deep-set eyes narrowing as Sævaldur took a seat, ignoring Rikki and his lawyer while he tapped at the computer to set up the recording.

'Chief Inspector Sævaldur Bogason. Interview with Ríkharður Rúnarsson and legal adviser Hans Hannesson,' he intoned. 'The time is ten forty, starting second interview.'

He looked up.

'We're seeking two weeks' custody,' Sævaldur said in a flat voice.

'We'll oppose that, naturally,' the lawyer said smoothly, with the air of a man relishing the prospect of a duel.

'So, Rikki,' Sævaldur said, ignoring the lawyer's comment. 'Tell me about yourself. What do you do for a living these days?'

'This and that. Freelance security and a few other things.'

'That's code for collecting debts and breaking arms, is it?'

'Ensuring that my clients' assets stay secure.'

'And of course you never overstep the mark, do you, Rikki?'

Sævaldur waited for a reply, but got nothing but a baleful glare from Rikki's deep-set eyes.

'So who were you collecting for last night? Did Thór owe someone money?'

Rikki shook his head.

'Nothing to do with me. I don't deal with low-grade street scum like Thór,' he said, his voice oozing disdain.

'But Thór is dead and I'm wondering if this was a debt you were supposed to collect or a little persuasion that got out of hand?'

'Chief Inspector . . .' Hans broke in. 'Facts, please.'

Sævaldur gave the lawyer a sideways glance before continuing.

'Rikki, you have a track record of beatings and assaults that goes back to when you were thirteen. You've been in and out of a cell for years and you've probably broken more arms and fingers than anyone else in Reykjavík,' he said. 'Although I'll grant you that you've got better at it in the last few years, at least in terms of getting caught and intimidating witnesses so none of them will say anything.'

'Chief Inspector, please,' Hans broke in again. 'Could you confine yourself to the facts of the case instead of the lack of facts?'

'Rikki here has a hell of a police record. That's a fact.'

'Maybe. But he's a reformed character,' Hans assured him for the benefit of the recording. 'He has no convictions whatsoever in the last eight years, as I'm sure you're aware. That makes his presence here ridiculous and I expect you to release him the moment this interview ends.'

'Yeah, and I'm sure he runs marathons for charity when he's not snapping thumbs,' Sævaldur rumbled, slapping the table. 'This is rock solid. We have a witness who places you at the scene. He's certain it's you; there's no doubt in his mind that you're the man. So let's get back to the start and you can tell me in detail exactly where you were and what you did last night.'

Rikki's face lost some of its colour and he leaned over to whisper in his lawyer's ear.

'A private conference?' Sævaldur asked before Hans could say anything.

'Rikki didn't do it,' Eiríkur said the moment he was able to speak without being overheard.

'I reckon you're probably right,' Helgi agreed. 'I wouldn't trust Fúsi Bjössa an inch, and he's the only witness. Is there anything from the uniform guys knocking on doors?'

Eiríkur shook his head.

'Sævaldur called them off, reckons he has enough to go on. I'll go through the statements, but I don't expect there's much there. It was midnight on a cold week night. Downtown there would have been a few people about, but Njálsgata is pretty quiet. There are houses one side of the street and that children's playground the other, and there are always drunks hanging out there after dark, so nobody's going to notice a few shouts.'

Helgi scratched his head.

'I don't know about you, but I've only been on this investigation with Sævaldur for a few hours and I'm missing Gunna already.'

'She wouldn't go for the easy option, would she?'

'She doesn't do anything the easy way.'

'But Gunna would have taken anything Fúsi Bjössa might say with a massive pinch of salt and then had a good look around . . .'

'For whoever really did this?' Helgi said, finishing Eiríkur's sentence for him.

Eiríkur glanced around before nodding in agreement. 'Yeah. So what do we do? Sævaldur's determined to nail Rikki to the wall on this. Do we challenge him, or what?'

'I'm reluctant to challenge Sævaldur,' Helgi admitted. 'Gunna would if she was here, but her balls are bigger than most people's.'

'Let's say we're reluctant to challenge Sævaldur without more to go on?'

'That's about it, I reckon,' Helgi decided. 'So, what do we have? I was there when we picked Rikki up this morning and he had no idea what was going on. He wasn't faking anything, but he won't give us an alibi. So my guess is he was up to no good last night and doesn't want to implicate himself in whatever that was.'

'But he will when the murder charge looks like sticking?'

Helgi grinned. 'Wouldn't that be poetic justice? Rikki having to admit to breaking some poor bastard's kneecaps to get himself out of something worse.'

'He'll get a couple of years inside either way? That would be sweet.'

'Exactly,' Helgi said with a broad smile. 'And that way everyone's happy; except Sævaldur.'

'Well, according to Miss Cruz, Thór's arm had been dislocated at the shoulder. That's not Rikki's style. He's a brute force and ignorance kind of guy.'

'Interesting,' Helgi mused. 'That'll come out in the autopsy report and we'll see what Sævaldur makes of it. I reckon he'll just shrug it off.'

'So where do we go from here?'

'You start with the witness statements as soon as you have them, but first, I'd really like you to go down to Njálsgata and knock on a few doors until you find someone who saw what really happened. I'll have a quiet word with Fúsi again and see how easily I can knock holes in his story, and . . .' He paused.

'And?' Eiríkur asked.

'Just before I got to the hospital this morning I saw Hallveig Hermannsdóttir coming out.'

'The lawyer?'

'That's the one. The dealers' friend, with her fingers in all sorts of sticky business. So I'm wondering what kind of business she had at the National Hospital at seven in the morning?''

Arndís and Agnar were already at their desks, engrossed in the screens in front of them.

'Morning,' Skúli said, dropping his bag onto a chair and extracting his laptop. 'What's new?'

'Stats are through the roof,' Agnar said, a grin spread across his face. 'Arndís's story on the Children of Freedom meeting is going viral. The comments are just nuts, completely wild. Every fruit-cake out there has an opinion.'

'And my Osman story?'

Agnar put out a hand and shook it from side to side.

'Not bad. I'm afraid you're in Arndís's shadow on this one, but still way above average. Loads of social media have picked it up, and I should imagine Steinunn Strand isn't a happy lady today,' Agnar said. 'I reckon we ought to have a follow-up on this; do you have any more rabbits to pull out of hats?'

'Working on it,' Skúli said, his attention elsewhere. 'Anything else new since yesterday?'

'North Korea grandstanding once again,' Agnar said with a yawn. 'Oh, and this year's murder happened last night.'

'This year's murder? What do you mean?' Skúli asked as his laptop came to life.

'Where have you been, Skúli? Iceland has an average of one murder a year, and this year's was last night,' Arndís said. 'Thór Hersteinsson,' she added.

'That blob of misery? I'm guessing Thór was the murderer?'

'You guess wrong,' Arndís said, spinning her chair around and propelling it and herself across the office to the coffee machine. 'Thór's the victim. That's all we know, except that it happened around eleven last night on Njálsgata, just along from the corner with Snorrabraut.'

Skúli nodded as Arndís propelled the chair across the floor again, this time to hand him a mug of coffee.

'So the famous Thór the Boxer is no more? Someone's put him in a box, have they?'

'Yep,' Agnar said. 'Iceland's number-one mugger, street thug, dope dealer, jailbird and all-round, headline-grabbing, fly-on-the-wall-TV-star bad guy is no more. We've knocked together an obit and it's ready to run as soon as he's confirmed as the victim, although it's pretty much public knowledge already.'

'So it's all under control? You don't need me for anything?'

Agnar grinned. 'You could have stayed in bed and left the hard graft to us hardboiled newshounds.'

'Yeah, the hard graft of rehashing a couple of press releases.'

'Come on, I had to do it the hard way and Google for all this stuff.'

Skúli sipped his coffee. He felt no less tired than he had been when he went to sleep the night before.

'So is there anything on who bumped off Thór the Boxer? And are we proposing a vote of thanks to the person in question?'

'No, and no,' Arndís said, looking up from her screen. 'His identity has just been confirmed, so I'll go live with his obit.'

'You can't ask me anything right now. I know my rights,' Fúsi mumbled as Helgi let himself into the room.

'Careful, Fúsi. Hallveig won't like it if you get to be a smarter lawyer than she is.'

Fúsi's mouth shut like a trap and Helgi silently congratulated himself.

'The doc will let me know when your statement can be taken, and the second I have a green light I'll be here to write down every word you say, Fúsi,' Helgi said. 'So let's just say this is another friendly chat as I'm concerned about your health.'

'What does that mean?' Fúsi spluttered through puffed lips that refused to obey him.

Helgi sat down at his side and gave Fúsi's arm an avuncular pat.

'It means that between now and the doc giving me the all-clear to take your formal statement on the events of last night, you have a few hours to reflect very carefully about what you want to tell us.'

'I already told you it was Rikki,' Fúsi spluttered, his face turning pale. 'It was Rikki who beat Thór up and then he turned on me.'

'That's what puzzles me,' Helgi said. 'All right, Rikki's a big lad. But Thór was a big guy as well, and he was always the first one to start swinging his fists. He could look after himself, and if I had to lay odds on those two going head to head, I'd have said it was pretty much even. And you, Fúsi, you've never shied away from a ruck like that. I'd have thought even Rikki the Sponge would have thought twice about taking on the two of you, especially as everyone knows you carry a blade.'

Fúsi's visible eye flickered in confusion.

'I don't know what you're talking about.'

'That's fine, Fúsi. Don't worry about it,' Helgi assured him in the same amiable tone as before. 'I just thought I'd mention to you that it might be worth thinking carefully over whatever Veiga had to say when she came to see you this morning.'

'Veiga?'

'Hallveig Hermannsdóttir. The lawyer. You know, the one who so skilfully got you off handling stolen goods last year. She was here this morning, and I've already checked that her mother isn't in hospital, so she must have been here to see an old friend,' Helgi suggested as he stood up. 'Such as you.'

Fúsi closed his good eye and lay back against the pillow.

'So what are you saying?'

'What I said just now: you've got a few hours until I can take a formal statement, and that doesn't have to be faithful to all the information you gave us earlier.'

'Let me think . . .'

Helgi opened the door to leave.

'Oh, by the way.'

'Yeah?'

'Rikki's in a cell right now and he's not a happy man. He doesn't know who put Sævaldur on to him. But once you've made a statement, then it's official and his lawyer will get to see it. Know what I mean? I'll see you later.'

Arndís answered the phone. '*Pulse.*' She listened, took off her glasses and looked over at Skúli, winking at him as she did so. 'No, he's on another line right now. Can I take a message?'

She nodded, scrawled on a pad and put the phone down.

'Who was that?'

'Your aunt.'

'Hansína?'

'That's the one. The permanent secretary herself.'

'It didn't take long for the shit to hit the fan,' Skúli said, a warm feeling of satisfaction spreading through him, until his mobile vibrated on the desk in front of him. He looked at the number and groaned.

Before answering, he counted to five, took a deep breath and touched his temples with his forefingers as the stress counsellor had advised him to do.

'*Hæ*, Dad.'

'What have you been doing now?' The voice was strident, his irritation bordering on anger. 'Your Aunt Hansína has called twice. She's been trying to find you all morning, and I can't imagine what's so important that she needs to get hold of you urgently.'

'Lovely to hear from you as well, Dad,' Skúli replied. 'How's Mum?'

'Don't play games with me, Skúli Thór. Where are you?'

'I'm at work, as usual. Where else would I be on a weekday morning?'

His father snorted.

'Then why hasn't Hansína been able to reach you?'

'Search me. Maybe she called when I was on the other line or in the toilet.'

'There's no need to be crude.'

'Sorry. That wasn't the intention. Hansína can call me whenever she feels like it. There's the office number, there's the mobile number you've just called me on, there's email and all kinds of social media, plus her office is about five minutes' walk from mine, so if it's really urgent, she can always knock on the door.'

'Well, you know now that she wants to get hold of you, so you had better call her and find out what's up.'

'Sure. I haven't spoken to Hansína since Grandad's funeral, so I can't imagine what she wants.'

'Oh, something official, she said. Just give her your attention, would you? She was quite agitated earlier and I'm not here to pass messages between you and the rest of the family, you know.'

'Sure, Dad. I'll have a word. How's Mum?' he asked, but the phone had already been slammed down at the other end.

Only a few yards from busy Snorrabraut, with traffic buzzing past well above the speed limit, Njálsgata was a quiet street. Children wrapped in thick coats and woolly hats played on the swings under the watchful eye of a young woman seated on a bench, counting heads under her breath to be sure that none of them had slipped out of the playground.

A coal-black pair of ravens perched on the roof of the nearby Austurbær cinema, waiting for the children to be shepherded back to play group before picking over the litter in the grass.

Eiríkur knocked on doors and rang bells, becoming increasingly frustrated as virtually nobody appeared to be at home, and the few people he did manage to speak to had seen nothing until blue lights had started flashing in the street outside the previous night.

He glanced around, hoping that someone would have a CCTV camera installed somewhere, but there were none to be seen. A camera dome in a corner or high on a wall had become almost standard practice for businesses, but not yet for the flats of this drowsy street.

'Yes?'

The door swung open in front of him.

'My name's Eiríkur Thór Jónsson and I'm a detective with the city police force,' he said before taking in the truculent face in front of him.

'And what do you want with me?'

'There was an incident in the street here last night, a serious one in which a man lost his life,' Eiríkur said, jerking a thumb along the street. 'It took place just over there, towards Snorrabraut.'

'I know where Snorrabraut is, thank you,' the man facing him through the crack of the door replied, a narrow nose and a high forehead visible in the gap. 'And how does that concern me?'

'We're looking for witnesses, anyone who might have seen anything last night.'

'And I know exactly what a witness is, thank you, young man,' he said as the door inched a little further open until it stopped on a length of chain.

'And are you a witness? Did you see anything last night?'

'It's possible. Look, I'm no admirer of the police and I really don't want to be involved in anything.'

The door made to shut, but Eiríkur quickly pushed it back until the chain caught again.

'If you saw something, anything, then it could be a huge help.'

'I have problems of my own. I don't want to be involved in anyone else's.'

'I'm sorry, I didn't mean to disturb you. But this is important. A man lost his life and we're doing our best to find the person responsible. Did you see anything? Even something that appears quite trivial could turn out to be important.'

The man's voice rose an octave in angry frustration.

'Leave me alone. I don't want anything to do with this, whatever it is.'

Eiríkur shrugged, his foot still holding the door against the chain.

'I can't force you,' he said and delved into a pocket to find a card. 'This is my name and number. If you have anything to tell us, please get in touch.'

He offered the card through the opening, but the man didn't take it. The moment Eiríkur's foot was removed, the door slammed and he was left still holding the card in his hand. He shook his head and, after a moment's thought, posted it through the letterbox.

He walked away, turning to look over his shoulder as he heard a metallic click. The letterbox had snapped shut and the card lay in the street by the door.

Carsten sighed. It was many years since he had felt so wretched, torn between what he knew was right and the consequences of doing the right thing.

Thirty years earlier, he had taken a stand against senior staff at the rural school where he was a brand-new teacher, choosing to believe the tearful girl with the bloodshot eyes who bawled and howled in an empty classroom. The girl seemed a child, but looking back she hadn't been more than a few years younger than he had been when the story came pouring out of her of what her uncle's weekend visits to the family home meant.

He could have stayed silent and sent her on her way, or simply referred her to a child psychologist. Instead, he had taken her to the police station where a report was filed, the bruises and razor cuts on Emilie Lund's skinny arms photographed, and once it had become part of the official system, it was going to stay there for ever.

It had cost people their careers; two people had lost their jobs and marriages, and he had long been convinced that it had cost him his own career. He still boiled with rage at the recollection of realizing that every one of the staff at that school, and half of the pupils, had been aware of what the girl had been going through, but not one of them had been prepared to say a word.

Carsten reflected that a whisper had followed him from school to school, a reputation as a troublemaker and a homewrecker, while Hanne's career had blossomed. The rumour attached to her husband hadn't carried across to her work in local government – and she had been fiercely proud of what he had done. She loved him for it, he was convinced of that.

At the time he had not thought for more than a couple of seconds before making a decision, bundling Emilie Lund into his car and not stopping until they were outside the police station.

Now he felt the situation was repeating itself, except that this time Hanne was blocking him from doing the right thing. He knew she was right, but he was right as well, and they both knew it.

'If we do nothing,' he said slowly, 'then this will stay with us for the rest of our lives, on our consciences.'

Hanne sat in silence in the passenger seat, staring at the grey waves hammering the porcelain-smooth boulders of the shore in front of them.

'It's not a question of right and wrong,' she said eventually. 'Whatever we do, it's going to be the wrong thing. Either way this will stay with us for the rest of our lives.'

She turned and looked at him, eyes red behind frameless glasses.

'I want to do the wrong thing that feels slightly less wrong, if that makes any sense.'

Skúli shivered and shut his eyes as the conversation with his father, their first in almost a year, replayed in his mind. The call had left him shaken and he cursed himself for having taken it. For years his relationship with his parents and brothers had been rocky, and he avoided contact as much as he could, mainly because he knew how restless and upset he would be left by the inevitable argument with at least one of them at any family gathering.

When the office phone rang again and Arndís politely answered it, he knew from the tone of her voice what was coming and he gestured for her to put the call through to him.

'Aunt Hansína,' he said, trying to sound breezy. 'What can I do for you?'

'Do you need to ask? I need to speak to you. Can you come here?'

'Right now? If Steinunn has a statement to make, then certainly I can.'

'Skúli.' The steel in Hansína's voice turned a shade harder. 'The minister does not have any comment to make at this moment. Steinunn isn't here right now. Elinborg is with her at the PM's office and there may be a statement later in the day.'

'Fine. In that case would you ask Elinborg to send me the statement when it's ready?'

'I don't for a second believe you understand how delicate a matter this is. You're causing untold trouble.'

'Trouble for whom? The minister who should have done her homework before inviting such a dubious person to sleep on her sofa? Or the government that I guess is expecting to be embarrassed because Steinunn did her own thing without clearing it with the PM's office first?'

There was a sharp intake of breath that he heard clearly through the phone.

'Skúli, are you aware who you're speaking to?'

'Actually, no. I'm not. I'm not sure if I'm talking to the Aunt Hansína who I've always got on very well with, or the permanent secretary pressured into speaking to her naughty nephew to get him to pull the plug on a story that could embarrass a government that doesn't seem to know what embarrassment is.'

This time there was a quickly stifled snort of amusement.

'All right, Skúli,' she said, her voice low. 'Let's not mess around. Can you pull this story?'

'Of course not.'

'Can you put a lid on it for a few hours?'

Skúli thought for a moment.

'And hang around waiting for an injunction to be served on us? No.'

'Smart lad,' Hansína said. 'So I can report back in good faith that I've asked and you've declined. Will I see you at the family gathering in July?'

'I'm not sure yet. It depends on whether or not we can afford a summer holiday in France this year.'

'Fair enough,' Hansína said. 'Given the choice of Skorradalur or Bordeaux, I know which one I'd choose. Thanks for the chat, Skúli. See you soon, I hope.'

The line clicked dead. Skúli met Arndís's gaze.

'I'd bet anything you like the ministry is seeking an injunction right now.'

He felt a sneaking elation at having stood his ground, although Hansína hadn't made any great effort to get the story suppressed. He wondered if she might have a motive that he wasn't aware of. It was no secret that Steinunn hadn't gone out of her way to make herself popular with her staff and that consequently there was little inclination among them to offer a helping hand. Skúli made a mental note to arrange to catch up with Valgeir before too long. The last few days had passed so quickly that he wasn't sure how long it was since they'd met and Osman's presence in Iceland had been confirmed.

'I'm going out for a few minutes,' he said, emerging from his thoughts. 'All right with you?'

Helgi scowled to himself while Sævaldur was scarcely able to contain his delight at the beads of sweat on Rikki's cheeks, cling- ing to the puckered skin around the tracery of scars that pitted his face.

Rikki's lawyer, a smooth, middle-aged man in a suit that Helgi decided would have cost him a month's salary, sat unperturbed at his client's side.

'The witness placing you at the scene is cast iron,' Sævaldur said. 'He swears blind it was you, that you attacked first Thór with punches to the head, and then himself, inflicting serious injuries.'

'Who's the grass?' Rikki snapped, and the lawyer placed a hand on his arm, shaking his head to tell him to keep quiet.

'My client requests that you disclose the identity of the witness in question.'

'I'm not able to do that until the witness has been treated and cleared by medical staff to be formally interviewed.'

'So you have one lowlife who claims he witnessed an assault taking place on a dark street and who's now high on painkillers. Come on, Chief Inspector. You have to do better than that,' the lawyer said in a mocking tone.

'The witness is reliable and the statements are being prepared,' Sævaldur retorted. 'Taking into account the serious nature of the offence – after all, there's a dead man down at the National Hospital – there is no option but to take this man out of circulation as quickly as possible. He's a menace to the rest of society. Unless he has a convincing alibi for the time of the murder?'

'Then you had better tell us when the murder took place so that my client can explain his whereabouts at the time of the incident he had nothing to do with.'

'Between eleven last night and half past midnight.'

Rikki's head jerked sideways and he whispered urgently to the lawyer, who nodded and frowned.

'I have to speak to my client in confidence,' he announced.

Forehead creased, Eiríkur typed in the address.

'Ketill Ómarsson?' he asked, looking up at Helgi.

'What?'

'Does that name ring a bell? Ketill Ómarsson?'

'In what context?' Helgi grunted, his mind elsewhere.

'Old guy. Bald head. Lives on Njálsgata. I knocked on his door and asked if anyone there might have been a witness to what happened last night, and got sent away with a flea in my ear.'

'So? Not everyone's happy to pass the time of day with us guardians of law and order.'

Eiríkur cracked his knuckles as he stared at Ketill Ómarsson's driving licence photograph on the screen in front of him. There was no doubt it was a smooth-faced version of the careworn older man.

'I know. But there was something about this guy that . . . you know. Something that didn't sound right. And he didn't say he hadn't seen anything, just that he didn't want to be involved.'

'It's an unusual name. Tried Googling him? Or checked to see if he has a record? There can hardly be many people with a name like that.'

'There are two in Reykjavík,' Eiríkur said. 'The other one's in his twenties, so it's definitely not him. This guy is suspicious. I'm wondering what he's not telling us, and why,' he said absently, fingers on the keyboard as he searched. 'Ah.'

'Ah?'

'Ah,' Eiríkur confirmed. 'Eight years for grievous bodily harm and attempted murder, served four, released in nineteen eighty-nine. Nothing since then.'

'Shit. No wonder he's no pal of ours. Did you get anywhere knocking on doors, apart from this guy?'

'Nothing. He was the only one who answered the door. I'll try again later when people are back from work. But this Ketill intrigues me. He was sentenced in nineteen eighty-five and there's no record.'

'It'll be on paper,' Helgi said. 'You'll have to go and look it up.'

'That could take half a day. Who's still about who would remember a case in nineteen eighty-five?'

'Thirty years ago? You'd have to go a long way up the ladder to find that out. Even Gunna wasn't here back then, and I was still on the farm.'

'Yeah, I know. Milking the horses, or whatever you hayseed types do out in the fields.'

Helgi looked up and grinned at Eiríkur's rare attempt at a joke.

'Cows, Eiríkur. It's cows that get milked. Or did you think milk comes from a factory somewhere that makes it out of coloured water?'

* * *

'You've been here a while, haven't you, Sævar?' Eiríkur asked.

Sævar tapped the number on his shoulder.

'Since before you were even a glint in your old man's eye,' he said, peering over the glasses that hung on the end of his nose like an ornament. 'What are you after?'

'After?' Eiríkur said with feigned innocence. 'What makes you think I'm after anything?'

'Because I wasn't born yesterday, as you've just pointed out.'

'True. Can you think back to nineteen eighty-five?'

'When Steingrímur Hermannsson was Prime Minister and Björk was still one of the Sugarcubes, you mean?'

'Er, sort of. I think,' Eiríkur said. 'I'm not sure I know about any Sugarcubes, but . . .'

'But you had a sheltered upbringing. I know. Come on. What are you after?'

'Ketill Ómarsson. Eight years for assault and attempted murder. Served four. Do you remember the case and who was in charge of it?'

'Páll Oddur Bjarnason was the officer who investigated that case. I went to his funeral six or seven years ago. That case wasn't long before he retired.' The warmth vanished from Sævar's face. 'Why are you asking?'

'The guy's a possible witness to a murder.'

'Thór the Boxer?'

'That's the one. Ketill Ómarsson lives a few doors away and I've spoken to him – routine knocking on doors – but he refuses to say anything. Then I found he'd done time for attempted murder, but it was so long ago that the records are all on paper, so I reckoned it would be quickest to ask someone who was here back then.'

Sævar grimaced.

'I joined the force in eighty-one, and I wasn't involved in that investigation at all, but it stank.'

'And? I guess this guy has every reason not to want to talk to the police?'

'Like I said, I don't know the details. But Páll Oddur was old school, if you know what I mean.'

'Meaning what?'

'Good grief, Eiríkur, you're dense today. Páll Oddur liked to have everything tied up neatly and wasn't fussy about stamping on people's toes. He got results, even if the means weren't always by the book.'

'He cut corners?'

Sævar glanced sideways, as if the ghost of the long-gone Páll Oddur Bjarnason might appear behind them to listen in and disapprove.

'Let's say he made sure things went his way,' he said after a moment's thought. 'There are a few dinosaurs like that still, but they seem to be a dying breed.'

Eiríkur nodded slowly.

'And this particular case? Don't tell me, he *helped* things come together?'

'You could say that,' Sævar said. 'Or that's the rumour. Only you didn't hear it from me.'

Osman took his coffee and sat in front of the vast television screen, flicking through the channels until he found a news programme, at which point he sat engrossed in reports from the US and Asia. Gunna cleared up the kitchen while Ívar Laxdal stalked around the house, checking windows and muttering occasionally into the communicator she had never seen him use before.

With their guest having found a Middle Eastern news channel in English, they sat by the window.

'Gunnhildur, we're getting queries from the Security Unit.'

'What about?' she asked, an eyebrow lifting in surprise. 'What do they want to know?' She nodded towards Osman.

'They're asking about a journalist called Skúli Snædal. D'you know him?'

'I do, although I haven't seen him for quite a while. He's a good lad, for a journalist.'

'Politics?'

'I think he writes about all kinds of stuff. He interviewed me a few years back for *Dagurinn*.'

'Before it closed down. Yes, I remember that. I mean his politics. Anything radical about him?'

'No, I don't think so. As far as I recall he comes from a blue-blooded Independence Party family, although I gather he's something of a black sheep.'

'A leftie?'

There was an unmistakable note of disapproval in Ívar Laxdal's voice.

'You mean a Left-Green type? No, more Social Democrat, I'd have thought. There's nothing radical about him as far as I know. He'd moved in with a girl the last time I saw him and they were expecting a child. That normally tends to knock the radical edges off people, doesn't it? Why are they asking about him?'

Ívar Laxdal tapped the table with a fingernail in irritation.

'You've not been checking the news, have you?'

'What's new?'

Ívar Laxdal looked ready to grind his teeth in frustration.

'This journalist works for a website called *Pulse*, and this morning he, or they, splashed our friend all over the news. Half a dozen others have picked it up. I can only assume that Steinunn has seen it, but I haven't heard any fallout yet.'

'Skúli? What does he have to say?'

'It's worded quite cleverly. No outright accusations, but a lot of hints that our friend over there is involved in arms and people trafficking.'

'Hell . . . And this article makes it plain that he's here in Iceland?' Gunna asked, deliberately avoiding saying Osman's name and alerting him to the conversation.

'The whole lot. That he's here, that he's been invited by Steinunn. Pretty much everything except giving directions to this place.'

Gunna stood up and looked out of the window at the bare expanse of Geldinganes opposite, with Reykjavík in the distance behind. An expanse of white horses had turned the grey winter sea of the bay into a patchwork, with wheeling gulls diving and swooping in the wind.

'It'll be interesting when he gets to Steinunn's place this evening,' she said. 'Although I don't imagine he'll be asked many awkward questions there.'

'And Steinunn has enough on her plate as it is, especially with the public meeting the Children of Freedom held last night. It all went peacefully, but there are some loud voices demanding that Kyle McCombie should be asked to leave, including some in Parliament itself.'

'I'm sure she's going to be in a delightful mood.'

'She'll be sweetness and light, as always in public,' Ívar Laxdal said with a morose sigh. 'What I'm not looking forward to is the one-to-one with her. Anyhow, I gather Skúli Snædal has been in contact with someone in mainland Europe who knows about our friend's movements, and that's a concern. If they know, who else does? And how do they know?'

'Questions and not many answers,' Gunna said sourly, tipping her head in Osman's direction. 'Welcome to my world. Look, Skúli's a decent enough lad. I can't vouch for him as far as his politics go, but he's been very fair and honest in all the dealings I've had with him. I can't imagine him being linked to anything illegal.'

'Good,' Ívar Laxdal said. 'I'll pass that on. But I think he's in for a rough ride.'

There was no doorbell. Eiríkur rattled the letterbox and rapped at the door just as he had done that morning.

It was late in the afternoon and a gaggle of children had taken over the playground. These were bigger than the morning's playgroup children, unaccompanied and raucous as they hurtled from one end of the playground to the other.

'What?'

The door opened a crack. Ketill Ómarsson's face appeared in the gap, mouth half-open in surprise, before the door slammed shut in his face.

'Ketill!' Eiríkur banged on the door as the children across the street fell silent.

'I've nothing to say to you,' he heard a muffled voice say through the door.

'Come on, Ketill. I just want to talk to you for a few minutes,' Eiríkur called, hoping his voice would carry through the door.

There was no reply. Eiríkur crouched down in front of the door, pulling open the letterbox.

'Ketill!' he called, peering through the letterbox at a narrow slice of the hallway inside.

'Who the hell are you?'

Eiríkur looked up from the letterbox to see two stocky men in running gear standing shoulder to shoulder, glaring down at him.

'I could ask you the same thing,' he said, rising to his feet.

'Look, pal. This is a quiet neighbourhood and we want to keep it that way.'

'Good for you,' Eiríkur said impatiently, glancing back at Ketill Ómarsson's door as if expecting it to open by itself.

'Go on, will you? Get out of here. We don't want anyone causing trouble.'

'Some kind of local militia, are you?' Eiríkur asked, his hackles rising.

The taller of the two stepped forward, chin thrust out.

'Make yourself scarce and there won't be a problem, understand?'

'And if there is a problem?'

'Then we'll sit you down on the pavement and keep you there until the police arrive. We've had enough trouble around here as it is.'

'Ah. In that case, I'm way ahead of you,' Eiríkur said, raising a hand and slowly delving into his coat pocket. 'As the police are already here, I think you two fine gentlemen can be on your way and not worry about trouble in your neighbourhood for the moment.'

He held up his identification card. The taller man squinted at it, deflated, and stepped back, while his shorter, broader friend relaxed.

'Sorry, man. No offence.'

'None taken,' Eiríkur assured him. 'Now, if you'll get your-selves out of here, I can get back to work.'

Eiríkur watched them jog down the street, and the sound of children playing resumed.

'Ketill!' he called again through the letterbox. 'Come on, I only want to talk for a few minutes. This is important.'

He rapped again on the door and heard his knocks echoing inside.

'Hey. Listen to me,' he called. 'I know what happened. I know about Páll Oddur Bjarnason. I know about Snorri and Pálína. I don't want the same thing to happen again. That's why I want to talk to you.'

'What the fuck do you know?'

The fury in Ketill's face was unmistakable as the door was snatched open and he stared down at Eiríkur, who was still crouched on his haunches where the letterbox had been a moment earlier.

Skúli huddled into his coat, wishing he'd worn a warmer one, and strode uphill and around the corner onto Laugavegur. He wasn't going anywhere, just intending to get some fresh air and a coffee in peace and quiet.

The cold was refreshing and he felt his earlier anxiety slip-ping away. The story was done. He had written the Icelandic angle alone, and Sophie in Paris had published her story within a few seconds of his going live.

It had been a stressful few days, with the uncertainty of how successfully they could keep on top of the story before, inevitably, other media stumbled across it, but they had; and he could feel in his bones that this was going to make waves.

He sat back with a flat white and a slice of carrot cake, shook off his jacket and placed his phone on the table in front of him. It was still early, and the coffee shop above his preferred bookshop was quiet.

He had taken one mouthful of cake when his phone began to buzz, and he saw the number of the lawyer who handled *Pulse*'s business on the screen.

'Skúli.'

'Hey, great story. Where did you dig that one up?'

'*Hæ*, Tommi. Thanks. It sort of dropped into my lap.'

'Well done. Like it. You're going to have trouble over this, let me tell you,' the lawyer cheerfully assured him.

'Why do you say that?'

'Skúli . . .' Tommi said, unable to hide his glee. 'You ought to know that you don't upset the establishment without having to answer for your misdeeds. Anyway, call me when you need me. Looking forward to hearing from you,' he said, ending the call suddenly.

Skúli shook his head and took another forkful of cake, then his phone pinged a couple of times in quick succession before buzzing with another call.

'You bastard,' Elinborg burst out before he had a chance to say anything. 'You said this wouldn't go live right away.'

'Come on, Ella. You know the score. I gave you fair warning.'

'You told me . . .'

'Yeah, I told you yesterday evening. I asked for a comment and you said there wouldn't be one. And . . .'

'Yeah, Skúli, and what?'

'We had to get it out there before the ministry could get an injunction.'

'Well, you're right enough on that,' Elinborg told him, and he wondered who else was listening to the call. 'You'll be hearing from legal today.'

Skúli didn't get a chance to say goodbye as Elinborg ended the call abruptly.

His phone immediately began to buzz again, so he declined the incoming call, found Tommi's number and pressed the green button.

'Skúli, my boy,' the lawyer said breezily. 'Need our services already?'

'Not right now, but I reckon we will. The ministry's losing its shit.'

'Excellent,' Tommi said and Skúli imagined him rubbing his

hands in delight. 'Get a statement written and email it to me before twelve, something about the story being directly in the public interest, essential that this kind of information is publicly available, all that crap. Got me? I'll tweak it and send it to all the other media outlets. Best to get your take on this out there right away, and if I were you I'd be ready to be on tonight's news.'

The door banged shut. Eiríkur stood in the hallway facing Ketill Ómarsson as he visibly struggled to contain his hostility.

'What's this all about?' Ketill demanded at last. 'I'm no friend of the police, and I imagine you've found out why.'

'I've heard half the story,' Eiríkur said. 'I haven't read the case files as it was so long ago they're stored away somewhere. But I'd like to hear the rest of it from you.'

'Why? After all these years?'

'Pure coincidence. I had no idea who you were until I knocked on your door. A serious crime was committed in the street outside . . .'

'Come on, everyone knows it was that thug Thór Hersteinsson who was given a hiding.'

Eiríkur hesitated, and was not surprised that gossip had travelled so fast. 'It hasn't been confirmed officially, but that's right, and it happened almost outside your door. He was murdered. Knocking on doors and looking for witnesses is standard practice.'

'Just like it was in nineteen eighty-four, you mean? That's not what your arsehole of a colleague did. He just threw me in a cell and it was a done deal.'

Eiríkur held out his hands, palms wide.

'I can't answer for Páll Oddur Bjarnason; he was long gone from the force before I joined. In any case, he's been dead a few years now.'

'And I hope the bastard rots for what he did.'

Ketill folded his arms and glared, challenging Eiríkur to defend him.

'All right. Tell me your side of the story.'

'I've told it before, often enough. It's all there in the case files, and the newspapers. Snorri did well enough for himself after he waved me off to prison.'

'How so?'

'He saw what happened to me, I suppose, and decided he'd be better off as an honest man. If you can call a salesman honest.'

'I know you got an eight-year sentence for assault and robbery,' Eiríkur began, watching Ketill carefully. 'I know you served four. I asked a few questions and heard right away that there was doubt about the case, but that nothing was ever done, and the gist of it is that Páll Oddur Bjarnason was too high up the pecking order to be touched.'

'I could have told you all that,' Ketill said, his shoulders sagging. His face had gone from furious to haggard and he leaned against the wall.

'All right. Tell me about it,' Eiríkur suggested. 'There's nothing new about a miscarriage of justice.'

'Miscarriage?' Ketill snapped, fury returning. 'It was so much more than a miscarriage. It was a fucking travesty, pure and simple.'

'Try me. Tell me what happened.'

'You know the names already, although I don't know where you got them from. Snorri's my cousin and Pálina was the girl he was living with back then. They were a pair of layabouts, petty criminals, small-time dope and thieving. One evening Snorri broke into an electrical goods shop that used to be on Ármúli years ago and the owner surprised him. I know exactly what happened, because I heard the whole story as the poor bastard slurred his way through his evidence at the trial. Snorri smacked him with a baseball bat, knocked half his teeth out, broke his nose and jaw, and ransacked the storeroom at the back of the guy's shop. I know exactly what happened,' Ketill repeated through gritted teeth, 'because I was the one in the dock listening to the victim give his evidence, instead of the real bastard who actually did it.'

'I know that,' Eiríkur said. 'That's pretty much what I've heard. But why? How come you were charged for this?'

'Because my dear cousin Snorri turned up in the middle of the night at the flat I was renting, woke me up and came in with a dozen boxes that he stacked by the TV, before disappearing back into the night, saying he'd return the next day to collect them.'

'I take it he didn't?'

'No, he didn't. Páll Oddur Bjarnason and three goons in uniform shoved their way through the door the next morning, picked up all those boxes and hauled me off to a cell. The rest is history.'

'But why?' Eiríkur asked. 'I still don't get it.'

'Because when Páll Oddur went to check on the usual suspects, including my cousin Snorri, who was pretty close to the top of the list, he found him curled up with his sweet little niece, Pálína Jónsdóttir. Anywhere other than Iceland Páll Oddur would have had to declare a personal connection and hand the investigation over to someone else, but not here. Páll Oddur found all the evidence he needed, plus his pregnant niece tucked up with his suspect. I imagine Snorri told him where he'd left the gear, and Páll Oddur came and got it, and me in the process. Rather than wreck his niece's domestic arrangements by arresting her boyfriend, he conveniently hung the whole lot on Snorri's country bumpkin of a relative, who'd only been in Reykjavík a couple of months.'

'So you had nothing to do with it?'

'Apart from letting my cousin Snorri leave a dozen stolen video cameras in my living room, nothing at all. Snorri had worn gloves when he broke into the guy's store, so there were no fingerprints, and he'd dumped the bat somewhere and it was never found. The victim said it was dark and he didn't see his assailant's face clearly; he just knew it was someone of around my build. That was enough for Páll Oddur to get a conviction, send me to prison, fuck up my studies and ensure that I'd never get a decent job for the rest of my working life,' Ketill said.

'Are you all right?' Eiríkur asked, concerned that the man's face had turned red and his breath was coming in alarming gulps.

'No . . .' he gasped, leaning against the wall to steady himself; Eiríkur stepped forward to take his arm.

'You need to sit down.'

Ketill nodded, his head lolling onto his chest.

'And you wonder why I'm no friend of the police,' he said

between hollow breaths as Eiríkur helped him along the passage to the kitchen at the back of the house.

Skúli wondered if the buzz of breaking a controversial story would ever be separated from the anti-climax that invariably followed it, the sneering voice inside his head that reminded him it wasn't quite good enough, he still needed to do better.

He checked the social media platforms to see what people were saying, then checked the website carrying Sophie's explosive article to read slowly through her text, which seemed oddly flowery as he translated it in his head.

He checked again to see if Lars had logged onto Skype, frowning when he saw he hadn't. Skúli checked the time. He knew Lars was virtually never unreachable, so he punched in Lars's mobile number and listened to it ring as he sipped his coffee. He was about to give up and go to join Arndís and Agnar in the café round the corner when the phone was answered.

'Yes? Who is this?'

'Hi. Is Lars there?'

It was a strange voice, suspicious. 'Who's speaking, please?'

'It's Skúli. Is Lars about?'

'You mean Lars Bundgaard?'

The voice dealt cautiously with the syllables of Lars's name.

'That's right. This is Lars's phone, isn't it? Is he there?'

'Yeah, he's here. But he can't talk to you. Where are you calling from, please?'

Suddenly Skúli was uncertain. There was something in the voice's authority that rang alarm bells.

'I'm calling from Iceland. Who are you?'

There was silence and he could hear muttering in the background.

'I'm a police officer. My name is Kerkhoeve,' the voice said, and out of force of habit, Skúli wrote down the name on the pad at his side, struggling with the syllables of the man's name and hoping he'd got it right. 'What is your name, please?'

Skúli felt a chill.

'Is Lars not there?'

'Yes. Lars is here, but he can't speak to you,' the sharp voice said again. 'Who are you, please?'

'My name's Skúli Snædal and I'm a friend of his. Why can't he speak? Is he busy? What's going on?'

'Give me your number, please. I'll call you back.'

Skúli reeled off his mobile number.

'Has something happened to Lars? What's going on?'

'Five minutes,' the voice said curtly and the line went dead.

Ketill sank onto a stool, his face red, breathing hard.

'Are you all right?' Eiríkur asked, taking another stool. 'Do you want me to call anyone?'

'Like who?'

'You live here alone?'

'No. But I don't want you calling anyone. Give me five minutes. I'll be fine.'

'Do you get these turns often?'

'No,' Ketill said, fighting for breath. 'It's only thinking back to what you've just reminded me about and that world-class arsehole Páll Oddur Bjarnason that brings it on. The bastard's six feet under, but it's as if he's still persecuting me from beyond the grave.'

Eiríkur took a glass from the draining board by the sink, filled it with water and placed it on the table within reach.

Ketill glared and wiped away a tear that had strayed from one watery eye.

'If you want to do something useful, boy, you can make some coffee.'

He waved a hand in the direction of the cupboard over the sink and an old percolator that stood on the worktop. Eiríkur fussed over this unfamiliar task, sitting back down once the machine had started to hiss and bubble to itself.

Ketill's colour had started to return and he supported himself with both forearms on the table, his lips pursed in a thin, angry line.

Eiríkur poured coffee into a mug.

'Is there any milk?'

'Fridge.'

A small carton of G-Milk joined the mug and Ketill squeezed it until a dribble of milk turned his coffee khaki brown. He took a lump of hard sugar from a packet and tucked it into his mouth, sipping coffee through it.

'Aren't you having any?'

'I don't drink coffee,' Eiríkur said and Ketill snorted. 'I'm sorry I gave you a turn. It wasn't the intention.'

'Remind me, what brings you here? You said something this morning about a fight.'

'A man was murdered last night in the street, a few metres from your door.'

'Thór the Boxer?'

Eiríkur hesitated. 'It hasn't been announced yet, but, yes. Thór Hersteinsson.'

'I guess he had it coming. He was an evil bastard and probably deserved it.'

Eiríkur shrugged. 'That's not for me to say. Do any of us deserve to have our life taken away?'

'Half of mine was snatched away,' Ketill snarled.

'I have to say I'm shocked. Páll Oddur had retired from the force long before I joined and I assure you things have changed a lot. That could never happen today,' Eiríkur said. 'That's one of the reasons I'm here.'

'Go on, officer,' Ketill said, taking another lump of sugar. 'Give me a good reason why I should help the police.'

'This is all stuff I shouldn't tell you. But we have a man in the cells who's been charged with Thór Hersteinsson's murder. He's not the most pleasant of people – a drug dealer with a whole string of misdeeds behind him – and I don't doubt that there are a good many things he's done that we'll never know about.'

'You've got the killer. So why are you here?'

'Because the officer who is heading this investigation has charged this man. My colleague and I, who are also working on this investigation, are sure the man's innocent. At least,' Eiríkur said, 'we don't believe he's responsible for this particular crime, whatever else he has on his conscience. That's assuming he has one, and I'm not sure he has.'

'This is hurting your conscience, is it?'

Eiríkur nodded slowly, taken aback by Ketill's question.

'It is. I have no love whatsoever for this person, but there's some evidence that he didn't do it, which the officer in charge of the case is ignoring. He's trying to browbeat a confession out of this man, and he's a hard-boiled sort of character, so it's an uphill battle.'

'Not some shrinking violet who gives way easily?'

Eiríkur thought of Rikki's scars and tattoos, and the fury on his face as he calculated the odds of taking on four police officers.

'No,' he said, 'far from it.'

'You're telling me there's an ethical dilemma of some kind here? Someone who deserves to be put away even though he didn't do it?'

'No,' Eiríkur replied. 'That's not it at all. My belief is that he *didn't* murder Thór, so he shouldn't take the blame for it, regardless of whatever else he's done.'

'A copper with a conscience,' Ketill said, his tone mocking. 'Who'd have thought it?'

'Like I said, we're not all like Páll Oddur Bjarnason.'

'But your colleague is?' Ketill said and coughed once, putting a hand to his mouth before his face turned brick red and he exploded in another coughing fit that left him trembling, his forehead in his hands. He took a long wheezing breath as he recovered. Eventually he straightened his back and leaned over to open a cupboard. He took out a flat bottle, spun the cap off and poured a slug into his coffee.

Eiríkur shook his head as Ketill offered him the bottle.

'I imagine you'd be happy to arrest me for having half a litre of moonshine in my kitchen cupboard,' he said, sipping his heavily laced coffee.

Eiríkur shrugged.

'I could, but I have better things to do. The paperwork would take up the rest of the day and you might get a tiny fine in a year's time once the whole thing has gone through the system.'

'If I'm still here in a year's time,' Ketill said, his voice dark. 'I could do with a refill if you can reach the coffee machine.' He pushed his mug towards Eiríkur, who stretched for the jug. Ketill added another slug, and the smell as the spirit hit the hot coffee filled the room a second time. 'Come on then. What are you after?'

'I want to know what happened last night. Did you see anything? And if so what?'

'And help put some poor bastard away?'

'Or keep some other poor bastard from being put away,' Eiríkur retorted.

Skúli waited for his phone to ring but nothing happened. He fretted as he took the bus home, sat in the kitchen and drank too many cups of coffee as the street outside slipped into darkness, all the while resisting the temptation to call Lars's phone again. Dagga took Markús for a long walk to the shops, and when they returned, cheeks red from the fresh wind, they found Skúli still sitting at the kitchen table, gnawing his fingernails.

When the call came, it wasn't the phone ringing, but the door, where a stern young woman stood with a barrel-chested man at her side.

'This is Skúli Snædal's residence?'

Dagga showed them into the kitchen, her eyes urgently questioning Skúli as the woman took a seat without waiting to be asked to sit. The man stood by the kitchen door and said nothing.

'Skúli?' she asked, as if Dagga weren't even in the room. 'My name's Birna Hreinsdóttir and we're from the police.'

'I thought so,' Skúli said, nervously extending a hand and glancing at the man. 'I know who you are.'

'That's interesting, because we've found out quite a lot about you,' Birna said. 'It'll be enlightening if we can work out how much of what we each think we know is true or not.'

She consulted a notebook as Dagga stood anxiously in the corner with Markús in her arms. 'University in Århus, a spell on a local rag there, *Dagurinn*, *Reykjavík Voice*, *DV*, now working for something called *Pulse*. Your father's Eggert Snædal, right?'

'That's right,' Skúli answered in a daze.

'It was around midnight. I don't know exactly,' Ketill said, as if overcoming an unwillingness to speak.

Eiríkur sat and watched and waited for the man's inner turmoil to resolve itself.

'I heard the noise outside. It's nothing unusual around here, though not so much on a week night, and they didn't sound like drunks on their way home. I was sitting in front of the TV and didn't think anything of it – just another argument, I thought.'

He sipped his coffee and grimaced.

'Cold,' he said. 'You could make another pot, you know. Now that you know how it's done.'

Eiríkur filled the percolator again, and once he was back sitting down, Ketill continued.

'It was the scream that made me stand up and take a look. I've never heard anything like it. A real howl, like an animal in pain. It made me shiver. So I took a look, just pulled the curtain back to see what was going on.'

'And?'

'You know, violence is normally very quick. It takes seconds. It's nothing like the movies. By the time I got to the window it was almost all over. There was a body on the pavement, not moving, and someone standing by it. There was someone else on the ground as well, and a big guy looking around. I reckon the big guy and the second man on the ground had a ruck where I couldn't see them, up against the wall.'

'Did you see these people? The big guy and the other one?'

Ketill shook his head.

'Not clearly. Don't forget it was dark and there's not a lot of light from those streetlights.' He sighed and jerked his head towards the percolator. Eiríkur dutifully filled a mug for him. Ketill slopped in a few drops of moonshine. 'What do you want to know? Jog an old man's memory.'

'To start with, I want as much of a description as you can give me of these two people, good enough to rule out the chap we have in a cell, and hopefully enough to be able to identify these people.'

'You'll be lucky. It was over in a few seconds.'

'Think. Please. Tell me what you *think* you saw.'

Ketill sipped his aromatic coffee and closed his eyes.

'The big guy was tall. Around two metres, I reckon. Big but not fat. He looked pretty athletic. Dark hair. Dark clothes, a leather jacket of some kind and jeans, I think.'

'Dark hair? You're sure?'

'Sure. That's about the only thing I can be sure of. A big guy with dark brown or black hair and a beard.'

'All right. And the other one?'

'The other one was a woman. I'm sure of it. Quite slight. Sort of mousy hair, shoulder length.'

'All right,' Eiríkur said slowly. 'So you saw a man on the ground, presumably the victim, and a woman standing next to him. Then there's another man on the ground and the big guy appears. Right?'

'Right.'

'So you didn't see the assault take place?'

'No.'

'And where did they go?'

'Up the street,' Ketill said, nodding in that direction. 'Towards Rauðarárstígur.'

'Did you see their faces? Even for a second?'

'The woman, yes. She looked right up at me. They they were gone, and they didn't hang about. A moment later there was some drunk who practically walked into the guy on the ground, and it wasn't long before the street was full of blue lights. Made me sick, it did. Seeing those lights flashing, just like the day Páll Oddur Bjarnason hauled me off to the cells.'

'You're certain it was a woman?' Eiríkur repeated. 'Absolutely sure?'

'Not absolutely, but sure enough. I watched them jog down the street, and if that was a man he had a lovely arse.'

* * *

Hans cleared his throat, perched a pair of frameless glasses on the end of his nose and peered at some hastily written notes.

Sævaldur folded his arms, cocked his head on one side and waited.

'Be my guest,' he said. 'I'm looking forward to hearing this.'

Rikki glared, beads of sweat forming in the stubble on top of his head.

'My client,' Hans said, looking up to check that Sævaldur was paying attention. 'My client spent yesterday afternoon at a gym, where he trained for two hours. There are witnesses who will confirm this.'

'You'll naturally supply me with all their names and addresses?'

'Of course,' Hans said. 'From four in the afternoon until six he was at the Laugardalur swimming pool, where he swam for thirty minutes and spent an hour in the hot tub. Again, there are witnesses who will corroborate this.'

'I don't give a crap about that,' Sævaldur said. 'This is all seven hours before your client beat the life out of someone on the street. Get on with it, will you?'

Hans looked mortified.

'Officer, you said just now that you wanted a detailed breakdown of my client's movements, so that's what we are providing you with.'

'All right, just get on with it then.'

'My client had a meal at Kúl on Frakkastígur and was there until ten that evening.'

'Now we're getting somewhere, I hope.'

'At ten my client went to the home of Geir Franzson and stayed there until approximately half-past midnight. He is unsure of the exact timing, but he states that he returned to Aneta Lisowski's home, and was asleep there when she returned from work at one in the morning, as I believe she has already confirmed.'

Sævaldur nodded slowly.

'And Geir Franzson's address? If it's the Geir Franzson I think it is, then he lives in Fossvogur, so I reckon your client could have left there at midnight, made it to Njálsgata, done the job, and been back at his girlfriend's place before one, knowing that's when she'd be back from work and could vouch for him being there,' Sævaldur said slowly, looking sharply at Rikki. 'So who's the patsy who'll confirm your client's presence at Geir's place until past midnight?'

'Her name's Aníka Björt,' Rikki said, coughing as his throat went dry. 'Geir's on holiday somewhere. There were only the two of us there.'

A grin spread across Sævaldur's face.

'And how old is Aníka Björt?' he said with gentle menace. 'Or does she belong to someone else, like Geir? Or is this just bullshit?' he said, shaking his head, then looking up as there was a knock at the door and Eiríkur's face appeared.

'Could I have a word, Sævaldur?'

'Sure, my boy. We're about to knock off while I run a few checks. Tell them to take this naughty boy back to the cells, would you?'

'Tell me about Lars Bundgaard,' Ívar Laxdal suggested.

'Hold on,' Skúli protested. 'How about *you* tell me about Lars Bundgaard? I spoke to some policeman in Belgium a couple of hours ago when I called Lars's number. What's going on here?'

'I know. That's how you were traced. How long have you known Lars Bundgaard?'

Skúli blanched. 'Am I some kind of suspect here? What's going on? What's happened to Lars?'

Birna leaned forward over the table.

'I'm uncomfortably aware that as you're a journalist, I have to be rather more cautious than I might otherwise be.' She looked steadily into Skúli's eyes, as if waiting for him to flinch, until she seemed satisfied that what she said would go no further. 'All right. All I can tell you is that your friend is dead. No,' she said, holding up a hand as Skúli opened his mouth. 'I can't answer any questions because I don't have any answers to give you. It's in the hands of the police over there.'

'Was it an accident, or was he murdered?'

'Why do you ask if he was murdered?'

'Because you're here asking me questions. If Lars had got drunk and fallen in the river, then I don't imagine I'd have some weird secret service outfit breathing down my neck.'

'That's a reasonable answer,' Birna admitted. 'And I'm not sure what you mean by some weird secret service outfit. But, yes. Lars Bundgaard was murdered, shot in his apartment. Now, how well did you know him?'

'I thought I knew him pretty well,' Skúli said, bewildered. 'But maybe I didn't after all. We both worked as interns for a few months on that local paper in Århus about ten years ago. We got on pretty well, although Lars was very politically minded and I'm not particularly.'

'You mean radical?' the man broke in.

'Call it what you will. Lars had a big social conscience. We kept in touch occasionally. Not regularly, but we'd talk a few times a year.'

'And when did you last meet?' Birna asked.

'Three, maybe four years ago. It was before Dagga and I got together, so more than three years ago.'

'Were you aware of his work?'

'Of course. As I said, we've stayed in touch, but not frequent touch. Lars was passionate about what he did. He could go on about social injustice for hours, and he'd get more and more angry in the process. So Lars was murdered?'

'Our colleagues in Antwerp believe so,' Birna said, arms folded on the table. 'I'll be honest with you, Skúli. We had an urgent request from Brussels to check you out.'

Skúli shivered and he could see Dagga hugging Markús tight.

'And what are you going to tell them?'

'Probably just what you told us – that as far as we're concerned, you're a fairly harmless journalist.'

'That's good to hear,' Skúli said bitterly, 'but it's not much of a professional endorsement.'

'That's what I'm going to tell my contact in Brussels,' the woman said, and all the warmth disappeared from her voice. 'But now *you* can tell *me* why you decided to contact Lars Bundgaard just as he happened to get himself murdered. There has to be a reason for it,' she said.

'What the fuck do you mean?'

Sævaldur's fury erupted; he immediately fought it back, though the anger was plain.

'What I said,' Eiríkur shrugged. 'Helgi thinks so as well.'

'Gunna's boys,' Sævaldur sneered. 'She's not around at the moment and I'm running this. I don't like it when my officers go off-script and do their own thing without telling me.'

'Sorry. I thought I was doing what the government pays me to do.'

'The government pays you to do what I tell you. Now, Aníka Björt, the tart Rikki's lawyer reckons he was with when Thór was murdered. You and Helgi had better go and find her and make sure she doesn't trip us up on this. I've been wanting to put Rikki the Sponge away for years.'

'Rikki didn't do it. There's a witness.'

'What?'

'There's a witness. Someone who lives on Njálsgata and looked out of the window. He saw Thór and Fúsi on the ground, and he said a man and a woman left the scene. A guy with hair and a beard. Rikki doesn't have a hair on his head, so it wasn't him.'

Eiríkur stopped himself feeling sorry for Sævaldur as his eyes narrowed.

'You're sure about all this? I don't want to see this case go down the drain.'

'There's more,' he said. 'We'll have Miss Cruz's report later, but she said that Thór's arm had been dislocated, pulled clear out of the socket. So we should be looking for someone with at least some martial arts skills. That's not the kind of injury Thór would have got in a fight with Rikki. There are plenty of marks on Rikki's face, but none of them are new, and I don't imagine he would have got away from Thór without taking at least a couple of punches.'

Sævaldur folded his arms and stuck out his chest, but there was defeat in his eyes for a moment, until he rallied and scowled.

'I'm not having this wrecked. Fúsi positively identified Rikki as the assailant.'

'What if Fúsi's telling tales?'

'Come on. Fúsi has to be terrified. He wouldn't point the finger at Rikki unless he was sure.'

'That's what I'm thinking. Will Fúsi back out of this?' Eiríkur said. 'He hasn't made a formal statement yet, and we won't get one from him until the doctor confirms he's in a fit state.'

'Then we'll make sure Fúsi doesn't back out of it, shall we?'

Hanne cooked and Carsten brooded. The camper van had been lovingly fitted out, with almost every convenience they could want in such a compact vehicle. They had been close for almost all of the years they had spent together, their lives entwined, going back for more decades than it was comfortable to think about. Everything had been shared, the good and the bad, and there had been an openness to their long relationship that some people found startling.

Now they had hardly spoken for days and the atmosphere between them had turned sour and hostile. Carsten felt adrift, wondering how Hanne could abandon the principles they had always lived by.

Social justice had always been something she had fought hard for, standing up for anyone she felt had been mistreated or marginalized, and often earning herself black looks and dark whispers behind her back in the process.

She had never failed to march to the nearest police station and bang the counter with her fist whenever she was sure the law had been broken, something that, fortunately, was a rare occurrence in her long career.

He felt too tired to drive any further. The camper was off the road, parked in a campsite, empty at this time of year. They had parked and walked in silence to the nearest shop to stock up on provisions, still managing to walk arm-in-arm, while Carsten had an overwhelming premonition that something had finally appeared in their lives that would surely tear them apart.

For the rest of the day they had spent the afternoon in the camper while flurries of snow hit the windscreen like handfuls of buckshot and a gusting cold wind rocked it on its wheels.

Normally it wouldn't have been a problem. They were both comfortable spending time together without the need to talk, each engrossed in a book or some writing. But now there was a new friction. Hanne's jaw was set like a rock, telling him she was in no mood for affection or even small talk. Carsten sat in the front seat with a book in his hands, staring at the pages without seeing the words.

'Are you all right?' Hanne asked eventually, driven to break the silence. 'You haven't turned a page for more than half an hour.'

'No. I'm not all right,' he said eventually. 'Any more than you are.'

The house stretched into the distance and Helgi decided that a place like this would suit him and his now large family, if only he could muster the income to match it. The white Range Rover in the drive would also have made a handsome replacement for his long-suffering Skoda.

'Yes?'

The woman who answered the door looked immaculate, but tight-lipped and brusque.

'Helgi Svavarsson, I'm a detective with the city police force,' he said, flipping open his wallet. 'I'm looking for Aníka Björt Sverrisdóttir.'

'What has she done now?'

The question was delivered with a combination of force and despair.

'Nothing that I'm aware of. But she may be a witness,' he replied, and saw the woman almost sigh with relief. 'I take it you're her mother?'

'I am. You'd better come in and I'll wake her up. I'm Elísabet Hákonardóttir, by the way,' she said, shutting the heavy door behind Helgi as he wiped his feet. He'd already checked on the family and knew exactly who the woman was.

The hall was hung with framed magazine covers, charting

Elísabet Hákonardóttir's progress from model to actress to arbiter of fashion, until the images gave way to a series of photos of a girl with her mother's looks but a surly pout that was all her own.

'Wait.'

Helgi raised an eyebrow and decided to do as he was told, standing with his hands behind his back as he inspected one framed cover after another of magazines that had been popular when he and Elísabet Hákonardóttir were considerably younger.

It was a while before she returned, lips pursed in frustration.

'She's coming,' she said curtly. 'I hope.'

'Thanks,' Helgi said, hiding his impatience.

'Can I ask . . . ?'

'What do you want to know?'

'Has she done anything? Something she shouldn't have?'

Helgi shrugged.

'I don't know. But as Aníka Björt is under sixteen, then you have the right to be present. In fact, you ought to be present.'

'Ah.' Elísabet took a sharp breath, her pointed nose lifting. 'I wonder if there are things that I'd prefer not to know about.'

'She's a teenager, so it's possible. Weren't we all young once?' Helgi asked gently, and tilted his head towards a figure in a thick white dressing gown approaching along the hall. 'Looks like she's here.'

'Hello,' the yawning girl offered. 'You wanted to talk to me about something?'

'Aníka Björt? My name's Helgi Svavarsson and I'm a detective with the city police force. Can we sit down and talk? I have a few questions for you.'

The girl nodded and looked at her mother.

'Yes, yes. Go to the living room,' Elísabet said, and Helgi could sense that she was keeping a tight rein on the tension inside her.

Aníka Björt curled in an armchair with languid grace, thin legs tucked beneath her, the dressing gown practically enveloping her. Fine, pale hair fell straight on either side of her face, giving her the look of someone peering through a narrow window.

'Can you tell me where you were last night, Aníka Björt?' Helgi asked, hoping to sound reassuring.

'I was out with Karin until about midnight. Then I came home and went to sleep.'

'And Karin is?'

'She's in my class at school.'

'And where did you go?'

'We went to see a movie in Kópavogur.'

Aníka Björt's voice was flat, devoid of expression.

'And when did that finish?'

'Around eleven. There's not much to do in Kópavogur, so we hung out for a while outside and then went home.'

'So you saw Karin last night. Anyone else?'

'Some of the others from school.'

'Nobody else?'

Aníka Björt shrugged.

'No. That's it.'

Helgi delved into his pocket and took out some business cards. He dealt them like playing cards, one for Elísabet and two for Aníka Björt.

'How did you get home, Aníka Björt?'

'Bus. It stops at the bottom of the hill.'

'So you're five minutes home from the bus stop?'

'Something like that,' the girl agreed.

'If you remember anything,' he said. 'Anything that might be important, I mean, then please call me.'

Aníka Björt nodded, her face blank, as Helgi stood up.

'That was painless. Thanks for your time,' he said. 'What was the film you went to see?'

There was a moment's pause.

'It was a *Star Wars* thing. It was a bit shit, but Karin likes those movies.'

The two Patrols appeared outside at exactly the appointed time. Gunna let Valgeir in and he stood awkwardly in the hallway as he waited.

'You can come in and sit down, you know,' Gunna told him, and he perched stiffly on one of the stools along the breakfast bar. 'Dinner with the minister? I don't suppose she's cooking herself, is she?' she asked, making an attempt to break the ice.

'I don't know,' Valgeir said, nonplussed for a moment before he realized it wasn't a serious question. 'Probably not,' he admitted.

'She's no domestic goddess?'

'I don't think so.'

Osman had dressed in a pale suit, which he wore with elegance and no tie, in contrast to Valgeir, who looked overdressed in what Gunna thought looked like a suit brought out only for funerals.

'Ready?' Osman asked softly, as always. His voice was never loud but could always be heard clearly, as if other people instinctively fell silent when he had something to say.

'Just waiting for you,' Valgeir said.

'Then let's go. I'm looking forward to this,' he said, and for a moment Gunna believed him, until he shot her a smile and a wink as Valgeir turned away. 'See you later, Gunnhildur,' he said, before walking out to the waiting cars.

The two Patrols disappeared into the night, their lights bright pools in the blackness until they crested the rise and vanished behind the houses in the distance.

'Just so you know,' Ívar Laxdal said. 'Your friend Skúli has stirred up a proper hornets' nest with his article today.'

'Yep. I read it. Is there any truth in all that stuff?'

'All that stuff?'

'About Osman being involved in organized crime. Weapons, slavery. How's Steinunn taking it? She must be livid.'

'She hasn't said a word to me,' he replied with a brief humourless smile. 'She doesn't talk to me unless she needs something or wants to point out the police force's shortcomings.' He sighed. 'On the other hand, it has completely diverted attention from the Children of Freedom thing, so she might very well be relieved. I've no doubt I'll hear all about it when the time comes. No need to wait up, Gunnhildur. I'll let you know when we're on the way.'

'You're not dressed up in your Sunday best like young Valgeir?'

He shook his head and looked at her with resignation on his normally impassive face.

'I'm not invited to the party. There might be some leftovers for the staff, if we're lucky,' he said. 'I've no idea when we'll be back. I'm hoping it won't be late.'

'Your guy's out of luck,' Helgi said, and the grin on Sævaldur's face made him wince inwardly.

'No alibi. I like that.'

Helgi twirled his phone in his fingers, as if willing it to ring.

'She's lying,' he said. 'The girl's not sixteen. Her mother's a dragon and she was in the room, so the girl chickened out. Said she'd been at the pictures with her friend.'

'You know, Helgi, that suits me just fine. I hope you're not feeling sorry for Rikki?'

'Of course not. The man's pond life.'

'Did he fuck the girl, do you think?'

Helgi scratched his head.

'I've no idea and I'm not inclined to speculate. It wouldn't be hard to put pressure on her; tripping her up would be like falling off a log.'

'Except you're not going to, are you?'

Sævaldur glared and Helgi met his gaze impassively.

'I have plenty to keep me busy, Sævaldur. But . . .'

'But what?'

'If the girl calls me at some point and decides to put things straight, then Rikki has an alibi.'

'In which case she'll go to court, where her underage sex life will be made very public,' Sævaldur said, folding his arms as if to underline the finality of his words. 'I'm sure her snooty mother wouldn't be keen on that.'

'True,' Helgi agreed. 'I'm not expecting to hear from her. But I wouldn't be surprised if she gets a call from Rikki's lawyer.'

'Until then we can pile the pressure on Rikki.'

'Sure we can. But we can't prevent Hans making contact with Aníka Björt. And if she gives him an alibi, then he's off the hook,

125

and instead of a dozen years for murder, he'll get a fine and a suspended sentence for screwing a fifteen-year-old kid.'

Gunna dozed on the sofa, stretched out under a blanket and with a book in her hands. She enjoyed the solitude, but wondered about her family. Would Steini and Laufey have been to Happy House for their dinner? Would Laufey even be at home this evening now that she spent more than half of her time in Reykjavík?

In the last year or so, since she'd started college in the city, Laufey had blossomed, much to Gunna's relief. She had gone rapidly from being withdrawn to an independent young woman with a new confidence about her. Instead of evenings spent hunched over a computer in her room, Laufey had found herself a new circle of friends in Reykjavík, leaving the village of Hvalvík behind. Gunna wondered how long it would be before Laufey flew the nest and settled in the city, or somewhere further afield.

She checked the time and felt her stomach rumble. On her own in the house, she hadn't bothered to cook anything and had made do with a couple of sandwiches instead. She wondered when they would be back, and couldn't help speculating on Osman's origins, which he'd been carefully evasive about.

Gunna levered herself off the sofa and walked around the house for the fifth time that day.

'Gunnhildur,' she heard Ívar Laxdal's voice intone in her ear as her communicator fizzed into life.

'Listening.'

'Ten minutes.'

'Got you. Out,' she replied.

She tucked the Glock back into its place under her armpit, pulled her fleece on over it and waited for the approaching lights.

A tight-lipped Ívar Laxdal got out of the black Volvo.

'Everything all right?'

'Fine. How was dinner?'

'Ask our friend when he gets here,' he replied in a sour voice. 'He's had a great time, and he's bringing company back with him. So much for security.'

The Patrols arrived together, followed by a squad car. Valgeir got out and opened the back door for Osman, who appeared as casually elegant as he had been when he'd left the house a few hours earlier. Behind him tripped a tall woman, long legs below a startlingly short skirt, and a mass of chestnut hair that seemed barely under control as she swept it back from her face with one arm.

'Is this it? Your hideaway?' She giggled. 'It's really cool, Ossie.'

Ossie? Gunna thought as Osman's arm snaked around the woman's waist.

The two Patrols disappeared into the night. Gunna and Ívar Laxdal talked in the lobby by the door as Gunna locked it.

'So dinner was a success?' she said. 'Who's the girl?'

'A relative of Steinunn's,' he said. 'I had her checked out and there's no record on file. No criminal record, that is. So we have to assume that she's clean.'

'Who is she?'

'Sif. She's Hallgrímsdóttir, but she uses her mother's family name. So she's Sif Strand.'

'Anything between those ears?'

'I've no idea.' Ívar Laxdal shrugged. 'You clearly don't keep up with the celebrity gossip about Steinunn's fashionable family, do you? If you did, you'd know all about Sif's colourful lifestyle.'

'All right. Are you leaving me to it?'

This time Ívar Laxdal grinned. 'I am. I'll leave you to deal with the lovebirds. He has appointments tomorrow that'll keep him out of our hair until the evening, so you can go home for a few hours if you like. I'll be back first thing.'

'Thanks a bunch,' Gunna said as she unlocked the door.

'You're tough, Gunnhildur,' he said, getting back into the black Volvo. 'You can handle it.'

The call came later than Helgi expected. He yawned and reached for his phone, glanced at the number he didn't recognize, and pressed the green button to answer the call.

'Helgi.'

'Er . . .' He could hear the crackle of wind in the caller's phone. 'Is that Helgi the policeman?'

'This is Helgi Svavarsson,' he confirmed. 'Is that Aníka Björt?'

He lifted his feet from the armrest at the far end of the sofa and got to his feet. Halla mouthed a question.

'Work,' he mouthed back and headed for the kitchen, where he perched against the table with the phone to his ear.

'I . . . er,' Aníka Björt floundered. 'I wanted to talk to you about . . .'

'What did you want to tell me?' He listened to the wind as she fell silent. 'Aníka Björt, are you still there?'

'Sorry. Yes. Listen, I didn't really tell you the truth today. You caught me off guard and my mother was there as well.'

'I know. But you're under sixteen, so she has every right to be there. Legally you're a minor, so she or a responsible adult has to be present.'

'Shit. I'm sorry.'

'Sorry about what?'

'About lying to you.'

'About what?'

'Did you speak to Karin?'

'No. Did you expect me to?'

'Well. Yeah.'

'I didn't need to,' Helgi said softly. 'It was pretty obvious you weren't telling the truth.'

'How did you know?'

'Because the cinema in Kópavogur closed about six months ago. You didn't go and see a film, did you?'

The lights in the living room had been dimmed. Osman and Sif were practically horizontal on the soft sofa where Gunna had dozed through the evening.

Osman chuckled and whispered in Sif's ear and she giggled appreciatively.

Gunna turned up the lights and Osman looked at her sternly.

'Is this your granny, Ossie?' Sif said with a smirk.

'My name's Gunnhildur,' Gunna said, taking off her fleece and folding it over the back of a chair. 'I'm here to look after this gentleman.'

Sif's face froze at the sight of the Glock in its holster.

'You're like a bodyguard, right? Wow! A lady bodyguard.'

'Sort of, Sif. Sort of,' Gunna said and the woman's face registered surprise at the sound of her own name.

Knowing that sleep wasn't likely, Gunna switched the coffee machine on and sat at the breakfast bar, flipping through a newspaper as she waited for the coffee to brew. At the other end of the long living room Sif's giggles became throatier and Gunna could hear Osman's voice becoming more urgent.

'Hey, where's the bathroom?'

Sif was on her feet and striding towards her, still tall with her heels kicked off and her hair artfully astray.

'Through there,' Gunna said, jerking a thumb towards the hall and looking down at the paper.

Osman was on his feet once Sif had clicked the lock behind her.

'Gunnhildur, would you be so kind as to leave us alone?'

'Actually, no.'

He glared back at her, as if the refusal were a personal affront.

'I will definitely raise this with Steinunn tomorrow.'

'Be my guest. I'm here to look after your safety, not be a nursemaid. I can't keep a lookout around this place if I'm locked away in a bedroom, can I?'

'This is ridiculous.'

'If you say so. I have a responsibility for security. If you want some privacy with your girlfriend, then there's a bedroom the size of most people's houses. But close the door, please. I don't want to have to listen.'

Every ounce of Aníka Björt's self-confidence had evaporated as she sat huddled in a heavy parka on a bench at the bus station. Earlier in the day Helgi had watched her tell him obvious lies without turning a hair – he wondered if her mother suspected.

Now all the maturity had been stripped away and she had become a vulnerable child again, ill-equipped to cope with the turmoil she was obviously struggling with.

'I need a coffee,' Helgi told her. 'Want one?'

She nodded and followed, watching as he helped himself to coffee, paid and asked for a Coke for her. He gestured towards a corner.

'So. What do you want to tell me?' Helgi asked when she had taken a seat and sipped her Coke.

'It's about what I told you earlier,' she said, shivering.

'I thought so but didn't want to push you too far.'

'Why? I mean, why didn't you?'

Helgi held his coffee mug in his hands, warming his fingers.

'We don't all bang the table and demand answers right now. Sometimes it works, but I didn't think it was going to work with you. I just gave you the opportunity to call me and put things straight. That's why I'm here now, and that's just what I'd like you to do.'

Aníka Björt slouched in her plastic chair, hands deep in the pockets of the parka that was wrapped tightly around her.

'Tell me how you know Ríkharður Rúnarsson,' Helgi suggested gently and watched her shudder as her eyes lifted to meet his.

'My brother knows Rikki.'

'And where's your brother now?'

'Prison. Mum won't talk about it. She said she's going to disown him.'

'And what's your brother's name?'

'Andri.'

'And he's in Litla Hraun?'

Aníka Björt nodded.

'I don't know him. What's he in prison for?'

'He was stopped at the airport with some drugs. They gave him two years.'

Helgi nodded to himself.

'He'll be out in less than a year if he behaves. When did he get put away?'

'A few months ago. I don't know the whole story. I wanted to go and visit him, but Mum said she wouldn't take me and it's a long way to the prison.'

'And your father?'

'He's not around much these days, and he isn't Andri's dad.'

'I see. You miss him?'

'Yeah. I do.'

'So how does Rikki fill the gap?' Helgi asked, his voice soft.

Aníka Björt rolled her shoulders, as if trying to pull herself deeper into her coat.

'He was at the gym one day. I used to see him there with Andri sometimes, so I knew who he was. He gave me a lift home a few times, and we'd drive around town,' she said and her voice faded away.

'And then?' Helgi asked, guessing where this would lead.

'We go to his friend's place sometimes,' she said in an almost inaudible voice. 'A few times in the afternoons, evenings sometimes if he wasn't busy somewhere, if his friend was away.'

'That's Geir Franzson's house?'

Aníka Björt nodded.

'Do you know what kind of work Rikki does?'

'Sort of. He trains hard and he said he does security work. That's why he's busy so often in the evenings.'

'I know you haven't heard from Rikki today.'

'How do you know that?' she asked, looking up to meet his eyes.

'Because Rikki is in a cell at Hverfisgata.'

'The police station?'

'That's it. And tomorrow he'll probably be shipped off to Litla Hraun.'

'Why?'

'Let's just say it's serious; he'll be looking at a lot more than just a couple of months or years in there. Look, Aníka Björt,' Helgi said, trying not to sound too earnest. 'Rikki's a pretty evil character, you know.'

'He's not a bad guy.'

Now it was Helgi's turn to shiver.

'I assure you Rikki is a very real criminal. He's under arrest for a very serious offence, and part of what I'm doing is tracing his movements yesterday to find out if they tie in with what he's supposed to have done. That means I need times and places, so I can nail down where he was and where he wasn't. Understand?'

'How did you know?'

'Because Rikki gave us your name.'

'He said he wouldn't ever tell anyone,' she said, the disappointment welling up inside her.

'Well, he did. I don't particularly want to defend him, what with Rikki being the person he is, but he didn't have a lot of choice in the matter. I need you to tell me where you were and when.'

'Geir's abroad somewhere. We were at his house until about midnight, then he gave me a lift home. Well, to the bus stop.'

'So your mother wouldn't suspect?'

Aníka Björt nodded miserably.

'Can I ask what you were doing?'

'What do you think?' she snapped, anger flaring up and her face flushing pink.

'Sorry, Aníka Björt. I know it's uncomfortable, but I have to be certain.'

'We smoked a couple of pipes and fucked. Are you going to tell my mother now?' she asked, no less furious.

'That depends.'

'On what?'

'It depends on whether or not Rikki is charged and it goes to court, in which case I'll need to have a formal statement, and that means your mother will undoubtedly have to be present at the interview.'

'Shit. No. I won't do it.'

'Well, if you watch the news tomorrow you might find out why your friend Rikki's in a cell,' Helgi said. 'Shall I give you a lift home?'

Gunna quickly looked through the handbag Sif had left on the living-room table. There was nothing in it of any interest, and

Gunna reasoned that if there had been anything suspicious she would hardly have left it lying around.

The wallet inside showed her Sif's driving licence, a couple of credit cards, a few photographs of Sif with a muscular young man. Gunna put it all back and shrugged on her fleece. There was no need for an outside circuit of the house after dark and it had been made plain that after dusk she was not required to leave the building. It was long after midnight and although Osman's groans and Sif's whoops from the bedroom had subsided, she decided she needed some air.

The cold breeze hit her like a slap in the face. She checked the garage doors, knowing that they were secure but checking them to justify being outside. The lights of the house cast long shadows over the threadbare garden, and at the end of the building Gunna found that the window of Osman's en-suite bathroom was cracked open, enough for someone to force it back and crawl inside.

She shook her head in disgust, knowing she would have to disturb the lovebirds to demand that the windows be properly locked from the inside, and walked back to the seaward side of the house in the shadow of the unlit wall when a moment's movement caught in the moonlight between the house and shore caught her eye. She sidestepped out of the light and stood with her back against the wall, eyes fixed and unblinking on the spot where she thought she'd seen something; her heart began to race.

She thought of clicking her communicator and asking if the team in the other house had noticed anything, but decided to wait until she was sure it was only a fox on the prowl.

The wind had dropped and so had the temperature. A luminous moon, clear skies and bitter cold were the perfect recipe for northern lights, she thought. She shivered and was a second from turning to go inside, having decided that whatever she had seen couldn't be anything significant, when a shadow lifted itself from the ground and loped, fast and stooping low, towards the house before dropping out of sight a second time.

Gunna held her breath, eyes on the spot, waiting for another movement.

She clicked the button on her communicator, thankful that she had taken it with her.

'You there, boys?' she murmured, simultaneously reaching into her fleece, extracting the Glock and clicking off the safety catch.

'Problem, Gunna?' a voice asked in her ear.

'Company. Looks suspicious. Somewhere on the seaward side of the house.'

'On the way.'

'OK,' she replied, eyes still glued to the spot where the figure had vanished from sight. She strained to hear the sound of the Special Unit officers approaching, knowing that she wouldn't be likely to know they were there until they let themselves be seen.

A peal of laughter could be heard from inside and she guessed that Sif and Osman had no idea what was unfolding outside, while she told herself it was nothing to worry about.

The shadow appeared again, and this time she saw it move deliberately towards the house on a course oblique to her view, aiming for the corner window. She drew breath in an involuntary gasp as the figure was silhouetted against the moonlit sea and she could clearly see the long finger of a weapon in its hand.

Her day's firearms training came flashing back to her. Weapon secure in right hand, support with the left, feet secure, knees slightly bent, look along the sight and make sure.

'Stop right there,' Gunna called, her voice decisive, although it sounded reedy and shrill to her. 'Police,' she yelled. 'Stop right there or I'll fire.'

There was no hesitation from the figure as it turned, and she saw the pistol lifted in the same two-handed grip as it sought a target.

Osman and Sif could still be heard laughing faintly through the calm night air. Gunna shouted again. Last warning, she thought to herself, hoping that she could keep the figure there, indecisive, until the Special Unit guys, who lived for this kind of thing, could arrive.

'I have you covered,' she yelled, her voice quavering as she took one step sideways and two paces closer to the figure, taking her

134

further away from the pool of light around the house. 'Put the weapon down. Now.'

This time the figure had an idea of where Gunna was standing and she saw it swing towards her. The crack of two shots echoed against the side of the house and one smacked into the wall where she had been standing a moment earlier. Aware that she was going to regret it, but knowing she had no choice, Gunna fired twice, hoping to hit her target but not to kill, knowing that with the man in her sights she had a good chance of doing some damage.

The reports were louder than she remembered from her firearms training, and for some reason she remembered that she had no ear defenders this time.

The figure dropped from sight. Ears ringing from the two reports in quick succession, heart hammering, Gunna froze.

'Drop your weapon and put your hands where I can see them,' she called, her voice hoarse as she made her way cautiously towards the place she reckoned him to be, the Glock trained on the position.

Her earpiece burst into life.

'What's going on, Gunna? Who's shooting?'

In the darkness the figure had been deceptively close. With the Glock still trained on the shadow as she stepped cautiously through heather, stiff with night frost, she pulled a torch from her pocket and played the light over the figure on the ground. There was no question that the man was dead. One of her two shots had hit him squarely in the chest and his head lolled sideways at a sickeningly unnatural angle.

'Gunna?'

The voice calling was no longer in her earpiece and a second torch played over the scene.

'Fuck, Gunna. That was fine shooting,' a voice said appreciatively.

'Save it for later, will you?' she snapped, her nerves stretched to breaking point. 'Both of you, spread out and check around. There might be another one somewhere. Check down by the shore.'

'OK,' the dark figure responded, a rifle cradled in his hands as he stalked down the gentle slope.

'Ívar, are you there?' Gunna said, clicking her communicator again.

'I am now.' He sounded drowsy. 'Problem?'

'You'd better get up here, and quick. I think we have something of a crisis on our hands.'

The warder opened the cell and Rikki looked up. His brows knitted in question as Helgi came in and the door clanged shut behind him.

'What the fuck do you want?'

'Sorry to disturb your beauty sleep, Rikki,' Helgi said. 'I thought a quiet word without Sævaldur anywhere around might be an idea.'

Rikki squared his shoulders and the muscles beneath his tight singlet rippled.

'Why?'

Helgi sat on the bunk and scratched his cheek.

'You know, Rikki, I'm off duty right now. I'd really like to be dozing in front of the telly with a beer in my hand. But instead I'm here with you. It's a hell of a way to spend an evening.'

Rikki glowered and perched stiffly in the bunk.

'Look,' Helgi said in an undertone. 'I've talked to Aníka Björt.'

'Right.'

'And you might find yourself being charged with having sexual relations with a minor.'

'Come on. She knows what she's doing, that one.'

Helgi shook his head.

'You know as well as I do that makes no difference. She's fifteen. What the hell were you thinking, Rikki? I thought strippers with plastic tits were your thing, not little girls like this one.'

'Shit. Let's not go there,' Rikki said, his head in his hands. 'What's the score, then?'

'Search me. I don't know whether the girl will make a statement to the effect that you were with her. She might, in which case you're probably in the clear on one count and in less deep shit on another. She might refuse, though, and then you're in deep shit.'

'So why are you here now?'

'Because you didn't finish Thór Hersteinsson off,' Helgi said, looking sideways at Rikki. 'And I want to know who did.'

Gunna had expected a team to be called out, but Ívar Laxdal arrived alone in his black Volvo, with the willowy young man from the ministry following close behind in the now familiar Patrol.

Ívar Laxdal surveyed the scene in the glare of the floodlights the two Special Unit officers had set up, a tiny portable generator chattering away close by to feed them with power. Valgeir looked sick as he surveyed the corpse and watched Ívar Laxdal go through the man's pockets.

He stood up empty-handed.

'Nothing at all, except for a set of picks and a torch. You have the weapon?'

Steingrímur, the raw-boned Special Unit officer Gunna had been belatedly delighted to see, handed him a revolver.

Ívar Laxdal cracked it open and emptied the bullets into his gloved hand.

'Two rounds fired.' He looked up. 'He fired at you, Gunnhildur?'

'Two rounds that I heard.'

'And that's when you returned fire?'

'I did. As soon as he fired, so did I.'

'And dropped the bastard,' Steingrímur said with admiration while Gunna shuddered at the thought of what she'd done.

'Who is the man?' Valgeir asked.

'How the hell should I know?' Ívar Laxdal snapped at him. 'My question is how this character turned up here with an old-style police revolver in his hand, nothing to identify him and camouflage paint on his face. How did he know Osman was here?'

Valgeir blanched. 'I . . . I really don't know.'

'Because only my officers know about Steinunn's friend in there. So if there's been a leak, then I can guess where it came from.'

'You'll have to take it up with the minister . . .'

'You're damn right I will, but between now and then I have to decide what to do with this corpse. I'm inclined to dig a hole right here and roll him into it,' he said, turning to Gunna, taking her arm and walking her away from the group clustered around the body. 'Are you all right?'

'I'm all right. Look, what the hell's going on? What are we doing about this man? You're not serious, surely?'

'About burying him in Steinunn Strand's back garden? I would if that damned boy wasn't here, but I don't dare to, Gunnhildur, much as I'd like to,' he said savagely. 'I should never have agreed to let Valgeir have access to our communications. That man was a professional killer and he'd have had no compunction about putting a slug in your head. Look, I want you to go back to the house and check on our guest. Are you all right to do that?'

'Of course I am.'

'Good. I'll make arrangements out here and be with you as soon as I can.'

By the time she'd unlocked the door, stepped inside and kicked off her boots, Gunna was shivering uncontrollably. She found Osman sitting in the living room, Sif nestled into his side with an expression of distraught confusion on her perfect face. She squawked as Gunna came into the room and sat heavily on one of the dining chairs, when she realized the Glock was still in her hand. She quickly took out the clip and put it and the weapon on the table.

'What happened?' Osman asked in a smooth voice.

'Someone looking for you, I guess.'

'And where is this person?'

'He's outside and he's not going to answer any questions.'

'He's dead?'

'Yes.'

'Good,' Osman decided, and Sif pulled away from him, hauling her legs up in front of her on the sofa and hugging her knees to her chest. 'You killed him?' he asked.

There was a new respect in Osman's eyes.

'No comment. But the man's dead.'

'We saw it from the window,' Sif blurted out. 'You killed him.'

138

Gunna felt her legs begin to tremble now that she was sitting down.

'I want to go home,' Sif said suddenly, standing up and wrapping her arms around herself. She looked so different, hair in real rather than carefully contrived disarray and wrapped in a shirt that presumably belonged to Osman. Gunna wondered if this was the same person who had breezed in, bursting with allure and confidence, a few hours before.

'I'm afraid that won't be possible for the moment,' Gunna said, looking up at Sif as she got to her feet.

'Why? It's a free country. I can do what I want.'

'To start with, it's the middle of the night and everybody here has better things to do than be your taxi driver. Secondly, you're in the middle of a serious security incident and it may not be safe for you to leave.'

'I'll call a taxi myself.'

'You can try, but your phone won't work,' Gunna told her.

'Don't be stupid. Of course it will.'

'There's a phone jammer here. Mobiles don't work within thirty metres of the house. You can go for a walk in the dark if you like. But my guess is that the dead guy outside with a gun in his hand wasn't working alone.'

Sif winced and perched on the edge of the sofa, her face in her hands. Osman watched with amusement as the shirt she was wearing flapped open, but he made no attempt to comfort her and yawned as he checked his watch.

Gunna groaned as she got to her feet and went to the distressed Sif, putting an arm around her shoulders. Sif buried her head in Gunna's chest and sobbed.

'I want to go home,' she repeated.

'You can't go home yet. Look, the best thing you can do is try and get some sleep,' Gunna assured her, longing to close her eyes herself and feeling the sting of fatigue in her eyelids. 'Use my room if you want to be on your own. Come on.'

Chapter Five

He inspected the beard critically. Trimmed close, it made him look slimmer and younger, different to the man with the full black beard who had grudgingly agreed that a closer look at the house would be worthwhile.

It had been a mess, he told himself, a complete wreck. He wondered if they had been expected, if the police had been tipped off. Had someone squealed on them? Maybe the cops had got lucky? He couldn't tell, not having been close enough to see what had happened.

He had followed the plan, heard the shots and withdrawn as soon as he heard the answering bark of an automatic pistol. Was Pino dead? He had watched him fall through the night vision glasses, but hadn't been able to see if it had been fatal, although that seemed likely. There had been four more bullets in the revolver's chambers, and as he hadn't heard any more shots, it seemed most likely that he was dead. From a safe distance he had seen lights set up, cars going to and fro.

Whatever had happened, the job was going to become ten times more difficult now that the police knew there was someone watching.

He had followed the contingency plans to the letter. The hire car had been returned and a replacement rented from another company under a different name. The apartment had been vacated for another in a quiet street, rented online.

It was with a heavy heart that he sent the jovial text message to his aunt reporting that he had extended his holiday – Ana would know what it meant and they would have to agree a course of action.

The sensible thing would be to disengage completely, to withdraw and return to the job later when routine had returned and complacency had set in. But he and Pino went back a long way and had done a good few dangerous jobs together in the past.

Finishing the job was almost a secondary consideration, he admitted to himself. A face-to-face meeting with whoever had shot Pino was what he was really looking forward to.

There was a hush over the house. Gunna huddled beneath a duvet on the sofa, sunk deep in its embrace, eyes closed but awake, numb after the unreal events of the night. She wondered if she would go down in history as a killer. Would she even keep her job? It was more than likely that she could be prosecuted, and there would certainly be an inquiry, which could become uncomfortably public.

Ívar Laxdal sat at the breakfast bar in the kitchen, muttering into his communicator while Valgeir sat along from him, nervous and unsure of himself. Osman appeared to be unaffected, while Sif had cried herself to sleep in Gunna's room. Steingrímur came and went, exchanging a few muttered words with Ívar Laxdal.

Gunna heard Valgeir stand up and leave the room. She gave up trying to sleep, got to her feet and poured herself a mug of half-stale coffee from the jug. As always when stress was becoming overwhelming, she ruthlessly stifled the craving for a cigarette.

'All right, Gunnhildur?' Ívar Laxdal asked, concern clear in his voice.

'Yeah. I'll get through it.'

'There's counselling, you know,' he said in an unusually gentle tone. 'Anything you need.'

'Just tell me what's going on.'

'It's a damned mess, I don't mind telling you. Not your doing, Gunnhildur. Not your doing at all,' he said thoughtfully. 'I'm trying to figure out how to keep this contained without putting a foot wrong, if you know what I mean.' He looked around. 'Where did that bloody boy get to? It's like having a toddler under your feet all the time.'

He strode to the door, banged it behind him and Gunna could hear raised voices outside.

She looked out of the window, wondering how far away dawn might be, and looked at the clock on the oven to check the time. She tried to remember the last time she had been awake all night.

Ívar Laxdal returned, fuming, with Valgeir's phone in his hand and Valgeir trailing in his wake. He threw the phone into the sink and dropped onto a stool while Valgeir sat down gingerly at the far end of the bar.

'Well,' he thundered, 'who were you on the phone to? And how?'

'I went far away enough to get a signal and spoke to Steinunn. Told her what happened.'

'And what did she say?'

'That she'd send someone.'

'You fucking idiot,' Ívar Laxdal seethed, getting to his feet and pacing the room. 'Dear God, where do they breed fuckwits like you these days?'

'The minister needs to know. I'd like to remind you that she's not just my boss. She's your boss as well.'

'I'm sure Steinunn is delighted that you've just taken a shit on her doorstep,' Ívar Laxdal said, a furious finger prodding Valgeir's chest. 'Doesn't it occur to you that what the minister doesn't know the minister doesn't have to deny knowledge of later? And if one of the minister's staff drops a turd on the minister's living-room floor, then the staff are going to be the ones who take the blame when the lid blows off. Understood?'

'I . . . er. I didn't think of it like that. I thought, naturally, that the minister ought to know.'

'Of course the minister ought to know. But this minister has ambitions, or don't you keep an ear to the ground? People who thwart political ambition tend to pay dearly for it sooner or later. Look, Valgeir. It's not even seven o'clock yet. The minister doesn't need to have heard anything until, say, nine, ten, maybe even later.

By then we'll have some answers, we'll have done all the damage limitation we can and, hopefully, we will have a nice tidy package to hand to the minister instead of a shit sandwich.'

'What have we done, Ívar?' Gunna asked. 'Is there any sign of an accomplice?'

'Steingrímur did some scouting around. Nothing to be found, but we'll see what tracks we can find once it gets light. The trouble is I daren't call in extra bodies. I had patrols watching for anything suspicious leaving the district last night, without giving them anything specific, but you know how short-handed we are these days.'

'Any idea who our boy might be?'

'Absolutely none.'

'He's still out there?'

'He's in the morgue now. Steingrímur and his team took the body and got Miss Cruz out in the middle of the night to take delivery. Now I'm wondering what to do with him.'

Gunna's eyebrows arched in surprise. 'Surely we need to go through the proper channels?'

'Well, we don't exactly need a post mortem. If I thought we could get away with it, I'd have rolled him into a hole in the ground before it gets light, but there are too many flapping ears about already,' he said meaningfully, with a pointed glance at Valgeir.

'What do you mean?' Valgeir demanded. 'Are you saying I can't keep my mouth shut?'

'Yes. There are too many people who would know where the bodies are buried, to put it crudely. I don't trust you to keep your mouth shut, or Steinunn's honoured guest, who I suspect is a lying, thieving opportunist crook, or the minister's decorative-but-dim niece in the other room.'

'And the Special Unit,' Valgeir added, before jerking a thumb at Gunna. 'And her.'

'I can trust the gentlemen in black, and I can trust Gunnhildur implicitly,' Ívar Laxdal said with quiet menace. 'You're the one who's the problem, and I have my doubts about our boss as well.'

★ ★ ★

Gunna scanned the shoreline and saw uniformed figures scouring the surf-rounded rocks, walking back and forth, heads down as they searched for anything that could indicate where the assassin had approached from and where his partners had disappeared to. Even if they were to find a few fading footprints, that wouldn't tell them much, Gunna decided, musing that the wind and rain had probably erased any traces of the man or men by now.

The man she had shot, with what she told herself was the luckiest shot imaginable, was probably now on a slab at the National Hospital, where Miss Cruz was undoubtedly scrutinizing the body in fine detail, checking his teeth for any distinctive dentistry, examining old scars and tattoos, any marks that could be significant. Maybe she would be slicing and dicing, as she liked to put it herself, looking for any sign that could provide a much-needed clue to the mystery man's identity – Gunna tried to push that uncomfortable thought to the back of her mind.

'I'm disappointed in you,' Helgi said gently and watched Fúsi's better eye snap open.

The swelling had gone down slightly, but his face was still a colourful mass of bruises. Helgi took a seat by Fúsi's bed and sat back, hands clasped comfortably over his stomach as he surveyed the room.

'What's that?' Fúsi croaked. 'What are you on about?'

'You heard. You told me a pack of lies. A complete load of bullshit.'

'I didn't,' Fúsi protested, but there was a helplessness in his voice.

'I'm guessing the delightful Hallveig got wind of Thór's premature demise some time early in the morning from one of her clients, and that said client sees Rikki as competition and reckoned it was the perfect opportunity to put Rikki the Sponge out of circulation for a good few years,' Helgi said, leaning forward. 'They knew the police would jump at the opportunity to lock him up, if only a suitable witness could be found to point the finger.'

Fúsi's eyes swivelled as Helgi sat back in his chair.

'How does that sound? Plausible?'

'I don't know what you're talking about.'

'That's where you're wrong, Fúsi. Rikki was hauled out of bed and down to Hverfisgata yesterday morning. He's still there and he's not happy; not happy at all,' Helgi said cheerfully. 'Now this is the interesting part, because Rikki has an alibi. Not as solid as I'd like, but good enough to tell me he wasn't anywhere near Njálsgata that night.'

'I still don't understand,' Fúsi said, lisping through the gap left by a missing tooth.

Helgi leaned forward again, planted his elbows on his knees and glared at close range at Fúsi's battered face.

'Rikki's a guilty man, I know that,' he said in a low, slow voice. 'But this is one thing he's not guilty of. So, Fúsi, you're going to come clean and give me the whole story. Exactly what happened and who was it who put you in hospital and your mate Thór in the morgue.'

'I don't know. Honest.'

'Because Rikki's going to be released pretty soon. He knows he's been in a cell for twenty-four hours on the say-so of someone who wrongly fingered him for the murder. So it would be terrible, wouldn't it, if he were to get even an idea that it was you? Not that I'm going to say a word, obviously,' Helgi said and paused, 'but I'm not the only one working this case, and you know what a vindictive bastard Sævaldur can be.'

Gunna recognized one of the two officers as they arrived at Einholt, wiping their feet carefully as they came in, looking around at their surroundings.

'Úlfur, isn't it?' she asked, shaking his hand. 'You spent a summer at the station in Hvalvík.'

'Hæ, Gunna.' The lanky young man's face broke into a smile. 'That's right. Seems like a lifetime ago, doesn't it? This is my colleague, Birna.'

Gunna almost did a double take, the angular young woman was

so similar to Úlfur, both of them tall, looking younger than their years with their short fair hair and dark business suits.

'You shot our John Doe, Gunna?' Úlfur asked in an undertone once the introductions had been made and the two officers had expressed a preference for water rather than the strong black coffee that Ívar Laxdal poured for himself and Gunna.

'So it seems,' Gunna said.

'Fantastic work. That must have been some quick thinking.'

Gunna shrugged. It wasn't something she wanted to discuss. 'He fired. I fired back. It all took a few seconds and then it was over.'

'All the same,' Úlfur said, a note of respect in his voice.

'Just looking forward to the inquiry now.'

Úlfur grinned. 'I'm not sure there will be one. But we'll see,' he said. Gunna sent him a questioning glance, but he had already locked his gaze on Ívar Laxdal, who had instinctively taken the lead.

'What do we have?'

'Not a lot,' Birna said. 'Nothing in the man's pockets. No identification. Nothing on a chain round his neck, no rings, no tattoos, a very old scar on his right forearm. The revolver is anonymous, no serial numbers on it and he had fired two rounds.'

'That fits,' Gunna said. 'I heard two shots.'

'We're getting a ballistics test to see if there's a match anywhere but I'm not hopeful. His face doesn't show up anywhere and his fingerprints don't match any records we have.'

'Description?' Ívar Laxdal asked.

'Mid to late thirties. One metre eighty-four, no health problems. It looks like he was very fit, someone who did more than just an hour at the gym once a week. Fair hair, clean shaven. There's a mark on his left ear where there may have been a piercing that healed over a long time ago. That's it.'

'It's his clothes that tell us more,' Úlfur said softly, as if he were apologetic at breaking into Birna's flow of words. 'The jacket, shirt, hoodie and trousers are all old, nothing special about any of them and there are no labels, except the label on John Doe's underpants which has Cyrillic lettering on it.'

'Russian?' Ívar Laxdal snapped.

Úlfur lifted his hands in question. 'Who knows? It looks like his underpants came from Russia. But they could have come from Bulgaria or Serbia, or Ukraine. We can't tell if he's from one of those countries or if he just went there to buy himself some underwear. It could be either. At any rate, I've sent pictures of the label to our Ukrainian translator and asked her to track down which language it is. That might give us at least a pointer in the right direction.'

'What's the strategy, Ívar?' Birna asked. 'How does the ministry want to handle this?'

'We'll find out soon enough, I expect. For the moment it's complete radio silence and we keep this totally under wraps until we know more. Not one single word to anyone. The corpse is at the National Hospital and only Miss Cruz gets to see it,' he said, counting items off on his fingers. 'Steinunn is off with her honoured guest for a trip round the tourist spots today, which is a bad thing if we need to get authorization for anything, or a good thing as we'll be left in peace and quiet.'

'Lovely day for it,' Birna said with a scowl, jerking her cropped head towards the rain tapping at the window. 'We don't think this can be kept quiet, but we can dress it up if it's done right.'

'In what way?' Ívar Laxdal asked, his forehead creased as he frowned.

'Listen. You have Osman. There's Valgeir from the ministry, and there's the Steinunn's niece in the other room,' she said, her voice dropping. 'Osman's an unknown quantity, as I told you a few days ago. Valgeir is under a ton of pressure from Steinunn; we're aware he has other problems as well. As for Sif . . .' Her voice tailed off. 'We can keep this hushed up, John Doe gets an unmarked grave up at Gufunes, but it's a ticking bomb. What if Valgeir or Sif have a skinful and blab? Then the damage is done. It's the kind of thing that will come back to haunt us all, especially the minister if she's not careful.'

'Careful isn't her style,' Ívar Laxdal said. 'Never has been. If it was, she'd never have invited Osman to Iceland to start with.'

147

'So we agree on that,' Birna said. 'Then there's the minister's husband.'

'What about him?'

'He has links with oddballs at universities overseas, all kinds of strange types.'

'You have files on everyone, do you?' Ívar Laxdal asked sharply.

'Not everyone. You have to be more than a member of the Left–Greens to warrant being watched.' She grinned. 'But only just.'

'Hello?' Skúli asked, his voice louder than it needed to be. 'Is that Plain Truth?'

'Who's asking?' retorted a curt voice on the other end of the line, and he was sure there was an underlying note of trepidation. It sounded like a young man or maybe a woman, but he couldn't be sure.

'I'm a friend of Lars Bundgaard.'

The line immediately went dead and Skúli slapped the table hard with the flat of his hand, wincing as it stung.

He typed in another number and tried again, listening as a phone somewhere in Europe rang.

'Yeah?'

This time it was definitely a woman's voice.

'My name's Skúli and I'm calling from Iceland. I'm a friend of Lars Bundgaard,' he said and listened to the silence. 'Hello, are you there?'

'Yeah. I'm here. What do you want?'

'I want to know what happened to Lars.'

'What's your name again?'

'My name's Skúli and I'm calling from Iceland. What happened to Lars?'

'Lars is dead.'

'I know that. What happened?'

There was a moment's tense silence and Skúli could hear the click of a lighter.

'Why do you want to know?'

'Because Lars was my friend,' he said.

'I don't remember him ever mentioning you.'

'Who are you, if you don't mind my asking?'

'I do mind your asking. You don't need to know about me.'

'All right. Look, Lars and I were at university together and we both used to work in Denmark, on *Jyllandsposten*. It's a local newspaper. Last week he called me with a lead for an article and we worked on it together. Then I tried to call him yesterday, and some policeman answered his phone. That's all I know.'

'What was this lead?'

'It was about someone called Ali Osman.'

'And how do I know you're not a policeman yourself?'

'I'm not,' Skúli said with a feeling of helplessness, wondering how he could prove himself. 'I work for an online magazine in Reykjavík called *Pulse*. You can look it up online. You'll see my name there, Skúli Snædal. You'll see the article about Osman.'

He heard a sigh through his laptop's speakers as the woman took another long lungful of smoke.

'It's not that I don't want to trust you, Skúli. I don't know if I dare trust you. I don't know if you're alone or if there's someone sitting next to you listening in to this conversation. I don't know if this call is being traced or recorded. We can't trust anyone at the moment.'

'What can I say? I want to know what happened to my friend and I want to know if it's anything to do with this guy he mentioned.'

'What did Lars say about him? Osman, I mean.'

Skúli could detect an interest there behind the feigned lack of it.

'He said that Osman is in Iceland. That's why he gave me the lead.'

'Ah. And what have you found out?'

'The article's online, you can see what we found out.'

'OK, I see,' the voice said after a long silence. 'I'll call you back later.'

'Please do that. I'll see what else I can find out before then.'

'Do that,' the woman said in an impassive voice. 'Goodbye.'

'Hold on!' Skúli yelped. 'Don't go . . . Listen, what happened to Lars? I still don't know.' He wondered if the connection had been broken as the silence continued for half a minute. But when the voice came back, it had a catch to it.

'One shot. Back of the head. Execution-style. In the hall of his flat on Veemarkt.'

'Who? Do you know who did this?'

'Speak to you later. Goodbye.'

'You fucked up.'

It wasn't a question and Michel felt a flush of resentment which he immediately suppressed. He had no choice but to admit she was right. There was a coldness in those grey eyes that made him deeply uncomfortable.

'Yeah,' he said at last.

'What went wrong?'

Michel sighed.

'I've no idea. But my instinct is that they got lucky and we didn't. If they'd known we were coming up the beach, then there would have been a squad of them, not one person with a popgun.'

Ana digested his words and looked over the car's bonnet at the drops of ice-cold rain pattering onto the street.

'Now they know there's someone out there, which is us. That means security will be ramped up and that makes our job so much harder.'

'True. But it won't be long before they get back into a routine again. That never takes long.'

Ana shrugged.

'All the same, they'll be more careful now. How about Pino? Anything they could use to identify him?'

Michel shook his head.

'No. We stuck with procedure. No marked clothing, no paper-work, nothing that could put anyone onto a trail.'

'And the weapon?' she asked.

'A revolver. No trail to follow there,' he said and fell silent.

Ana clicked her fingers softly a couple of times as she thought.

'All right. I'll check in later and see if anything's changed.'

'And until then?'

'We watch and wait.'

'Wait for what?'

'Instructions to eliminate or pull out, or the chance of an opportunity we can't ignore.'

Hans looked even more self-satisfied than usual as he arrived at the Hverfisgata police station to take Rikki away. He sat in reception, his leather-gloved hands elegantly folded in his lap.

'He's all yours, Hans,' Helgi told him as Rikki rolled his shoulders and pulled on an anorak.

'Thank you,' Hans replied smoothly. 'So pleased you saw sense on this one.'

'You behave yourself, Rikki,' Helgi said, ignoring the lawyer. 'I'll be wanting a word with you later on, so don't go into hiding.'

The lawyer's eyes darted from one to the other.

'What's that about?'

'All part of the service,' Helgi told him. 'Public relations. Keeping the general public happy.'

'Yeah, yeah,' Rikki grunted, scowling in frustration. 'Get me out of here, will you?'

Helgi watched the mismatched pair walk away, and once they were out of sight, he took the lift back upstairs.

'Where's Sævaldur?'

'Fuming somewhere, I expect,' Eiríkur said. 'You and I are now public enemy number one and two as far as he's concerned.'

'Until Gunna's back and she can take over the role again.'

Eiríkur jerked a thumb at a newspaper on the edge of his desk.

'Seen the papers?' he asked sourly. 'Thór Hersteinsson's obituary is in *DV*, and an interview with his mother. You'd imagine from reading it that he'd been some kind of sweet angel who spent his days off reading stories to orphans in hospital rather than a thug who liked nothing better than punching anyone who stood up to him.'

'I'll keep that pleasure for later,' Helgi decided.

'Do that. You'll have tears in your eyes by the time you've finished it. Anyway, we have descriptions, so it's noses to the grindstone. The description you got from Fúsi pretty much matches what Ketill gave me.'

'Fúsi said he and Thór tracked these two from Laugavegur, where they crossed at the lights, and followed them up Snorrabraut. Fúsi followed them and Thór doubled around the block to head them off, so we have a time and that street from Laugavegur up as far as Njálsgata, where they disappeared towards Rauðarárstígur.'

'So we start knocking on doors again?' Eiríkur said.

'Exactly. We can start on Laugavegur and see what we can dig up.'

Now it was Steingrímur's turn to look tired. There were black folds under his eyes and his cheeks were red from a morning in the biting wind.

'Any joy?' Gunna asked, handing him a mug of coffee that he cradled in his huge hands to warm them.

'Not much. The wind's taken away anything that might have been lying around and the rain's washed out any footprints. So we're back at square one there. I knocked on a few doors further up and asked if anyone had seen any unusual traffic, but nothing. Hell, it's bitter out today. Roll on spring.'

He shivered and sipped coffee gratefully.

'Still you and your pal up at the other place?'

'Nope. We have reinforcements. Two more guys so we can take turns and get some sleep as well. There's one with his eyes glued to a pair of binoculars watching this place and another one watching the road. One asleep and me here for the moment. What's the thinking at the moment? Any ideas who John Doe is, or was?'

Gunna shook her head.

'Nothing so far.'

'Will you stop beating yourself up, Gunna?' Steingrímur said gruffly. 'You did what any one of us would have had to do in the circumstances. He fired first and he had four more rounds in the chambers of that revolver.'

Gunna sighed.

'I know. But it was a lucky shot on my part. A few inches one way or the other and he'd still be alive. He'd be badly hurt, but he wouldn't be dead.'

Steingrímur shrugged.

'You did what you had to do,' he repeated. 'It's not as if you had time to think about it. You did a fine job and you deserve a medal, in my opinion.'

'You think so?' Gunna brooded for a moment. 'I'm sure his wife probably wouldn't agree, or his children.'

'If he had a wife and children. You couldn't know. We don't even know who he was or where he came from, or even what he was doing. Like I said, stop beating yourself up about it.'

'Looks like we have another one to run with right away,' Arndís said, a ballpoint between her lips and her eyes locked on the screen in front of her.

Agnar was on the phone, muttering into the microphone in his hand as he lounged in his chair.

'What's that?' Skúli asked.

'Thór the Boxer. The police have released a description of the guy they want to interview in connection with the killing the other night.'

'I thought they'd arrested that dope dealer?'

Arndís shook her head.

'It turned out he had an alibi, and now they have a new suspect they want to track down. Unidentified male, aged thirty to forty, one metre ninety, dark hair.'

'You're putting the story up?'

'Of course. Right now, this very minute,' she said. 'Everyone else will have this, so we can't be left behind.'

Skúli retreated into his own thoughts. He had gnawed his fingernails since his conversation with the two police officers and he was under no illusions about what their role was.

At the same time, his own anger and frustration were starting to boil over as he wondered if the story he had worked on with

Lars and Sophie had led in one way or another to his friend's death. He was startled by the sudden thought that Sophie might also be in danger, or that he himself could become someone's target. The thought set him shuddering with a sudden terror and he felt faint for a few seconds.

Skúli stood up and walked a few paces to what they laughingly referred to as the boardroom, a small room with a ceiling that sloped at one end under the eaves of the building, where they would go for privacy, a confidential interview, or simply to take a break from the screen. This was just what he wanted, and he lay down on the lumpy sofa, closing his eyes as he fought to keep his mind from the thoughts that made him shiver with uncertainty.

Instead, he concentrated on Lars, the two-room flat they had shared in Århus for a year, the amicable arguments over beer and pizza, and the occasional girls who could be persuaded to pay them a visit.

He asked himself whether Lars had lost his life because he'd exposed a side of Ali Osman that had been kept carefully out of sight, or if there was another reason?

Skúli told himself he couldn't afford to be brave, that his family were now his priority and he couldn't place them in any jeopardy just to fuel his own ambitions – or to seek out what had happened to an old friend he'd hardly heard from for three years.

The key had to be Valgeir. He was the only route he had to Osman and the truth that he might be better off pretending didn't exist. But maybe he would be better off taking Osman's example and hiding in plain sight?

Gunna told herself that Úlfur and Birna weren't twins, not even siblings, but it was hard when they looked so alike, with similar suits and haircuts. She toyed with the idea of telling them to dress differently so she could tell them apart at a glance.

'Who has access to the minister?' Ívar Laxdal rumbled. 'I mean, there must be someone she actually listens to, surely?'

'Apparently not,' Birna said, putting down a cup of coffee that

Ívar Laxdal had poured for her. She pushed the cup to one side and opened a sleek silver laptop. 'She listens to people within her party, but doesn't pay much attention to her department's advisers. We may have to take this higher.'

'That's practically treason, isn't it?' Ívar Laxdal asked. 'After all, she is the minister with responsibility for justice, law and order and public safety. She's our boss.'

Birna allowed herself a hint of a smile. 'For the moment,' she said quietly. 'You can never tell with politicians, can you? There could be a reshuffle next week, and someone new in charge.'

'And if this blows up in Steinunn's face and her position becomes untenable, then that's just what'll happen,' Úlfur said.

'After she's denied everything and declined to stand down for a week or two,' Ívar Laxdal added. He frowned and glanced around. 'And where's our guest, Gunnhildur?'

'In his room, feet up and watching the TV.'

'Good.' Ívar Laxdal squared his shoulders. 'Now. What do we know, and what do we need to find out? Birna? Úlfur? Start with the dead man.'

'We don't know any more than we knew yesterday. His face isn't known anywhere.'

'Flights have been checked?'

'It's being done. We've been going through CCTV from Keflavík airport, which could narrow down which flight he might have arrived on, but it takes time and we don't have the option of bringing in additional manpower on this, so we have to do it ourselves. We've been through four days' worth so far and we'll be going through more today.'

'Go back another four days. Then another four if you don't get anywhere,' Ívar Laxdal decided. 'The only thing I can add is that Miss Cruz feels his dentistry work could be Eastern European, which doesn't narrow things down a great deal.'

Úlfur shrugged. 'That could give us something to go on. We're waiting for enquiries to be answered.'

'Let me know when you've chased it up.'

'I'm not exactly overworked here,' Gunna pointed out. 'If you can get me access to the footage, there's no reason why I can't go through it when I'm not darning our guest's socks for him.'

Birna looked sideways at Ívar Laxdal, who nodded.

'Good idea. Fix it up, will you? Now, Osman. Tell me anything I haven't already seen in the confidential report I wasn't supposed to see.'

'What we know is that Osman has some determined enemies,' Birna said, one finger on the trackpad of her laptop as she peered at the screen. She looked up. 'I spoke to Brussels this morning and they've been keeping an eye on him for a while. Osman has been linked to several groups in the Middle East, but only on a peripheral basis, family links as much as anything else. Nothing concrete. The organization he runs – the White Sickle Peace Foundation that supports refugees from war zones – is very wealthy. My contacts in Brussels tell me that he more or less treats the foundation as a personal piggy bank, but it's not easy to tell where all this wealth comes from.'

'We ought to know something about that in Iceland, surely,' Gunna said.

'Precisely,' Birna said with a touch of frost in her voice. 'But in this case we don't. Brussels say he has accounts here and there, including what's effectively a working account at a Dutch bank with a balance of around a quarter of a million Euros. Then there's the fact that White Sickle is registered in Panama and maintains its finances there, so that's also where the trail ends.'

Gunna crossed her arms and laid them on the table in front of her. She wanted to yawn, but resisted.

'All right. Let me be devil's advocate here. Let's suppose our man really is what he says he is, a philanthropist who runs a peace foundation and has managed to make a few enemies. What do you have that tells us that's not the case?'

Úlfur looked startled and Ívar Laxdal stifled a smile.

'Well, to start with, someone tried to kill him.'

'Do we know that? Can we be sure Osman was the target?' Gunna asked.

Birna shrugged. 'I think we have to assume that.'

'Birna's right,' Ívar Laxdal decided. 'Even if Osman wasn't the target, we have to work on the assumption that he was until we know better. Next question?'

'As I asked, can we be sure that whatever information you're getting about him is accurate?' Gunna said. 'Does he have terrorist links? Is this simply conjecture and hearsay? Could he genuinely be a peace advocate?'

Birna and Úlfur exchanged glances.

'I'm not quite sure where you're taking this?' Úlfur said, his voice rising in irritation.

'I'm asking you to be certain of your ground, and to convince us.'

'I'm not sure we need this kind of scrutiny from uniform,' Úlfur said, his eyes flashing towards Ívar Laxdal.

'Valid questions, young man,' he growled in reply. 'This is extraordinarily sensitive and we must be sure of where we stand. If there's a terror angle, then this becomes a national security matter and we'll all be taking early retirement if we fuck things up.'

His words hung in the air as Úlfur looked taken aback and Birna looked intently at her laptop.

'We have to assume a few things,' Ívar Laxdal decided, counting them off on his fingers. 'One, we have to assume a terror link until we know better. Two, we have to assume whoever tried to kill Osman wasn't working alone. Three, we have to keep this under wraps as Osman is a guest of the minister, who wants his presence to be kept strictly confidential. This also ties our hands as we can't bring in help from outside. Four, we have to convince the minister that Osman may well be something other than an advocate for world peace, rainbows, unicorns and all that stuff. Five, we have to keep him alive and send him back where he came from unscathed. Anything else?'

'Yes,' Birna said. 'We need to convince the minister that we ought to ship him out of the country as quickly as possible, and if she won't do it we have to go over her head.'

'You mean if she doesn't play ball, her head's going to roll?'

'Exactly. And if this comes out, which could happen if we're not very careful, then it will roll, and our heads with it. Steinunn has never been known for being what you might call a generous politician.'

'Not bad,' Ana said. 'Other entrance?'

'Fire escape through the kitchen.'

The apartment was centred around a large kitchen–living room with the blank white cupboard doors of the kitchen occupying one end.

'Bathroom?'

'Through there,' Michel said, jerking a thumb towards a passage that opened out from between two stylish bookcases. 'Two bedrooms. Or are you staying somewhere else?'

Ana hung up her coat and scanned the room. 'How long do you have this place for?'

'We can stay here until the end of the month. The owner is studying abroad somewhere and won't be back for a while. We won't need it that long.'

'So he's not going to come knocking on the door?'

Michel grinned. 'I don't think so. When she gave me the keys, his ex-wife took care to let me know that she was his former wife and was only looking after the place under protest. I think we could trash the place and she wouldn't care.'

Ana sat on a handsome but worn couch and sank deep into its upholstery as she tucked her legs under her. Her eyes travelled around the room, taking everything in, the window locks, and the bolt and chain on the outside door.

Michel watched his companion and liked what he saw; young but not too young, wiry rather than petite, but with muscular curves under a stylish business suit and a confident way of moving that told him she could handle herself. She had already proved that the other night when that idiot mugger had been stupid enough to try his luck. He was sure that after what she'd done to him, even with the best medical treatment, the man's shoulder would give him pain and trouble him for the rest of his life.

'So,' she said, 'do you have the hardware here or stored some-where safe?'

'It's hidden. We'd have to be incredibly unlucky for anyone to find it, and even if they do, it can't be traced,' he assured her. 'How are we off for intelligence? Do we know for sure what happened?'

Ana's face hardened.

'No. And my contact doesn't have access to everything. I'll see what I can find out.'

Helgi felt he had stepped into a different world. What had once been Reykjavík's main street was a place he rarely went near now that it had become largely devoted to the booming tourist business.

He dimly remembered the street as having been studded with jewellery shops, but now the gaps between them had been filled with cafés and eateries, with signs in their windows in English and German, and only occasionally in Icelandic.

It didn't take long, and he silently congratulated himself as the young woman who managed the pizza place scrolled through Sunday night's CCTV recording.

'Is that what you're looking for?' she asked, as Helgi stared at her computer screen.

'Looks like it,' he said. 'Scroll back a little, will you?'

The girl did as she was asked and the pair walked jerkily back-wards across the screen in the Sunday night darkness.

'You were already closed at that time, weren't you?'

'Yeah. We close at eleven. There's normally someone still here until about midnight, clearing up and prepping for the morning, but they'd have been out the back.'

'That wasn't you, was it?'

'Two nights ago?' She thought. 'No. That would have been Ewa. But she wouldn't have seen anything from the prep room.'

The image on the screen wasn't as clear as he would have liked, but it showed a heavily built man and an average height woman walking side-by-side, and the time stamp on the recording matched perfectly.

'If you were closed, why didn't you turn the recording off?'

'It's easier just to let it run all the time. That way nobody forgets to switch it on,' she said. 'Plus there's stuff that can happen when we're closed. You'd imagine the camera would discourage people from taking a piss in the doorway, but we get two or three of them on camera every weekend.'

'Can you save that for me?'

'Sure,' she said. 'I can email it to you.'

'Yeah, please. But let it run for another minute, would you?'

The wide angle lens above the door showed a deserted street, then a minute later Thór Hersteinsson's distinctive round-shoul-dered bulk appeared, slouching in the same direction with Fúsi at his side.

'That's what I need. Can you give me that clip, from eleven thirty-six to eleven forty-one?'

'No problem,' the girl said, clicking the mouse. 'Give me your address and I'll send it to you right now.'

'Thanks. Are there any more cameras about?'

'Try the bank. There's one above the cashpoint further down.'

Osman's schedule had been arranged and had to be adhered to, regardless of events. Valgeir drove the Patrol, with Osman and Gunna in the back, while Ívar Laxdal followed in his sinister black Volvo.

The minister had planned on an informal day's travel around some of the sights that could be easily reached from Reykjavík – Gunna guessed that Thingvellir and Gullfoss would be on the agenda. She could have asked Valgeir, but didn't feel inclined to speak to him and was just relieved that their guest would be some-one else's responsibility for a few hours.

Steinunn Strand's residence was in a suburb on the northern outskirts of Reykjavík, a newish spread of big houses, of which hers was one of the largest, stretching back deceptively far from an unimposing frontage.

'Ali, good morning,' the minister greeted Osman as Valgeir opened the door for him, and he stepped out of the car. 'We have a lovely day planned for you. I do hope you enjoy it. Come in,' she said with a welcoming smile, flashing a quick glance at Gunna and then a questioning look at Ívar Laxdal as he arrived seconds later.

The minister took Osman's elbow and guided him into the living room, where her husband was waiting. Gunna could sense the husband's discomfort and tried to recall if he had any political links other than being married to a woman who had politics running through her bone marrow; she decided the unfortunate man had just been unlucky.

There was an imperceptible nod to Ívar Laxdal as Steinunn's husband shook Osman's hand. The minister's children had been persuaded to make an appearance and introductions were made to a young woman Gunna guessed was in her early twenties and a young man a year or two older whose features were a youthful version of his mother's.

Steinunn's face hardened as soon as Osman was out of immediate earshot.

'What the hell happened?'

There was no greeting or pleasantry, just a direct, sharp question.

'We have a casualty. He was observed outside the property where Osman is staying. He had made it past the lookouts. When he was challenged, he didn't respond,' Ívar Laxdal said in terse phrases.

'And he's dead?'

'He is.'

'Fucking hell.' The words sounded jarringly out of place on the lips of a woman who normally spoke so smoothly in Parliament or in TV interviews. 'Who is this bastard? Or was?'

'No idea. We're working on that. No identification. He was armed, and he also fired two rounds before my officer returned fire.'

'Armed? With what?'

'A handgun – an old-fashioned revolver. It's a nasty piece of work that doesn't have a safety catch, just a long-reach trigger. Not exactly an amateur's weapon.'

'Good grief. Ívar, this has to be kept absolutely quiet,' Steinunn said in an urgent undertone. 'Don't let this get out. I'm counting on you to wrap this up. I don't want to hear any more until it's dealt with. Understand?'

'It's not as simple as that.'

Steinunn's expression hardened again.

'In what way?'

'It's unlikely that this person was operating alone, so we can't rule out the fact that he may have an accomplice with him, or even a team.'

'Come on. You can't be serious?'

'I'm deadly serious,' Ívar Laxdal retorted. 'This man didn't find his way to Einholt on foot, and he didn't blunder into the place by accident. It was pure chance that my officer was outside and saw him approach. We daren't assume this was some kind of solo effort by an amateur fanatic. I can't advise you to go haring around the country with this man while there could be someone else gunning for him. And I can't guarantee to keep this quiet. There are too many people involved who can't be trusted.'

'Who?'

'Valgeir for one, and your niece.'

'Sif?' Steinunn's mouth tightened into a white line as she thought. 'Sif spent the night there with Osman? Shit. The little slut. I should have known better than to invite her last night,' she muttered. 'Leave Valgeir to me. And leave Sif to me as well. Where is she now?'

'Still at Einholt.'

'Good. Keep her there. On my authority. Spin her whatever yarn you like, but keep her there and keep her away from the phone. Now, where's Valgeir?'

Ívar Laxdal jerked his head towards the living room.

'In there with your husband.'

'Good. Tell him to come here. We'll call you when we have an ETA for this evening.'

'Aren't you going to commend my officer for protecting your guest?' he asked as Steinunn was about to walk away.

'Why? Who was it?'

Ívar Laxdal nodded at Gunna and Steinunn took a step back, as if noticing her there for the first time.

'You shot this man?'

'Not willingly. But yes.'

'Oh.' Steinunn seemed at a loss for what to say. 'Good work, I'm sure. Good work,' she finally said lamely. 'Quick thinking.' She looked past Gunna and her eyes zeroed in on something behind her. 'Valgeir, a word, if you please,' she said, beckoning him to follow. 'Berlin,' Gunna heard her say in her familiar crystal-clear voice. 'Was it Berlin or Washington that you were so keen on?'

It was a twenty-minute drive back to Einholt and it passed in silence as Ívar Laxdal glowered and Gunna wondered how she could tell him that he ought to get someone else to babysit Osman for the rest of the assignment.

'Well, we have a few hours to think things over and take it easy while Steinunn shows our guest around,' he said, switching off the engine. He turned to her and placed a hand on her forearm. The sudden moment of intimacy was such a surprise that Gunna almost jerked her hand back. 'Gunnhildur, are you all right? If you want to bail out of this, then I'll understand.'

Gunna retrieved her hand, ran her fingers through her hair and rubbed her eyes with the heels of her hands.

'I'm all right,' she decided. 'I could do with an hour's sleep.'

'Good.' Ívar Laxdal grinned and she could see the relief in his eyes. 'But you had to think about it, didn't you?'

'I did. But I don't like to walk away from something that's not finished.'

'Come on. We deserve a chance to put our feet up for half an hour.'

The atmosphere inside the house was tense. Steingrímur sat at the breakfast bar looking through the previous day's newspaper while Sif sat on the sofa, her knees drawn up and her arms hugged tight around them. She was still wrapped in the dressing gown she had thrown on that morning.

'She all right?' Gunna muttered to Steingrímur.

'No, I don't reckon she is. Refuses to speak to me and she's just sitting there without a word.'

Gunna wanted to yawn and lie down for an hour, but instead she went over to where Sif was huddled on the sofa and sat next to her.

'Listen, I'm sorry about everything last night. It wasn't what any of us had expected.'

Sif turned her head to look at her, eyes wide and blank.

'I'm afraid you're caught up in something more serious than anything we could have expected and we're trying to work out how to deal with it,' Gunna continued. 'Osman is rather an enigma, and we need to find out who was trying to kill him.'

'Are you sure he was trying to kill Osman?' Sif asked, speaking for the first time, her voice cracking.

'I think it's fair to assume that. There were only three of us here and I doubt he was after an obscure middle-aged police officer. Or is there something about your private life we ought to know?'

'How dare you!'

'I'm just asking. You suggested this character might have been after someone other than Osman, and since I'm unlikely to be the target, the implication is that it's you. Do you have any reason for someone to come after you with a firearm?'

'Don't be stupid. Of course not.'

Gunna nodded. 'So this person must have been looking for Osman.'

'The person you shot.'

Gunna shivered. 'You were watching. He fired first.'

'You didn't have to kill him.'

'I didn't mean to kill him,' Gunna said, with more heat than she'd intended. 'You think I want someone's life on my conscience?'

'No,' Sif allowed. 'I don't suppose so.'

'Did Osman seem nervous? Did you get the impression he might be expecting anything like this?'

'He had something on his mind,' Sif said sourly. 'And once that was out of the way he had a nap before suggesting a repeat performance.'

'So what did you talk about?'

'We talked all evening at Steinunn's house. About all kinds of things: travel, films, art, all that stuff. I'm sure she put me next to him deliberately. Once we got here he didn't want to talk a lot. Like I said, there was only one thing he was after. It was only when he heard you shouting outside that he woke up and went to look out of the window. Look, when can I go home? I asked your gorilla there to drive me home earlier and he said he couldn't leave the building.'

'I'm sorry, but he's right. Nobody's leaving here for a while,' Gunna said, an added decision creeping into her voice. 'Until we know more about all this, we're all staying put.'

'And when Osman's back tonight, we're just one big happy family again, are we?' Sif sneered. 'Well, if he wants company then you can keep him warm because I'm not inclined to.'

'We must.'

'We can't.'

'All these years, we've never disagreed on anything important. We both know what's right.'

Hanne shook her head violently and banged the table with the flat of her hand, setting the plates rattling.

'I know what's right, and my family comes first,' she hissed.

The people at the next table looked up in surprise and then turned their eyes away in embarrassment at the sight of a couple in respectable middle age arguing so quietly and yet with such vehemence.

'We should go to the police and tell them what we know, tell them what happened.'

'Don't you dare even think of endangering my family,' Hanne said, glaring at him. 'Dorthe is my daughter. Inge is my grand-child. I won't have their lives put in danger.'

Carsten sat back as if she'd slapped him. His astonishment could hardly have been greater if she had taken a fork from the table and stabbed it into his hand.

'Thirty-four years,' he said. 'Thirty-four years ago I accepted

165

that child in your belly wasn't mine and I've brought her up as if she was my own. How dare you suggest . . .'

'You've never threatened her life before.'

Carsten felt a flush of heat and his breath came in gasps. After a moment the dizzy spell passed and he brushed the back of a hand across his forehead to find it damp with sweat.

'I need to . . .' he muttered, struggling to his feet.

'You need to what?'

'I need to stand outside, get some air. I feel sick.'

Hanne sat still, numb with her own anger at the two men who had appeared from nowhere one evening on the way to the ferry, politely telling them that they had no choice but to do as they were told. Her hatred for them ran deep, a loathing more virulent than anything she had ever felt before.

She stared through the window, watching Carsten in the cherry-red anorak he'd bought in Copenhagen for their dream trip to Iceland as he walked to and fro in the evening darkness, his breath a plume of vapour in the freezing air.

Hanna clasped her hands together, squeezing them tightly, until she could almost feel the bones of her fingers crack with the pressure.

'Hey, lady.'

The voice seemed to come from somewhere distant, a sound that had no relevance to her as she sat and waited for something she knew could never come.

'Hey,' the voice repeated, this time with greater urgency, and she heard the scrape of chairs being shoved back as people quickly got to their feet. 'Is that your husband?'

They were running for the door, while others looked up from their half-eaten meals, wondering what had happened.

Registering their urgency, Hanne looked up. A young man in a blue work overall was looking into her eyes.

'What?'

'The guy in red? He's your husband?'

'Yes,' she said, her heart hammering as she looked out the window and saw, with horror, a small group gathered around a figure on the ground, one of them tugging open the red parka while another felt for a pulse in his neck.

'They're at Thingvellir,' Ívar Laxdal said.

'You spoke to the escort?'

'Yep. Steinunn's showing him around in the rain and Osman's pretending to enjoy himself.'

'So what else? Any word on the dead man?'

'He's in the morgue at the National Hospital. No way around that, sadly.'

'And Steinunn seriously thinks this can be kept quiet?' Gunna asked. 'She must be nuts. She'd be better off making a clean breast of it all.'

'There are ways and means, Gunnhildur. Ways and means.'

'And there'll be an inquiry at some point – soon, I'd guess. Staff at the hospital must be aware that there's a gunshot fatality in the morgue, and they'll all be carefully not asking questions while they wonder what happened and who it is.'

'It's being contained as far as possible. Miss Cruz is in charge. We have key people who have been taken aside and told this is a sensitive matter of national security.'

'Is that what it is?'

'I don't know. We have to assume it is until we know different. There'll be someone from the National Security Unit along soon to brief us, once they've asked as many questions as they can.'

'How time flies when you're having fun.' Gunna yawned. 'Do you think Steinunn has told her boss about all this yet?'

Ívar Laxdal looked startled. 'The Prime Minister? I doubt it. Not if she has any sense.'

Ana jogged across the road, ordered a coffee and sat at one of the computers in the almost empty café. It was one of the rules she took care to adhere to, and she made sure the others did the same.

She used a smartphone only when necessary and made sure the others used only old-fashioned nineties-style mobiles, switched on when needed and regularly discarded. All other communication was through a series of rotating social media profiles accessed through computers in cafés and libraries to avoid building a trail that could easily be followed.

She logged in and reflected that this was becoming more difficult. Smartphones that contained everything in a single device had begun to sound the death knell for internet cafés, making access to public computers less easy.

Once she'd checked both accounts, she sat back and digested the information she'd received while finishing her coffee and sandwich, logged off and looked around the empty café. The bored barista looked up, wondering why his customer had frozen with her eyes on the TV screen behind him.

A few seconds showed her a face she couldn't fail to recognize, before going back to a newsreader.

'What's that about?' she asked the barista.

'That? Oh, there was someone murdered in a fight a few nights ago. The police are looking for the guy who did it.'

'And that's him, is it?' she asked. 'How much do I owe you?'

'Four thousand six hundred,' he replied. 'Yeah. They think so.'

'Who got murdered?'

'Him? He was a proper bastard. He sold drugs and had a protection racket going with a few places in town.'

'But not here?'

'Nope. I suppose we're too far from the centre for him to bother with us.'

He handed her change.

'So nobody's shedding tears for this guy?'

'Thór? Hell no,' the barista muttered. 'Maybe his mother. But nobody else.'

'Hi, how's things?'

'All right. Why?'

Skúli knew he was pushing friendship further than was wise. Valgeir sounded flustered, answering the phone with a monosyllable instead of cracking the usual joke.

'Coffee? Usual place in half an hour?'

'Well . . .' The uncertainty in Valgeir's voice was unmistakable. 'Yeah, but not right now.'

'Steinunn's keeping you busy, is she?'

'She has been, no doubt about that.' This time Valgeir chuckled. 'Actually, I'm off.'

'Off? Off where?'

'Vienna. It turns out I've been a good boy and good boys get rewards.'

Skúli hid his surprise. Valgeir's unexpected departure would deprive him of one of his best ministry contacts, someone with an unofficial insider's insight into the workings of government. Valgeir might be a relatively low-level official, but it had been clear for some time that he was a bright candidate being quietly groomed for better things. His occasional meetings with Valgeir generally gave him a snippet of information that cast the ministry's workings in a different light to the official viewpoint, and Skúli had also taken care to be discreet in using information gleamed from these occasional meetings.

'Wow. Vienna. That sounds good. More money as well?'

'Yep. Up a pay grade and a promotion.'

'No time to say goodbye to your old pal?'

'Look, Skúli, I'm packing as we speak. I'll have time in the next couple of days, but it'll have to be really quick.'

Hanne closed her eyes and kept them shut tight, willing herself not to watch and wishing she could blot out the whine and whiplash crack of the defibrillator.

It was the relief in the voices of the people around that told her Carsten was still alive, prompting her to open her eyes to find one of the filling station staff by her side, her hand in his.

It seemed a long time before a police car arrived with a pair in uniform who calmly took control, making sure that Carsten was brought inside, and watching the trio of volunteers holding his hand and keeping him awake.

Hanne stood frozen to the spot until one of the officers took her to one side, sat her down with her back to the scene being played out and wrote down a string of details. A mug of coffee turned cold on the table in front of her.

'What happens now?' Hanne asked, her teeth chattering.

'The ambulance should be here shortly. They'll take him to Blönduós if things look stable, or south to Reykjavík if it looks risky. But Blönduós is closest.'

'I know. We spent the night there,' Hanne said, as if in a dream. She wondered if they could have spent their last night together, both of them angry and hurt, with hardly a word passing between them.

The officer cocked his head to one side as he listened to his earpiece.

'They'll be here in a couple of minutes,' he said. 'I expect the medics will do what they can to stabilize Carsten and they won't hang about. They'll want to be off right away and you'd best go with them.'

'What about . . . ?'

The first tear found its way down Hanne's cheek, not so much because of Carsten as in frustration at her own helplessness.

'Give me the keys to your truck and my pal will drive it to Blönduós. He'll only be half an hour behind you,' he said, as if he knew what she was going to say.

Hanne fumbled in her pocket and dropped the keys with their big cork fob onto the table.

'It's the . . .'

'The only one outside with Danish plates? Listen, the police station is just across the street from the hospital in Blönduós. I'll hang on to the keys until you're ready. All right?' he said and looked up, listening to his earpiece again. 'That was quick. They're here,' he said, standing up. 'Don't worry. We'll look after him.'

She sat numbly as the crew appeared in the doorway, the ambulance's light bouncing through the windows and flashing off the walls.

A hand descended on her shoulder and squeezed gently. She opened her eyes, terrified of what would greet her.

'Come on, Hanne,' the police officer said gently. 'They're taking him to Blönduós, there's no time to waste.'

She picked up Carsten's cherry-red coat from the floor as she shuffled to the door on the policeman's arm, following the stretcher her husband was on as it was wheeled smartly through the doors and into the biting cold.

On the way she caught sight of a newspaper in a rack by the door and stopped, transfixed by the face that stared back at her from the front page. In a brief moment of clarity she wondered if it was time for her to have a heart attack of her own.

'Come on, Hanne.'

The door of the ambulance was open and a man in a green overall with a broad smile on his round face held out a hand for her.

The man would hardly be smiling if her husband was dead, she thought.

He had to be alive, surely?

Osman looked invigorated by his day in the fresh air and Steinunn looked delighted that a day of Iceland's rainswept countryside, just as it was about to shrug off winter, had been such a success.

Gunna and Ívar Laxdal arrived at the minister's house as the sightseers were finishing dinner, a three-course affair, Gunna noted, judging by the stacked crockery in the kitchen where the au pair and an assistant brought in from the ministry canteen were sitting exhausted at the kitchen table.

'Ali, would you excuse me, please?' Steinunn said, rising as she saw Ívar Laxdal and Gunna approaching, escorted by Valgeir, incongruous in skinny jeans and a sweater instead of his usual suit. 'This way, please,' she instructed and they followed her down the spiral staircase to the study in the basement.

She closed the door of the study behind her and sat down behind a cluttered desk while Ívar Laxdal cast around for a chair and finally waved Gunna to the only spare seat available.

'Well?' Steinunn said, elbows on the desk and fingers in a steeple in front of her face. 'What do you have to tell me?'

'Not a lot,' Gunna replied, perched uncomfortably on the stool like a naughty schoolgirl. 'No identification whatsoever. All we can tell you is that the dead man could be of Eastern European origin, judging by his clothing.'

'I see. I take it you've met the National Security Unit today. What's their take on this?'

'They'll tell you themselves, but they don't know enough to have one,' Ívar Laxdal said. 'We don't know who this man was and we don't know where he came from. All we know is that he had a weapon and he was quite happy to use it. We're certain he's not a local. Gunnhildur?'

'I'm with you on this. I've encountered all kinds of homegrown villains and we've had a few firearms incidents, but never a situation like this.'

'So what are you doing?'

'Contacting Interpol to see if we can identify him. We have fingerprints and we're fast-tracking a DNA sample through the lab in Sweden. But even ultra-fast means days, maybe even weeks. If Interpol don't know who he is, then we're stuck, unless something new comes to light.'

'Such as?'

'An accomplice. Or several. If this guy's a professional, then he's likely to have been part of a team. I can't imagine that he walked up to Einholt, so how did he get there? If he came by car and then walked along the shore, where's the vehicle and who's the driver?'

There was an awkward silence as Steinunn digested the information. 'So you said. Do you really think there are more of these . . . these people out there?'

Her eyes darted towards the narrow window high in the wall.

'I told you before, I'm certain of it. It's highly unlikely the man was working alone. On the other hand, maybe your guest can provide a little insight?'

'Osman? He's not going to know who was trying to kill him, is he?'

Gunna shrugged. 'We won't know unless we ask him, will we?'

Steinunn shook her head impatiently. 'Ask him if you must, but I won't have him interrogated like a common criminal. He's an increasingly important figure on the international stage. We have to treat him as such.'

'That's not what the National Security Unit say about him,' Ívar Laxdal said in a soft voice.

'What?' Steinunn blanched as if she'd been struck. 'I don't listen to gossip, Ívar. You know that.'

'Sometimes gossip is all we have to work with, and sometimes it's remarkably accurate.'

'Not in this case. I don't want to hear another word.'

'Steinunn, there are serious questions about this man's integrity,' Ívar Laxdal growled, and Gunna could hear the frustration adding urgency to his voice. 'There's every chance he's not what he appears to be. Have you seen what's in the media about him already?'

'Gossip. Bring me evidence,' Steinunn snapped. 'Has any of this leaked out?'

'It's only a matter of time, I expect,' Gunna replied, aware that Ívar Laxdal's frustrated anger had left him tight-lipped. 'We can't hope to keep this out of sight. And there's the question of whether we *should* keep it out of sight.'

'What do you mean?'

'A man has lost his life. This isn't a police state. There will be questions. We feel the best thing is to pre-empt the media and at least get this into the open before the rumour mill does it for us; and it will. You don't take a corpse to the National Hospital with a fatal gunshot wound and expect nobody to bat an eyelid.'

For the first time Steinunn seemed to be genuinely disturbed and Gunna wondered if it was the threat of adverse publicity that was causing her discomfort or the possibility of a situation spiralling out of control. She could see a twitch starting to show under Steinunn's jaw, just as she noticed the fingernails bitten short.

The minister's chair was pushed back hard, stopping against a bookcase on the wall. Steinunn sent Ívar Laxdal a look that told him the interview was at an end, but he remained where he was.

'Has the Prime Minister's office been informed?' he asked, his gravel voice low but distinct.

'No,' Steinunn snapped back. 'Not that it's any of your concern.'

'It is my concern,' he replied. 'Especially if I'm not convinced this is being handled correctly.'

'You do your job, Ívar, and I'll do mine. For your information, the PM knows there's a situation but hasn't asked for details. I've assured him it's under control. Until it's not under control, I'm not going to bother him with this.'

Gunna could see the furious twitch spread to Steinunn's lip while Ívar Laxdal stood unmoving.

'We can't keep this quiet, Steinunn. We need to take the initiative.'

'What are you talking about?'

Ívar Laxdal scratched his chin with his thumb and the rasp cut through the quiet. A tinkling laugh from upstairs could be heard faintly through the closed door.

'I mean we need to take the bull by the horns and release at least part of what's happened. You know damn well that if we don't, it'll get out anyway, and by then we'll be playing catchup, trying to kill rumours instead of pre-empting them. We have to manage this, not react to it.'

Steinunn's eyes went from Ívar Laxdal to Gunna and back. Gunna tried to keep her face expressionless until the minister's gaze had moved on.

'All right,' Steinunn decided. 'I want a plan. Tell Valgeir and he can bring it to me to be approved.'

'There isn't time for that. We have to do this fast,' Ívar Laxdal said and Gunna expected Steinunn to slap him. 'We announce that an unidentified individual has died of injuries sustained during a suspected terrorist incident. Male, rough age, and we release a photofit good enough for anyone who's seen him but not too accurate. That's it. They can ask all the questions they like, but no details. We can cite security issues and nobody will argue. We'll give them the absolute bare bones and no details.'

Steinunn stood for a moment in thought. 'When?'

'Right away. In time for the late news bulletin.'

'No,' she said in a sharp voice. 'Absolutely not.'

le gradually

g, and she

s, Steinunn. We'll need to release
ooner than later.'
e more facts before we say anything.
w when you can release something,
my department,' she said, eyes fixed
me. Understood?'

ed to con-
lationship

Osman.'
t.'

hink you

fter him knows where he is. We need to
t of sight.'
stion?'

just took
t on the

much anywhere but Einholt would be

cused somewhere beyond Ívar Laxdal's

ked. 'I
they'll

the Special Unit watching the place, so it
place in the country. But bring me options
it over.'

cold, Gunna withstood the temptation to dig

s and   e ribs.

to   he was going to slap you,' she said with a laugh that

n half relief at the tension having been broken.

dn't have come as a surprise if she had,' he grunted as he
e car door. 'Steinunn has a reputation.'

at now?'

rst, we have to dispose of Sif. Could you do that? Then I
guess we're back to square one.'

'And I'm back to babysitting, am I?'

'Ready to leave the country?'

Valgeir had grudgingly agreed to meet at a burger bar near the
harbour.

'Next week,' he said and registered Skúli's surprise. 'Yes, I
know it's really quick. But I'm taking up my post in a month and
I wanted a holiday first, so there's a week to pack my stuff. I can't
wait.'

'Why Vienna? Not Berlin or somewhere bigger?'

Valgeir looked sheepish and Skúli saw a warm smi[le] appear.

'Well,' he said, 'there's this woman I've been seei[ng] lives in that part of the world.'

'A girl? Wow, congratulations.'

'Oh, go to hell, Skúli,' Valgeir said in a voice that fai[led to con]ceal his delight. 'We've been having a long-distance r[elationship] for a while, and I've kept it quiet. But now you know.'

'I'm sure Dagga will be relieved. She was starting to [think you] were the other way inclined.'

'Way wide of the mark,' Valgeir said and smirked. 'I [have had] my time, and now I need to get my place ready to pu[t on the] market.'

'You're selling?'

'Sell at the top of the market, they say.' Valgeir wi[nked]. reckon things are going to keep going up for a while, but [it'll] drop again.'

'Is that secret inside information on the next crash?'

'It's no secret. I have contacts in investment business[es and] they're dropping property to buy currency. I can't wait [to get] away. A couple of years as cultural attaché in Vienna will su[it me] perfectly, and by the time I'm posted home again all the shi[t will] hopefully have died down.'

'What shit's that?' Skúli asked, feigning innocence and che[wing] his sandwich.

'Hell, Skúli. The shitstorm you unleashed, plus the Children of Freedom thing. Steinunn's days in the cabinet are numbered. Anyone close to her has failure written all over them. I saw your piece this morning. You're not going to be popular for a while.'

'I can live with that.'

'I should never have told you anything.'

'Did I mention your name?'

'Of course not,' Valgeir snapped, hurt. 'But anyone can put two and two together, and if Steinunn hadn't approved this posting, then I'd be worried.'

'But I didn't and you're clear,' Skúli replied. 'As long as nobody notices us here.'

'Why do you think I told you this place? It's not because of the cuisine.'

'In any case, Steinunn has more to worry about with the Children of Freedom than with Osman, doesn't she? I gather the Prime Minister isn't happy and he wants her out.'

'True,' Valgeir said. 'The PM doesn't like her. To be quite honest, without wanting to be quoted, a moderately intelligent nine-year-old wouldn't do a worse job than Steinunn does. Not that the PM's much closer to the top of the class, but he's as sly as any fox.'

Skúli snorted with laughter, relieved that Valgeir's sense of humour had been coaxed back to the surface.

'So will the Children of Freedom be the PM's opportunity to dump Steinunn, or is the Osman thing more likely to be the straw that breaks the camel's back?'

'You could put it like that. She ignored public opinion on Kyle McCombie and the Children of Freedom, which was a mistake. That guy's a complete lunatic.'

'I'm aware of that. My colleague interviewed him and said he's totally batshit crazy.'

'So she got the full force of it?'

'Not at all. She said he came across as fairly balanced, it's just his underlying beliefs that are crazy. The fact that he's so articulate and has all kinds of figures at his fingertips makes him sound reasonable; it's only afterwards that you think through what he's said and realize it's all just ranting. The presentation is so polished he doesn't sound like a fruitcake.'

'I'm relieved to hear it,' Valgeir said, absently pushing a sliver of tomato around his plate. 'I had wondered if I was the only one who thought he was nuts.'

'No, it's not just you,' Skúli said. 'Anyway, the skids under Steinunn?'

Valgeir shrugged.

'Do I care? Probably,' he said. 'Maybe not right now, but she's stepped in the shit so many times already that I can't see her being able to stay on much longer. The PM can't abide her, but they're from the same party, so he can't shoot her down without raising hell among the faithful. But then he doesn't have a huge majority, so a few false steps and a couple of rebels – you know who I mean – and the government could crash and burn.'

'So Steinunn and the PM are joined at the hip?'

'Precisely,' Valgeir said, selecting a toothpick from a jar on the table and applying it to the gap between his front teeth. 'Unless she manages something massive, some monumental disaster that gives him a chance to shove her out into the cold.'

'It's not as if we have a tradition in Iceland of politicians apologizing and resigning when they screw up.'

'True. But if there's some colossal clusterfuck, then there's no option,' Valgeir said, the toothpick between his fingers. 'Then she might have no option but to fall on her sword,' he said with a look of deep satisfaction, snapping the toothpick between his fingers.

'So what's he like?' Skúli asked. 'Osman, I mean.'

'He's . . .' Valgeir said and stopped, wondering how to describe Osman. 'He's one of those people who's used to being obeyed, used to getting his own way, but he's not grand at all. Very Middle Eastern, incredibly charming. You know, he kisses women's hands and all that stuff. Handsome with it, big nose, black hair. Looks a bit like a vulture.'

'But he's not popular in some quarters. So why's Steinunn brought him here?'

'She met him at a human rights conference in Helsinki,' Valgeir said, his voice low and his eyes darting from side to side, as if frightened of being overheard. 'He can turn on the charm like a tap. He fixed her with those brown eyes and she was bowled over.'

'The Iron Lady's smitten?'

'She thinks the sun shines out of his arsehole. He's . . .' Valgeir cast around for words. 'He's charismatic. It's something in the way he talks. The only one I've seen so far who wasn't blown away by him was one of the cops looking after him. Steinunn's niece was all over him and he took her back to . . .'

'Back to?' Skúli prompted.

'Sorry. That's strictly secret.'

'When you say Steinunn's niece, you mean Sif Strand was all over him?'

Valgeir looked pained.

'You didn't hear that from me, all right? In fact, you didn't hear it at all.'

'Fair enough,' Skúli agreed. 'Steinunn doesn't know all the shady shit about him, does she? Didn't you do background checks on him?'

Valgeir twisted in his seat and craned his neck over the heads in the café.

'We did. The National Security Unit did a report on him in double-quick time. Steinunn just read the summary and dropped it in the bin. It looked to be mostly hearsay and not much hard fact.'

'But you read it?' Skúli asked and Valgeir nodded. 'And what did they make of him? Is he a fraud or for real?'

Steingrímur's impatience was obvious when Gunna returned to Einholt and Ívar Laxdal drove away. She looked around the living room and shot an enquiring glance at Steingrímur.

'Where is she?'

'TV room.'

'Are you in a hurry to get away?' Gunna yawned. 'They're supposed to be bringing our guest back here at ten on the dot.'

'I ought to relieve my colleague at the watch post in an hour or two. Why?'

'I need to sleep. Only had a couple of hours last night and I'm almost asleep on my feet. Could you keep watch while I close my eyes for an hour?'

Steingrímur grimaced and Gunna could tell that he longed to say no.

'All right. It's almost six now. Call you at seven?'

'Eight would be good.'

'All right. Hey, what's happening in the big outside world?'

'Not a lot. The Laxdal tried to persuade the minister to let him make a statement later about the dead guy, but she wouldn't have it.'

'Your victim . . .'

Gunna felt a jolt pass through her at the words. 'Yes,' she said in an ice-cold voice. 'If that's what you want to call him.'

'Come on, Gunna. He fired two rounds at you. If you hadn't got him first he wouldn't have hesitated to kill you.'

'I know. But I can't get it out of my head. I still can't believe it.'

'Believe me, that guy meant business. I'm just glad it was him and not you.'

Gunna found herself shivering as she sat on one of the stools, huddling into her coat in spite of the warmth indoors.

'I need to get some sleep,' she said. 'I hope I *can* sleep.'

'You do that. Get your head down and I'll call you in a couple of hours. I'll call my mate next door and tell him he'll have to look after things on his own. Go on.'

'What would you need to secure that place?' Ana asked.

The microwave pinged and she put a ready meal on the table, a second one ready to go in.

'On my own or just the two of us?' Michel asked. 'Difficult.'

'No, just if you had what you needed. Go on, I'll have the other one.'

Michel ran a fork through the unappetising stew, sprinkled it with chilli flakes and stirred it.

'It depends how much damage and noise you're happy with. I'd say two to take out the security detail along the street and three to take the house itself. A stun grenade through the window and a grenade for the door, and we'd be in. Grab the guy, tape him up and we'd be in the truck and away in under a minute, I guess. Even better if we could go via the beach. Why? What are you thinking?'

'You've done this before?'

'Many times.'

The microwave chimed a second time and Ana tasted her ready meal.

'This is shit, but I suppose you can eat it,' she said, looking with distaste at the finished product that bore little resemblance to the picture on the packet. 'Unfortunately that's the easy part. What happens afterwards is the problem.'

'I get you. Dead is easy, but snatching him alive is more of a headache?'

'That's about it. I'll have to tell them that we can do dead, but if they want a snatch it'll have to wait until he's back in Europe.'

'Where he's surrounded by his own people.'

'True. But here the headache is getting him back to the mainland alive.'

'He could be sedated?'

Ana frowned.

'It's complicated, and it's risky. Too much to go wrong,' she said and looked up brightly. 'Anyway, we might have a change of plan.'

Steingrímur's hand on her shoulder shook her awake.

'How long have I been asleep?'

'It's almost nine. Osman should be back soon and Sif is determined to talk to you.'

Gunna forced her eyes open. 'Five minutes.'

She splashed her face with cold water and decided she was alert enough to face the world.

'I've been here for almost twenty-four hours now and I need to go home,' Sif said as Gunna emerged from her room. Sif's eyes flashed with frustration. 'This guy said I couldn't leave.' She jerked a thumb at Steingrímur.

'I was given instructions to keep you here,' Gunna said, still far from fully awake.

'I've committed some crime, have I?'

Gunna hesitated. 'No, but there's an unprecedented security situation here.'

'I don't give a shit,' Sif snarled. 'I haven't committed any crime and I'm being held here against my will. Even my phone doesn't work here. It's like being in prison. What's going on? Either I get taken home or I'm going to walk out of here.'

Gunna found herself sympathizing but was unable to say so.

In the turmoil, Sif had become a minor consideration. Still numb after the shooting, and with Ívar Laxdal preoccupied with the dead man's identity, Gunna realized she should have paid Sif closer attention earlier in the day.

'I'm sorry,' she said finally. 'Things have been pretty dramatic over the last few hours. I'll do my best to get you taken home as soon as possible.'

'I have to go to work tomorrow.'

'I understand. Like I said, I'm sorry. I'll talk to my boss.'

'Half an hour and I'm out of here,' Sif said, swinging a thick tress of hair over her shoulder. 'If I have to walk until I can find a cab, I will.'

'Half an hour. Leave it with me.'

Gunna stalked the living room, concentrating on her communicator earpiece until Ívar Laxdal responded.

'We have a problem. Sif is demanding to leave.'

'Hell. Keep her there, can you? At least until I come back?'

'Ívar, we can't keep her here against her will. She hasn't done anything wrong.'

'I know, but she's seen too much.'

'And we should have talked to her before. Can you get Steinunn to speak to her? She said to leave Sif to her, didn't she?'

There was a long pause.

'Sort it out, will you? I'm tied up right now.'

'Fair enough.'

Gunna pulled out her earpiece and went to where Sif sat upright and angry at the bar.

'You're going home. Steingrímur will drive you.'

'At last. That took a while.'

Gunna glared. 'I'm sticking my neck out here. I'm asking you to give me an undertaking not to discuss anything that has happened over the last twenty-four hours with anyone who hasn't been here today. Understand?'

'Of course I understand.'

'Not a single word to anyone, not family, not friends. Nobody at all. As far as they're concerned, you just vanished for a night and a day. You had a stomach bug and spent the day on the toilet.'

'Yeah, yeah. I get it,' Sif fretted. 'Come on,' she said, standing up and turning to Steingrímur. 'I want out of here. This place is creeping me out.'

'Not a single word out of place. This could be a terrorist incident, so you'll be as silent as the grave until this is sorted out. Is that clear?'

'Yeah. I won't even tell my boyfriend where I've been. All right?'

The lights of cars arriving swept across the ceiling, and Gunna switched the television off just as the ten o'clock news began.

The travellers trooped in, Steinunn with a practised smile, Osman looking drawn and irritable, while Ívar Laxdal brought up the rear.

The smile died on Steinunn's lips as Osman disappeared into his room, shaking his coat off. Ívar Laxdal stuffed his beret into his coat pocket

'Is there a problem?' she asked, a glint of steel in her eye.

'Can we have a word without Osman listening in?'

'Now?'

'Now.' There was no mistaking the determination in Ívar Laxdal's tone. 'We have a problem,' he said before Steinunn had a chance to ask a question. 'In fact, we have a whole bunch of problems.'

'Then bring me solutions.'

'I have a whole range of solutions, but I'm not sure you're going to like any of them.'

'Try me.'

'Firstly, get him out of Einholt. As I said before, it's no longer a safe place.'

Steinunn stared at Ívar Laxdal, her lips pinched in anger, which she quickly controlled.

'Why?'

'I told you – it's been identified as his location,' Laxdal said. 'As long as he's here, we're just waiting for another attempt on his life. My officers could be in the firing line.'

'And? Do you have somewhere safe for him?'

'Somewhere well outside the city. But out of the country is the best option.'

Steinunn chewed a lip, the first sign of indecision Gunna had ever seen the minister betray.

'There's more you need to be aware of,' she said, and Steinunn looked up sharply.

'What?'

Gunna took a deep breath and glanced at Ívar Laxdal, who opened his mouth to speak, and then stopped.

'You must have seen what the media has been carrying about Osman, that his foundation is a front for a trafficking operation. The foundation is a cover to launder cash that goes through the accounts, ostensibly as charitable donations.'

Steinunn's mouth hung open for a second before shutting like a trap.

'You can't be serious. I don't believe this.'

'And I can't believe you haven't seen this, or been briefed on it. What we have from the National Security Unit doesn't contradict the press reports.'

'And you didn't tell me? Why not?'

'You were told,' Ívar Laxdal snapped. 'At least, the possibility that this was the case was mentioned in the report those baby-faced twins produced before Osman arrived in Iceland.'

'Shit,' she breathed, glaring across the desk at them. 'I don't have to tell you what damage this could do,' she said, pointing a finger at Ívar Laxdal.

'What I'm concerned with is the body we already have on ice, the safety of my officers and getting this colossal liability out of the country before something goes massively wrong. This was supposed to be a four- or five-day assignment, and it's already turning into something open-ended. We don't have resources for an extended security operation.'

'I had hoped he'd be here for a few weeks,' Steinunn said, as if lost in her own thoughts. 'I want confirmation of these allegations first thing tomorrow. I cannot accept that my own judgement has been so wrong. I've known Osman for some time now. I've even been to one of the shelters he runs in Greece. I'm convinced he's an honourable man, so you'll need to persuade me otherwise.'

Osman looked tired. With Steinunn and Ívar Laxdal gone, for the first time he showed a vulnerable side to his character.

'Good evening,' Gunna said. 'Had a good day?'

Osman looked at her suspiciously through narrowed eyes, as if he were wondering whether she was being sarcastic.

'It has been a long day,' he said at last and sighed. 'A very long day.'

'There's coffee in the pot and food in the fridge,' Gunna told him, taking a seat at the end of the long dining table.

After a moment's indecision he poured himself coffee and sat down stiffly, as if the day's exercise had been more than he was used to.

'Where is . . . ?' he said and hesitated. 'Where is Sif?'

'She's been taken home. She's not happy and I'm hoping she can keep her mouth shut.'

Osman sipped his coffee.

'That's a shame. I'd hoped she would still be here. A lovely young woman,' he said. 'So we are alone again, Goon-hild-oor?' he asked, rolling the syllables of her name slowly across his tongue with a smile. 'Just the two of us?'

'That's it. Just us again.'

'And you are still armed?' he asked, tapping a cigarette from a packet and hunting through his pockets before clicking a cheap lighter. 'You don't mind if I smoke?'

'I'm still armed, and yes, I do mind if you smoke. This place has some very sensitive smoke detectors, and if you don't want a couple of fire engines and police cars turning up outside, then I suggest you open that door and stand outside.'

'Like being a teenager, eh?' Osman grinned, standing up and opening the door that led to the shoulder-high enclosure around the hot tubs. 'You want one?' He proffered the packet through the open door where he stood half outside, his profile silhouetted by the moonlight.

'Not for me, thanks.'

'You never smoke?'

'Not any more.'

He smoked moodily and stubbed out his cigarette in a tin by the door before pulling it shut, shivering. He dropped back onto the chair, a languid leg draped over the armrest, and laid his head back. He rubbed his eyes and Gunna checked the door, shooting the bolts into place.

'You look tired.'

Osman's eyes snapped open.

'Today I have seen mountains, a lot of rocks and six different kinds of weather, and although Steinunn is a wonderful lady in many ways, I don't think she has stopped talking for more than a minute since this morning.'

'You're a distinguished guest, so I guess you've been given a VIP tour.'

'Maybe. I should feel honoured, if that's what you mean?'

'No comment,' Gunna said and suppressed a smile. 'You mean Steinunn doesn't make the best tour guide?'

'Maybe,' Osman said, crinkles appearing at the corners of his eyes as he laughed. 'You did well last night, Gunnhildur. I'm impressed,' he said, the smile disappearing from his dark eyes. 'You have killed someone before?' he asked softly.

'No,' Gunna said sharply. 'Of course not. There's only ever been one police firearms incident in this country that resulted in someone's death.'

'One? Is that all?'

'It's a very peaceful place. We don't generally see gun crime and police officers aren't armed.'

'And now there are two.' He smiled, eyes still fixed on hers. 'You were all so worried last night that I thought this had to be something unusual.'

'This isn't unusual where you come from?'

Osman laughed, this time with little humour. 'I was brought

up in the shadow of a civil war and there is nothing unusual where I come from about people settling differences themselves. I could strip down and reassemble a Kalashnikov with my eyes closed when I was ten years old. You have to learn to defend yourself if you intend to stay alive,' he said in a slow voice. 'As you have found out.'

Gunna felt a chill pass through her at the recollection.

'So do you have any idea who the man is?' Gunna asked and watched as Osman shook his head. She saw his eyes flicker rapidly to one side before settling to a steady gaze again. 'Who would want to do you harm?'

'There are plenty to choose from,' he said with a short bark of laughter. 'I don't know where to start.'

Gunna swung a kitchen chair around and sat on it backwards, folding her arms on the chair back as she returned Osman's stare.

'Let's have a few ideas, shall we? Who would be so keen to come after you with a gun that they'd travel all the way to Iceland to do it?'

Osman sat up, taken aback by Gunna's determined line of questioning. He lifted his chin up and to the side, and raised one long leg off the arm rest.

'Why do you need to know? Does it matter?'

'Of course. A man has lost his life and we need to identify him. There's also a real chance that he wasn't working alone and we can expect someone else to try the same thing.'

'Gunnhildur,' Osman said. 'Where I come from you don't get involved in politics without making enemies. They may not even be my own personal enemies. My father also had no shortage of people wishing him harm. My uncles have even more.'

'And you inherited your father's enemies?'

'Of course. That's the way things work. My enemy's son is also my enemy.'

'This wasn't someone from the Middle East. At least, he wasn't . . .'

'Wasn't what? An Arab?'

'Definitely caucasian. Fair hair. Uncircumcized.'

Osman's eyebrows rose a fraction of an inch towards the thick dark hair that spilled over his forehead.

'Interesting,' he said eventually after staring at his hands. 'Unlikely to be a traditional enemy, then. In any case, they would not travel so far. To them I am only a threat if I am present.'

'That's what I thought. So, any ideas? I can understand you being unpopular, but you have to be seriously unpopular for someone to come all this way to try to kill you.'

'I have no idea, officer.' Osman stood up and stretched, his midriff a few feet from Gunna's face. He stepped forward and placed a hand gently on her shoulder. 'It's been a long day and I'm going to sleep,' he said with a grin. His white teeth flashed in the half darkness. 'I'll leave the door open in case you feel like keeping me company.'

Chapter Six

Michel sniffed the air and gauged the wind as they got out of the car. It was the deadest time of the night, with many hours before dawn would break over the mountains to the east. This was his favourite time, when no people were to be seen and he could walk almost unseen among the homes of those who had no idea they could be being watched.

He led the way, footsteps crunching on the gravel underfoot, and only switched on the lamp on his head as he turned the corner, taking them out of sight.

'Ready? You've done this before?'

'Why do you think I'm here?' Ana replied, dropping her rucksack on the ground and snapping open the catches. 'How far is it?'

'The other side of the headland there.'

She shook off her shoes and jacket and unrolled the drysuit, pulling it on and scowling.

'Sorry. It's Pino's and he was taller than you,' Michel apologized.

'That's all right,' she said, squatting low to force air out of the suit. 'Come on.'

The two kayaks, once orange and now roughly painted matt black, rocked in the waves lapping at the shingle.

'Here,' Michel said. 'In case there's a problem or we get separated, this place is waypoint one. Hit the home button and it'll take you right back here.'

She nodded, stowed the GPS set in the drysuit's waterproof knee pocket and pulled on a balaclava and a pair of neoprene gloves.

'Ready?' she prompted.

'Yeah. Stay close. We don't want to lose each other and that's easy to do in the dark.'

'Black boats and black clothes. You don't need to tell me,' she replied. 'You know where we're going, so you go ahead and I'll be on your tail.'

The night wind was a lazy one, a breeze that gnawed at exposed faces. Half a moon appeared at intervals from behind the clouds and Ana followed behind Michel as his firm strokes set a steady pace towards the black shadow across the water.

It was as the two kayaks rounded the headland and left its shelter that the wind hit them harder and the chop of the water buffeted the boats. Keeping close together, and with frequent sideways glances, they paddled closer to the beach that could hardly be seen. Michel back-paddled and Ana caught his arm, keeping the two kayaks bobbing in the choppy water.

'There,' Michel said. 'That's the place.'

He slipped off a glove, opened a pocket and handed her a night vision scope. Ana peered through it, watching the shoreline jump into clarity as if it were only a few steps away.

'That's the house?' she asked, peering at the long, low building where lights gleamed from two large windows.

'That's it.'

'What happened?'

'We went up the beach about four hundred metres to the south. Pino went to take a look. I stayed on the shore and we agreed that if anything went badly wrong, then I was to back out quick.'

Ana could hear the anger in his voice overcoming his cool manner, while the wind whipped at his words.

'And?'

'I watched through the scope, so I could see it happen. Someone came out of the house, one of the security people. He must have opened the door and stepped outside just as Pino was moving, because I heard the challenge. There were a couple of shots, two his, I think, and two or more of theirs. Pino dropped. That cop must have got lucky with a shot like that in the dark.' He shrugged. 'It happens. It's part of the job. Come on, we've seen everything and we shouldn't hang around here.'

Gunna swung open the door and the visitors trooped inside.

'Welcome to the garage,' she said, zipping her fleece up to her throat. 'We're in here for obvious reasons. Our guest is still asleep, but we don't need him to appear in the middle of a conversation. There's no heating in here, so we ought to keep it quick.'

The new arrival looked exhausted and slightly bewildered in the chill of the pre-dawn darkness, but shook first Ívar's hand and then took Gunna's, holding it for slightly longer than was comfortable.

'Luc Kerkhoeve.'

'Luc is from Brussels,' Birna said, slipping seamlessly into English. 'State Security Service. He got here last night and he's interested in our guest.'

'We've been keeping an eye on him for a while, almost three years; since he arrived in Brussels and set up this Sickle Foundation. Yet another foundation,' he said with a shake of his head.

'Can we share information freely?' Ívar Laxdal asked quickly in Icelandic, glancing at Birna. 'Is there anything that stays off limits?'

'We don't have any secrets to keep,' Birna replied in soft English. 'Anything Luc can help us with would be appreciated.'

'Good. No hide-and-seek,' Ívar Laxdal grunted. 'Let's keep it that way. Luc, Gunnhildur has been in charge of Osman's security since he arrived in Iceland. I'm a senior officer at the city force and this operation is my responsibility, supposedly. Osman has been here for almost a week, at the invitation of the minister. In fact, he has an outing organized this afternoon, a visit to Parliament with her. His presence here was supposed to be kept under the radar, but the press is already sniffing around all this and there's been an incursion on this building, with one fatality. I think that should put you in the picture.'

Luc looked up sharply.

'Fatality?'

'Just down there, between here and the shore. An intruder was seen, he was challenged, and instead of putting his hands up, he fired. There was an exchange of fire and the intruder was killed. No identification has been possible so far.'

'Do you have a picture of the dead man?' Luc asked.

Úlfur scrolled through his phone and passed it to him. Luc stared at the image.

'Email it to me,' he instructed, and reeled off an email address. 'The face isn't familiar, but I can leapfrog the official channels.'

He concentrated on his own phone, fingers flickering over the screen.

'Got it,' he muttered to himself as the photo arrived in his inbox. He plugged the earpiece in and made a call, speaking in staccato French, stabbing a finger at his phone's screen as he spoke. Birna listened carefully and Gunna guessed that she was the only one present who understood Luc's side of the conversation.

Finally, he nodded in satisfaction and ended the call.

'My contact thinks he knows who this man is, or was. He'll call me back when he has something. Now, you want to know about Osman and I want to know what he's doing here.'

'We dug out what information we could in the two days we had between the minister remembering to tell us Osman was coming and would we please look after him, and him arriving here,' Birna said, sitting on a workbench set against the breezeblock wall of the garage. 'So we don't have much.'

Luc put a hand in the pocket of his jacket and took out a notebook and a sheaf of papers that he opened on a workbench next to Birna, who moved along to give him space.

'He calls himself Ali Osman. In fact, his name appears to be Osman Deniz, according to the passport he managed to get courtesy of the Italian wife who left him a few years ago,' Luc said and looked up. 'At least, that's the official story. We believe he's originally a Turkish national with links to Syria. That part of the world is totally upside-down at the moment. Ankara doesn't reply to many requests for information and you can imagine what it's like trying to get information from Syria.'

'I think he's originally from Lebanon,' Gunna said, and Ívar's eyes widened.

'Really? He told you that?'

'I've no idea if he was telling the truth, but he said he had grown up during a civil war, and judging by his age, that could be Lebanon.'

'Interesting . . .' Luc said thoughtfully as Birna and Úlfur shared glances and raised eyebrows. 'There are so many conflicting myths about this man that it's hard to tell what's lies and what isn't. This is interesting background, but I'm not sure it changes our analysis.'

'Which is?'

'That as far as we can make out, he has been one of the key figures getting refugees into Europe.'

'Which is the White Sickle Peace Foundation's work? Assisting refugees from war zones?' Birna asked and Luc shook his head.

'No. You misunderstand me. The foundation he created does some work trying to make life easier for refugees once they reach Greece or Italy, with tents, water, that kind of thing. But we're sure it's a front for his real business. Forget all the humanitarian and political shit. Osman is all about the money.'

She had already checked the dining room, watched as he ate breakfast, drank a second cup of coffee and headed for the lift.

Ana took the stairs, watching for the cleaning staff, and found them on the third floor, where trolleys loaded with cleaning materials waited in a line. With nobody to be seen, she lifted a pile of towels from the end trolley and stepped back through the door to the stairs that nobody used when the lift was so much easier.

On the sixth floor she folded her coat under a fire extinguisher, pulled on a pair of blue rubber gloves, held the towels in her arms and knocked on James Kearney's door.

'Housekeeping.'

The door swung open and he looked at her quizzically, failing to recognize the woman who had spent part of an evening watching him in the bar from behind a book and a glass of white wine.

'Excuse me. I bring towels,' she said, giving herself a guttural accent.

'I don't need towels.'

'Excuse me. Supervisor say, towels to rooms.'

'Look, I don't need towels. Leave it, OK?'

Ana looked confused, peering at him over the pile of white towels in her arms.

'She tell me, towels to this room, next room.'

'All right, if you need to,' he said grudgingly and stepped aside.

She watched him go back to his chair in front of the TV and went into the bathroom, placed the towels on a high shelf that she had to stretch to reach and half-closed the door. She took one of the two tooth glasses, stood behind the door, and hurled the glass at the floor, enjoying the crash as it shattered and giving a passable impression of a squeal of pain.

'What . . . ?'

A moment later he was in the doorway, feet crunching on shards as he looked at the floor beneath the washbasin where the glass had smashed.

'What happened? Where are you?'

As he swung open the shower cubicle to look for her, Ana stepped from behind the door, hands already crossed. She slipped the loop of twine over his head, smartly uncrossed her hands and felt it tighten.

Unable to shout, he gurgled, his hands clawing frantically at his throat as she maintained the tension, waiting for him to stop thrashing as his life ebbed away. It felt like an age before he sank to his knees in a widening pool of urine. Ana grunted with the effort as she steered his bulk towards the bathtub, toppling it in and lifting his legs, one after the other, neatly making it look as if he had curled up there.

She quickly looked around, stepped out into the passage and pulled the door shut behind her, hooking onto it the cheerful door hanger declining room service, which she hoped would mean the room remained undisturbed for at least another twenty-four hours.

A moment later she had retrieved her coat, made her way down the stairs and dropped the blue gloves in a bin by the door as she walked away from the hotel.

Skúli felt his shoulders ache. The slush was more than his shoes were made to cope with and now he would have damp feet for the rest of the day. Much as he loved his work at *Pulse*, family life had made him appreciate closing his laptop and pushing the rough-and-tumble of news to the back of his mind for a few hours every day. Evenings with Dagga and Markús had become the part of the day he looked forward to from the moment he closed the door behind him each morning to catch the bus into town.

It had been a few years since the tell-tale lethargy had last stalked him, creeping up on him quietly while his attention was elsewhere. A week ago, under the hot water of the shower, the thought had come unbidden to mind that something wasn't right, and he had searched his mind for what it might be. Old failings and embarrassments sprang to mind with increasing regularity, making him quail as he roughly took his thoughts by the scruff of the neck and sent them packing.

It was the moments of quiet that he dreaded, the times when his mind would wander unerringly to places he would prefer to leave unvisited. The minutes falling asleep with the welcome warm pressure of Dagga's back nestled against his, or the silent mornings, waking to find their legs tangled together, were the difficult ones; seeking or emerging from sleep had become a familiar gauntlet to run, with unwelcome dark thoughts unexpectedly popping up before he was ready for them.

During the day he could keep the gathering darkness at bay, smothering it with bustle and activity so that only occasionally something would sneak through the gaps in his armour, reminding him that the black dog was waiting, panting with its red tongue lolling out between white teeth, and it could wait far more patiently than he ever could.

Skúli shivered. The wind was a chill one from the north with snow on its breath, just when it looked like spring should be about to make an overdue appearance. He wondered if winter and the weeks of low daylight were what caused his problems, and reminded himself that in the past these assaults on his peace of mind had not respected the seasons, appearing at various times of the year, taking him by surprise throughout his teens until he had come to recognize the signs.

Was it time to go back to the doctor? He worked his chin into the comforting insulation his woollen scarf offered while the wind whipped at his hair. No, not the doctor. Not again. Last time the tablets had lasted for months, and when he finally stopped taking them he felt such a surge of relief that he had promised never to go down that route again.

Laugavegur was practically deserted. On a weekday afternoon there were no revellers either setting out on their night's epic journey around Reykjavík's nightspots or making their weary, hungover way home after a heavy night out. There were also no tourists, and half of the shops catering to Iceland's new status as a fashionable travel destination were closed, waiting for the weekend.

Skúli turned down Klapparstígur, contemplated for a moment whether or not to spend half an hour browsing through the unpredictable shelves of his preferred second-hand book shop, and decided against it. His bedside table was already groaning under the weight of books waiting to be read, plus he knew he should get back to his desk. The wind hit him square in the face as he turned onto Hverfisgata and walked up the slope to the shabby building where *Pulse*'s office was located.

The walk had helped and his mind was made up, which immediately made him feel better.

He shook off his coat and hung it over the back of his chair. He took a deep breath, spent a minute searching online for a phone number, punched it into his desk phone and listened to it ring.

'Yeah?'

'Hello. My name's Skúli Thór Snædal and I'm a journalist at *Pulse*. I was wondering if we could talk?'

Gunna told herself that cabin fever was setting in as she watched CCTV of airline passengers waiting for their luggage. The morning's visitors had departed, Kerkhoeve with Birna and Úlfur, and Ívar Laxdal on some mysterious errand of his own, and now Gunna was chafing at the isolation. Regardless of how often she had craved solitude in the past, she'd had enough, and found herself longing for normality – even a mundane walk to the local Co-op would be welcome right now.

Hundreds of faces had passed by on her computer screen already, and only a dozen had needed a closer look to compare them with the starkly lit photograph of the dead man.

She paused the CCTV replay again to give herself a break and found herself staring at the dead man's face, his pale hair in a rough crewcut, a week's worth of stubble and a hint of blue peering from half-closed dead eyes as the man lay on the slab.

The house was silent. The door to Osman's room was open and Gunna could hear the mutter of his laptop keys. She stood up and set the percolator to make another pot of coffee, telling herself she needed the caffeine jolt to keep concentrating on the faces on the screen.

She couldn't help thinking about the dead man, whether or not he had a family expecting him to return home, or elderly parents who might be wondering where he was. She reflected that she hadn't seen the man's face in life, or heard his voice, just seen the shadow in the darkness; she'd been taken aback by the swiftness of his shots as soon as he had heard her call out. There had been no hesitation, as one shot had gone into the dark while the other had smacked into the wall. She still hadn't summoned up the courage to go outside and check by how much it had missed her.

Gunna found her mouth dry and her heart pumping fast as she put both hands on the kitchen worktop, the percolator rumbling and spitting in front of her as she thought of what *could* have happened; she could be the one on the slab at the National Hospital. Ívar Laxdal would have had to make the trip out to Hvalvík in his best uniform to give Steini and Laufey the bad news. Gísli's ship would have to be called and he would have to endure the hours before docking wondering what had happened to her. Then there were the boys, Ari and Kjartan, Gísli's two sons by two different mothers. They would have had to grow up with nothing but the haziest memories of their grandmother.

'Is everything all right, Gunna?'

Osman's voice was soft, concerned and understanding. A hand settled lightly on her shoulder. Gunna stayed still, her breaths returning gradually to normal.

Dry-eyed, she turned towards him. The hand remained on her shoulder.

'Fine, thanks. It feels like it's been a long day already.'

Osman looked down at her.

'It gets to you, doesn't it?'

'What do you mean?'

'Killing someone,' he said in the same soft voice. 'It's an emotional business the first time.'

She felt the pressure of his hand increase, pulling her towards him, gently but insistently. Gunna hesitated, surprised that she was even tempted to move closer, and allowed herself to be folded into his embrace. She clasped her arms around him, resting her head against his chest and feeling his chin against the top of her head as he held her tight.

She felt a warm glow of comfort for a few moments, took a deep breath, let go of him and stepped back, folding her arms as a barrier between them.

'It gets easier, you mean?'

'Of course.'

Gunna stopped herself from asking how many people Osman had killed.

'It's not something I plan to make a habit of doing.' She poured coffee into two mugs and handed him one. 'It'll be a while before there's a meal. I asked Ívar to bring us a takeaway. I'm afraid the kitchen isn't my natural habitat.'

'You are busy? Working?'

'I am. And I need to get back to it,' she said, nodding towards the laptop open on the dining table. 'I have a lot to get through before our lunch arrives.'

★ ★ ★

Ana started the engine and waited for the car to warm up. The walk along the causeway and out on to the rocky promontory of Geldinganes had left her chilled through. The icy wind had found every gap in the layers of clothing she had put on, despite her care to be as windproof as possible.

It had been a worthwhile few hours. The place was almost an island. A narrow causeway emerged from the grey sand to curve out to Geldinganes, its surface too uneven for wheels, and Ana picked her way across. Once out there, she had walked in a circle around the promontory, binoculars in hand, making a passable imitation of someone there to spot birds and seals as she examined the long, low building at Einholt.

For a while she sat in the lee of the island and watched people coming and going. Some of them she had seen before, such as the man and woman in their practically identical suits; she guessed they were with the police.

Ana unzipped an inside pocket of her thick coat and extracted a smartphone of exactly the kind she had forbidden Michel and Pino to carry, and powered it up.

It had taken her a day or two, and a conversation with one of their technical consultants, to figure out why Osman's phone had failed to appear, when they had realized that Einholt was either in a dead zone out of phone coverage, or else a jamming system was in operation. The previous day, when he'd left the house with the minister, she had been quietly jubilant when the tracker that had been hacked into Osman's phone suddenly appeared again. Now she could be more confident that her target was safely where she wanted him, and that she would know if he were to make a move.

She was relieved to have time to herself again. It seemed that Michel had been surprised at how quickly she'd arrived on the scene, but he had failed to realize that she had already been there, keeping a discreet eye on both the target and the two former mercenaries, hoping that they would finish the job by themselves.

Admittedly Michel had followed procedure to the letter and, as far as anyone was aware, the hapless Pino remained a mystery man, although she doubted that Luc Kerkhoeve would fail to identify him.

Once the car had warmed up and she had rubbed some warmth back into her numb fingers, she powered down the smartphone and drove away from the deserted shore, taking the road through the suburbs towards the city centre. After having been on her feet since midnight, she needed to sleep. But first she needed to check in and confirm that the assignment at the hotel had been carried out.

Gunna watched the video sequence again and again, pausing it every time there was a clear view of the man. At first glance there was nothing out of the ordinary about him. His clothes were non-descript, jeans, a coat that gaped open to show a hooded sweater, trainers on his feet. The only striking thing about him was his eyes, pale and mobile, which flickered around the arrivals hall, taking in everything as he waited for a kitbag to arrive on the carousel, and then marching towards the exit. He seemed neither young nor old, with a timeless look about him.

Gunna played the sequence repeatedly, trying to assess whether or not the man was travelling alone, all the while telling herself that an accomplice would hardly have travelled on the same flight. She stared at the man's face, zooming in until he filled the screen, freezing the image as he looked unblinkingly at the camera he must have known was watching him.

'So who are you, young man?' she breathed, having reverse-tracked his movements through the terminal to see him arrive on a flight from Amsterdam.

She wondered what his name was, where he came from and if anyone were waiting to hear from him. A wife or a lover? Maybe some soft-cheeked young woman was wondering why her calls weren't being returned. There could be children, she thought, and felt sick. Was there a house or an apartment somewhere that would remain silent and empty until one day a bank or distant relative claimed it? And where? Where was this man's home? He had travelled through Amsterdam in his Eastern European underwear, but he could have come from practically anywhere and would almost certainly have travelled in a dog-leg route of some kind to throw off anyone trying to track his movements.

Again she told herself to calm down, to stop letting herself be frustrated by inactivity. It wasn't her job to dig into the dead man's life and past; other people would do it better than she could. All the same, she found herself running through the options. There must have been CCTV at Schiphol, and there had to be footage of him there that could be tied to his arrival there; he would certainly have been photographed as he checked in for his flight. That would provide a name, and a name and a picture were a start. Even a false name was a start, she decided. There had to be a credit card attached to that name, an address, and so on. Much would depend on co-operation with forces in other countries, although the terror tag that went with the incident would ring alarm bells and push the case close to the top of every priority list.

But where were these people staying in Iceland, assuming the dead man hadn't been working alone, she asked herself again. There had to be a bolt-hole, a hiding place, somewhere in or around the city. There had to be a car somewhere, rented or purchased. And where had the revolver come from, she reflected, wondering if they had brought it with them, and if so, how had it got through airport security measures? Or had it come some other way? It was more likely it had been acquired in Iceland, she decided, as anyone bringing in a weapon would hardly have gone for such an antique.

Much of what needed to be done required team effort, but she was shut away in this comfortable out-of-town cage, left to hope the work was being done.

She was still looking into the dead man's eyes as she felt Osman appear soundlessly, padding on bare feet with a glass in his hand.

'Gunnhildur, do we have orange juice?' he asked.

'What?' she replied, shaken from her train of thought. 'Sorry. I was miles away. Look in the fridge.'

'There is no orange juice.'

Osman's voice was soft, with a hint of petulance.

'Sorry. It's on the list, so it should be in the next delivery when Ívar comes back.'

'I see.'

Osman sat down on one of the dining-room chairs opposite the laptop that had claimed Gunna's attention. He looked at his watch and yawned while Gunna continued to frown at the screen in front of her.

'What are you doing?' he asked with a suddenness that took her by surprise.

Gunna looked up and saw Osman's frown of disapproval. It occurred to her that someone not giving him their full attention was something he was unused to.

'Since you ask,' she said slowly, turning the laptop around, 'I'm looking at the man who came here to kill you. Does that face look familiar?'

Osman's eyes widened and Gunna watched his face intently, waiting for a hesitation or some reaction that would tell her something. Instead, he looked at the pale man's face with non-chalance and shook his head. He sat back on his chair and lifted his feet onto another, crossing his bare feet across it. Gunna was struck by the size of them, and the wiry black hair that grew across his insteps.

'I've never seen this man before,' he said, and Gunna was inclined to believe him.

'Well, we think he and his friends know who you are, and it seems they travelled a long way to do you harm.'

Osman shrugged. 'That's nothing new. You don't do good work without attracting enemies.'

'What do you call good work?'

'I run a charity. I founded a charity,' he said, eyes flashing. 'My work is to help my people, to make their lives better.'

Gunna turned the laptop back round and closed it. 'Who are your people?'

'Anyone who has suffered. Those are my people.'

'Everyone? All around the world? That's ambitious.'

'I mean in my country, the part of the world I come from, the place that is my home.'

'So far you haven't said much about where you come from. You still haven't told me where that is.'

'You wouldn't understand.'

'Try me.'

Skúli had never been entirely comfortable behind the wheel. Dagga had decided that they needed a car, and had set about finding something small enough to be handy around the city while still big enough to accommodate a child seat and any amount of toddler paraphernalia. Occasionally she dropped a hint that sooner or later a second child seat would be required.

Normally he relished the bus journey into town as twenty minutes of uninterrupted reading time plus a healthy walk. Dagga looked surprised but said nothing when Skúli muttered that he'd need the car for a change.

He was earlier than usual, and although normally he would have started with a mug of coffee and half an hour spent checking messages, this time he went straight for the competing news outlets and social media.

Few of the mainstream media had followed up on *Pulse*'s scoop of the previous day. But he saw that most of the other digital media had mirrored the story, and social media feeds had snapped hungrily at the report with all sorts of comments, including outlandish conspiracy theories from familiar names that normally made him either chuckle or despair.

His Osman scoop had failed to oust Kyle McCombie from the headlines, as an irascible TV interview with him aired the night before had inflamed more passion that spilled over into angry exchanges.

'Good for business,' Skúli mused as Arndís hung up her coat and went to her desk.

'What's good?'

'Extremist nutcases spouting venom.'

'That racist guy again? How long's he staying here?'

203

'I think he left late last night. I don't imagine he'll be missed.'

'Only by his white supremacist friends. Did you get any feedback on your story yesterday?'

'Not much,' Skúli said. 'I thought there'd be more. There's a lot of shouting on Facebook, but that happens all the time anyway. No word from the ministry, no injunction, nothing.'

'That's a shame,' Arndís agreed. 'An injunction would have told us you were on the right track, and it would have been great for circulation. Silence doesn't do much good.'

'It's not as if dignified silence is Steinunn Strand's style, though. I'm still waiting for the secret police to come calling in the middle of the night.'

'If she could send them, I'm sure she would.'

'And . . . we have news,' Skúli said as his inbox bleeped a new message and he peered at the screen. 'Hey, come and look . . .'

With Arndís looking over his shoulder he clicked the link and they watched as the news report began to play.

'Where's this from?' Arndís asked as a barrage of French burst from the speaker.

'My contact in Paris. She must have found something more on Osman.'

The wide-angle, hand-held footage with rapid-fire commentary showed beach scenes of refugees overjoyed to have sand under their feet, children held tight as family groups waded through the shallows, and street scenes of people with no belongings other than what they could carry making their way through dusty villages.

Skúli took a sharp breath as the scene switched suddenly to a brass plate screwed to a concrete wall among a line of others.

'White Sickle Peace Foundation,' Skúli breathed. 'She's been to Brussels. Brilliant, Sophie.'

The camera followed people entering and leaving a building as he struggled to make sense of the commentary in a language he was only barely familiar with, until an indistinct figure, muffled in a sheepskin coat, appeared at the door, and he could make out the back of Sophie's head as whoever held the camera hurried to keep up with her.

'Do you have any comment to make on the allegations made about White Sickle Foundation by the Plain Truth?' Sophie called in hoarse English at the figure striding away from her.

'Are you going to agree to make White Sickle's finances public?'

A hand waved dismissively.

'How is White Sickle linked to the death of Lars Bundgaard?'

The figure stopped and turned to the camera, eyes burning with furious indignation.

'I have no comment to make,' the man snarled in abrupt English as he marched along the street with Sophie at his heels, repeating the same questions, until he vanished through a door that slammed in her face.

'We didn't manage to get any answers from the White Sickle Foundation,' Sophie's voice said as the screen returned to an image of the brass plate, before it dissolved into a now familiar portrait of Osman. 'Except for a statement telling us that the only person authorized to comment is the director, who is currently abroad and not contactable. That's Ali Osman, or Ali Osman Deniz, or Suleiman Ali Osman, or whichever name he's currently using.'

Skúli drummed the table in excitement.

'She's done it,' he crowed. 'She's fucking done it!'

'A parallel investigation by our team in Iceland has revealed that White Sickle's director is in fact currently in Iceland as the guest of a senior government figure,' Sophie said to the camera as Skúli whooped with delight. 'Don't forget to be with us again tonight for the second part of our investigation.'

The report ended with the camera showing a boat abandoned on a sunlit beach, rocking in the waves lapping around it, panning to a shoe lost in the sand and lines of footprints disappearing into the grass in the distance.

'My home was within sight of the blue sea,' Osman said. 'We lived ten minutes from the beach and an hour from the village in the hills my father's ancestors had come from. That was always home even though we had lived in the city for three generations.'

He spoke in a slow, dark voice, deeper than his usual conversational tone and with a mesmerizing rhythm to his words.

'My father and his brothers had always been involved in politics. The eldest of my uncles had been to university in France and when he came home, he entered politics instead of business. The family as a whole is branded with his name and reputation. He was murdered during the second conflict. Or we believe he was murdered. He was taken and we heard nothing more of him. He has to be buried on a hillside somewhere, along with the other victims of whatever faction took him, and that was never clear.'

Osman paused and his eyes glittered. He poured water into a glass from a jug on the table and sipped.

'All we could do was leave. In the first conflict – the first of many – the hundred days' war, the family home had gone, somewhere in the empty zone in the centre of the city that nobody dared visit. My grandfather's business had come to a standstill. He had traded in almost anything, spices, fruit, leather, clothes, but there was nobody left to produce anything. The country people were starving. In the village that we still think of as our home, my cousins had joined militias and gone to fight. The eldest son of my father's brother was killed outright by a mortar shell. His brother was injured only a few days later, and now he does what he can with half a hand and one foot. The youngest brother survived the war and is now a prosperous landowner, although he's worried about what is happening only a few miles away across the borders. Damascus is not far away.'

The thin morning daylight that had flooded the house faded as a cloud drifted over the sun, giving the room a sudden chill. Gunna stood up and switched on the kitchen light.

'My father took us north along the coast, driving an old van – the kind that European students used to drive all the way to India when the roads through Iran and Afghanistan were still safe for wanderers of that kind. Maybe that was where that old VW came from. I don't know. We were all crammed into it, my father and mother, two grandparents, four children and three of my young cousins, as well as whatever we could salvage. We became refugees in our own country, until my father was able to grease the right palms and we went to a town on the coast, a pretty, friendly place where people were suspicious of us to start with, but not for long.'

'To Turkey?' Gunna asked as Osman paused.

He waved a hand in impatience. 'Quiet. I will tell the story. My grandfather had many friends throughout the region. He was a trader. A trader has to have friends and he has to be trusted. There was no electronic money in those days. Business was done in cash, or gold, or sometimes between banks, which was slow. Anyway, there were men in Turkey, in Cyprus, in Egypt, even in Italy and France, who had known my grandfather and trusted his word, and in turn they were prepared to trust my father because of whose son he was. They could see my grandfather in him, so he was able to trade. He had some money that he had been prudent enough to hide. At the end of our journey I helped him take up the floor of the old VW – I could not believe my eyes when I saw the gold coins in cloth bags hidden there. If the militias he had bribed along the way to let us pass had suspected, we would have all been corpses by the side of the road – my parents, my grandparents and seven children.'

'You were lucky.'

'Lucky? I don't know. All I can be sure of is that there was no shortage of prayer. Maybe we were helped. Maybe someone was watching over us. Do you believe?'

Osman gazed intently, his eyes like dark pools in their growing intensity.

'No,' Gunna said. 'No, I don't believe in anything upstairs or afterwards if that's what you're asking.'

'You are truly an unfortunate woman, in that case.'

'Perhaps. But I like it that way,' she said. 'Your father was able to rebuild his business and a new home?'

'He did.'

'Where is the rest of the family now? Your brothers and sisters?'

'This is the hard part to tell. The whole thing happened again.

In my part of the world it seems to happen once in a generation. We are sent a plague. There was a drought and people became unhappy, poor, hungry. The government did nothing except tell them to be quiet. The result was another war.'

'You were involved in that?'

'No, Gunnhildur. I left long before it started. My father was prosperous enough after a few years to send me and my eldest sister to be educated properly. I went to Europe; she went to the capital – it was not proper for a girl to travel abroad, otherwise she would have gone. The others went as well, apart from the eldest, who became an officer in the army. He is still there, I think. I have not been able to contact him and I do not know what has become of him. One day I will find him.'

A lilting reggae beat pulsed from invisible speakers. A man at the counter didn't look up as Skúli approached, unwinding his scarf as he made his way across the distressed wood floor, feeling his feet squelch in damp shoes.

'Hi. I'm looking for Sif.'

'So is everyone, darling.'

The guy still hadn't looked up. Skúli had become used to all kinds of treatment by people he approached in his line of work, but this kind of scorn was on a new scale.

'How would you like to tell me where she is,' he said slowly. 'Considering I'm expected? Darling.'

The guy looked up and peered at Skúli through half-closed eyes, screwing up his narrow face.

'And who did you say you are?'

'I didn't. Sif asked me to come here, so how about you tell her she has a visitor?'

'All right. There's no need to be rude, is there?' he drawled and went to a door set in the wall furthest from the entrance, opened it and called, all without taking his eyes from where Skúli stood by the counter.

Skúli felt his breath snatched from him as Sif appeared in the doorway, beckoning to him, while the sharp-faced man went back to the counter and whatever he had been doing behind it that was more important than looking up.

The chestnut mane was alluringly disarrayed, as usual whenever Sif Strand was photographed in public, but he was unprepared for her sheer presence and height as she looked down at him, her face a question.

'Skúli?'

'That's me. We spoke earlier,' he said, trying to sound detached.

'Cool. This way.'

'You work here?' he asked as he followed her along a corridor, squeezing past racks of clothes that were lined up along its length.

'Sometimes. When I'm needed to help out,' Sif said, turning to glance at him. 'My sister owns this place and she thinks I can drop everything and help out just like that.'

She snapped her fingers to illustrate the point and swung open a door that squealed on its hinges.

'Now. What do you want to know?' Sif draped herself across a chair, her endless golden legs elegantly crossed. 'You work for what? *Pulse*?'

'That's right. I'm one of the news team.'

'I thought you didn't do fashion stuff? Too highbrow for that kind of thing.'

Skúli fumbled in his pocket and took out his phone, looking for the text message Lars had sent him a few days earlier.

'This guy,' he said, turning his phone around to show her. 'You've met this guy. That's who I'm looking for.'

Sif's face froze.

'Who are you? You're not from some fucking scandal sheet, are you?'

'*Seen & Heard*?' Skúli replied and tried to smile. 'No, far from it. I'm tracking this man's whereabouts and I understand he's keeping a very low profile.'

'You're not going to mention me anywhere, are you? Because if you do . . .'

'If I do, what?' Skúli asked, stung at the crude threat.

'I'll make your life hell,' Sif leaned forward and hissed. 'Now tell me why you're really here.'

Skúli shrugged. 'Like I said, I'm trying to find out what this man is doing in Iceland, and I have it on good authority that you know him quite well.' He looked into sharp eyes that stared back at him angrily. 'Or so I'm told.'

Ívar Laxdal blew on his fingers as he stamped slush from his boots and banged the door behind him, handing her a bag that smelled enticing.

'Locked it?' Gunna asked without looking up as he took off his coat, dropping it and a pile of newspapers onto a chair.

'Both locks.'

He shook the Thermos to check if there was coffee in it and poured himself a mug.

'It's only damned well snowing,' he grumbled. 'That's all we need.'

'Sounds good to me. I can't imagine any bad guys will want to sneak up on the place in a blizzard.'

'One should never underestimate an opponent,' Ívar Laxdal said, coughing as the steam from his coffee hit his throat. 'Good. Any joy with the CCTV?' he asked with little hope in his voice.

'Actually, yes,' Gunna said, turning and grinning at him. She nodded her head towards the bedroom. 'You'd better come and have a look. And bear in mind that I've been staring at these faces all morning, so I'm not as wide awake as I'd like to be.'

She scrolled back through the raw footage to find the time-stamp, and set it to run as Ívar Laxdal sat and gazed intently at the screen. The picture was remarkably clear, capturing passengers walking along the passageway that would take them through the airport terminal.

She could hear Ívar Laxdal's heavy breathing at her shoulder as he peered at the screen with an intensity that furrowed his brows. On the screen a queue of people shuffled towards the desks, pass-ports in hands, bags over shoulders, sweltering in heavy coats. The vaguely unreal images seemed somehow clearer than reality. Ívar

Laxdal fumbled in his pocket, taking out his rarely worn spectacles and jamming them on the end of his nose without taking his eyes off the computer.

'There,' Gunna said, slowing the replay and then stopping it as a pair of bright eyes under tousled pale hair flashed past the camera lens, framed between two other impatiently waiting passengers. 'I reckon that's him.'

'Time?'

'It was a late flight, last Monday.'

'Monday? You're sure? Osman arrived in Iceland on Thursday night.'

'Ívar, of course I'm sure,' Gunna said with a measure of disapproval. 'I've checked and double-checked. He arrived on a flight from Amsterdam. He was here four days before Osman, so they knew he was coming here well before we did. So how did they know and have time to prepare?'

Ívar Laxdal was busily jotting down times and flight numbers in his hardback notebook.

'Amsterdam. Right. Leave it with me. I'll have the flight checked out and see what else we can dig up on this man.'

'Who's doing that?'

'Birna and Úlfur are handling that side of it. But I can go straight to airport security for this.' Ívar Laxdal took off his glasses and folded them as a humourless smile crossed his lips. 'Steinunn wants this handled by the Security Unit, not by us plods.'

'It's a stupid question, maybe,' Gunna sighed, jerking her head towards Osman's partially open door, 'but how long is this going to go on?'

'At the initial briefing it was a week. Now, I've no idea.'

'I was under the impression that this was to be a couple of days, and then I'd be able to sew on my chief inspector's star.'

'That's what I was hoping for as well. I'm down one of my best officers at the moment and I could do with her back. I've told Steinunn that either this is the National Security Unit's baby or it's ours, but she more or less told me to wind my neck in and do as I'm told. You're getting frustrated out here?'

'Not yet, but it's not far off. I haven't seen my bloke for a week, and I think it's the first time we've been apart that long since . . . But the really frustrating thing is that I should be banging on doors, not sat here as a glorified housekeeper.'

Ívar Laxdal scowled and shook his head. 'This is your assignment. I can't bring in anyone from outside.'

'Maybe Birna could come and wash his underwear for a day or two? Or Úlfur?'

'Let me see what I can arrange. But don't be too hopeful. Steinunn wants him watched like a hawk,' he said. 'Speaking of which, Osman is due at the ministry at two, and has a tour of Parliament at three, before we bring him back here. That's assuming Steinunn is still a minister by then. She's seeing the PM later and I'd love to be a fly on the wall when that conversation takes place. The opposition has been calling for her to resign and even the press that normally supports the government is turning against her.'

'We'd best get Osman fed and ready, then.' Gunna sighed. 'It's almost like having a small child again. But first, hold the fort for ten minutes, will you, while I take a quick shower? You being here will discourage our guest from accidentally bumping into me when I'm wrapped in a towel.'

Osman took Steinunn's hands in his own. Gunna wondered if he was going to kiss them.

'So happy you found time to see me, Steinunn,' he said, his voice a deep purr. 'I know how busy you must be.'

'I'm so sorry. I have forty minutes before I have to leave to see the Prime Minister,' Steinunn said. 'I really would like you to explain a few things for me before I see him.'

She gestured towards a deep sofa at one end of her office.

'Leave us, would you?' she said curtly. 'Give us twenty minutes.'

Steinunn's new adviser hesitated and looked ready to protest, but then nodded, quickly shepherding Ívar Laxdal and Gunna from the minister's presence.

'Let's leave them to it, shall we?'

'You're going to give us a cup of coffee and tell us what's really happening, are you?' Gunna suggested.

'Coffee I can do. Reality I'm not so good at,' he said. 'By the way, I'm Matthías, parachuted in to take Valgeir's place in the hot seat,' he added, striding along the corridor until he found an unoccupied office and closed the door behind them.

'I imagine you already know who we are and you've done some homework on Osman?' Ívar Laxdal said.

'I have. Valgeir gave me a run-down. I've also read what *Pulse* had to say about the minister's friend.'

'So where do we stand?' Gunna broke in. 'Do we have any idea what's happening?'

Matthías lifted a couple of thermos flasks on a sideboard until he found the one that wasn't empty.

'I don't know what's going on in there right now. She's under a heap of pressure at the moment and Osman isn't her priority.'

'What is?' Gunna asked.

'One is Kyle McCombie and the public meetings he's been holding, plus the Patriot Party that seems to have burst into existence overnight. Osman is number three for the moment, but he might shoot up to the top of the list once Steinunn has seen the PM.'

'Patriot Party?' Gunna asked. 'I'm sorry, I've been living under a rock for the last week and I have no idea what you're talking about.'

Matthías shrugged. 'It didn't exist until two days ago, and as far as I can see it exists mainly on social media. You know how these bubbles pop up and then disappear. The concern is that this might become a bubble that doesn't disappear.'

'Some kind of extremist movement?'

He nodded slowly. 'Pretty much. A nationalistic soapbox for people with anti-immigrant, pro-white views. The same as we've seen pop up in other countries. We just have to wait and see if it develops beyond Facebook into something tangible.'

'What are the odds?' Ívar Laxdal asked.

'No idea,' Matthías said after a moment's thought. 'It could be a flash in the pan that disappears as quickly as it began, and dies away now that McCombie has left the country and his sidekick leaves tonight.'

'Or it could become a movement that brings all the nutcases out into the open,' Gunna suggested. 'Do they all deserve a secret file like the lefties do?'

She reflected that Matthías's expression had nothing friendly or funny about it.

'Well, I'm fairly new. I only jumped in to cover for Valgeir at short notice,' he said with a smile that was even more wintry than before. 'But I've had a pretty in-depth briefing from the National Security Unit.'

'The terrible twins?' Ívar Laxdal asked.

'That's them,' Matthías said, and this time there was a spark of humour in his grin. 'I have as much of the picture on Osman as they have, and they've brought me up to speed on the Children of Freedom. So I'm probably better informed on all this than Steinunn is right now.'

'Or ever will be,' Gunna said, and immediately regretted her words as Ívar Laxdal scowled at her.

'It appears that the reason for McCombie's visit to Iceland was primarily to meet Osman. The meeting and the media noise is a sideshow that we expect to fizzle out,' Matthías said. 'They had a meeting at the Vatnsmýri Hotel, as you know.'

'Of course. I was there,' Gunna said.

'McCombie and the Children of Freedom are putting four million dollars into a venture that Osman is organizing.'

'What?' Ívar Laxdal demanded. 'How do you know this? Does Steinunn know?'

A wry smile flashed across the adviser's face before he replied.

'There was a listening device under the table, and I've listened to the recording of the entire conversation. We know exactly what they agreed. Four million dollars goes to White Sickle, and Osman's people will ensure that a shipment of arms and ammunition reaches a particular militia. The agreement was "the usual route", so while we don't know what route that is, we can conclude that this isn't the first time.'

'Hold on,' Gunna said. 'This isn't legal, surely? How did you manage to bug the right table at the hotel?'

'Of course it's not legal,' Matthías said with brusque impatience. 'But this isn't the kind of evidence that's going to end up in court, so let's just say it's vital information even though it's not legally admissible. As for the table, well, it wasn't possible to be sure where they would sit, so your colleagues had a listening device under every table in the room, plus one in his room. Just in case. The other material has been wiped, even though some of it would have been very interesting if I were a divorce lawyer.'

'Hell,' Ívar Laxdal swore under his breath. 'Does the PM know about this?'

'He will before Steinunn gets to his office.'

'And then?'

'She's going to have to make a choice,' Matthias said as his phone buzzed discreetly. He glanced at it and stood up. 'Steinunn,' he said. 'I'll be right back.'

Ana longed to sleep for another hour. She could feel the soreness in her eyes even before she'd opened them. She willed herself to get out of bed, not silencing the insistent buzzing from the phone until she had pulled on clothes and was sure she was awake.

Michel was dozing on the sofa and opened his eyes as she appeared.

'Coffee,' Ana muttered, heading for the bathroom.

She returned refreshed and alert to find the percolator spluttering and Michel with a questioning look on his face.

'What's the plan?'

'I need to check our boy's whereabouts. But it looks like we're disengaging, with or without a result.'

'Tomorrow?'

'Tonight. You'll be travelling home tomorrow.'

'That's a relief. I thought I was going to be stuck in this place for ever.'

He lifted an eyebrow as Ana took out the smartphone and waited for it to come to life.

'I thought . . .' he began.

'Yeah. I know what you're going to say,' she interrupted.

'No, I was just going to say I wondered how you always seemed to know where he is.'

'Only some of the time. It took a while to figure it out, but our guess is that there's a jamming system at the house, so we can only tap into his phone when he's away from there and it connects to a phone network.'

She peered at the screen, zoomed in on the map to identify the blue dot's position and nodded to herself.

'He's on the move,' she said, to herself rather than to Michel. 'He's not far away, but out of reach.'

'You mean he's at the police station?' Michel said with a bark of laughter.

'Somewhere even more secure than that. It looks like he's in the Parliament building. That's probably about as safe as he can be anywhere. Until he leaves,' she said. 'So we'll watch him come back, see what happens, and wait in case the plans change again.'

Matthías was back quickly, with a grim look on his chiselled face.

'Problem?' Gunna asked.

'We'll find out soon enough. There's a security alert at Hotel Vatnsmýri. I'm not sure what it is, but the Special Unit's there,' he said. 'That's the Special Unit guys we have left who aren't already watching Einholt.'

'No idea what's going on?'

'No. But it's serious. A fatality as far as I can make out, and a whole floor of the place has been closed off completely.' A bleak smile crossed his face. 'I expect you could find out more quickly than I could,' he said.

Ívar Laxdal got to his feet and walked over to the window, muttering into the microphone of his communicator.

'And our friend?' Gunna asked.

'Ah. You have an hour to relax,' Matthías said and shook the Thermos on the table again to check how much coffee was left in it. 'He's gone over to Parliament with a couple of the ministry people. Your colleague Úlfur and the guy from Brussels are with them.'

'It would be perfect if he were to come to grief just as I've put my feet up.'

'I think you've done enough already, Gunnhildur,' Matthías said with a look of respect in his eyes that told her he had heard about the intruder at Einholt.

Ívar Laxdal sat down heavily and took his earpiece out, scowling with frustration.

'One fatality on the eighth floor of the airline hotel. The deceased is a foreign national. That's all I can get out of them. Every officer in the city is there, apart from us.'

'Murder?' Gunna asked.

Ívar Laxdal shrugged.

'I'll tell you when I know,' he said. 'Osman's over at Parliament, so where's the minister?'

Matthías's bleak smile returned.

'She's with the PM. So I guess we'll find out in half an hour or so if she's still a minister.'

Hanne crunched through the frozen grass outside the hospital, wrapped in her thoughts. Yesterday had been bitterly cold but clear. Today there was a breath of warmth in the air, as if winter was thinking about giving way to spring, but not right away.

They had been through Blönduós before, spending the night in the campsite in the middle of the little town. On the way out, they had passed the hospital on the outskirts without realizing what it was, or knowing that many of its facilities had been shut down and shifted to Akureyri in the north or to the Reykjavík hospitals.

Clouds had settled on the mountains in the distance, low and heavy, the grey merging with the grey water of the bay beyond the town, little more than a village as far as Hanne could see.

She clenched her fists in their thick woollen gloves and strode across the road, looking both ways and not seeing a car anywhere in sight.

'I'm looking for the police station,' she said to the first person she encountered in the civic offices. It hadn't been a long walk – not long enough for her to change her mind and go back to the hospital.

'Through there,' the man said with a bleak smile, pointing a finger. 'I'm not sure there's anyone there right now. But you might be in luck.'

Hanne pushed open the door.

'Hello?'

'Hi.' The police officer who had hurried her into the ambulance the day before gave her a welcoming grin. 'How's Carsten?'

'He's very weak and he's not happy. He's had a huge fright,' she said. 'We've both had a huge fright. But he's alive.'

'Pleased to hear it. I expect he'll be well enough to fly home soon.'

'I don't know . . .' Hanne said. Going home wasn't something she had thought about, and now she realized that she would have to decide what would come next.

'I expect they'll transfer him to Reykjavík as soon as he's stable.'

'I'm sure they'll let us know. They've been so good over there at the hospital. I . . .'

'Yes?'

'Well, first I wanted to thank you for everything you did yesterday. You and your colleague were fantastic. And thank you so much for bringing the camper for us. I couldn't have driven it yesterday.'

'All part of the job,' he said, going from jovial to concerned as he picked up on Hanne's uncertainty. 'Is there a problem?'

Hanne sank into a chair and felt her hands trembling.

'Yesterday. At the place where . . .'

'Staðarskáli, yes.'

'That's right. As we were leaving, I saw a newspaper there, just for a moment, with a man's face on the cover.'

His eyes narrowed.

'Do you know which newspaper?'

She shook her head. 'I didn't see the name, but it had a red border.'

He left the room and she could hear him rummaging through papers.

'This one?' he asked, a folded newspaper in his hand.

'I think so.'

'This is yesterday's paper,' he said, unfolding it and looking at the cover. He pointed at the CCTV picture of a burly man. 'This man? What about him?'

'I've seen him. It's a long story.'

Skúli found himself trembling with nerves as the car made leisurely progress up the long slope. He furiously debated with himself whether or not he was doing the right thing, certain that Lars's murder had to be linked to his having revealed the reality behind Osman's organisation. He told himself that Lars deserved someone making an effort to get to the truth, by some means or other, and the key had to be the man at the centre of it all, hidden away in Steinunn Strand's second home.

Skúli stopped at a busy filling station by the main road and pumped fuel into the tank while his mind buzzed with conflicting opinions.

He moved the car away from the pump and went inside the building, where he sat at a bright red plastic bench and drank a cup of rank coffee that the first sip told him he didn't really want after all.

'You all right, pal?'

He looked up to see a man in a blue overall looking down at him with concern, and realized that he had shut the world out as he'd hunched over his coffee, his head in his hands.

'Yeah,' he muttered. 'I'm all right. Just a headache,' he added meekly.

He wondered how long he'd been sitting there wrapped in his own thoughts, and realized with a sudden shock that he hadn't told anyone where he was going. If anything were to go wrong, nobody would know where he was.

Turn round and go back to the office? Or call in sick and go home?

Those were two options. Or he could keep going. What would Lars have done?

His father and brothers suddenly came to mind, unbidden and unwelcome. What would they do?

'You'd better get your DNA checked, Dad. I'm not sure Skúli's one of us.'

His eldest brother's mocking jibe surfaced suddenly when his patience ran dry and he aired an opinion, knowing beforehand that nobody else present would share his point of view. That had been the last Christmas he had spent in the family home. An argument had been brewing for hours as his brothers had swapped business gossip with their father, while Skúli had sat in silence, excluded from their banter.

'I don't know,' the other brother had drawled. 'I always thought he was a gay, but now he's got a girlfriend, there could be hope for him yet.'

Skúli had ground his teeth. He hadn't mentioned his relationship with Dagga to the family, but gossip had a habit of moving alarmingly fast around Reykjavík. It had made him long to be back in Denmark, where nobody knew or cared that he was Eggert Snædal's youngest son.

He swung the car off the main road at Grafarholt and began to wonder if he was on the right road as he drove through the suburbs, using the bulk of Korpúlfsstaðir – once an out-of-town landmark, now firmly surrounded by housing estates – as his reference point for the map he had in his mind.

He made a few wrong turns, reversed out of silent dead-end streets, and eventually found the tarmac give way to a gravel track as he finally saw Einholt for himself. The place hadn't been easy to find, even though he knew exactly where it was. The narrow gravel track at the far extremity of what looked like a cul-de-sac kept Einholt hidden, and he had no doubt that the house's owners preferred it that way.

The low house, with its narrow windows on the landward side, hunched in a dip in the tussocky scrub that undulated down to the shore beyond, the track looping round to reach the seaward side of the house, which was out of sight. Beyond, he made out the brooding mass of Geldinganes and, on the inland side, the last of a line of houses at the end of the housing estate, which stopped a kilometre of heather-covered ground short of Einholt.

As he wondered whether to park by the track and walk, or drive right up to the house, he reflected how isolated this place must have been in the past. Only a few years earlier there had been no houses here at all, and Einholt must have been well beyond the city limits. Yet here, almost inside the city, it had been left as a secluded enclave that hardly anyone other than the occasional bird-watcher visited. It was little surprise that Steinunn Strand had been a firm opponent of further housing development in this direction back when she had sat on the city council.

Birna brought them an update, pushing open the door and stuttering.

'There's a massive alert,' she said finally. Gunna watched her clench and unclench her fists as she sat down.

'And?' Ívar Laxdal rasped. 'What's happened?'

'A fatality at the Vatnsmýri Hotel. The victim is James Kearney, the young guy you saw there a few days ago with Kyle McCombie.'

Ívar Laxdal looked blank for a moment and Gunna filled the gap.

'The sidekick? You're sure it's murder and not an accident?'

'Strangled,' Birna said. 'I saw the body. No doubt about it.'

'Any details?'

'It must have happened this morning, because he had breakfast in the restaurant. There was a Do Not Disturb hanger on his door, so he was left alone, and he had booked a late checkout. It wasn't until he wasn't there to meet someone from that brand-new Patriot Party who was supposed to be taking him to the airport that the staff checked the room and found him in the bathtub.'

Gunna glanced at Ívar Laxdal, just as Matthías returned.

'Where's Osman?' Gunna snapped.

'Still over at Parliament. Why?'

'You'd best get him back here fast,' Gunna replied, and turned to Birna. 'Better still, go over to Parliament and haul him back here right away. Then we can get him back to Einholt as quick as we can.'

Birna sat with her mouth half open for a second, then shut it quickly and stood up.

Matthías looked from one to the other as Birna left the room at a trot.

'What's all that about?'

'The victim over at the Vatnsmýri Hotel is Kyle McCombie's sidekick,' Ívar Laxdal said. 'We're going to have to get Osman away quickly.'

'Shit!' Matthías breathed. 'A US citizen murdered in Iceland, and not just some redneck tourist. This could be a real crisis.'

'Yep. It can be someone else's crisis,' Gunna told him. 'We have other stuff to worry about. Are you going to tell Steinunn we have something of an emergency on our hands?'

'I'll tell her,' he said and the wintry smile returned. 'But she has a crisis of her own to manage.'

Ívar Laxdal shook his head.

'What now? Don't tell me she's been sacked.'

'Steinunn has been given a golden handshake, and I have to hand it to the PM, he could hardly have done it more elegantly.'

'And?'

'Steinunn stands down with immediate effect as both a Member of Parliament and a minister. She gets a job as the deputy director-general of the United Nations World Tourism Organization. That means she goes to live in Madrid for five years and gets a fat UN pension at the end of it. This isn't to become public knowledge right away, mind.'

'So the PM gets rid of his biggest bugbear,' Ívar Laxdal said, 'while she gets a comfortable berth, and nobody loses face.'

'I told you the PM was a sly bastard, didn't I?'

'Are you sure about this?' Michel grumbled.

Ana checked the smartphone for the blue dot as she shivered in the chill of the gathering dusk. They were on the lee side of the headland, but this still gave them little shelter from the wind.

'He's moving,' she said. 'Coming this way. I reckon we have about twenty minutes.'

'Are you sure about this? It's the busiest time of the day.' He gestured towards the line of lights making slow progress in the distance. 'I don't like it. Too many people about.'

'Exactly,' Ana retorted. 'We finish the job, and in two minutes we're on our way where nobody's going to be looking for us. And by then it'll be dark, which is even better.'

'If you say so,' Michel grunted.

He assembled the long rifle carefully, placing it on its bipod and snapping a magazine into place.

'You know, if I was them,' he said as the parts clicked together, jerking a thumb towards Einholt, 'this is about the first place I would have swept before putting anyone down there in a safe house.'

'But you're not them.'

'So I'm asking myself why? Is there a reason they didn't check this place out? What was it anyway?'

'I don't think there's ever been anything here. Maybe just a few sheep, and that was a long time ago,' Ana replied and squatted on her haunches, watching Michel lie carefully down behind the rifle, shifting to make himself comfortable. The weapon slotted into his grasp as if it belonged there. He squinted through the sights and sucked his teeth.

'It's extreme range for this thing,' he said doubtfully.

'But you've calibrated the sights, haven't you?'

'Of course,' Michel said, his voice laden with disdain that she should even suggest the weapon might not be ready.

'So what's your problem?'

'This is a bargain-basement imitation of a sniper's rifle and it's good for around nine hundred metres. That looks more than a thousand.' He shivered as the sharp breeze nipped at his face and ears. 'At least in Africa when we did this kind of thing it was warm.'

'Well, tomorrow you can be in Africa, if that's what suits you.'

* * *

The car's suspension groaned in protest as Skúli bumped it as gently as he could through the potholes. He heard the grinding from the exhaust as it scraped over the ground more than once, holding his breath and wondering if he'd done any damage.

He suddenly imagined Dagga slowly shaking her head, lips pursed, which was her usual reaction when something displeased or disappointed her. This time there would be no pursed lips when he brought the car back with its exhaust intact.

Skúli wondered what the reception would be at Einholt, assuming he was in the right place.

Sif Strand had finally confirmed that this was where her aunt's mysterious guest was staying, although he'd already formed an idea that the farmhouse, which had become an exclusive residence, was the most likely place.

The car bumped off the worst part of the track and onto the smoother stretch leading to the house, before coasting down the last of the slope to a crunching halt in the gravel.

The place was silent. There were no cars to be seen, no lights in any windows, even though it would soon be dusk.

Skúli sat stiffly in the car. Was he too late? Had Osman been moved elsewhere? Or had he left the country?

All the possibilities passed through his mind like a kaleidoscope of vivid images, each one telling him that he had gone wrong, should have acted earlier, ought to have been quicker off the mark and now he had missed out.

He swore quietly to himself. It was an old habit. A profanity when he had been growing up had meant a punishment of some kind, and he had never got into the habit of swearing profusely in English as most of his contemporaries had.

Getting out of the car, only the shrill calls of birds could be heard over the rush, rattle and hiss of the surf on the stones of the beach.

Osman arrived with a frown on his face and Birna at his elbow.

'What is happening?' he asked, his voice soft but determined. 'Is there a problem?'

'Several,' Ívar Laxdal said shortly, a finger to his ear as he listened to his earpiece.

Gunna glanced at him and Ívar Laxdal nodded imperceptibly.

'The situation is that James Kearney has lost his life,' she said, keeping her voice flat and watching carefully for a reaction.

Osman's eyes widened in surprise.

'James . . . ? I was talking to him only . . .'

'Yes, we know. I was there as well,' Gunna reminded him. 'This is all getting uglier by the day. People seem to get suddenly dead when they get close to you. Who could have done this? You seem to have known him well, so do you have any idea who would want to harm him?'

'No, of course not. I've been in contact with James, and with Kyle, for some time. But I have only met them in person a couple of times. How did this happen? An accident?'

Gunna shot a questioning look at Ívar Laxdal, but Birna answered instead.

'It was not an accident,' she said curtly.

'And Kyle?' Osman asked. 'Is Kyle safe?'

'Mr McCombie could hardly be safer,' Birna said.

Osman looked from face to grim face.

'I am shocked,' he said finally. 'Do you know who did this? Do you have the person?'

'I don't know the details, but we have to get you back to Einholt right now,' Ívar Laxdal said, and muttered into his communicator.

Gunna pulled on her fleece and zipped it up, hiding the Glock from view.

'Where is Steinunn? I ought to speak to her,' Osman said.

'I'm sorry, but that's not possible,' Matthías said from the doorway.

Osman's eyes flashed.

'Why? Is she not here?'

'I'm sorry, but Steinunn is with the Prime Minister right now and they're not to be disturbed,' Matthías lied with a smooth half-smile. 'I'm sure she'll be in touch as soon as she's available. But as

I'm sure you understand, there's an unprecedented situation that she and the PM are closely concerned with.'

'And Kyle? Where is Kyle?'

'His flight left the country last night,' Ívar Laxdal said. 'Come on. Steingrímur is outside with a squad car so we can get an escort back to Einholt.'

'Something's happening,' Michel said, his eye to the sights of the rifle. 'There's someone there.'

Ana looked up from the smartphone in her hand and frowned.

'Police?' she asked. 'The target is moving now and fast enough to be in a vehicle, but that can't be him.'

'No. It's a guy in a crappy old 206. He's got out of the car and is walking round the house.'

Ana took a compact pair of binoculars from her backpack and focused on Einholt.

'No idea,' she said eventually. 'Someone lost? A pizza delivery? What the fuck are they playing at?'

Michel watched through the rifle's sight, the cross hairs neatly intersecting across Skúli's chest as he stood on the seaward side of the house, gazing at the imposing bulk of Geldinganes.

'Take him out if you like?' he suggested with a snigger.

'Don't talk such shit,' Ana snapped, eyes on the smartphone's screen again. 'The last thing we want to do is tell them where we are before the target shows up, and he's moving this way.'

'I'm joking,' he said sharply, and settled back to look through the sights. 'No point knocking off some guy who's just delivering a takeaway. But if it was the guy who shot Pino, then he'd be pretty high on my list,' he grunted.

'Target first,' Ana said. 'Settling scores comes a long way behind.'

'Hey, wait a moment. There's company. Let's see how good these guys are.'

The suddenness of it took Skúli by completely surprise. There was no warning until a voice bellowed so loudly that he almost missed his footing and fell over.

'Stay where you are,' the voice roared in English. 'Hands over your head right now.'

Skúli looked from side to side in confusion, slowly raising his arms.

Hands grabbed his shoulders and propelled him hard against the wall, knocking the breath out of him, and he gasped as his face was pushed into the concrete. A moment later his hands were hauled hard behind his back and cuffed, before the door was opened and he was half-dragged, half-pushed inside.

He could hear voices muttering behind him and lifted his head, only to find it roughly shoved back down; the hands rapidly went through his pockets, extracting everything from them and heaping the contents on the tiles.

His head was buzzing by the time he was hauled into a sitting position and propped against the wall, by which time he realized he had failed to notice that cable ties had been used to bind his ankles together.

One black-clad man squatted next to him, hard blue eyes glaring through the holes of a balaclava that hid the rest of his face, while a second cradled a sinister black machine gun in his arms as he muttered into a microphone on his jacket.

The squad car was ahead of them, its flashing lights and occasional bursts from its siren clearing a path through the late afternoon traffic. They were quickly past the city centre and took Sæbraut at a steady speed until the siren howled again as they slipped onto the cloverleaf interchange and up onto Vesturlandsvegur, heading out of the city.

Ívar Laxdal drove, while Gunna sat in the back with Osman, his face etched with concern.

Gunna's communicator burst into life and she listened.

'Understood,' she replied. 'I'll be back to you in a few minutes.'

'Problem? Another one?' Ívar Laxdal asked from the driving seat.

'Something's up,' Gunna replied as the squad car ahead of them took the next slip road off into another cloverleaf and the traffic lights ahead of them changed neatly to green as they approached. She clicked her communicator again.

'Steingrímur, we have a problem. Pull over when you get a chance, will you? There's a trading estate up ahead at Fossaleynir and we should be out of sight there.'

Osman's eyes went from Gunna to Ívar Laxdal and back.

'What's going on, Gunnhildur?' he asked.

'We don't know, but we don't want to take any chances,' she replied as the lights of the squad car ahead turned off and they followed it down a side road, coming to a halt outside a row of industrial units.

'Come and talk to us, will you?' Gunna muttered into her communicator and saw the squad car's door swing open and Steingrímur's long figure unfold itself.

'What's happening?' he asked, shutting the Volvo's door behind him as he twisted round in the passenger seat.

'An intruder at Einholt. The pair from the watch post yomped down there as soon as they saw this person show up and took him by surprise. No identification so far. That's about all we know.'

'Shit, hell and damnation.'

Ívar Laxdal's fist hammered the steering wheel in front of him.

Gunna glanced sideways at Osman.

'As you've probably guessed, we have a problem. There's an intruder at Einholt and we're not going anywhere near until we have an idea of what's going on.'

'It's not just that we don't know what's going on up there,' Ívar Laxdal said. 'We also don't know how far security has been compromised, who knows you've been staying at Einholt, and so on.'

'And I thought Iceland was such a safe country,' Osman said softly.

'It was until you turned up. Now suddenly we have two corpses and a possible international incident to deal with,' Ívar Laxdal rasped back. 'So what are the options? A cell at Hverfisgata would be my ideal choice,' he said. 'We need somewhere so secure it'll throw off any pursuit, reset the clock.'

'We can do that,' Gunna said. 'It won't be comfortable, but we can do it.'

'Nothing?' Michel asked. He lay behind the rifle, huddled with his arms folded in front of him, watching through a pair of binoculars balanced on a stone.

'They've stopped,' Ana said, frowning as she watched the blue dot that hadn't moved for twenty minutes. 'And it's going to be dark really soon.'

'So this is a no-show?'

'Let's see. We don't need to be in a hurry, but we need to figure out if they're coming this way or not.'

Michel got stiffly to his feet and stretched his arms.

'Careful,' Ana admonished. 'Don't let yourself be seen.'

'Just going to empty the tank,' he said, unzipping his drysuit and walking away.

Ana shifted into his position behind the binoculars and watched as a vehicle came down the track to Einholt. It came to a halt in front of the door and three figures got out.

'Anything?' Michel asked.

'Luc, there you are,' Ana said to herself and chuckled, this time with her eye to the rifle's sight as she made out the figure of the little man in his shabby grey suit.

'Someone you recognize?' Michel asked, lying down next to her. 'An old friend?'

'Not exactly a friend; he'd happily lock us both up and throw away the key. It's a guy from State Security. He looks like a cuddly teddy bear with a bad hangover, but he's as sharp as a razor.'

'You speak from experience?'

'No. Fortunately not. But he has a reputation and he's someone to keep clear of.'

'Change of plans,' Ívar Laxdal said as Steingrímur got out and went back to the squad car, and Osman's eyes opened wide in unspoken question.

Ívar Laxdal swung the black Volvo out of the car park back into the traffic. Darkness was falling, bringing a sharp frost with it as the weak winter sun dipped out of sight.

'Where are we going?' he asked as Ívar Laxdal's Volvo rejoined the afternoon crush of traffic heading for the city centre.

'Since your safety's compromised, we have something special lined up for you,' Gunna told him, suppressing a smile.

'We aren't going back to Steinunn's house?'

'No. We're going somewhere else.'

'And my things? My computer and the rest?'

'Steingrímur will bring your belongings.'

Osman looked suspicious.

'Gunnhildur, what is this?' he asked, his voice hardening in concern. 'Have they bought you?'

'What?' Gunna said in surprise. 'Don't be ridiculous. Like I told you, we're going somewhere these people won't be able to follow, and as Ívar and I are the only ones who know where we're going, there's no chance of a security leak.'

'You're sure?'

Ívar Laxdal kept the Volvo moving through the traffic, slowing for lights and powering through them as they changed to green, ensuring there would be no opportunity for anyone to approach the stationary car anywhere along the way. It was only when they were in the thickest of the late afternoon traffic that Ívar Laxdal had no choice but to stop, his eyes darting from mirror to mirror.

Gunna leaned over to Osman, who was sitting very straight, concern on his face as the orange lights by the road flashed across his face, rigid with concern.

'Tell me, Osman. Who knew you were here?'

'Why do you ask?' he replied quickly, startled by her question.

'Because someone knew about your movements and we want to either find them and put them away, or at least keep you away from them. The man who came to Einholt . . .'

'The man you killed, Gunnhildur.'

Gunna gulped, felt her heart race for a second, and told herself to concentrate.

'The man with a gun who was looking for you. He was here in Iceland several days before you, before *we* knew you were coming. They were prepared. So who knew? The aircrew of the jet you arrived in?'

Osman shook his head.

'The jet is owned by one of our benefactors. The crew didn't know until an hour before we left that I was the passenger.'

'All right, your staff?'

'The foundation only has three staff and I can vouch for them all. They are all thoroughly dedicated and I trust every one of them. As well as that, without me there is no foundation and they would have no jobs.'

'Unless they were paid a serious amount of money? Or blackmailed, threatened?'

'Of course it's possible. But I don't believe so.'

'All right. Who else?'

'The obvious ones. Steinunn. You.'

'Not me,' Gunna replied. 'I didn't know who you were until you got off the plane, and whoever is after your skin knew long before that you were on the way to Iceland, long enough to prepare.'

'That's it. Steinunn. My three colleagues.'

'And the American guy,' Gunna reminded him. 'He knew you were here. When did the Children of Freedom know about your movements?'

Osman glared.

'Kyle is like a brother to me. I trust him completely.'

'Maybe. But maybe Kyle told someone he was coming here to meet you, and what about the guy he was with?'

'James . . . ? I don't know,' Osman admitted and the first glimmer of doubt appeared on his face.

'Almost there,' Ívar Laxdal grunted from the front seat.

'So,' Gunna continued, 'from my point of view, it seems your security is full of holes. Steinunn may have informed her staff that you were coming, and they may have told someone else. You understand? Or it could have been one of your people, although I'm inclined to discount that if you're so certain they're trustworthy.

231

Or the Children of Freedom? If you had to make a guess, which one would it be? What's your gut feeling?'

Ívar Laxdal brought the Volvo to a gentle halt.

'Where are we?' Osman asked, looking out in to the darkness and leaving Gunna's question unanswered.

'This is your route out of the city, and nobody has a hope in hell of following you,' Ívar Laxdal said, grinning over his shoulder in the darkness as he opened his door. 'But it's a windy night so it's not going to be comfortable.'

'We've lost him,' Ana said.

'Sure?'

'Yeah. The signal's back in the city centre now and there's something strange going on there.'

'Like what?'

'I'm not sure. The signal's right down by the harbour.'

'It's all restaurants down there. Maybe they've gone for dinner and we can sit it out until they get back?'

She switched off the smartphone and stowed it in an inside pocket.

'We disengage. They wanted a snatch, but we can't pull that off here. I reckon they really want this guy alive so it doesn't look like they're going to authorize a kill. My decision, we pull out and wait for the target to relocate. It'll be a lot easier to deal with him once he's back in Europe.'

'Yeah? So no bonus.'

'No bonus . . . yet,' Ana told him. 'Come on, break everything down and we'll make our way back.'

He got to his knees and began to dismantle the rifle and pack it into its case, while Ana watched Einholt in the distance. Nothing had changed and nobody had left the building.

'Done. Are we taking this with us, or stashing it here?'

'Bury it,' Ana instructed, disappearing into the deepening gloom. A fierce rain shower had come out of nowhere and beat down for a few moments, simultaneously hiding the lights at Einholt across the bay.

Ana carried the two packs down to the beach, where their kayaks lay on the stones. She quickly turned over the one Michel had used and knelt down, fumbling at the same time for a stone big enough to fit her hand comfortably. She dealt the kayak one sharp blow with the stone, hoping it would be enough, and was satisfied to see that a long crack had appeared in the plastic before she righted it again.

At the lookout position Michel scraped a hole in the wet earth, rolling aside stones until it was deep enough for the black case to be covered with a thin layer of soil.

'What was that noise?' he asked when Ana reappeared.

'What noise?'

'Just now. A bang.'

'Nothing. I slipped on the rocks and caught my elbow on one of the kayaks.'

She knelt down beside him and together they rolled a few stones on top of the hole where he'd placed the weapon, in a rough triangle shape that was enough to mark the spot.

'Happy with that?'

'No. Not really. But we don't have a lot of choice. Come on. There's no point hanging around here.'

Steingrímur appeared out of the darkness, with Osman's bag slung over his shoulder and a laptop case in his hand.

'Here's the gear,' he grunted. 'You're sure about this, Gunna?'

'If I wasn't sure, we wouldn't be here,' she replied. 'Drop those by the gate. Our pal can carry his own luggage from now on.'

Steingrímur sniffed the wind.

'Rather you than me on a night like this,' he said.

'It'll be fine. A bit of a breeze blows away the cobwebs. All I want you to do is go back to Einholt and make it look like nothing's changed. All right?'

Steingrímur vanished back into the darkness. Gunna punched a series of numbers into a keypad on a high steel mesh gate and watched it swing open. Osman followed, bags in his hands, the wind tugging at the tails of his coat.

'Gunnhildur,' he said, his voice plaintive with anxiety. 'Where are we going?'

'Watch your feet,' she instructed. 'It can be slippery here.'

The pontoon echoed under her feet as she marched past the boats tied up to their finger berths.

'Here we are,' she told Osman, sitting on the gunwale and swinging her feet over and onto the deck of the boat. 'Pass me your stuff and jump aboard.'

Osman followed in a daze, watching as Gunna unlocked the door to the little wheelhouse. She used the torch in her phone to light her way, and pointed to a narrow bench at one side.

'Sit there,' she instructed and disappeared through a low opening. A moment later lights flickered into life and her face appeared at the top of the couple of steps to the cabin.

'Bags?'

Osman handed them to her without a word and they disappeared into the cabin. A grubby orange overall was thrown into the opening and Gunna clambered over it back to the wheelhouse, before going back out into the darkness on deck.

Osman could hear the bang of a hatch being opened, and he peered into the night and saw Ívar Laxdal swing himself over the gunwale.

'Everything in order, Gunnhildur?'

Gunna scrambled back on deck and closed the hatch behind her.

'All shipshape. I'll just turn her over, then you can throw the ropes off.'

'I should be doing this, you know.'

'I reckon I can manage as the skipper on my own boat.'

'Your boat?' Ívar Laxdal asked in surprise.

'Well. Let's say it's half my boat and I know my way around it, so it's going to be fine. I'll tell you the story later. Right now I'm more concerned about our guest.'

Ívar Laxdal shrugged grudging agreement as Gunna turned the key on the wheelhouse dashboard, pressed the starter and the engine grunted, hesitated and gurgled into life before settling into a reassuring rumble below their feet. An alarm whined for a few seconds and faded away.

Osman sat on the bench, his smart topcoat and polished shoes incongruous under the brightness of the wheelhouse lights. Gunna watched as the electronics came to life and nodded to herself, satisfied that everything was working.

'Ready,' she called out to Ívar Laxdal and followed him out on deck. He stepped onto the gunwale, steadied himself with a hand on the wheelhouse roof and jumped for the pontoon.

'Let go aft,' he intoned and Gunna coiled the rope away.

'Let go forward,' she said. 'We don't need to spring off here.'

Ívar Laxdal stretched to hand the forward rope over the gunwale and Gunna stowed it away.

'Have a good trip. Give me a call when you're there,' he instructed as Gunna slipped the engine into gear and eased the lever forward until the engine's rumble grew to a roar.

The boat moved smoothly away from the pontoon and its pool of light. Gunna waved to Ívar Laxdal as he became an indistinct shadow on the quay. She left the wheelhouse door hooked open, went to the controls inside and clicked off the lights, leaving Osman in the gloom, with only the faint glow from the radar to see by as she spun the wheel with one hand, the other on the throttle.

'Gunnhildur,' he asked. 'Where are we going?'

Gunna pressed a button a couple of times to increase the scale on the radar display and pointed at the corner of a green shape that covered the top half of the screen.

'There,' she said. 'That's where we're going. And you'd better put that on,' she added, pointing at the orange suit on the top step. 'It's a cold night.'

Skúli had been propped on a chair in a bedroom. Once the two men in black had heard him speak Icelandic, their guard relaxed and one of them snipped the cable ties at his ankles, although the handcuffs still manacled his wrists together.

'What's going on here?' he asked, trying and failing to sound angry and truculent. 'Why am I being held like this?'

The two men exchanged glances and one shook his head.

'Well?' Skúli demanded. 'Do you . . . ?' he said and stopped himself.

He realized with a sick feeling that he had almost asked them if they knew who he was, and while Eggert Snædal's name undoubtedly carried weight, he immediately despised himself for having almost fallen into the trap of using it.

'You're not supposed to say anything, right?'

'Right,' one of the masked men confirmed.

'Who are you? Police, or what?'

'The National Commissioner's Special Unit,' the shorter of the two men said, leaving the room and closing the door behind him. 'And that's all you need to know, so save your breath.'

Skúli sat in the half-darkness for what seemed an age, listening to doors open and close as people came and went. He wondered whether to shout and complain, but decided to follow the man's advice and sat quietly until one of them finally came to fetch him, leading him to the kitchen and pushing him onto a chair.

Ívar Laxdal walked straight past him, went to the counter and filled the percolator.

'All quiet apart from . . . ?' he asked, jerking his head in Skúli's direction.

'All quiet.'

'Good,' Ívar Laxdal said as the percolator hissed and bubbled. 'Thanks for your efforts, gentlemen. Good to know that you're on the ball. You can stand down now.'

The two figures in black withdrew silently without a word or a backward glance. Ívar Laxdal pottered in the kitchen while the two men and the woman muttered in English over a laptop on the table where cups and plates had been pushed aside.

'Well, Skúli,' Ívar Laxdal said at last, handing him a mug of coffee that he had no choice but to take in both hands. 'Ah, I see the gentlemen of the Special Unit have been thorough,' he muttered to himself and fished in his trouser pocket for a bunch of keys.

He unlocked and snapped open the handcuffs, depositing them on the table. Skúli rubbed his wrists.

'They were fairly gentle with you, I gather. No broken bones, just a little injured pride, maybe?'

Skúli recalled the indignity of being slammed against the wall outside and the speed and force with which he had been cuffed and hauled inside.

'I suppose so,' he admitted. 'A few bruises, though.'

'What brings Eggert Snædal's black sheep of a boy up here?' Ívar Laxdal said. 'As if I didn't know already, but I want to hear it from you.'

'Osman,' he said shortly, and the three faces around the laptop looked up sharply. 'But you probably knew that.'

'I read your article, and the one your opposite number in France produced. I'm impressed at the information you pulled together, and most of it was remarkably accurate.'

'Accurate, meaning there was stuff there you didn't know?'

Ívar Laxdal smiled briefly.

'Possibly. But tell me why you were so determined to track our guest down? Incidentally, he has left and won't be coming back here.'

'He's left the country?'

'Possibly,' Ívar Laxdal said.

'That's a very cautious answer,' Skúli replied. 'I imagine you've moved him somewhere quieter.' He sighed and felt a wave of fatigue rise through him. He was still trembling from the shock the two men in black had given him, and his head was buzzing. 'A friend of mine was working on Osman, and he was murdered, as you know. I don't know who by. I wanted to confront Osman, ask him face-to-face if it's true that his foundation is a massive money-laundering scheme and that he's up to his neck in trading arms and desperate people. That's why I came here today. I didn't imagine I was going to get an answer, but I felt I couldn't live with myself if I didn't ask the question.'

Ívar Laxdal looked at Skúli with grudging respect.

'That was remarkably courageous of you, considering what happened to your friend.'

'His name was Lars Bundgaard. He worked for a human rights

organization called Plain Truth, and he was shot in his apartment in Antwerp.'

'Antwerp?' Ívar Laxdal got to his feet. 'Luc? Would you?'

The pair of them went to the far end of the long lounge and talked in an undertone, before he came back and sat next to Skúli again.

'Your friend's death is being investigated. That's all I can tell you. That's all I know.'

'And now that Steinunn presumably knows all about Osman, is he being kicked out of the country?'

'Steinunn . . .' Ívar Laxdal said with a smile. 'She has other things on her mind at the moment, what with the death at the Vatnsmýri Hotel . . .'

'What?'

'I guess you didn't know? It's been on the news already, and I think it was your colleague Agnar who reported it first, admittedly by a very narrow margin. James Kearney, one of the two members of Children of Freedom present in Iceland, was found dead in his hotel room today. So Steinunn is in the middle of an international incident, considering the controversial nature of the man's visit.'

'Shit.'

'As you so rightly say, shit. Watch the news in the morning. Steinunn will have something to say, but probably not what you're expecting.' Ívar Laxdal stretched. 'And now, young man, I have work to do, so you'd better go home. Your wife is probably wondering where you've got to.'

'I'm not under arrest?'

'What for? You blundered into a security area, but you can hardly have been aware of that. There's the trivial matter of trespassing on private property, but I don't imagine the house's owner will have any inclination to pursue that.'

'I thought . . .'

'Well, you thought wrong. Go home, Skúli. And keep your head down. There's nothing more you can do for your dead friend.'

★ ★ ★

The two kayaks slipped into the water as another furious squall of rain battered Geldinganes, beating down with an intensity that blotted out the lights of the city which should have greeted them as they passed the outer point. There the wind also set a chop to the waves that buffeted the two tiny boats.

Ana concentrated on the GPS set strapped to her wrist, making sure that Michel's kayak stayed close, until he called out.

'Hey! I've sprung a leak!'

'What?' she called back.

'A leak,' he yelled in fury. 'How the fuck did that happen?'

Ana back-paddled to bring herself level with him.

'What's the problem?'

'This thing's leaking. It's not going to make it.'

'You'd best paddle fast, get as far as you can while it's still afloat.'

He dug the paddle deep into the water, and Ana had to admire the man's animal strength, powering the almost submerged kayak through the waves while she fought to keep pace with him, until it finally gave way and he swam free of it.

'How far? Come closer so I can hold on to your boat.'

'You'll pull it under. You'll have to swim the rest. It's not far.'

Michel swam a steady breast stroke, making heavy going against the waves, and Ana could see that he was tiring rapidly.

With a few quick strokes of her paddle, she brought the kayak close up behind him and fumbled for the carpet knife stowed inside her kayak. She reached out and slashed at Michel's back, the razor-sharp blade slicing a long gash in his suit. He yelled in shock as the freezing water flooded into it.

'What? My fucking suit's split!'

He trod water for a moment and looked around in desperation as she let the knife drop into the water.

'Help me, will you?'

Ana back-paddled again and watched him without a word as he fought to swim towards her, weighed down by the suit as it filled with water.

'Ana! Help me . . .'

She was surprised at how long he lasted, impressed by the man's stamina as he swore, threatened and set off for the nearest shore-line, too hopelessly distant for him to reach. The hatred in his eyes once he realized she was going to let him die was no surprise, but she decided against telling him it was nothing personal. From the moment she'd seen his face on the TV news bulletin, there had been no other way that this was going to end.

'You let him go?' Birna said in disbelief as Skúli's car bumped along the track away from Einholt.

'What do we need to keep him here for? He hasn't committed a crime and I've no intention of going before an inquiry to explain why he'd been held against his will. Not that there would ever be an inquiry,' he added.

'And where's Osman?' she asked. 'Why isn't he here?'

'He's in Gunnhildur's hands, until such time as we can put him on a flight, and I don't think there will be any real objections now that Steinunn's position is changing.'

'You know about that?' Úlfur asked.

'It's my job to know things,' Ívar Laxdal replied stiffly.

Luc had been listening to the exchange and held up a hand.

'If you don't mind me interrupting,' he said, 'I have some information for you.'

He raised his phone to show them a picture of a man glowering from the screen.

'The dead man?' Birna asked.

'Your victim,' he said.

'And?'

Luc's finger swept and stabbed at the screen.

'His name's Carlos Pino. South American origin of some kind, according to my contact in Paris. He's been living in Bulgaria for the last ten years. No criminal record.'

Birna frowned.

'So why's he on your system?'

'As a person of interest. He had a military background and had been a security consultant, which means he was a mercenary, active mainly in Africa. He was part of a group providing security for an oil company about five years ago and they found themselves outgunned and outnumbered. A French unit bailed them out, interrogated them all, photographed and fingerprinted each one before they let them wait a week to get on a transport flight to Europe.'

'They weren't arrested?'

Luc shrugged. 'They hadn't committed any crime in Europe, so I think the French just wanted to get rid of them. But they've been keeping tabs, and this guy has been flagged up as having been active in the region again since. Not that he'll be doing that any more.'

'Where do we send the body?' Ívar Laxdal asked, saying what everyone had been thinking. 'You said South American, so Chile? Argentina? Wherever he's from, it wouldn't be a surprise if they're quite happy for him to be quietly buried here.'

'They may well say he's nothing to do with them,' Luc said with another laconic shrug.

'So who was he working for? And why was he here?' Úlfur asked.

'Who knows? But he wasn't here for the scenery or the nightlife.'

The boat bucked and juddered. Spray cascaded over the windows of the wheelhouse that was just big enough for Gunna to perch on the stool, its steel stalk bolted to the floor, with a hand on the wheel as she peered into the darkness while Osman's face became progressively paler.

'The weather,' he said. 'Is this safe?'

'I've slowed down so it'll be more comfortable. But it's still going to be bumpy,' she told him, looking at the radar screen. 'We have the wind going one way and the tide the other, so that's always going to whip the waves up.'

'How long will this go on?'

'Like I said, we're fighting the tide, so we're only making five knots. It's another eighteen miles, so let's say a bit less than four hours. Do you want to lie down?'

'No. I'm fine,' Osman said and she could see he was making a huge effort to control himself.

Gunna slid from the stool and stepped down into the little cabin, clicked on the light and hunted for the five-litre container she knew was there. She slopped water into a kettle, lit the gas on the camping stove that was built into the bench and put the water on to boil before going back up to the wheelhouse.

Osman's face was ashen. She wondered whether to offer him a bucket, just in case, but decided not to dent his pride.

'There's no coffee on board, but there are a few teabags down there, so you can have a hot drink in a few minutes.'

Osman nodded and sat in unhappy silence while she checked the radar and adjusted the autopilot a couple of degrees.

'Gunnhildur, this is your boat?'

'Not exactly,' she said. 'Well, sort of.'

'I don't understand what you mean.'

'On paper it's half my boat. My son bought it last year, but for all sorts of reasons it's in both our names. He's been fixing it up, which is why it doesn't look much. But everything under the engine hatch is as good as new.'

With a glance at the radar, Gunna swung herself back down the steps into the cabin, turned off the kettle, poured water into a couple of mugs, dropped a teabag in each and stirred with an almost black teaspoon. She handed one mug out of the cabin's opening. Osman opened his eyes and took it, cradling it in both hands to warm his fingers.

'Sorry, there wasn't time to get any stores,' she told him cheerfully. 'If you're hungry you'll have to wait until we tie up.'

She followed at a distance, the occasional sweep with the paddle enough to keep herself within sight of him but far enough to be out of reach, while his strength ebbed away.

It wasn't until she was sure he was finished that she came closer and grabbed a handful of sodden hair. To be certain, she held his head under the surface and counted slowly to a hundred.

She checked the GPS on her wrist, calculated how far they had drifted and took a length of cord from her knee pocket. She tied one end under the dead man's arm and put her own arm through the loop at the other end, hooking it around her elbow.

It was heavy work paddling the kayak with the drag of the dead man behind it, and she dug deep into her reserves of strength. Here in more sheltered waters the sea was almost calm, and with the black shadow of the beach within sight, she abandoned the kayak and waded the rest of the way, dragging the corpse behind her into the shallows.

It wasn't easy hauling the drysuit off him, and she almost gave up, sitting down in the lapping waves more than once to catch her breath. Once it was off, she stuffed the cord into an inside pocket of his jacket and rolled the body back into the water, wading out again and helping it float off, wondering how far the tide would take it.

It was a struggle to tramp through the heather, and for a few minutes she wondered if her sense of direction had let her down, until she made out the landmark of the solitary house that stood back from the shore. Keeping it to her right, she struck out across the scrub and hit the gravel path she was looking for. Behind a shipping container she stripped off her own drysuit, noticing with distaste that her clothes were damp with sweat. She rolled both her suit and Michel's into the tightest bundle she could and pushed it deep between stacks of pallets before jogging to the car park.

Ana clicked the fob of the car key in her pocket and saw the lights flash. It was time to go.

It was almost midnight by the time Osman looked hopeful at the sight of the approaching lights of Akranes. Gunna cut the engine revs and pushed open the cabin door, hooking it back and shivering at the chill.

Osman was on his feet, his face to the wheelhouse window.

'What is this place?'

'It's called Akranes.'

'And what is here?' he asked.

'A few thousand people, a few factories, some shops, a cinema, and I think there's a museum as well. That's about it.'

'So why are we here?' he asked as Gunna clicked off the auto-pilot and gave the wheel a turn, feeling the rudder bite.

'We're here because it's quiet, and because the only people who know you're here are you, me and Ívar. We didn't even tell Birna or Úlfur, or Steinunn for that matter. Nobody followed us across the bay; if they had, I would have seen them on the radar. So if you're followed here, then there's something very wrong.'

'So this is a safe place?'

'It's quiet. It should be safe, as long as we don't stay for long,' Gunna confirmed as the boat slipped past a couple of ships tied up at a long quay snaking into the water. She peered through the window, looking for the berth. 'Now, this is what I need you to do . . .'

She brought the boat up to the pontoon with the engine ticking over, sliding the bow up to it, and quickly put the engine back into gear with a brief burst of power astern to bring it alongside.

'Go on!' she called to Osman and he stretched awkwardly across the narrowing gap, finding his footing on the planks of the pontoon, much to Gunna's relief, as she had imagined him floundering in the black water.

She went to the stern and handed him a rope, pointing at a cleat on the pontoon.

'Put the loop around that,' she ordered, hauling at the rope as it was made fast and whipping it quickly around the bitts. 'The same at the bow,' she instructed, and uncoiled the bow rope from where it had been secured by the wheelhouse door.

Osman took it, looped it over another cleat and stood back with a smile on his face, his motion sickness miraculously gone.

'What happens now?'

'Now? Now we have to walk.'

Chapter Seven

They walked up the hill from the harbour and were soon among silent houses. The wind had eased, although rain pattered softly on the ground around them. Gunna could see that Osman was drenched, the elegant overcoat he had worn to visit Parliament only a few hours earlier had picked up smears of grease and was heavy with water.

She could hear his shoes squelch with every step, and he looked around curiously at the dark houses lining the silent street.

'This way,' Gunna said, pushing open an iron gate into the gloom of a garden and leading the way around a high-sided house that loomed above them.

She went down a couple of steps at the side of the house and punched a series of numbers into a glass-fronted box screwed to the wall by the door. To her relief, the box dropped open, releasing the key, and she opened the door, fumbling for the light switch inside.

'Shoes off, please,' she instructed, kicking off her own boots and striding through the apartment, clicking on lights and peering into rooms. 'I know it's late, but I think we deserve some coffee, don't you?'

'Please.'

Osman stood uncertainly, dripping water on the kitchen floor.

'Hang your coat up by the door and come in here.' Gunna quickly set the percolator to run, and found mugs and a carton of long-life milk. 'We're in luck,' she announced, placing a packet of biscuits on the table. 'But that's all the food there is.'

She patted her pockets for her phone and tapped in a text message.

Docked. G

Seconds later her phone buzzed with a response.

Good. See you tomorrow. ÍL

Gunna wondered if she ought to send Steini a message, and suddenly felt very alone.

'Gunnhildur, what is this place?' Osman asked, looking around the cramped kitchen and gingerly sitting on a stool, as if he expected it to give way beneath him.

'This place? It belongs to my son. He inherited it when his father died,' she said gruffly. 'It's no business of mine, but I think he'll probably sell it, or else rent it out.'

'Your son? His father?' Osman said softly.

'It's a long story and I don't want to go into it.'

'But I have told you my whole story,' Osman said in a low, slightly mocking tone. Under the dim kitchen light he looked more tired than she had seen him before, with lines under the dark eyes that drew her in. 'And we have been through so much together.'

Gunna stripped off her fleece and hung it on the back of a chair, hoping it would be dry by morning. As she sat down she realized that she still had the Glock under her arm. For a moment she was surprised that she had become accustomed to its presence there.

'I have a son from a short relationship when I was young. I hadn't seen my son's father for more than twenty years, and then he turned up not long ago, terminally ill. My son and his father had been in occasional contact, but they weren't reconciled until close to the end. He had a lot of children, with half a dozen mothers, as far as I know. But my son – our son – was the only one who was with him during his illness and when he died.'

'So he left this place to your son?'

'He left him everything he had, which was this place, which he hadn't lived in for seven or eight years,' Gunna said slowly and looked up.

'I see,' Osman said, still huddled in his coat. 'But you have other children?'

'I have a daughter, and her father was the man I was married to. And that's about all I have to say.'

'I think you don't trust me very much, Gunnhildur.'

'Trust?' Gunna said, standing up to fill two mugs. 'We've been living under the same roof for a week now and I still don't know what to make of you. I don't know if you're the philanthropist you claim to be, or the criminal the newspapers claim you are, or if you're some kind of terrorist.'

She sat down and pushed one of the mugs across the table to him.

'I see. You don't believe me.'

'It's not that I don't believe you, Osman. My job is to weigh up evidence. It's what I do every day, trying to get to the truth, whether it's a murder or someone caught shoplifting. But with you I simply don't have the evidence, so I'm not in a position to decide whether you're for real or not.'

She sipped her coffee and yawned.

'But you are not afraid?'

'Afraid of what? You?'

'If you think I might be a terrorist, then you should be afraid for your life.'

Gunna shrugged.

'I may have saved your life. So should I be afraid?'

His smile was dazzling in the half-darkness, but there was a flash of frustration in his humourless bark of laughter.

'I don't think you need to be afraid. But tell me, I've been out of touch. What are the newspapers saying?'

'That you're involved in trafficking arms and people, and that your foundation is a smart way to launder money. That's what it adds up to.'

'In that case I can guess who they've been speaking to. There's an organization that has pursued me relentlessly from the moment the foundation was set up. The accounts are there for anyone to see. There is nothing to hide.'

'That's precisely what they're saying; that you're hiding in plain sight. Making yourself too important and prominent to be questioned.'

'And what do you think, Gunnhildur?'

'Like I said, I don't have the information I need to form an opinion one way or the other. But I would make a guess that your hands aren't as clean as you'd like us to think, considering there are people who seem to be very keen to shut you up,' Gunna said. 'Now, Mr Osman. The question is, what are we going to do with you?'

'Where is Osman?'

Steinunn's voice was shrill and far from her usual measured tones, which indicated argument would not be tolerated.

'He's safe,' Ívar Laxdal replied. 'I hope.'

'Safe. Where?'

'Not in Reykjavík.'

'Don't play games,' Steinunn snapped, one finger drumming a slow beat on the desk in front of her.

'With respect,' Ívar Laxdal replied in a tone that carried very little respect, 'we have a shitstorm to deal with at the moment after James Kearney's murder, in addition to the fact that it may be directly linked to Osman's presence in Iceland. The US media is going to latch onto this soon enough and they're not going to be fobbed off easily.'

'You're defying me, and that's not a wise thing to do.'

'Again, with respect,' Ívar Laxdal said, speaking slowly and clearly, 'we have a leak somewhere along the line. Somehow these people knew exactly where your friend was. I can only assume that when they couldn't get to him, they went for McCombie's associate, who was much easier to reach in that hotel. As far as I know there's no motive for James Kearney's killing, other than that he was a member of this strange group, and that he was involved in some business with Osman's organization. We have no idea if he became a target because McCombie was out of reach, or if he was the target. My intuition is that in this instance the underling was murdered as an example to the others, a warning to stay out of whatever they had been cooking up between them, in the same way that a young man who had exposed the activities of Osman's foundation was murdered in Antwerp. This is something way beyond anything we have seen in Iceland before, and we're not equipped to deal with this.'

Steinunn stared back at Ívar Laxdal.

'And?'

'I don't know if the leak was here, or with Osman's people, or the Children of Freedom, but I've taken measures to plug it. Now only Gunnhildur and I know where he is, nobody else. When I'm confident it's safe, I'll bring him back.'

'I want him back here tonight.'

Ívar Laxdal shrugged.

'Until he has a ticket out of the country or somewhere genuinely secure, then he stays where he is,' he said, and watched Steinunn's eyes flash with fury.

'How's Carsten?' Helgi asked.

Hanne looked as if she hadn't slept properly for a long time and Helgi decided that was probably the case.

'He's all right. He was brought to Reykjavík yesterday and he seems to be stable. I hope they'll let us fly home soon.'

Helgi wanted to smile, but found he couldn't. The mortuary always did that to him.

'You're ready for this?'

Hanne nodded once.

Miss Cruz lifted the sheet from the man's face. The beard was shorter, the dark hair lying in black tangles, but the heavy brows and flat nose were the same.

Helgi saw Hanne's face tighten and knew before she spoke that this was the man.

'It's him. One of them.'

'You're sure?'

'Absolutely. No doubt about it. It's a face I'll never forget.'

'Good,' Helgi said quietly and Miss Cruz let the sheet fall back over the corpse's face.

Hanne wanted to shed tears, for Carsten and for her own guilt at finding herself rejoicing in the man's death. But she stood immobile, staring at the shape under the sheet.

'How did he die?' she croaked at last, her throat dry.

Helgi glanced at Miss Cruz.

'Drowning,' she said quietly.

'Good. Thank you. I think I've seen enough,' Hanne said.

'Thank you for coming in. I'll have to take a statement from you, and then I can drive you back to the hostel if you like.'

In Miss Cruz's office Helgi took notes, enough for the short statement needed to confirm that Hanne had identified the man as one of the two who had threatened her and her husband, presumably hiding contraband in their vehicle.

Hanne surveyed Miss Cruz's office.

'One of my uncles was an undertaker,' she said at last. 'So I sort of grew up with death in the family. I thought I was more immune to this than most people.'

'I'm not sure you ever build up complete immunity,' Helgi said, still writing, while Hanne looked over his shoulder at the row of data sheets clipped to the wall, her eyes drawn to a photograph stapled to one of them.

'God . . .' she muttered.

'What? I'm sorry?' Helgi said, looking up and seeing the look of confusion on Hanne's face. He twisted around in the chair to see what had caught her eye.

'There. That picture. I swear,' Hanne muttered. 'I swear that's the other man, the second one.'

'You're sure? The other guy?'

Helgi went to the door and opened it.

'Miss Cruz?' he called. 'Could you come here for a moment?'

Hanne stood up and went over to the whiteboard festooned with notes held in place with little coloured magnets.

'I'm sure . . . I think it's him. He's in here as well?' she asked, a feeling of fierce joy surging through her.

* * *

250

'How did this happen?' Ívar Laxdal rasped into his phone.

'Helgi brought in a woman to identify a body, a man who was pulled out of the water. He'd been found on a beach. There's no sign of any trauma, and it looks like drowning. I'm expecting the blood results to come back telling me he was either drunk or high on something,' she said and gulped.

'Go on.'

'Helgi brought the lady here to identify him. They used my office so he could take her statement, and she saw the ID pic of the gunshot victim on my pinboard. It completely slipped my mind that it was there. She couldn't take her eyes off it, said she recognized him.'

'Where are they now?'

'In the coffee room. Helgi can't understand why he couldn't see the other body, and I said you'd have to be here.'

'All right,' Ívar Laxdal decided. 'I'll talk to Helgi. Will you get the body ready?'

'Yes, of course,' Miss Cruz said with an impatience he'd never seen before. 'There's something else here you really need to see.'

Gunna woke later than she usually did. She deliberately hadn't set the alarm and revelled in the pleasure of still being wrapped in a duvet as the first rays of sunlight made their way into the room around the edges of the living room's blinds.

The muted sound of Osman snoring in the apartment's only bedroom told her he was still asleep.

She hadn't undressed more than necessary the night before and she felt clammy; she was longing for a shower, but decided against it. Hunger overcame any thoughts of hot water and she pulled on her boots.

Outside it was a fresh morning, no warmer, but brighter than the previous few days had been. The wind came off the sea, bringing with it the sharp tang of seaweed, and she took deep lungfuls as she walked down to the quay to check on the boat.

'All right to leave her here for a while?' she asked at the fuel berth, where it had been tied up the night before.

The harbourmaster looked at her curiously.

'You came across the bay last night?'

'That's right. Tied up here just before midnight.'

He scratched his chin, a thumbnail rasping on bristles.

'I thought so. Bumpy night, was it?'

'Just a bit.'

'Staying long?'

'Not sure,' Gunna said. 'But the boat might be staying longer than I am.'

'No problem. Put her on one of the pontoons on the other side if you're going to be staying any longer than tomorrow. The weather's supposed to ease off tonight, so there might be people wanting fuel.'

Gunna thanked the man and left him to check over the pilot launch. She walked back up the slope, in no doubt that Kallabakari was the next essential place for her to visit; sure she could already smell the fresh bread on its shelves.

Ana lay in the bath for a long time, enjoying the solitude and the chance to read a book until the water began to cool. She turned the last page, put the book aside, and her thoughts went back to her reasons for being in Iceland and what the next step would be.

The completed assignment would keep her solvent for a good long time to come and allow her to spend the next few months in the near-solitude she preferred. Maybe even a few weeks in this odd little country, she wondered, and immediately dismissed the idea. Work and personal lives needed to be kept as separate and remote from each other as possible.

She had a leisurely breakfast of tea and toast with honey, without Michel's silent but irritating presence in the apartment. She wondered how long it would be before he was found, and guessed it wouldn't take long before some dog walker stumbled across his corpse on a beach. It was always people walking dogs, she reflected, people who went where normal people didn't, and at ridiculous times of the day and night.

She would have to check in using an anonymous computer

somewhere, in either a café or at the city library, where she could log into one of her dummy social media accounts to confirm that she could travel now that the operation was over, suspended as being too hazardous to achieve on this remote island.

Ana took out the smartphone, switched it on and watched it come to life. She activated the application that monitored the trackers, which were so laughably easy to embed in phones if people didn't take care. All it took was for the target to answer a call from a sender's unknown number, even for a few seconds, and the process began to implant an inconspicuous nugget of software that piggy-backed on the target phone's location software. Every time the phone was in contact with a mobile network, it would discreetly update the little blue dot on the screen of her phone.

She was intrigued, as she munched her toast, to see that Osman's blue dot had left Reykjavík and was now on the coast across the bay from the city, while the red dot's position was still in the city. Maybe it was time to pay this one a visit at last.

In the cubicle that served as a break room, he found Helgi with a bony woman in late middle age, with dark rings under her eyes and an air of tension about them both.

'Miss Cruz has filled me in,' Ívar Laxdal said. 'I'm sorry, Helgi, but I'm going to have to keep a few secrets from you. Do you mind if this lady comes with me?'

'Sure,' Helgi said, clearly perplexed. 'Do you want me to wait here?'

'For a few minutes,' Ívar Laxdal said; the grim look on his face was enough to silence Helgi's protests. 'I'll be back soon, and I'll explain then – as far as I can.'

They left Helgi muttering under his breath, and Hanne felt the chill of the mortuary as Miss Cruz opened the door for them.

Another gurney had been wheeled into position and he beckoned Hanne over.

'I understand there were two men, Hanne,' Ívar Laxdal said. 'All I want from you is a yes or no.'

Hanne gulped and nodded. Miss Cruz lifted the sheet.

'Yes,' she whispered and looked up at Ívar Laxdal. 'Yes,' she said again in a firmer, louder voice. 'This is the other man. I have no doubt about it.'

Miss Cruz dropped the sheet.

'I can put him away again now?'

'Please do,' Ívar Laxdal said, taking Hanne's arm and escorting her back to where Helgi was quietly fuming as he waited for his witness to return.

Gunna dropped the bag of rolls and pastries on the table, set the percolator to run, and with Osman's snores still audible through the thin wall, she made for the shower and stood for a long time under the scalding water, regretting only that she had travelled light and had no clean clothes to change into.

She emerged freshly scrubbed to find that Osman's snoring had ceased and the smell of coffee filled the apartment. She elbowed his door open an inch.

'Morning. Breakfast is here.'

'Good morning, Gunnhildur,' he said, and coughed. 'No breakfast in bed?'

'Not a hope. Breakfast is on the table, and if you're not quick I'll eat it all.'

She rooted through the contents of a chest of drawers in the hall, and found a pair of socks that would fit, but decided that if they were going to be here for long, then she would have to pay a visit to a shop for some clean clothes.

Osman appeared drowsily and sank into a chair by the table. Gunna pushed a mug towards him.

'There's coffee in the machine and a carton of fresh milk in the fridge.'

To her surprise, he stood up and, without a word, helped himself to coffee. A week earlier he would have stayed in his chair, eyes going from mug to machine, expecting her to do it for him.

'You're in the news,' she said as he sat down and reached for a pastry.

'What?'

Gunna showed him the freesheet newspaper she had picked up from a rack in the bakery.

'Admittedly this is something of a scandal sheet,' she said as Osman chewed a sweet roll. 'But you're in there.'

His brow furrowed and he rubbed his eyes.

'What does it say?'

Gunna ran a finger under the type on the front page as she translated.

'It says that a suspected arms and people trafficker is linked to the death of James Kearney at the Vatnsmýri Hotel this week, in what they call a surprise revelation by a source who declined to be named.' She looked up at Osman. 'I guess that means they made it up, or that it's guesswork on their part. Not that I know anything about the Kearney case, so I can't even guess who they might have talked to. Look,' she said, turning the paper round to show him the picture that filled a quarter of the page, directly below a grainy photograph of refugees on an anonymous beach. 'You're front-page news.'

Michel's belongings fitted neatly into the backpack she found in his room. She went through everything, methodically emptying the pockets and placing everything personal in a pile. There wasn't much: a French passport, a health card and driving licence that she knew to be fakes, a couple of photographs in a plastic wallet of a smiling family with a white beach in the background. She peered at the pictures, seeing a smiling African woman and three small children gathered around a barbecue. It was a far-from-new photo, and for a moment she hoped that the children were grown up now, old enough to cope with the fact that their father would not be making any further appearances in their lives.

The clothes folded neatly into the bag, and she slung it over one shoulder as she left the apartment.

She dropped a carrier bag folded around Michel's passport and other documents into a bin along the street, wondering when the next collection would be. It would have been better to burn them, but lighting a fire anywhere in the city was too much of a risk.

'Hi. These are for you, if you want them,' she said to the man with an ash-grey ponytail.

The charity shop was a ten-minute walk from the apartment. She had noticed it a few days earlier, when she'd been tempted to spend half an hour among the cast-offs to see if there were any interesting vintage items there. Clothes could wait, though.

'God bless you. You want the bag?'

'No, keep it.'

He unzipped the bag and shook the shirts and trousers onto the counter.

'Good clothes,' he said. 'Not yours?' he asked, eyeing her from beneath one bushy eyebrow.

Ana shrugged.

'My ex-boyfriend went back to his wife and left all this at my place. I've given up waiting for him to come and get them. If he wanted his clothes, he'd have been back by now, I suppose,' she said dismissively.

'I'm not sure we should take these without his consent . . .'

'He's had eight months to come and get them, and I'm moving, so I have to do something with his shit. It's up to you,' she replied. 'I'd rather someone had some use out of them. If you don't want them, they'll just be thrown out with the rest of the rubbish.'

He smiled and Ana knew that he had his eyes on Michel's multi-pocketed trousers.

'In that case, your ex's loss is the Mission's gain.'

'You're taking me off this, are you?' Sævaldur said, his habitual surly tone betraying even more irritation than usual.

'Not at all,' a brusque Ívar Laxdal said. 'You're doing a fine job under difficult circumstances, but there are aspects of this case that you're not familiar with, and that's why I wanted to bring you up to date.' He paused, as if for effect. 'Or as up to date as I can.'

Sævaldur sat back, arms folded, glancing around the room at Birna and Úlfur, and glaring at Helgi and Eiríkur. He looked Luc Kerkhoeve up and down without a word.

Ívar Laxdal immediately recognized the signs and inwardly braced himself for a struggle.

'We have a shitstorm to deal with,' he said. 'Three dead people, and somehow it all ties in together.'

'Three?' Sævaldur snapped. 'I know of three. The American at the hotel and the drunk who was hauled out of the water over at Gufunes this morning, plus Thór the Boxer. Are we talking about the same three?'

'This is where I have to be secretive as there are things I can't tell you. All I can say is that if you're counting Thór the Boxer, then we have four. That's Thór, James Kearney, and we have two dead males, one of whom appears to have drowned in the creek on the west side of Gufunes,' he said, counting them off on his fingers. 'Now we must switch to English, for Luc's benefit,' he said, watching Sævaldur scowl again. 'Luc is from State Security in Brussels and has some knowledge of the two fatalities that we're not going to go into too much detail about. But Helgi and Eiríkur have established that the unnamed Gufunes guy was involved in Thór the Boxer's death. Right, Helgi?'

Helgi raised a finger. 'Er . . . Well, Eiríkur did a lot of this,' he said in awkwardly stiff English. 'Do you want to . . . ?'

'We found the Gufunes guy on CCTV twice on Laugavegur,' Eiríkur said. 'That's once outside a pizza shop and once on an ATM camera. Thór and his pal Fúsi were following them.'

'Them?'

'Yes, them. Thór and Fúsi were following a couple. Fúsi finally admitted that this was their usual tourist mugging technique. They'd follow someone leaving a restaurant or a bar, corner them once they were somewhere out of sight, and lift their phones, cash or whatever.'

'This was a mugging that went wrong,' Helgi chimed in. 'They thought they were safe, and cornered this couple on Njálsgata, round the corner from the cinema. But it didn't work out as they'd planned.'

'The Gufunes guy beat the two of them up, you mean?' Sævaldur said.

Luc's patience could no longer be contained and he slapped the table.

'Will you please understand,' he said. 'These people are not amateurs. A couple of clumsy muggers are not going to be a problem for them.'

'It was the drowned man who put Fúsi in hospital,' Helgi said. 'But the woman was the one who put Thór in the morgue.'

Skúli was surprised at himself. After the previous day's ordeal he had found his way home almost on autopilot, relieved that he had made his way through the city; it was almost as if the Peugeot with the cracked windscreen knew its way home.

Dagga had growled and pursed her lips as he'd told her the story. Her eyes narrowed in anger, she shook her head in disbelief and Skúli wondered how she could be more angry about the whole thing than he was.

He had slept for almost twelve hours, called in to let Arndís and Agnar know that he was ill and wouldn't be in that day, then spent the morning writing down every detail of what had happened at Einholt.

He sat back and read through what he had written, made a few additions and notes, and was satisfied, even though he was sure these words would never be read. All the same, he wanted his own record of what had taken place before the details faded from his memory. He rubbed his wrists, still sore from the handcuffs, and wondered what his next move should be. Osman had clearly been moved from the minister's house. But where to?

Halfway through the morning, the phone buzzed at his side, and seeing Arndís's number, he answered.

'You all right, Skúli?'

'Yeah, I think so. Tough day yesterday.'

'What was that all about?'

'I'll tell you later. What's new?'

'The reshuffle. Wondering if you have any inside info from your pal?'

'Reshuffle?' Skúli scratched his head and had the immediate sinking feeling that he had been asleep on watch.

'That's right,' Arndís said patiently. 'Two out, two new faces in. One of them's Steinunn Strand, and I know you have someone on the inside there, so have you heard anything?'

'Shit,' Skúli said. 'No, not a word. Like I said before, I feel lousy and haven't been paying attention. I think my contact there is burned out, but I'll see if I can track him down.'

She wondered whether to check the smartphone for the red dot's location, but decided against it. She knew where to go and had memorized the route. The walk would do her good, and for the first time since she had been in Iceland, there was some real warmth in the sunshine.

It wasn't as far as she had thought as she strolled through a part of the city she hadn't paid much attention to before, with streets that meandered rather than strode straight from place to place as they did in the newer districts.

Öldugata was quiet, with more trees between the buildings than she had seen anywhere else, and houses that looked as if they belonged there rather than having been built in a hurry a few weeks earlier.

When she found it, the house was a large one, surfaced in rough grey concrete and with its front wall directly on the pavement. The windows were small compared to the expanse of wall between them, as if it had been built back when glass had been an expensive luxury. There were six apartments, she guessed, or maybe eight if those tiny windows in the gable also had people living behind them.

Ana peered at the line of doorbells and failed to see the one she was looking for. Rather than ring one at random and ask, she walked past the house, and saw there was a flight of steps at the side leading to a basement, with narrow windows that were almost flush with the ground in the bare but well-tended garden at the back.

She went down the steps, saw the name she was looking for and heard a bell chime inside as she pressed the button.

'Hello, Valgeir,' she said and smiled broadly as he opened the door.

'We're looking for a woman?' Sævaldur said, failing to hide his incredulity, and then guffawing suddenly.

'What's so funny?' Ívar Laxdal asked, hesitating to issue a rebuke.

'Well, Thór the Boxer being murdered by a woman, considering the number of women he'd abused over the years. He was no knight in shining armour, was he? But I still find it hard to believe a woman could have done this. Thór was a real bruiser, so she must be something special.'

'She probably is,' Luc said, his voice icy. 'I told you, these people are not amateurs. You can be confident these aren't the first people they've murdered. This person could also have killed the American.' He paused and glanced at a sheet of notes in cramped handwriting in front of him. 'Kearney,' he said at last. 'James Kearney.'

'We have something on that,' Ívar Laxdal said, swiping at a tablet. 'The Gufunes guy had this in a pocket of his jacket.'

He placed the tablet on the table in front of him so the others could see the coiled length of cord.

'It's just under a metre long, with a loop at each end that's easily big enough for a hand,' he said and swiped again, this time bringing up an image of a livid discoloured line on flesh that it took a moment for them to realize was James Kearney's neck. 'It fits perfectly. The marks on the man's neck have precisely the same dimensions as this rope. Miss Cruz noticed. She's doing tests to see if the rope has any traces that can link it definitively to the killing.'

'So you think your dead man is the killer because of this?' Luc asked. 'Be careful, is all I will say. It's easy to lay a false trail, and that's what this could be.'

'Right,' Ívar Laxdal said quickly. 'Of course, we don't jump to conclusions.'

'The two men. The man who was shot and the one who drowned,' Luc said. 'Are they connected? And if so, how are you sure?'

'Helgi?' Ívar Laxdal prompted. 'The Danish lady?'

'We had a sighting of the drowned man on CCTV and we let the press have images,' Helgi said in his slow, careful English. 'There were quite a few calls, but the convincing one was a Danish lady who went to the police in Blönduós.'

'Where?'

'It's in the north. She and her husband had been travelling around the country in a camper van. On the way to the ferry in Denmark, two men came to them at a campsite and told them to go for a walk. They showed them pictures of their children, parents and family, and said if they co-operated, nobody would be hurt. So they did. When they got off the ferry in Iceland, the two men met them somewhere in the east, she wasn't sure quite where, and took whatever it was they had hidden in the camper.'

'And why did she go to the police?'

'It seems they'd been arguing about it for days. He wanted to; she didn't. Then he had a mild heart attack, which he survived and is now in hospital recovering. She saw the drowned man's photo on the front page of that day's paper and apparently changed her mind, told the local cops and they got in touch with me. I asked her to go to the mortuary with me to identify the man, as I was fairly sure it was him, and she also saw a photo of the other guy while we were there, and recognized him as well. So we can place the two men together, no question.'

'Not a word of this leaves the room, by the way,' Ívar Laxdal said, looking from face to face. 'With these two men dead, we have no idea if this woman's family is still under threat, but we have to assume so.'

'And you place this mysterious woman with the drowned man, the Gufunes guy,' Luc said, as if Ívar Laxdal hadn't said anything. 'Let me tell you. These two men were the muscle, the ones who do the dirty work, the usual ex-military types with all kinds of skills and not a shred of conscience. Whatever they hid in that Danish couple's camper will almost certainly be some kind of hardware, I'd guess firearms and ammunition. Something of that nature. The woman is different,' he said, wagging a finger at Ívar Laxdal. 'Her tracks will be very carefully covered, but she'll be the brains of this outfit.'

There was a hush as Luc's words sank in, until he broke the silence himself.

'It's an open secret that there's a price on Osman's head. You get him out of your country, and all this shit will follow him somewhere else.'

'And James Kearney?' Birna asked.

Luc shook his head.

'I don't know,' he said. 'I can only guess. We know he was doing some kind of deal with Osman, and not for the first time, right? Well, I'd guess it's a warning, something to tell these crazy people to keep their money and their noses out of the Middle East. The same with the activist who was murdered in Antwerp, the journalist's contact.'

Úlfur coughed quietly, opened his mouth to say something and closed it again.

'Well, this other guy,' Sævaldur asked in a slow drawl. 'The drowned man's partner. Do we get to know what happened to him, and is there a reason it's all so secret?'

The white walls of the lighthouse glittered in the morning sun and Osman craned his neck, squinting against the brightness to make out its full height.

Waves gnawed at the shoreline, the stiff wind off the bay filling the air with moisture and the tang of the sea. Gunna shivered in her fleece, and envied Osman his thick coat, even with the smears of grease it had acquired on the boat.

'And where did we come from yesterday?'

'Over there. You can see Reykjavík in the distance.'

'And the weather was like this in the night?'

'Worse,' Gunna assured him. 'It's just as well you couldn't see it in the dark.'

'I think I would have refused if I had known,' he said after considering the crash and roar of the waves hitting the long finger of the breakwater jutting out into the bay.

'Nobody knows you're here, I hope. Isn't that what you wanted?'

'Of course,' he said, looking around. 'Can we find lunch some-where here?'

'I guess. We can see if there's a café open somewhere.'

They walked side by side, crunching through the gravel back towards the town. Gunna zipped her fleece to her throat, hiding the Glock under her arm. She was unsure what to do with it, aware that carrying a firearm in a provincial town like Akranes was a potential minefield. On the other hand, she was conscious that she was on duty and responsible for Osman's safety, and with any back-up an hour's drive away in Reykjavík. Her other concern was where to put the weapon. She wasn't prepared to put it down anywhere within Osman's reach, or out of her own reach.

All the same, the Glock remained unloaded, with the clip in her pocket, where she rolled it between her fingers as they walked.

'Gunnhildur, what are these . . . these logs?'

Osman pointed towards the empty frames that stood aban-doned near the shore.

'Those? They're for drying fish.'

'Fish?'

'Yep. I don't think it's done any more. In the old days fish were hung on the bars, high up where animals couldn't reach them, and it was a smelly job hanging it up there.'

'You have done this work?'

'Of course. I was brought up in a fishing village back when all the kids worked in the fish every summer. I've spent plenty of time up there on the drying racks.'

'Gunnhildur, you are full of surprises.'

'Like I said, I don't think it's done these days. The fish is all frozen now.'

They skirted the harbour, where Osman stared at the boat tied up at the fuel berth.

'It's so small,' he said in disbelief.

'It's not a big boat,' Gunna agreed.

Osman shook his head.

'We came through that weather last night,' he muttered, 'in that little thing?'

They took a corner table in a café, where Osman wolfed two sandwiches and a bowl of soup, and asked for more. Gunna realized that, apart from the rolls at breakfast, they had both hardly had time to eat since the previous afternoon.

She tapped a message into her phone while Osman finished a second bowl of soup.

What's new? G – and dispatched it to Ívar Laxdal.

Osman sat back with a smile on his face that looked to her to be forced, and her phone buzzed a reply.

Everything in order in Ak? Frantic here. I'll call when I get a moment. ÍL.

'News?'

'Nothing yet. They'll be in touch later today.'

'What happens next, Gunnhildur?' Osman asked, leaning forward over his empty plate.

'Well,' she said, and looked over Osman's shoulder to catch the eye of the man behind the counter. 'My inclination is to have a coffee and a piece of the cake.'

'No, I mean after that?'

'After that I need to do some shopping. My colleagues brought your bags to the boat last night, but my clothes are still at Einholt, and I really need some clean stuff. But I guess you mean what happens after that, and the answer is, I don't know,' she said and looked up as the barista sauntered over.

'Can I get you anything else?' he asked.

'An Americano and a slice of walnut cake.'

'Sure,' he said and gestured to Osman. 'The same for your husband?'

Gunna grinned.

'He's not my husband, but he'll have the same.'

'What brings you here?' Valgeir asked, unable to mask both his astonishment and his delight.

'You know. Just being a little adventurous for once.'

'I'm leaving tomorrow,' he said, feeling foolish. 'When did you get here?'

'Yesterday afternoon,' Ana said, enjoying seeing his boyish happiness and feeling slightly sorry at the prospect of puncturing it. 'Just scouting things out.'

'So this is business, not pleasure?'

'Contrary to the old saying, it's perfectly possible to mix the two,' Ana assured him. 'I couldn't let you know, for the usual reasons. Well,' she added, 'I suppose I could have done, but I liked the idea of surprising you.'

'Wow!'

Valgeir's smirk stretched from one side of his face to the other as Ana took off her coat and folded it over the back of the only remaining chair in his apartment.

'We're cool to talk here, right? We're not being listened to by your spooks?'

Valgeir laughed.

'Spooks? No, the nearest thing we have to spooks are pretty busy at the moment.'

'So what's the situation?'

'Well.' Valgeir took off his glasses, polished them on his shirt and grinned. 'I'm pretty much out of the loop now that I'm on leave and leaving for a new posting. But I dug up some gossip. The press officer's an old friend and she lets me know what's going on.'

'She? What kind of friend?'

'We were at university together.'

'Not together at university?' Ana probed.

'No, not at all,' Valgeir said, suddenly flustered.

'All right. I believe you. What did she have to tell you?'

'Just that Osman has been moved out of the house he was staying at because it wasn't secure. This is just between you and me, but things are going crazy at the moment and I'm not sorry to be on leave and on my way out of the country for a few years. That's four deaths so far, which is completely off the scale for this country.'

'Four?'

'Yeah, the guy the grumpy policewoman shot to start with, then they found someone they think was the dead man's partner, drowned not far from the house where Osman was staying. On top of that, there's been a scandal going on with some American far-right group that's been holding meetings here over the last few days. One of the two men was murdered in his hotel, and they reckon the killer was the guy who drowned,' Valgeir said, shaking his head. 'Normally there's one murder a year here, so this is like four years' worth in one go. The police are going crazy.'

'What was the fourth one? You only mentioned three.'

'Oh, some lowlife drug dealer. They seem to think it's connected to the others, but I don't see how.'

Ana felt the excitement inside as she flexed her fingers.

'And our friend?' she asked quietly.

'He's been moved somewhere out of the city for the moment, but Elinborg reckoned that he'll be leaving the country very soon, probably tomorrow, she said.'

'They've decided to get rid of him?'

'Pretty much,' Valgeir said. 'In fact, I'm not the only one who's leaving. Steinunn Strand, that's the minister whose department I was working in, is going as well. She's been bumped up to some fat UN post, so if she's no longer in the country, then I reckon Osman's welcome is about to expire.'

Valgeir reached out and took her hand, clasping it in both of his as a smile spread across his face.

'I'm so happy to see you,' he said. 'What a surprise. We'll be travelling together, won't we?'

'Yeah, why not?' Ana gently disengaged her hand and looked around the apartment. 'You've sold this place?'

'Not yet, but I have a couple of offers already. I'm holding out for a few more days to see if I get a better one.'

'And you're packed and ready to go?'

'Pretty much.'

Ana slipped out of the door and went along the hall, glancing into each room along the way.

'You haven't packed the bed yet?'

'I'm not going to. A friend of mine is taking the fridge, the sofa and the bed.'

Ana gave him a sly look that set Valgeir's heart pumping.

'In that case, we can make use of it, can't we?'

Osman was patient, just like a model husband, Gunna thought. He sat quietly with his hands folded in his lap as she bought what she needed, then carried the bag of new underwear, a bottle of shampoo and enough from the supermarket's food aisle for an evening meal.

'We're not going to be able to stay here for long,' Gunna said as they walked back to the flat.

'Why?'

'You didn't notice people looking at you? They've seen your picture in the papers and I'd guess that you've been noticed. We should have just stayed indoors.'

'I would go crazy if I had to stay in that tiny place for much longer.'

'This is a small town. There are a lot more visitors these days, but people still notice a stranger, especially at this time of year, when it's quiet.'

'You mean you can't hide in Iceland?' Osman asked.

Gunna laughed.

'You can try, but it's not easy. If you don't want to be noticed, then you have to blend in, until people stop noticing you.'

'And how long does that take?'

'In Reykjavík, a few years. Where I come from, it would take at least a lifetime.'

'So Iceland isn't a place to hide?'

'Not at all,' Gunna said, pushing open the front door, which was stiff in its frame. 'It's pretty safe, but it's not easy to stay out of sight. You can be sure that someone will have whispered to someone else who has a cousin who works for a newspaper, which means there's only so long that we can sit it out here. One more night, maybe. I'm hoping Ívar Laxdal will have figured something out before then.'

Osman went into the little living room, ran his eyes over the spines of the dozen or so books on the shelves and picked one. Gunna switched on the radio in the kitchen, then the percolator, and picked up her phone.

Any news? she punched in and sent the message.

Be with you at 1530, the reply came seconds later.

She looked through to the other room and saw that Osman was sitting with the book in his hands, staring past the pages into space.

'Hey.'

'What?' he asked, startled out of his thoughts.

'There's coffee in the machine,' Gunna said. 'Help yourself. Ívar Laxdal will be here in a couple of hours. Maybe we'll learn something then.'

'I have to brief the PM,' Steinunn said, her voice bleak. 'What's the situation?'

She had become a lonely figure behind the desk so wide that there was a chasm between her and anyone who wanted to speak to her. A few days before, the desk had been piled with reports and files in neat stacks, but the workload had already been discreetly taken away to be prepared for her successor.

Ívar Laxdal raised an eyebrow in Birna's direction to suggest that she could deliver the news, or lack of it.

'Well . . .' she began. 'One of the dead men has been identified as a former mercenary. The second one—'

'The drowned man?' Steinunn broke in.

'That's him. He's been conclusively linked to the first man, so the assumption is that the two of them were working together. There's a third person linked to them who hasn't been traced.'

'And James Kearney? Have you identified his killer? As I said, I have to brief the PM on this, and he's going to be climbing the walls if I don't have anything for him, and for the Americans.'

Birna opened her mouth and Ívar Laxdal could see her wondering how much to say.

'We can be confident that these people were responsible for

Kearney's murder,' he said. 'We don't have the details of who did what, but there's enough evidence to link them to him.'

Steinunn stared into Ívar Laxdal's eyes.

'Why?' she demanded. 'What on earth is their motive?'

Ívar Laxdal stared back.

'Cash,' he said. 'That's what we believe, according to our opposite numbers in Europe.'

'Just money?'

'Exactly. These people were paid to murder James Kearney, possibly as a warning to the Children of Freedom to keep their activities to their own back yard. And your friend Osman has a price on his head. Five million dollars. That's quite an incentive, so it's no surprise it brings in people ready to run risks and take chances.'

Steinunn sank into her seat and her eyes bulged. She hunched forward, elbows on her desk, the fingers of one hand nervously twisting a lock of hair.

'Shit. I thought . . .'

'It seems,' Ívar Laxdal said slowly, sitting down and looking Steinunn in the eyes, 'that your friend is a little of everything, but he managed one very unwise deal when he sold the same shipment of military hardware to two rival organizations. Neither of them got what they wanted, and now they both want Osman's head on a plate. Hence the five million. That's the rumour, at any rate.'

'No wonder he's a frightened man,' Steinunn said in a hollow voice.

'Frightened, yes,' Ívar Laxdal said. 'And with good reason. The question is, what are you going to do about it?'

Ana strolled back through the town, enjoying window shopping and knowing that there was nothing she needed to buy, until a bookshop tempted her. After half an hour among the shelves, she emerged with a couple of novels under her arm.

She knew where she was going, stepped out of the way of the ambling tourists, took a turn and walked uphill.

'Good morning,' the girl at the counter said.

'Hi. I booked earlier. My name's Susanna.'

'You're a little early, so take a seat, please. Someone will be with you soon. Would you like a coffee while you wait?'

'Yes. That would be lovely,' Ana said, taking a seat in the corner and opening one of the two books. 'Take as long as you like. I'm in no hurry.'

For the first time, Osman looked lost and Gunna pushed a mug towards him.

'You're in the news again,' she said. 'Questions are being asked of the minister, and Steinunn is going. Did you know?'

'What?' He looked around in astonishment. 'Going where?'

Gunna scanned the pages of the copy of *DV* she had picked up at the supermarket.

'A United Nations post,' she said. 'It seems it's something pretty prestigious, although the subtext is that she's being given a way to step down from government without having to be sacked.'

'She's going? Why hasn't she told me?'

There was real alarm in his voice.

'Well, to start with, there was something of a panic yesterday. I reckon she had a lot on her mind, and on top of that, we whisked you away, and I don't imagine Ívar has told her where you are.'

'What now?' Osman said, looking blankly over the top of Gunna's head at the wall behind her.

Gunna sat in silence and waited for him to continue or emerge from his thoughts.

'I had hoped to stay here for a few weeks,' he said eventually. 'To think, consider my options and find some solutions.'

'To what?'

His eyes were pools of darkness in the gloom beneath the low ceiling.

'To where I can be safe,' he whispered. 'But now I'm not sure there is any such place.'

Steinunn's office felt cold, and she glared at Ívar Laxdal over the expanse of desk between them as if she were defending against an invading army. She held Ívar Laxdal's gaze. The door whispered open and Matthías came in.

'You're telling me I have to betray him, withdraw the offer to allow him to spend time here?' she said.

'That's exactly what I'm telling you. Count the bodies,' Ívar growled. 'Four so far. How many more do we need?'

Steinunn looked aside and chewed her lip.

'What does my new adviser think?' she asked, her eyes snapping into focus on Matthías.

'With respect,' he began, before Steinunn cut him off.

'Less of the "with all due respect" bullshit. I didn't come into politics yesterday, so I know what that phrase means and I'm no stranger to it.'

Matthías clasped his hands together, fingers entwined.

'With all due respect,' he repeated, and this time without being interrupted, 'it's out of your hands. You're not going to be in the country. Once you've taken up your new role in Madrid, it's not as if you're in a position to offer the gentleman in question hospitality, either personally or on behalf of the state.'

Steinunn's face darkened as Matthías continued.

'In fact, it has never been entirely clear on whose authority he is here – yours personally, or the government's – and there are questions that could arise about allocation of public resources. So far they haven't, and hopefully they won't be raised either in Parliament or in the media,' he said in a pleasantly musical intonation. 'However, the PM has more or less made up his mind already.'

'And?' Steinunn said.

'He said, and I quote, "Get that piece of trouble out of my back yard." He also requested an update as soon as the situation has been resolved.'

Steinunn bowed her head.

'You mean he wants confirmation as soon as Osman is out of the country?'

'That's about it. And he has to be gone before you leave for Madrid.'

★ ★ ★

271

Ana liked the look and admired it in the mirror as the hairdresser stepped back.

The brown hair that had brushed her shoulders had been cut high and sharp to the tops of her ears. It was a shade darker than it had been, mahogany instead of chipboard, she decided.

'That's lovely, thank you,' she said as she pulled on her coat.

'See you again.'

'Maybe,' Ana said. 'Next time I have a holiday in Iceland.'

Outside she looked both ways. Food or work?

It had to be work, so she walked back downhill the way she had come earlier, back towards the western part of town with its endless souvenir shops and bars that wouldn't be open until later in the day.

She made for the imposing building she had made a habit of visiting over the last few days, sat at one of the library's computer terminals and logged in to the first of several social media accounts that she used.

Astrid's Facebook profile page, with its avatar of a cartoon puppy, looked back at her, and a moment later it had been deleted.

She punched in another address and a password, and Peter Eriksen's profile appeared, this time with an avatar of a young man with long hair that curled down to his shoulders and glasses with heavy black frames.

Ana clicked a few like buttons, ignored a couple of friend requests, added a few non-committal comments in places to keep the profile alive before opening the messages folder. She read the two most recent messages from a sender she recognized and ignored the rest. She replied in the usual format, informing the other person that Michael had decided to go back to school – a code reporting that Michel was no longer in circulation – and that she would be in class in the next few days, so should they meet for a coffee in the usual place? That meant a debriefing was needed. She noticed that the message had been received, but no reply appeared.

She could return later in the day and check if there was an answer that needed her attention. In the meantime she could take it easy. A sandwich and a beer in one of the cafés would suit her, and then a quiet hour in one of the galleries looking at stark Nordic art that she felt had an alien quality to it.

She logged out, cleared the usage history and stood up, wondering as she did so if that naïve boy were dead yet. The look of surprise and dismay on his face when reality had dawned on him had made her want to laugh at the time, but now it was just saddening.

She would have to check on him soon to make sure and remove the evidence. But lunch could come first.

It was a shame, as she had genuinely liked him when they had met in Helsinki, and again when he had been besotted enough to meet her in Berlin. She reflected that with a little moulding and some prodding under her guidance, he could have turned from a nervous, gauche young man into a pleasantly interesting companion.

It was too late now, though, and there were plenty more interesting men around, even if most of them had already been snapped up. She shrugged. It wasn't as if that had ever been a problem.

'I like it here,' Osman said. He looked around the bare walls and the cupboard doors painted in pastel colours.

'What do you like so much?'

'Listen.'

Gunna sat still. Around them the old building creaked almost imperceptibly and the wind whispered at the window that was open a crack.

'I don't hear anything.'

'That's just it. Not a car to be heard. No people. No noise. Not even children playing outside,' he said. 'Just quiet.'

'It's not always like this. It was quieter at Einholt.'

'Maybe. But it was almost like being a prisoner there. A prisoner in great comfort, but still a prisoner. What we have done today – gone for a walk, had a meal – is something I have not been able to do safely for a long time.'

'Because you're a wanted man?' Gunna said. 'You must have upset someone pretty badly.'

'That doesn't matter now,' he said a with a dismissive shake of his head.

Gunna craned her neck to look at the kitchen clock high on the wall.

'Well, I reckon Ívar should be here soon, and we'll find out what the plans are. This place is fine for a few hours, I suppose, but it's not going to be once word gets out that you're staying here.'

'You haven't heard from Steinunn?'

'Of course not,' Gunna said. 'She doesn't communicate with people at my level. Ívar or one of the ministry staff will pass on whatever she's decided. I don't imagine we'll be the first ones to find out what's going on.'

Skúli rang the bell, and when there was no answer he hammered on the door.

'Valgeir? You there?' he called out.

The house seemed deserted. He peered through the grubby panes of glass in the front door and saw the narrow hallway stacked with neat lines of boxes taped shut, the walls bare of the pictures that usually hung on them.

Valgeir had to be out somewhere.

Skúli took a step back and took out his phone, scrolled through the numbers and hit the call button by Valgeir's name. He listened to the phone ring, and ring some more, until the voicemail message cut in and he ended the call.

In a meeting? Hardly, he decided. Valgeir was on gardening leave so there was nothing official to occupy him. He thumbed the redial button, and in the distance he was sure he could hear the electronic chime he recognized as Valgeir's ringtone.

When voicemail cut in yet again, he put his ear to the door, called again, and this time there was no mistaking the faint ringing inside the flat of the phone that never left Valgeir's side.

He wondered whether or not to call the police, but his experience the previous day helped him make up his mind as he tried the door handle and wasn't surprised to find it locked.

Could he pick the lock, he wondered? He scanned the heavy

wooden door and knew there was no possibility that he could break in this way. He went up the steps and checked all of the flat's windows, finding one that was open the crucial inch that let him get his fingers behind it. He pulled it open halfway, far enough to get a hand inside and release the mechanism holding it in place, then felt something break as he wrenched it fully open.

It didn't occur to him until he was halfway through that the window might not be wide enough, and it was a squeeze to get through the narrow gap, adding scratches to his knuckles to go with the grazes he had acquired the day before.

The window was the smallest one, leading to the smallest room in the flat, and he felt for a foothold, managing to step onto the toilet and lower himself down, gasping with exertion and nerves. If anyone had seen him scrambling through a window, he could expect a knock at the door before long and someone in uniform wanting to ask a few awkward questions.

Unsure of himself, he called out.

'Valgeir?'

There was no reply. He switched on the hall light, checked the living room and saw nothing but more boxes in neat stacks. Valgeir's phone lay on the armrest of the only remaining chair.

It was when he pushed open the door to the bedroom that he saw him and stood rooted to the spot in confusion, before a voice at the back of his mind told him to do something, and he wondered for a second, What?

Skúli snatched at the cloth that had been stuffed in Valgeir's mouth, slapped him gently and called his name.

'Hey, come on. Wake up, will you?'

He felt in Valgeir's neck and was overjoyed to feel a pulse confirming he was alive. After what seemed a long time, one eye opened.

'Skúli?' he said and retched, gasping for air and retching again. 'Get this off me, please, Skúli.'

It was only then that Skúli stood back and saw what he meant.

His clothes were in a heap on the floor and Valgeir had been trussed up in towels and the same broad brown tape used to seal his removal boxes. His legs were behind him and one end of a cord had been tied around his ankles, while the other looped around his neck, so that every time he straightened his body, the cord cut off his airway.

Skúli's fingers tugged at the knot and failed to release it. He looked around in panic as Valgeir choked again, and ran from the room. The scissors had been laid neatly next to the now empty tape dispenser on top of one of the boxes. He guessed they were sharp enough for the sticky plastic tape, but he had to saw at the thick cord.

'Take a deep breath,' he ordered as Valgeir's eyes bulged and then closed tight. 'This is going to hurt.'

The boat's engine coughed and grunted into life. Osman watched as Gunna coiled away the mooring rope. She leaned over the gunwale to check the cooling water was circulating and pointed to the coiled rope.

'I want you to jump onto the berth and make that rope fast when we get there. All right?'

'Where?' Osman asked. 'Where are we going?'

'Not far.' Gunna gestured at the pontoons on the other side of the harbour. 'Just over there.'

Osman looked visibly relieved.

'So we're not going back to the city?'

'Well, we are, but not in this.'

The wind had shifted direction, a cold blast coming off the land. Gunna shivered and lifted the collar of the coat she had pulled on over her fleece. If she were to need the Glock now, she reflected that she would need to take off two layers to reach it, and then she would still need to dig into her pocket for the clip to load it.

She put the boat into gear and increased the engine revs from the gurgle of tickover to a full-throated roar, taking it astern with the wheel hard over to leave the fuel berth.

Osman watched with fascination as she gave the wheel a few turns back to amidships, and opened the throttle to take the boat at a gentle pace across the open water of the harbour.

Overnight the place had become busy as a couple of larger fishing vessels had docked – the occasional gust of wind brought them the pungent sweetish smell from the factory on the quayside.

Gunna took the boat through the harbour entrance, enjoying the feeling of it buck as it caught the waves and the wheel in her hands. Osman stood in the wheelhouse doorway, holding on to the door frame, his face already turning pale.

'Where are we going? I thought . . .'

'Don't worry. We're not going far. Just enjoying the breeze.'

She took the boat a few minutes past the entrance, steered in a long curve around the bay beneath the shadow of the mountain above them and toyed for a moment with the thought of a trip into Hvalfjörður, before telling herself to be sensible and get Osman back to dry land.

He relaxed as the boat slipped into the smooth waters behind the arms of the harbour entrance and Gunna cut the engine revolutions back to tickover. As she approached the finger berth, she put it into gear astern and gave a burst of power. The boat responded obediently, losing way and sliding neatly to the berth.

'There,' Gunna said as the boat bumped against the timbers. 'Jump up.'

Osman stepped gingerly onto the pontoon, placed the loop over a cleat and stood back.

'Now that one,' Gunna said, taking in the bight of the rope and jerking a thumb at the bow rope she had laid over the gunwale. 'And quick.'

She made the stern rope fast, took in the slack of the bow rope and hauled herself up and along the narrow walkway around the wheelhouse to make it tight on the cleat on the casing. She rapidly passed the rest of the rope back through her hands.

'Hey, take this,' she ordered, passing the end to Osman, who stood with it in his hands, wondering what to do with it.

'What?'

Gunna slid down from the casing and swung her legs over the gunwale on the pontoon.

'A ship should always be tied up properly, whether it's a

cockleshell like this or a battleship,' she said, whipping the rope around another cleat on the pontoon, and doing the same with the stern rope's end. See?'

She stood back and Osman could see that the boat was neatly secured four ways.

'Very good,' he said.

Gunna shut down the engine and listened to the gurgle die away, before lifting the hatch and dropping herself down below alongside the engine. She shut off the sea cocks, lifted herself back on deck and slid the hatch into place. In the wheelhouse she lifted the bench seat, isolated the batteries and wondered how long it would be before she got another chance to spend a little time at sea. She shook off her thoughts as she locked the wheelhouse, and let her fingers trail across the timber of the wheelhouse door's frame. Next time, she thought, giving it a pat.

'Come on, then.'

The steel gate pushed open and clanged shut behind them. They walked back up the slope towards the town, shoulders hunched against the biting wind, and Gunna could see Osman wrinkling his nose.

'Gunnhildur, what is that smell?' Osman asked.

'That? That's the money smell,' she replied with a laugh.

'Money?'

She turned and waved a hand towards a large blue and white ship laid to one of the quaysides where figures bustled to and fro around it.

'See that one there? It's the time of year when they catch a little fish, I don't know what it's called in English. But they catch huge amounts for a few weeks, and it goes to the factory over there. That's where they turn it into fishmeal. Like flour, but made of fish.'

'Flour? For what?'

'You wouldn't want to try and make bread with it,' Gunna laughed. 'It's used for fish feed, animal feed. That kind of thing. They call it the money smell because the crews used to earn so much money while the season lasted. So for the fishermen it really was the smell of money.'

* * *

'What the fuck happened?' Skúli demanded as Valgeir gasped down lungfuls of air. 'You got robbed or what?'

'Shit . . .'

Valgeir fumbled for his trousers, but gave up and dragged the duvet around him as he shivered. His hands shook as he gathered the folds of the bedclothes around his throat, where a red mark had formed as the cord had cut into his neck.

'Is the door locked?'

'Yes, of course. I had to climb in through the bathroom window.'

'Please, Skúli. Go and bolt the door. Put the chain on, and lock the bathroom window.'

'The door's locked. Why bolt it as well?'

'Just do it,' Valgeir pleaded.

Skúli went out into the hall and shot the bolt at the bottom of the door and hooked the security chain in place. The bathroom window was less easy, as he found that he'd wrenched it almost clear of the frame, but he managed to pull it back into place, where it wouldn't be easily noticed.

When Skúli returned, Valgeir was hunched with his eyes closed, sobbing between deep breaths.

'It's all locked up. Nobody's coming in here without a battering ram. Do you feel like putting some clothes on and telling me what happened? And how about I call the police and you report whatever happened here?'

'No!' Valgeir's eyes were wide open. 'Not the police. Definitely not.'

'Shit, Valgeir. Someone almost murdered you, and you're seriously telling me you don't want to take it to the police?'

'No. Not a word.' He shook his head. 'Nothing. It never happened. Get me some water, would you?'

In the kitchen Skúli hunted for a glass in the empty cupboards, gave up and let the cold tap run for a moment before filling a plastic mug.

Valgeir had pulled on his trousers and a shirt by the time Skúli

279

handed him the mug, and he drank the water down in one long draught before sitting down on the edge of the bed and holding his head in his hands.

Skúli sat on a stool.

'All right, explain. Give me a reason not to report an attempted murder.'

'Because I've almost sold the flat. I've got a new job in Vienna and I'm supposed to be leaving tomorrow. I just want to forget all this. Pretend it never happened. Get on with my life from now on.'

'So who was it?'

Valgeir took a gulping breath.

'Her. Astrid.'

'What? The woman you were seeing in Germany? She turned up here in Reykjavík? When?'

'This morning,' Valgeir mumbled and looked up. 'Fuck, Skúli. I'm in so much shit if this gets out. Up to my neck. I'll be dismissed, career over in a flash.'

'Explain, will you?'

'I met her in Helsinki, at the same conference where Steinunn got on so well with Osman, a couple of months ago. She told me her name was Astrid and she was there undercover, supposedly with an EU delegation. She said she was tailing Osman, that he's a known criminal and her team was gathering evidence.'

'And you fell for it? And her?'

Valgeir moaned quietly. 'Totally. I even took a couple of weekend breaks and met her twice in Berlin before Osman arrived here.'

'But you knew Osman was on the way here?'

'Yeah. Steinunn told the team that she was making arrangements for him to come to Iceland, but we weren't to tell anyone, not even family.'

'So you told this woman?'

Valgeir hung his head and a teardrop landed on the tiled floor with a splash.

'Yeah. Everything,' he groaned. 'Not a word, Skúli. Don't say a thing. I thought I was doing the right thing, that she really was working for Europol, and it was all part of a massive investigation into people trafficking.'

Skúli's thoughts went to the two men in black and the lines on Ívar Laxdal's face.

'What have I done?' Valgeir crooned to himself, and Skúli had no answer to give him. He looked up and his eyes were filled with tears. 'I lost it. Completely lost it. I've never had much luck with girls, then suddenly there was this smart, attractive woman who showed real interest in me, and I couldn't see what was right in front of me.'

'You fucked up, Valgeir,' Skúli agreed.

'Now I've lost her, not that I ever had her, I suppose. And I don't want to lose my career as well. So please, Skúli. Don't say a word to anyone, let me finish packing and I'll be gone tomorrow,' he said and shivered. 'I'm not staying here, though. The freight company can collect my stuff and I'll go to a hotel for tonight. I don't want to see this place again as long as I live.'

It took Osman half an hour and two mugs of hot coffee cradled in both hands before he stopped shivering enough to take off his coat. Gunna hung it on the hook behind the door.

ETA 10 minutes ÍL, flashed the message on her phone.

'Ívar is on the way,' she said. 'I imagine we'll be going back to town, but I have no idea where we'll be staying.'

'We can't stay here another day? It's peaceful here. I like that.'

Ívar Laxdal's black Volvo appeared soundlessly in the street, and as he got out and looked around, Gunna tapped on the kitchen window, pointing towards the end of the house and the steps down to the basement flat.

'Nice place, Gunnhildur,' he said as he stamped his feet in the hall. 'Can I ask how . . . ?'

'It's my son's. I'll tell you about the boat later.'

'Ah, that explains things,' he said, moving aside to let Luc and Birna crowd in behind him.

'Osman's in the kitchen. There's enough coffee for everyone, but not enough chairs.'

Ívar Laxdal shook Osman's hand and planted himself firmly on a stool next to him, leaving Luc to take the only one remaining, while Birna scowled at being left to stand.

'How was the trip across the bay?' he asked Osman.

'It was an adventure. Not one I would like to repeat, but an adventure all the same.'

'Ach. You were in capable hands. Gunnhildur comes from a long line of sea dogs and knows her way around a boat. I wouldn't have let you go if it hadn't been safe,' he said and turned to Gunna. 'Everything all right? No problems?'

'Nothing so far. No sign of anyone snooping around. But Akranes isn't a big town, so it's only a matter of time before someone joins the dots.'

'Exactly,' Ívar Laxdal said. 'We have a place for you overnight near Reykjavík, and you'll be leaving the country tomorrow.'

'Tomorrow?' Osman said, his mouth open. 'But . . .'

'The thing is, we don't have the resources to ensure your safety,' Birna broke in.

'And we've had four fatalities in a week, all apparently connected to your presence here. That's as many murders as Iceland would normally have in five years,' Ívar Laxdal added. 'So you can understand my position, not least that we don't want you to be the next fatality.'

'Is this because Steinunn is going?' Osman asked. 'I thought she was a true friend, and now she's abandoning me.'

'That may have something to do with it,' Ívar Laxdal said and shrugged. 'Politicians . . .'

'So you're going to send me away? I thought I had at least a few weeks of safety here.'

'This gentleman here is from Brussels, and even if you don't know him, I gather he knows you pretty well,' Ívar Laxdal said. 'Luc?'

Ana pulled her scarf up over her mouth and her hat down to her eyebrows. It went against all the rules, but she wanted to check. In spite of the sunshine, the wind had a bitter quality to it as it ate

282

its way through however many layers a person was wearing, so she buttoned her coat up, lifted the collar high and walked fast.

Öldugata was deserted. A few flakes of snow scudded along the ground, driven by the knife-edge wind that bit at her cheeks. Apart from a shabby car that had been parked half across the pavement, there was nothing to be seen at the house where Valgeir's flat occupied part of the basement.

There was no movement anywhere. There were few lights behind the windows, no cars on the move and no pedestrians. It was as if this part of Reykjavík had been deserted. Encouragingly, there was no sign of life at Valgeir's flat. She saw the door was shut and noticed, as she strode past, that there was a pristine covering of frost on the steps, so nobody had come in or out for an hour or two, and it was inviting trouble to go around the back of the house and peer through the windows.

It nagged at her that she hadn't finished the job there and then, instead of trying to make Valgeir's death look like a kinky sex game gone wrong.

She fingered the key in her pocket and decided against going in.

Ana strode back to the library and made up her mind on the way. If the instruction came through to stay in Iceland and try to re-establish monitoring Osman, she would return and make sure Valgeir was dead. If it was time to disengage, she would be on the first flight out.

Valgeir hunched in the passenger seat, nervously looking around, a scarf wound around his neck to hide the red mark that had eaten into his skin. He clutched a laptop bag in his arms, and Skúli threw the case containing Valgeir's clothes onto the back seat. All his remaining belongings had been quickly stuffed into boxes, taped and added to the pile in the hallway, and the flat had been locked and left without a backward glance.

Dagga's battered blue Peugeot coughed and complained.

'Come on, will you?' Valgeir muttered.

'I'm doing my best,' Skúli retorted. 'It doesn't start easily in the cold.'

He turned the key again and the starter motor whined, hung, and unwillingly turned the engine over a couple of times before it burst into life.

'Come on, let's be going.'

'It's all right. There's nobody about, and certainly not your ladyfriend.'

The car bumped off the kerb and into the road, while Valgeir sighed with relief. His eyes were red and his hands were trembling.

'I'll see if I can get a flight tomorrow.'

'To Vienna? Is there a direct flight?'

'No. I'll need to make a connection somewhere, but it's not a problem.'

'Where are we going?'

'Going?' Valgeir looked confused.

'I ought to be taking you to A&E, or at least to the police,' Skúli grumbled. 'But as you won't have either of those, where do you want me to take you?'

'Hell, I don't know. A hotel.'

'Yeah. Which one?'

'Hotel Vatnsmýri? By the domestic airport?'

'Expensive,' Skúli said, bringing the car to a halt at the lights at the bottom of Gilsgata. 'There's a hotel there,' he said, pointing across the street.

'Yeah, but I don't like that place. Vatnsmýri is away from the centre and I can get the flybus to the airport tomorrow. Don't go that way,' he muttered. 'Go left instead. I don't want to go through town.'

'You're going tomorrow?'

'Yeah. I don't want to hang around.'

'And tonight? What are you going to do tonight?'

'Room service and an early night.'

Valgeir lapsed into silence and settled deep into his seat, the scarf wrapped around his face, and didn't relax until the car was on Hringbraut and leaving the western part of town behind.

'Tonight,' Skúli said, signalling and slowing to take the turning off the main road, 'I'm sure Dagga would like to see you before you go. Get a taxi to ours and you can have a meal with us tonight.'

Valgeir grimaced.

'I'd like to,' he began, 'but right now I just want to shut myself away.'

'Come on. She's about the only relative you have in Reykjavík. You ought to say goodbye, surely?'

Valgeir sighed.

'All right. If I must. But don't go to any trouble.'

The car came to a halt outside the hotel and Valgeir opened the door to get out.

'See you at six,' Skúli said as Valgeir reached into the back seat for his case and struggled to lift it.

'Like they say in the movies, I'm making you an offer you can't refuse,' Luc said, shifting his stool up to the table and planting his elbows on it, staring Osman in the eye.

'If it's an offer, then I can refuse if I choose to.'

'Hear me out. You're in the shit up to your neck. There are two rival factions battling it out, who have been united by you. They've discovered they have one thing in common; they both want you delivered to them in one piece, alive. And you know what that means,' Luc said in a stuttering, rapid delivery. Osman opened his mouth to speak, but Luc held up a finger in his face.

'You have a choice in this, sure. Your option is to get off a flight in Brussels tomorrow and my people collect you before you even get to passport control. From there you do business as usual, except that we're watching every step you take. Your foundation continues as before, except that you tell us every detail about the people you're dealing with, what they're doing, where the cash comes from, and we see every cent that comes in and goes out, who put it there, what dog-leg routes it took and why it came to you. Understand?'

Osman's eyes became the impassive black pools that Gunna had seen before.

'And the other option?' he asked in a low, clear voice.

Luc folded his arms.

'You get off a flight in Brussels tomorrow,' he said. 'That's it. You get off the flight and do whatever you like.'

'And?'

'I know how big the bounty on your head is, and these people really, really want you. If they don't get what they want, the price tag will just keep going up until someone delivers. But I don't believe it will go that far,' Luc said and paused. 'I put your chances of staying free at a week . . . ten days at the most.'

A tremor passed through Osman and his jaw trembled.

'You think I am afraid?'

'Maybe not. But I also know you're not stupid. You know what will happen to you when you're delivered. You'll tell them every single thing they want to know, give them access to all your businesses and bank accounts, and by the end you'll be begging them for a neat finish with a bullet.'

'I'm to be thrown to the wolves. Is that what you're offering, Commander Kerkhoeve?'

Luc shifted in his seat and took his time answering. If he was surprised that Osman knew his name, he did not show it. The atmosphere in the room was electric as everyone waited.

'That you get to live.'

'For how long?'

'For as long as you're needed. You run the foundation as usual.'

'And when I'm no longer needed?'

'You surrender the foundation to a charity of some kind and we help you disappear.'

'I know about disappearing,' Osman replied with bitterness. 'It's not as easy as you think.'

'True,' Luc agreed. 'But we have resources, and sympathetic contacts. A new identity is easily created when you have access to the apparatus of government. Making it work is down to the individual. If you have the discipline to keep your head down and abandon what you were before, it's perfectly possible. Of course, you have to be aware that it's very much in our interest for you to live to a ripe old age without being discovered. So it's a long-term commitment on our part, not an offer that would be made to just anyone, you understand.'

Osman sighed and clasped his hands in front of him on the table as his eyes stared at the wall above Gunna's head, where the kitchen clock ticked away the seconds.

'There are conditions,' Luc said, breaking the silence.

'Such as?'

'One strike and you're out. We are talking complete co-opera-tion, no hesitation, no deals on the sly, nothing held back.'

'Meaning what? Punishment?'

Luc laughed. There was no mirth in it, just a bark of cold amusement that nobody shared.

'There would be no need to administer any punishment. We would simply withdraw and the wolves could have you. It wouldn't take long.'

Ana unwound the scarf from around her neck and opened Peter Eriksen's profile page again on the library computer.

She was nervous now, sure that she had made a mistake in deal-ing with Valgeir. She wanted to return to the flat on Ölgugata and make sure, but kept telling herself that it would simply compound one mistake with another.

She clicked on the messages, and saw with satisfaction that she was asked to arrange a meeting with Michael's teacher whenever it might be convenient.

She deleted the messages, closed the profile and opened the airline's web page.

The next morning's nine o'clock flight could get her home in time for lunch.

Ívar Laxdal's Volvo was packed for the journey back to the city. Osman sat in the middle seat, squeezed between Birna and Gunna as Luc glowered in the front seat.

Leaving Akranes behind, Osman craned his neck for a last view

287

of the colourful little town as it disappeared behind them. A few trails of powder snow snaked lazily across the black tarmac of the road, driven by the wind, and the top of the mountain looming over the town disappeared into fat grey cloud that threatened more snow.

As the Volvo approached the Hvalfjörður tunnel, a police patrol car slipped into position ahead of them, before they dipped down the long slope into darkness. Gunna could feel Osman's nervousness magnified and glanced to one side to find his eyes shut tight.

'All right?' she asked.

'Just a little claustrophobia,' he muttered and gave her a thin smile. 'It'll be fine. I just have to convince myself we're going to come out the other side.'

Once out of the tunnel and into the remains of the daylight, the patrol car escort's lights flashed blue and it picked up speed, overtaking trucks and cars along the road skirting the coast.

Always nervous as a passenger, even with Ívar Laxdal at the wheel, Gunna wanted to close her eyes as well.

The city had the feeling of hatches being battened down. The morning's sunshine had gone and a few shallow white drifts began to collect by the roadsides and against walls and cars parked facing the north-east wind. The patrol car's blue lights stopped flashing and Ívar Laxdal eased the car off the main road and through the cloverleaf onto Reykjanesbraut.

'We are leaving the city?' Osman asked, looking around.

The road was packed with traffic and the patrol car's lights flashed a few times to clear a path.

'Through it and out the other side,' Birna said.

'So where are we going? I would like to see Steinunn. Is it not possible to meet her?'

'I'm afraid not,' Birna said in a tone that was both apologetic and firm. 'Steinunn is very busy right now and sends her kindest regards. She said she regrets that your visit couldn't be longer.'

'I see,' Osman replied. 'She feels she made a mistake in asking me here and I guess she's thinking of the headlines?'

Birna weighed her words for a moment.

'Yeah. That's about it,' she said.

'I'm now an embarrassment rather than a welcome guest,' he said with a touch of bitterness.

Ívar Laxdal muttered into his communicator and the patrol car peeled off as they approached Hafnarfjörður. At the next intersection a pair of motorcycles swung onto the road and flanked the Volvo through the traffic, escorting it past roundabouts with barely a slackening of pace, and out onto the main road again. They overtook everything on the road, and this time Gunna shut her eyes in spite of Ívar Laxdal's skill at the wheel and the blue lights that flashed in the gathering gloom with snowflakes spinning in the beams of the Volvo's headlights.

'Where are we?' Osman asked as the two motorcycles fell back and Ívar Laxdal took the suburban streets at a more sedate pace, pulling up on the tarmac gap between the ends of two terraces.

'This is Keflavík,' Gunna said, as nobody else seemed inclined to answer him. 'The airport is just over there,' she added needlessly as the sound of an aeroplane circling to land could be heard.

'Here we are,' Ívar Laxdal said. 'Your place for tonight. It looks like a jail, but it's not, and it's comfortable inside. I'll be back early tomorrow, and until then Steingrímur and some of his boys will be watching over you.'

Valgeir ate his curried chicken in near silence while Skúli fed Markús, and Dagga tried to have a conversation with the cousin she'd rarely had much contact with.

'Why did you ask him here?' she hissed to Skúli as Valgeir disappeared to the bathroom.

'I told you, he's had a rough time. He needs some support.'

'Who was this person? Do you know?'

'Not really. It's all to do with Osman. Valgeir got unlucky, I guess, and got himself tangled up in all this.'

They fell silent as Valgeir reappeared. His eyes were red and he was unable to hide having spent five minutes of solitude in tears behind the locked door.

'I'm really sorry,' he said in a thick voice. 'I'm shit company. Can you call me a cab?'

'Sure. Or one of us can drive you back to the hotel?'

Valgeir shook his head.

'Just get me a cab,' he said and dropped heavily into one of the kitchen chairs.

Dagga went to find her phone and Skúli handed Valgeir a mug.

'You've got time for coffee, haven't you?'

'Yeah. I suppose,' he said as Skúli poured. 'Sorry, Skúli. I'm feeling lousy. I just want to crawl into bed for a few hours and then get the bus for my flight in the morning.'

'You know who this woman is?' Skúli asked in an undertone, leaning forward over the table.

'Nope. Not a clue. I just knew her as Astrid Szabo, which you can bet isn't her real name. We communicated mainly through social media and her profile has vanished. Not blocked, completely gone, and her phone number is out of use.'

'Where did you meet?'

'Hotels. I don't know exactly where she lives, or lived. She said it was a boring suburb where nothing ever happens.'

'So you don't have anything?'

'Not a clue. I don't even have a picture of her. Just the image in my head of her face, and the fact that her German is flawless enough for her to be a native, although for all I know she could be from anywhere.'

He sipped his coffee. For a second Skúli was tempted to put out a comforting hand, but he held back.

'You know, Skúli? I really thought I'd hit the jackpot with her, absolutely won the Eurozillions. She's pretty and fantastically smart, way smarter than I am,' he said and sighed. 'I wonder if I'll ever see her again, and what I'd have to say to her?'

Gunna shut the door behind her, kicked off her boots and put the security chain in place.

'Gunnhildur, what is this place?'

'Someone's apartment. I guess it's used for short-term lets for tourists. I imagine Ívar booked it online.'

The flat was warm, but minimally furnished in a way that made it feel cool. Gunna had the feeling that nobody ever lived here any more, that this place had become one of the many used solely for a night or two by travellers passing through.

She opened cupboards and the fridge to find that milk and a couple of pizzas had been provided, then she switched on the oven.

'Quick and easy dinner tonight,' she said, turning to see that Osman was still wrapped in his coat, hands in his pockets. He sat at the table in silence as Gunna prepared their meal, shaking off his coat and looking morose while Gunna shook salad from a bag, squeezed a sachet of dressing over it and took the pizzas from the oven.

'Help yourself,' she said, slicing each pizza into six. 'They've even left us a bottle of wine if you'd like a glass.'

Osman chewed pizza and nodded. Gunna opened the bottle and filled one glass for him, half a glass for herself.

'Our last night together,' Osman said with the first glimmer of a smile she had seen since the conversation with Luc in Akranes a few hours before.

'It is,' Gunna said, raising her glass to clink against his. 'It's been interesting, and a little crazy, so I won't be sorry to go back to normal duties again.'

'And to your . . . boyfriend? Husband, or whatever you refer to him as?'

'Of course. I think this is the longest we've been apart, so it goes without saying that I'm looking forward to seeing him again, and my children, and the grandchildren.'

'You are fortunate. You have a family around you. I have nothing like that any longer.'

'So what was your decision, if you don't mind my asking? Are you going to accept Luc's offer?'

Osman shrugged, drained his glass and held it out for Gunna to refill.

'I have no choice. Kerkhoeve is quite right. There are more people who want me dead than I can stay away from, so I either accept his terms or the rest of my life will short and probably extremely uncomfortable. Coming to this place was an attempt to disappear from sight, but the secret was out before I even got here.'

'You mean there are people you can't trust?'

'They are everywhere,' he said gravely, 'but they don't wear a badge, so I can't be sure who is trustworthy and who isn't. Except you, naturally. You are honest. I can feel that in my bones.'

'And Luc?' Gunna asked, ignoring the compliment. 'Are you sure you can trust him?'

'Kerkhoeve is someone I can rely on. I won't say trust. But I can rely on being kept safe for as long as I am useful to him. I will have to live in a cage, though. Everything I do or say will be watched and recorded, until I have told him everything I can give, and then . . . Then I don't know.'

'A new identity?'

'It's possible. Somewhere far away.' There was a hopeful look in his eyes. 'Or maybe by then everyone will have forgotten all about this.'

'You told me before that these things are never forgotten.'

'You're right. There are places I'll never be able to go, people I'll never see again, including most of my relatives. Being seen with them would put them in danger.'

Gunna picked up the last piece of pizza and bit into it.

'Tell me,' she said, 'between ourselves. This swindle that Luc talked about. Did you do it?'

Osman sat back and frowned. His eyes sparkled with an anger deep inside.

'Swindle? No.'

'So what happened? Can you tell me? So I know what kind of a man I've spent the last week with.'

'If you think you can believe me, then I will tell you.' He sighed and was silent for a moment as he collected his thoughts. 'You understand that I don't know the whole story myself,' he said at last. 'Some of this is a mystery to me as well.'

'Go on,' Gunna said, finishing the last of the pizza and sipping her wine.

'There were two shipments, two days apart.'

'Can I ask what was in the shipments?'

Osman smiled. 'Medicines, a whole variety of drugs, mostly antibiotics. But also ammunition, thousands of rounds of small arms ammunition, and drones. These eyes in the sky are becoming very sought after. So, from your point of view, some good and some bad.'

'Understood.'

'The first shipment was warned off, diverted. The plan was to bring it up the beach in the south. It's better there as the road is near the shore, but there aren't many places where it's possible to land unseen, as most of that coast is inhabited. In the end, they went to the backup plan, a landing place further north. It's more difficult there as the coastline's rocky, with mountains and bad roads, but fewer people and less chance of being seen.'

'And they were able to land?'

'The first one. The larger, second shipment was stolen.'

'Do you know who took it?'

'I can only guess, but it was cleverly done. The boats were intercepted offshore and simply taken. The men on board were lucky in that they were only beaten and thrown in the water, so they were able to swim to shore. But the goods were gone and the group that was due to take delivery never saw anything. They claimed we had sold the same goods to two rival militias. These people don't take kindly to being wronged. It's a matter of pride for them to seek revenge if they've been wronged, and that's what they want to do.'

'So someone robbed them, and you get the blame?'

Ana trudged through the scattering of powder snow.

The apartment had been left clean and tidy, with nothing left behind that could raise any suspicion. She had searched the place with care, just in case Michel had hidden a weapon somewhere, but there was nothing.

She left the key on the kitchen counter, along with a note thanking the owner for a pleasant stay and a promise to leave a positive rating on the letting website.

A taxi took her to the bus station and she ate a solid meal at the cafeteria as she waited, killing time, watching people coming and going, deciding that the majority of them were tourists in their thick, bright thermal coats and heavy walking boots.

Nobody took any notice of the woman in a long brown overcoat who sipped coffee after her meal and leafed through a local newspaper, pausing as the face of a man with deep brown eyes and a black beard appeared across half a page.

With a finger under the text, she puzzled her way through the headline and the picture caption, consulting the dictionary in her phone for the words that escaped her.

She folded the newspaper, already well thumbed after having been on the cafeteria tables for most of the day, and stood up, leaving a few coins on the table for the staff.

The coach hummed into the darkness and Ana stared into the gloom as snow settled on the darkening landscape at the side of the road, forming a soft covering over the jagged lava.

The hotel in Keflavík was overheated and stuffy, and she shook off her coat the moment she stepped into the lobby.

'One night?'

The young man behind the desk eyed her curiously.

'One night,' she confirmed. 'Early flight tomorrow, so could you please order me a taxi for five?'

'Going somewhere nice?'

'Yeah,' she said, passing a credit card across the counter. 'Home.'

She punched in the number, took her key and shouldered her bag.

'Your room's on the first floor. Would you like me to help you?'

'I can manage, thanks. Is there a bar here?'

'Through there. Open until midnight.'

'Cool. I'll be down for a nightcap.'

'If there's anything you need, I'm here to help,' the young man behind the desk said with an unmistakable hint of suggestion.

'And in the unlikely event there's anything I need, then you'll be the first to find out,' Ana assured him.

'What you were doing was illegal?'

Osman smiled properly for the first time.

'Illegal? What is illegal in a lawless land? I can't say if what we were doing was right or wrong. We were just meeting a demand. If I hadn't done it, someone else would have been there to take the money.'

'And the risks.'

'And someone else would have found themselves staring a pistol in the face. This is life.'

'So the other side of the business, the refugees. You were happy to do that as well?'

'Again,' Osman said, 'there was a demand, a very strong demand. People wanted to escape a war zone, and they were prepared to pay with practically everything they had. Business is business. If someone wants to give you money, you don't turn them away.'

Gunna shook her head.

'It's difficult for me to understand how you could do this. We see on the news here—'

'You see half the story. You see penniless migrants. What we see on the beaches are people desperate to escape the bullets or persecution. They don't ask the price of a place in a boat; they just pay it, and we made sure they were able to wade ashore and weren't put to sea in some hulk that was ready to sink.'

'And the same in North Africa?'

'That is not my affair. White Sickle is active with the refugees who come to Italy from North Africa, but I've had nothing to do with bringing them across. Gunnhildur, I have been there. If I were to try and steal business from the people who are there, then my throat would have been cut within an hour. I may have been unlucky sometimes, but I'm not stupid.'

He yawned and lifted the wine bottle. He poured himself another glass, then held the bottle over Gunna's. She put her hand over it.

295

'I'm on duty. Remember?'

'Of course. I don't think you are ever off duty, Gunnhildur.'

'It does happen. I'll be off duty for a week once you're on your flight.'

'And what will you do?'

'Relax. Try not to think about this last week. Read a book and play with the grandchildren.'

Osman shook his head.

'I can still hardly believe they appointed a grandmother as my bodyguard.'

His smile returned, broad this time, his teeth a brilliant white. Osman reached across the table between the glasses and the pizza crusts, his fingers seeking out her hand. She did not withdraw it as his fingertips trailed across the back of her hand.

'Gunnhildur, I admire you tremendously.'

'Thank you.'

He held her hand and squeezed it, and Gunna felt her stomach flutter as he gazed into her eyes with a warmth she hadn't seen before.

'Gunnhildur, this is our last night,' he murmured. 'Maybe we should spend it together?'

Gunna lifted her hand, laid it over his and squeezed back, hard enough to make Osman wince.

'Thanks, but no thanks,' she said at last. 'No offence, but I have a guy of my own and it just wouldn't be right. We can both just have an early night and go to bed with a good book.'

The look of disappointment on his face was clear and Gunna wanted to laugh, but restrained herself. Her own momentary hesitation in refusing had taken her by surprise, and she wondered why she had even thought about it. Osman was an undeniably attractive man and capable of being captivating when he wanted to switch on the charm. Maybe if he hadn't treated Sif so coldly on the night of the shooting, which now seemed so long ago, she would have taken his suggestion more seriously – how much more seriously, she wondered?

She reminded herself that she was on duty, and while that did

not have to be a reason to turn down an adventure, she knew there
was a good chance that every word they said was being recorded.

'Go on. You can take a shower while I clear up here. Old
grandmothers like me need our beauty sleep. We have to be up
early; Ívar will be here at five.'

Chapter Eight

Bundled in a woollen hat that came down to his eyebrows and a coat that reached his ears, the taxi driver said not a word until he pulled up at the terminal.

The young man at the hotel's reception desk had been equally taciturn; either he was tired at the end of a long shift or disappointed that she hadn't required his assistance with anything during the night.

Ana handed the driver cash, waved away a receipt, and shivered as she marched through the cold darkness and into the building. She felt as if she were on holiday, with one job done and another called off. Now there was the flight home, a debriefing in yet another anonymous central European hotel, followed by a few days of relaxation. It had been a long assignment – for five months she had tailed Osman, then for the last few weeks she'd tried to manage those two knuckleheads; she felt she deserved a rest.

'Sandra Blondel?'

She nodded as the check-in clerk scanned her passport, pressed a button for a conveyor belt to whisk her case away, and handed her a boarding pass.

'Enjoy your flight,' he said, giving her the first welcoming smile of the day.

She had nearly finished breakfast when the sight of a familiar figure almost made her spit coffee out before she froze.

Valgeir walked past as if in a daze. His eyes were red and there

298

was a scarf wrapped high around his neck as he stood peering at the screen showing the departure gates.

Ana turned away and pulled her collar up as she fumbled for her phone. She switched its camera to selfie mode and looked at her own face in the screen, while watching Valgeir as he stood behind her shoulder. Her heart hammered and she bitterly reproached herself for not having dealt with him conclusively the previous day.

She quickly took stock, wondering what her best option was. The safest one would be to leave the airport and get a later flight. But she had the advantage of having seen Valgeir while he was unaware of her, and as long as he didn't get a clear look at her face, she could probably avoid being recognized. The problem was he could be on the same flight, and that would be fraught with problems.

Squinting at the phone's screen, she watched him shamble towards the bookstall where he scanned the rows of magazines and foreign newspapers on display. Ana quickly gathered her belongings, stuffed the phone in her pocket and set off for one of the souvenir shops, keeping Valgeir at enough of a distance that he would be unlikely to recognize her if he turned around, but close enough that she could watch and avoid him.

'Sleep well?' Ívar Laxdal asked with a shadow of a smirk, confirming her suspicion that the flat had been bugged.

'Very well, thanks,' Gunna replied and placed Osman's case on the back seat.

'No problems?'

'Were you expecting any?' Gunna asked.

'Not at all. I knew everything was in safe hands. We need to be quick, so where's our boy?'

Osman appeared, bleary-eyed and shivering in the wind that seemed to be even colder in the pre-dawn gloom.

'Good morning,' he said, extending a hand for Ívar Laxdal to shake.

A surly Luc huddled in a thick anorak, stamping his feet, taking puffs from a cigarette cradled in one hand. He gave a surly wave, trod the butt of his cigarette into the snow and got back into the passenger seat of Ívar Laxdal's car.

There was silence on the way to the airport until Ívar Laxdal pulled up behind a black Mercedes outside the terminal. Inside the building he led the way, glancing from side to side as he strode through the half-empty building, with Osman at his side, Luc hurrying to keep up and Gunna following, aware that somewhere behind them Steingrímur and his team were outside.

'No formalities here,' Ívar Laxdal said, rapping on a door that opened to admit them to a meeting room where Steinunn and a glum Matthías were waiting.

'Ali, I'm so sorry,' she said, standing up to take Osman's hands in hers, leading him to a corner of the room where they talked in undertones. Gunna could see tears begin to well up in Steinunn's eyes and Osman nodded as she talked rapidly.

'Ready for this?' Ívar Laxdal asked Luc, who looked as if he were reining in his impatience.

He shook his head and pursed his lips.

'Yeah. There's a welcoming committee at Brussels, so once our friend is their responsibility, I'll be happier. I don't like flying, even when I don't have someone to escort safely to the other end,' he added and turned to Gunna. 'Did he tell you anything that might be useful?'

'You can listen to the tape,' she growled, and Ívar Laxdal looked uncomfortable.

At the other end of the room, Osman and Steinunn stood up, and she again clasped his hands in both of hers as he looked into her eyes.

'I'm so sorry,' she said again. 'I do wish . . .' she continued, without finishing her sentence.

'I appreciate what you've done, and what you tried to do,' Osman told her, his voice raw. 'It's unfortunate that so much trouble came with me to your peaceful country. I would have liked to stay a little longer.'

'We have to go,' Ívar Laxdal said as Steinunn squeezed Osman's hands again before letting them go.

'We should go,' Osman agreed, with a parting look at Steinunn.

Ívar Laxdal led the way, this time with an airport official at his side, who opened doors for them as if by magic.

'You're going all the way to the gate?' the man asked. 'Or just to the departure lounge?'

'The gate.'

'No problem. It's a bit of a mess at the moment, I'm afraid. The place is being rebuilt.'

'Again.'

'Yeah, as if we haven't had enough building work here. But winter's the time to get it done.'

He pulled open a door that Gunna noticed only had a handle on one side, and they stepped out into the departure lounge.

Ana's heart sank as she saw Valgeir join the queue for the departure gate she wanted. He seemed completely absorbed in his phone, and she wondered if she could safely take the same flight without being seen. What could he do even if he were to see her? If he'd reported what had happened yesterday, he would hardly be leaving the country so soon afterwards, or would he?

She joined the end of the line and could see the back of Valgeir's head some way in front of her, almost at the front of the queue. Ana put on a baseball cap with a puffin motif that she had picked up at a souvenir stall, pulling the brim low to hide most of her face, and took a deep breath. She told herself there was still time to bail out if things looked awkward, and there was every chance that she would make it home in time for lunch without Valgeir having any idea that she was on the same flight.

The queue moved in fits and starts as the passengers boarded, a sleepy attendant checking passports against names on boarding passes – Ana quickly checked that she had a passport in Sandra Blondel's name in her hand.

She saw with satisfaction that Valgeir was in the middle of the aircraft, while she had paid extra and booked a window seat near the front. Confident that she would be able to avoid him, she handed her documents across.

'Is it a full flight?'

'Pretty much,' the attendant said. 'It doesn't help that we have a VIP on this flight, so he gets a row to himself.'

'Anyone famous?' Ana asked.

'No idea. But it's short notice, so that normally means it's some politician.'

'So this is goodbye. Luc is travelling with you,' Ívar Laxdal said, and turned to the airport official. 'And this gentleman will take the two of you to the gate once the other passengers have boarded.'

Gunna thought Osman looked a completely different man to the self-assured figure who had stepped out of a private jet what seemed like an age ago. The coat he was wearing still carried the stains from the boat, but he stood upright, with the bearing of a man accustomed to being listened to.

Osman extended a hand to Ívar Laxdal.

'Thank you, Commander. I'm deeply grateful for all your efforts. I appreciate I have made life difficult for you.'

'It's been interesting,' Ívar Laxdal replied.

'And Gunnhildur,' Osman said. No hand was extended and instead he opened his arms. Gunna could feel the Glock in its holster pressed against her side as Osman's arms closed around her in a fierce embrace and she hugged him back.

'I won't say it's been all fun and games,' she said, disengaging, 'but it has been an experience. I hope everything works out for you, Osman.'

'I hope so too, Gunnhildur. I hope so. And I hope that one day we can meet again.'

'And with that, we must go,' Ívar Laxdal said. 'Look after him, won't you, Luc, and thanks for all your efforts.'

Luc coughed. 'And you. I'll be in touch next week, and I'll send you the information you asked for on your cases. All right?'

Ívar Laxdal gave him a wave that was almost a salute, and Gunna had to hurry to keep up with him.

'What now, Gunnhildur?' he said as they walked back through the terminal. 'What now? Back to the shop?'

'For you, maybe, but I haven't been home for more than a week, so you could start by giving me a lift to Hvalvík. Steini might even make us breakfast if we're lucky.'

Squeezed into the window seat next to a man in a suit who had merely nodded as he took his place before absorbing himself in a movie on his computer, Ana wanted to laugh. What were the chances of all three of them being on the same flight?

The man she had somehow failed to murder was seated a dozen rows behind her, while the one she was still hoping to deliver to angry men who wanted him dead had taken a seat at the front of the cabin. Osman had been ushered on board by an official, accompanied by a dishevelled man she knew as Commander Kerkhoeve. She knew him by sight, and sincerely hoped he wouldn't recognize her; not that there was any reason he should. As far as she knew, she didn't appear on any police records, either under her own name or under any of the various aliases she used.

The man in the next seat looked sideways over his glasses and closed his laptop for takeoff. Ana had no desire to strike up a conversation and closed her eyes, pulling the brim of her cap down over her face.

She was surprised to wake well into the flight, having dozed off while the aircraft climbed into the skies over Iceland. The movie the man in the suit had been watching had finished, replaced on his laptop's screen with a spreadsheet that looked less interesting, but which he seemed to find just as absorbing.

What next, she wondered. Would there be an opportunity to shadow Osman? It was unlikely. Kerkhoeve's shabby figure might not look much, but the man had a reputation for ruthlessness and results. At least she knew where he would be going, should the not entirely reliable tracker in Osman's phone fail.

Then there was Valgeir. Should she simply avoid him at the other end, or give him a wave and a smile before disappearing into the crowd?

* * *

'You're coming in, aren't you?'

Ívar Laxdal switched off the Volvo's engine and they sat in silence.

'You know, Gunnhildur,' he said at last, 'you have no idea how relieved I am that Osman is no longer our problem.'

'I think I can guess. But now we have to clear up all the mess he caused.'

'Some of it. The two mercenaries haven't been formally identified, although Luc gave us a rough idea of who they were. One of them was responsible for the murders of Thór Hersteinsson and James Kearney, before drowning in an as yet unexplained accident. Neat, isn't it?'

'Yes. Much, much too neat. Certainly too neat to have been an accident.'

'Whatever went on there, it's a mystery that you and I will probably never get to the bottom of.'

Gunna chewed her lip.

'Now you're wrapping all this up, hopefully you can tell me if there's likely to be an inquiry.'

Ívar Laxdal frowned. 'What do you mean?'

'The dead man. The one I . . .'

'Ah, you mean the unidentified individual who accidentally shot himself with his own illegal handgun?'

Gunna stared at him. 'Tell me you're joking.'

'Gunnhildur, I'm serious. Nobody wants an inquiry. Not me, not you, and certainly not anyone higher up.'

'But there are people who know. You, Steingrímur, the twins, Sif Strand, Valgeir, Steinunn, plus a few others. This can't be kept secret.'

'An open secret.' Ívar Laxdal shrugged. 'Whispers. You'll have to live with the rumours. But if I have anything to do with it, that's as far as it'll ever go.'

'It feels wrong, totally wrong,' Gunna said. 'This will be hanging over me for ever. Suppose the press get a sniff of it? Or some future government? I think I'd be happier if there were an inquiry and it was all out in the open, whatever the consequences.'

'I don't know what I can tell you, except that there's no appetite for an inquiry.'

'And the two dead men? Someone knew they were here. Supposing their families decide to start digging into what happened to them? How can I be sure there won't be a knock on the door one day?'

'The simple answer is that you can't. But there's not going to be an inquiry. If there were to be one, there's no doubt that you'd be exonerated. I wish I could put your mind at rest, but I'm not sure I can.'

'You said right at the start that this assignment was a poisoned chalice, and you were absolutely right. I'm going to be like Osman, constantly looking over my shoulder from now on,' she said, punching a fist into the palm of her other hand. 'Do we know who's replacing Steinunn?'

'Steinar Jakobsson, as far as I know. A safe pair of hands, nothing flashy, zero imagination, does what the PM tells him to do.'

'Wonderful. Another lawyer running the show.' Gunna pulled the handle and felt the door open. 'Come on. Steini will be happy to see an old shipmate. That's his van there, so he must be home, but I don't know who that yellow Polo next to it belongs to.'

Gunna pushed open the front door, stamped her feet and kicked off her boots.

'Hello! Does anyone live here?' she called out, opening the inner door and stopping in the doorway as Steini looked up and grinned from where he sat at the table under the kitchen window, a bowl of cereal in his hands and yesterday's newspaper in front of him.

'Hey! Welcome home, and the Big Man as well,' Steini said with a delighted look on his face, standing up and spreading his arms to hug Gunna. She buried her face in his neck and closed her eyes, suddenly feeling deeply tired.

He squeezed her tight and she felt the Glock pressed into her side.

'What's . . . ?' he asked, loosening his embrace.

'Shh,' she said, pulling him tight against her. 'Don't ask.'

'I had no idea you were coming back today,' he said and held out a hand for Ívar Laxdal to crush.

'So, how did it all go? Operation mystery all over?' Steini asked, banging mugs onto the table and pouring coffee from a Thermos. 'You want some breakfast? I boiled a couple of eggs, and there's the usual stuff on the table,' he said, sweeping the newspapers into a pile.

'It's all over,' Ívar Laxdal confirmed.

'And the boat's on a pontoon in Akranes,' Gunna added.

'Akranes? What? When did that happen?'

Gunna looked at Ívar Laxdal. 'Two nights ago, was it? Or three?'

'Whichever. It was blowing like hell, at any rate,' he growled, a hand clasped around a thick mug. 'How's tricks, Steini? Keeping busy?' he asked, quickly steering the conversation away from what he and Gunna had been doing for the last week.

'Ach. There's always stuff to keep a man occupied. I promised I'd go and look over an engine down at the quay today, an overheating Yanmar. Good engine, runs perfectly at tickover, but gives trouble at high revs.'

Gunna cracked an egg and buttered herself a couple of slices of bread as Steini and Ívar Laxdal talked engines.

'By the way, you were going to tell me about that rather handsome boat of yours,' he said. 'Something of an antique, isn't it?'

'The boat?' Gunna said, taken by surprise. 'It was my dad's boat years ago. The old man and I used to go lumpfish netting in the spring, and he always said it was a shame it was too small to rig for shrimping. Anyway, when he died, neither of my brothers were interested, so it was sold.'

'And?'

'Gísli heard it was up for sale last year. It was a bit of a mess and had no fishing licence, so it wasn't expensive, pretty much just scrap value, so we paid the asking price, brought it down here and it's been tied up in Vogar. Steini and Gísli have been working on it, and it was on the pontoon in Reykjavík because someone Gísli knows was fitting the new radar. We were going to take it over to

Akranes last weekend, but now we've already done the delivery trip.'

'I wouldn't mind doing some lumpfish netting if we get a chance,' Steini said wistfully.

'Well, you're almost too late for this season,' Ívar Laxdal said.

'There's always next year if you feel like coming along as crew,' Gunna said through a mouthful of egg and black bread. 'By the way, Steini, the yellow car outside, is that Laufey's friend's?'

'Yeah,' Steini said after a pause. 'Nice girl. Shy.'

'Someone from university?'

'I'm not sure. I haven't been here much, so I've hardly seen them.'

Ívar Laxdal drained his mug.

'And with that, I have to be going,' he said, turning serious. 'I don't expect to see you at Hverfisgata today, Gunnhildur. Tomorrow would be fine.'

'I was hoping for after the weekend, considering it's been a pretty full-on few days, however many it's been. I've lost track.'

'It's been a week,' Ívar Laxdal said and got to his feet. 'Can you come in for a debriefing with Birna and Úlfur tomorrow afternoon? Once we've done that, I don't expect to see you until next week. How's that?'

'Sure. And you can give me a lift to Einholt. My car's still in Steinunn's garage.'

Gunna went to the door with him.

'Not a word to anyone, not that I have to spell that out to you,' he said in the doorway.

'Not a word,' Gunna assured him, and he waved once as he stalked over to his car.

Steini was making himself sandwiches when she returned to the kitchen and wrapped her arms around him from behind.

'It's good to be back.'

'Tough week?'

'Yep. But it's all a big secret, so I can't tell you anything about it.'

★　★　★

Osman was the first off the aircraft, escorted out of the cabin ahead of the other passengers, with Luc Kerkhoeve holding him firmly by the elbow. Catching up with them or seeing who was there to collect them wasn't an option, but Ana was satisfied that there would be no great obstacles to picking up his trail, although it appeared likely that Osman would be watched carefully around the clock.

She guessed that Iceland had been anxious to relieve itself of this troublesome visitor, and Commander Kerkhoeve had engineered some deal by which he had a hold over the fugitive.

Ana lifted her collar high, shouldered her bag and, without a backward glance, followed the line of people leaving the aircraft. Once she was clear of the walkway and following the signs towards baggage reclaim, she dawdled, kneeling to tie a bootlace, checking her phone, waiting for Valgeir to overtake her.

When he walked past, still in a daze, she followed him at a discreet distance until he stood at the carousel, looking around like an owl blinking in the daylight.

Ana took a position at the far end, where she could watch him without being seen, but he was again too engrossed in his phone to notice her, only occasionally looking up to see if his luggage was on the way.

To Ana's relief, her case was one of the first to appear. She pulled off the puffin cap and stuffed it into a pocket, extended her suitcase handle and marched towards the exit.

She took a deep breath, walked over to where Valgeir stood, wrapped in his thoughts, and touched his elbow.

'Hello, Valgeir,' she said, and he swung his head to look at her. His jaw dropped as he realized who was standing at his side with a broad smile.

He stood frozen to the spot and stared, first with incomprehension on his face, turning slowly to fear.

'Astrid?' he croaked.

'Shh, Valgeir,' Ana said, putting out a hand and touching his lips with one finger. 'I just wanted to say sorry. It was nothing personal. And goodbye,' she added, turning and striding smartly to the exit, her case bumping at her heels, before Valgeir could decide whether to say anything or keep quiet for ever.

Gunna looked up, hearing a door squeak open, and saw a slim young woman appear in the doorway, with long fair hair hanging loose; it hid most of her face, but not the look of surprise on it.

'Er, hi,' the young woman said diffidently. 'I'm Ingunn. You must be Gunna? I've heard a lot about you.'

'I am,' Gunna said with a quizzical look, and the girl looked awkward.

'Pleased to meet you,' she said. 'I'm sorry . . . I was just on my way to . . .'

The bathroom door swung shut behind her.

'That's Laufey's friend?' Gunna asked.

'That's her.'

Steini put his sandwich box into a carrier bag, added an apple and scratched his head.

'Not taking coffee?'

'No, Jói makes coffee on the boat,' he said, and then fell silent as Ingunn made a fleeting appearance again, tiptoeing barefoot as she tripped silently back down the passage.

'What's Laufey's friend like?'

He pursed his lips in thought.

'Not sure. Quiet as a mouse, hardly says a word.'

'Well,' Gunna yawned, 'I might be asleep by the time Laufey wakes up, so there's a chance I could miss them both. It's been a long week and I could easily sleep for a whole day.'

'I'll wake you up when I get back. Shouldn't be all that long.'

He leaned down, squeezed her hand and was gone. The front door banged shut behind him and she could hear his pickup mutter into life outside. The house seemed eerily quiet and Gunna realized that, out of the habit she had acquired over the last few days, she was still wearing her fleece jacket zipped halfway up.

She took it off, threw it over the back of a chair and took the Glock from its holster, telling herself she should have put the weapon firmly in Ívar Laxdal's hands before he left for Reykjavík.

'Mum, what the hell are you wearing?'

Gunna turned to see Laufey behind her, a questioning frown on her face.

'Firearms duties, sweetheart,' Gunna said. 'The first and last time. How are you? How's it been without the old lady under your feet?'

'Y'know. Peaceful. Very quiet.'

'So, anything happened while I've been away?'

'Nope. Gísli's at sea. Drífa's fine, except that Kjartan's teething. We went over there yesterday to give her a bit of a break.'

'You and Steini?'

'Me and Ingunn.'

The blonde girl appeared behind Laufey, in jeans and a hooded sweatshirt but barefoot, and placed a hand on Laufey's shoulder.

'Is there something happening here that I ought to know about?' Gunna said, eyeing the two of them standing close together.

'Mum!' Laufey exploded as the frown deepened across her freckled face. 'Can't you take off your detective's hat, stop being so suspicious and just be off duty for five minutes?' She glanced at the Glock, still in Gunna's hand. 'And are you going to put that bazooka away?'

Gunna sighed and felt a rush of fatigue, the aftermath of the last week's tension coming to an end.

'Sorry, sweetheart. I can't tell you how tough the last few days have been.' She opened one of the kitchen drawers, put the pistol inside and shut it, then unclipped the holster, slipping it from her shoulders with relief and draping it over her jacket on the chair. 'That's better. Never again.'

Acknowledgements

I'm particularly grateful to Lilja Sigurðardóttir for allowing me to borrow her human gorilla Rikki the Sponge. But if you want to know where Rikki's nickname comes from, you'll have to read Lilja's outstanding Reykjavík Noir series.

Thanks to many friends in Iceland, especially my cohort of informers, Bylgja, Lúlli and Gummi, who are always ready to come up with answers to the strangest questions.

Much love to the magnificent Elves . . .